ICE PALACE

BOOKS BY EDNA FERBER

Autobiography: A PECULIAR TREASURE

Short Stories: ONE BASKET · NOBODY'S IN TOWN · BUTTERED SIDE DOWN · CHEERFUL—BY REQUEST · HALF PORTIONS · GIGOLO MOTHER KNOWS BEST · THEY BROUGHT THEIR WOMEN

The Emma McChesney Stories: ROAST BEEF MEDIUM PERSONALITY PLUS · EMMA MC CHESNEY & COMPANY

Novels: ICE PALACE · GIANT · GREAT SON · SARATOGA TRUNK · DAWN O'HARA · FANNY HERSELF · THE GIRLS · SO BIG · SHOW BOAT · CIMARRON · AMERICAN BEAUTY · COME AND GET IT

Plays: THE ROYAL FAMILY (with George S. Kaufman) MINICK (with George S. Kaufman) · DINNER AT EIGHT (with George S. Kaufman) · $1200 A YEAR (with Newman Levy) · STAGE DOOR (with George S. Kaufman) · THE LAND IS BRIGHT (with George S. Kaufman)

Ice Palace

by EDNA FERBER

1958

DOUBLEDAY & COMPANY, INC.

GARDEN CITY, NEW YORK

In Alaska there is no town of Baranof.
There is no village of Oogruk.
There is no building called the Ice Palace.
No character in this book is meant as a portrayal of a real person.

The quotation from Alaska, *by Merle Colby.*
Copyright by The Macmillan Company.
Reprinted by permission.

Library of Congress Catalog Card Number 58–5936

Printed in the United States of America
Designed by Alma Reese Cardi
First Edition

ICE PALACE

1

Every third woman you passed on Gold Street in Baranof was young, pretty, and pregnant. The men, too, were young, virile, and pregnant with purpose. Each, making his or her way along the bustling business street, seemed actually to bounce with youth and vitality. Only an occasional old sourdough, relic dating back to the gold-rush days of fifty years ago, wattled and wary as a turkey cock, weaving his precarious pedestrian way in and out of the frisky motor traffic, gave the humming town a piquant touch of anachronism.

An exhilarating street, Gold, though the stores and office buildings that lined it—one- or two-story cement or wooden structures—were commonplace and even shabby. The enlivening quality was inexplicable, but ardent Alaskans sometimes attributed it to the piercing quality of the Arctic light and the dryness of the atmosphere. Middle-aged tourists, weary after thousands of miles of travel over this seemingly boundless territory—whether by plane or by a combination of plane, train, ship and automobile—were puzzled and plaintive as they viewed the haphazard town of Baranof for the first time.

"Everybody walks as if they had springs in their shoes. Or maybe it's because you're all so young."

If the visitor's guide happened to be Ott Decker, Secretary of the Baranof Chamber of Commerce, he would reject this with the mysterious lightheartedness that seemed to suffuse most near-Arctic citizens.

"Young's got nothing to do with it. Around here you can live to be a hundred, easy, unless you're shot, or your plane cracks up on you, or a bear sees you first."

"Well, it's something. A kind of a crazy something. No offense. I just mean, what makes them bounce?"

"My opinion, it's the violet rays or the magnetic pole—we're not so far from the North Pole, you know, when it comes right down to geography—or it's the radiant northern, uh, isotopes or something."

"Now wait a minute. Just a minute. Radiant. I always understood you had winter about eight months in the year, and no sun to speak of."

"That's right. But you feel great. And summers! Say—summers! Like today. Daylight round the clock twenty-four hours. And you know what? You don't need sleep. You feel hopped up all the time. Take the Eskimos up there in Kotzebue and Oogruk and Barrow and around where it's really tough going. Always laughing their heads off. For what! They got nothing to laugh at. They just feel good. Everybody feels good. I don't know. It's a kind of a balloon feeling."

It was true that everything in Baranof seemed exaggerated. Edges sharper. Skies bluer. Mountains higher, snow deeper, temperature lower, daylight longer, sunlight briefer, depending on the season. The very air sometimes seemed more utterly still than anywhere else in the world, yet it pulsed almost palpably with life. When the wind blew it blew harder. Down in southeast Alaska—the region facetiously called the Banana Belt—the Taku screeched and whistled about your ears in season. In the remote north villages on the Bering Sea or the Arctic Ocean the polar blasts in February could strangle the breath in your throat and force it back into the reluctant lungs. Deceived by the dry air, you could freeze your face and walk about, unknowing. Baranof wore parkas, fur-hooded, through the winter. This gave pedestrians the anonymity of dominoes at a masquerade. There was a favorite joke, often quoted. "Winters in Baranof, speak to anything that moves. If it's standing still, call the ambulance."

Off to school on the bitter black winter mornings the children were round bundles of wool and fur, their eyes peering out like those of small woodland creatures in a nest. Mothers, standing briefly in the doorway, would call, "Now remember, don't run! Even if you're late—don't run." They knew the danger of the quick intake of breath like icy knives into the warm scarlet lung tissue.

Across the winter night sky swept the northern lights, eerie dazzling curtains of swaying green and blue and orange. Then, miraculously, June came, it was summer, it was daylight round the clock. The thermometer that had registered sixty below zero in January now might show ninety above. Yet there was Baranof and much more of Alaska besides, dry and cool, energetic and somewhat crazily high-keyed in an agreeable way under the constant compulsion of the weird Arctic sun. Up, up far north in Barrow on the shore of the frozen Arctic Ocean the United States flag whipped aloft in the wind for eighty days and eighty nights, for there was during that period no sunset hour in which to lower it. If you happened to be soaring in a comfortably cosy plane above Bering's ice-locked coast, nibbling a ham sandwich and sipping hot strong coffee, you could see just over there, beyond the two island dots that were the Big Diomede and the Little Diomede, the black strangely menacing line that was the coast of Siberia.

But here in mid-Alaska a kind of carefree mood took hold. Baranof stayed out of doors every possible minute. You played baseball at midnight. Your wife tended her garden at eleven P.M. Your children frisked like leprechauns far into the night. Perhaps you slept from midnight through the hour or two of rosy twilight until, like a blindingly dazzling scimitar thrust through a scarlet velvet curtain, the sun rose again at one or two o'clock in the morning. This brief interlude of repose seemed, magically, to suffice, both for the sun and you.

If you were young and in love you might stroll hand in hand down to the water's edge to delight romantically in the glorious color above and the pastel reflection below. Mount McKinley, king of all the peaks on the North American continent, white-crowned in the summer, white-robed in the winter, looked in this midsummer midnight light like the gods' Valhalla—or a gigantic scoop of raspberry and orange sherbet. Baranof citizens adjusted to this summer-winter variant of one hundred and fifty degrees as nonchalantly as they digested the local moose steaks in January or the monster home-grown strawberries in August.

As for grubby Gold Street—it compensated in scenery for what it lacked in architectural grace. At one end the shabby thoroughfare met the mountains that reared their incredible height, peak on peak, a screaming white. At the other end the water curved to hold the town in its icy arms. It was a setting of diamonds and pearls surrounding a blob of agate.

If you were an Important Person arriving by air to visit Baranof you were officially met at the smart little airport by Bridie Ballantyne or Ott Decker or both. If you were a Very Important Person you were met by Chris Storm. Christine Storm. Only her grandfather Czar Kennedy and her grandfather Thor Storm called her Christine. As First Assistant to the General Manager of Alaska Public Relations, Christine Storm's appearance was likely to mislead the average tourist; but then, she never was assigned to small fry. She was reserved for any visiting President of the United States who condescended to the Territory (none in her day); Senators and Congressmen (National); Big Business Types (with Wife); Big Game Hunters (minus Wife) with guides flying small maneuverable planes in search of polar white or mammoth brown bears.

Born in Alaska, the daughter of a father and mother born in Alaska, the granddaughter of two grandfathers who were considered Alaska history, Chris Storm was almost as outstanding as Mount McKinley. Certainly in the wintertime, if assigned to a Very Distinguished Visitor, Chris was a striking figure there at the airport gateway as the big four-engine plane from Seattle drummed down out of the heights to the runway that now stretched its impressive length in what had been, less than a half century ago, literally a howling wilderness.

Dramatically, she dressed the part of native daughter. Her official winter greeting costume was a pure white fox parka intricately bordered with a delicate frieze of Eskimo symbols in black sealskin. Her grandfather Thor Storm had told her that some of these symbols were phallic or otherwise sexual, which interested her, as did all Eskimo lore, and sometimes, quite matter-of-factly, she would obligingly explain these to inquiring visitors.

"My, that's a lovely coat!" the wife of a V.I.P. from Outside would exclaim.

"It's called a parka, and we pronounce it parky, no one knows why."

"All those little figures and things in the border. Now that one—it looks like two little hills with a valley between. Do the signs have any significance, do they mean anything, sort of like the writing on caves and tombs in the Orient? Mr. Rauschenbusch and I took a trip around the world last year."

"Oh, that. That's part of a legend in which an Eskimo sees the back of his wife as she bends over the cooking pot, he dreams he must find his way through the two hills to the valley."

"What! Sh! The men will hear you. What's this one?"

The white fox parka, with its hood of white wolf, was a fitting frame for the girl's brilliant face. Slim white fur mukluks and gloves completed the dazzling effect—too dazzling, her enemies said. In the rather rueful way she sometimes had when speaking of herself Chris agreed with them. "In this outfit I look like that girl in the beer ads. But it's good Alaska publicity."

Then, in summer, hot or cold from June to September, Chris's costume as Greeter and Guide was the most feminine of cottons or silks, her golden arms bare, the bodice fashionably low cut, as proof that Alaska was a summer resort.

Visitors often mistook her for something purely ornamental, like the scenery. They were completely wrong. They were wrong about the scenery too. Hidden in those fabulous peaks and creeks and torrents were copper and gold and uranium and platinum and cobalt and tin and tungsten and nickel and lead; in the tundra and flatlands coal and oil; in the vast streams and inlets and seas millions of finned and furred creatures from salmon to seals to whales. But they were not for the casual passer-by. Beneath Chris Storm's shining surface, too, there were hidden treasures and wonders of mind and heart and spirit.

The three Baranof Professional Public Relations stars used three quite different weapons with which to do battle with the world known as Outside. Christine, deceptively blithe and débonnaire, tickled you with a poniard of gaiety, but you never felt sure that she might not drive it suddenly into your ribs. Bridie Ballantyne used a verbal shillelagh wrapped in cotton velvet. Ott Decker, good Chamber of Commerce Secretary that he was, just laid on with a shovel.

For example, though her laugh was merry, her way lighthearted, Chris's statements were sometimes dramatic. Listeners were likely to recall them, thoughtfully, following the more spectacular moments of their trip.

"Yes," she would agree, apparently in charming deference to the stranger's comment. "Yes, this is a gigantic wilderness. With neon lights, of course; and hydrogen bombs and dog sleds and radar and Eskimos and crab meat *au gratin* and skin boats and juke boxes and art exhibits and symphony concerts; and moose sometimes ambling down Gold Street in a real tough winter."

The Visitor from Outside, puzzled and vaguely resentful, would wave an arm with a gesture that embraced the incredible landscape.

"Some country you got here, that's for sure. I thought it would be different. Of course, it's different, all right, but other ways it's more like back home than I thought. Not like it, exactly, but——"

"We're people—all kinds of people—just like you in the States. We're white and black and brown and young and old and smart and dumb. But we're absolutely different in one way."

"How's that?"

"Would you like to pay government taxes if you couldn't have a voice in the state you live in, and couldn't vote for President of the United States? Would you like taxation without representation?"

This challenge they found disconcerting in a girl as attractive as Chris. "I'll say I wouldn't like it. I wouldn't stand for it. Why don't you write your Congressman and Senator in Washington, tell 'em to get on the job, or out?"

"Don't you know that Alaska has no Congressman or Senator in Washington! We're a Territory. Everything we do, and everything the Territory yields, goes out. Outside. Everything goes out and nothing stays in. Gold. Copper. Timber. Fish. Millions and millions and millions a year. Outside. We're slaves."

"Oh, now, say!" After all, the Visitor had not come all this long distance to listen to soapbox speeches, even though delivered by a pretty girl. "What's a girl like you bothering her head about whether you vote for President? Let him worry. I know what I'd do if I was President. I'd appoint you a Cabinet Member. Secretary of Beauty. You'd send bunches of beauty delegates over to Russia, they'd send bunches over here. No more war. The Russians keep sending over those bullet-headed fellows with eyes like mean oysters. Who loves them! Nobody."

Perhaps, casually, an Outsider undergoing the Visitor's Treatment might say, "Where's your home, Miss Storm? You certainly don't look like an Alaskan."

They did not know that Christine Storm had been known to Alaskans since the day of her fantastic birth. She had become a legend.

"I don't know how you think Alaskans should look. But I'm an Alaskan."

"That right! Born right here in Baranof?"

"I was born in a caribou in a blizzard up in the Wood River country."

Baffled, smiling uncertainly, the visitor might catch the word caribou and cling to it. "Caribou? Let's see now, there's a town called Caribou, I think it's in North Dakota though. Or was it Canada I saw it? But I understood you to say you were Alaska-born."

"I didn't mean a town called Caribou. I meant a caribou."

"I don't get it. I must be dumb."

"A caribou is a huge sort of reindeer and I was born inside of one that my father shot when he and my mother were caught in a blizzard on a hunting trip. I wasn't due for another three months but they say my mother was one of those dauntless girls—a kind of Alaska version of the Scott Fitzgerald type that was the fashion then. Grandpa Kennedy—her father—had sent her to Vassar, she knew Edna St. Vincent Millay. Anyway, what with the blinding blizzard and the stumbling around, and no shelter, and only the dog sled, I started ahead of time. Even if my father had had a chance to build a snow-block shelter, there wasn't time. By some miracle he shot a caribou. He slit the caribou's belly and gutted it and put my mother inside on the furs from the sled, it was blood-warm for a little while, and sheltered, and it kept her from freezing and me, too. And that's where I was born."

The listener would appear somewhat hurt. "Who you trying to kid?"

"But I'm not. It's true. Ask anybody."

"Now let me get this. There was a caribou handy, and he shot it and slit it and gutted it, you said, and then your mother——"

"My mother died. I don't know why *I* didn't, but I didn't."

"Now look here, Miss Storm, I may be what you Alaskans call a —what's that word?—uh—che——"

"Cheechako. We here in Alaska pronounce it cheechawker, it comes from a word in the Chinook language, it means——"

"I know what it means. Same as tenderfoot in the West. But I don't buy that story of yours, Miss Storm, cheechawker or no cheechawker."

But then, even the girl's appearance had a tinge of incredibility. Her eyes were black, her hair golden. Baffled by the unusual combination, strangers assumed that the yellow hair was tinted. The eyes were long, narrow, and ever so slightly pinched at the outer corners. The skin warmly golden, but this, too, was complicated by a faintly pink touch on the rather high cheekbones like the flush on the cheek of a good English peach espaliered against a sunny brick wall in, say, Kent. Most people considered her quite a beauty, but the cynical said, not with that jaw line, you could break your knuckles against that, and your heart, too. A lot have. Heart, I mean. Ott

Decker, and they say that son of Dave Husack in Seattle, and practically every young guy in the Territory. But a lot of them think she's too bossy and independent. I'll say this for her; anybody who knows her will say she isn't stuck up. I guess Bridie Ballantyne saw to that. And Thor Storm. Maybe Czar Kennedy, but I've got a hunch he isn't as democratic as he pretends. But Bridie! She'd get my vote for President.

Bridie Ballantyne, in her own way, and within a more limited geographical area, was perhaps as well known as Chris. In Bridie as guide and hostess the tourist was treated to an exhibition of local pride unexcelled since Chauvin himself. Though no one knew her exact age it was roughly estimated at between sixty-five and seventy. She lied about it or ignored it.

In a region of almost fanatic joiners Bridie Ballantyne was a member in good standing of practically every group banded together in gregarious Baranof. With five hundred or even a thousand miles between you and the next town, Baranof—and all Alaska—had to manufacture its own fun. A lonely people in a far-off wilderness long before the airplane began to weave its gossamer web from the Atlantic, from the Pacific, across land and water to the Arctic, they had perforce contrived their own social life as pioneers have since the wandering tribes of Israel.

Bridie was President of the Pole Star Chapter of Women of the Moose; luck-struck player in the Ice Palace Canasta Club; Charter Member of the Far North Poker Poke; the Pioneers of Alaska, the Sourdoughs, the Daughters of the Midnight Sun, the Eaglets Eyrie, the Chamber of Commerce, the Hostess Dinner Club, the North Stars, the Garden Club, the Optimists, the Art Guild, the Music Circle (she couldn't carry the simplest tune), the Dinner Speakers. She appeared weekly on the local television program. She knew the town from the spanking new airport at one end to the primeval tundra at the other; from the latest rookie's frightened bride arriving at Kinkaid Air Force Base to the most desiccated sourdough in his leaky log cabin in the weeds at the edge of town. She belonged to the Baranof City Council and there was talk of her running for Territorial Congresswoman against Shaw Gavin, a hard-core politician of twenty-five years' standing and a minion of the Big Boys in Seattle and Washington.

Though Bridie's interests were myriad her chief delight was the job of piloting visitors around town. She invited them for a cup of tea or a mouthful of sherry in her cluttered one-room apartment at the Ice Palace. She loved company, she loved Baranof, she loved life. Ott Decker said that to hear her carry on you'd think Alaska was the Promised Land with built-in refrigeration. She talked. She talked incessantly with an enthusiasm that was contagious. In fifty years of Alaska she had seen the worst and the best of it. She held forth to strangers, to friends of half a century. As she talked, her elaborately coiffed steel-gray hair and her blue eyes and her good clear skin seemed to give off sparks. She always spoke of Alaska as We.

"We're one fifth the size of the whole United States, did you know that, now? And two times the size of that little bitty Texas they're always yawping about. And bigger than a whole parcel of European countries put together. Folks don't know. Folks Outside just don't know a thing. Ignorant as moose. Here in Baranof and Anchorage and Fairbanks and Nome and even towns more north it's no colder than towns in Finland and Norway and Sweden and Denmark—let alone that Russia. But all those millions of American tourists traveling over there, you don't hear them complaining about those places being cold or uncomfortable. Oh, my, no! They're quaint and novel and so different, and the scenery! And here we are, a mass of beauty, can you picture now what any of those countries in Europe would give for a grand big lovely rich place like Alaska! The highest mountain, old Mount McKinley. And Matanuska Valley can grow you the biggest cabbages in the world, let alone strawberries and potatoes and greens and grains. And you could graze cattle by the million but those witless ones in Washington won't let us own the land, let alone work it. Look at it! Sun all day and all night, summertime, and you feel as if you'd had two glasses of good dry champagne."

"Mosquitoes?" her listener might venture, timidly.

"Who minds a mosquito now and then! It's exercise. Winters you relax and enjoy your home and your friends and read, and just when you're beginning to be tired of all that comfort, why, next thing you know the ice goes out with a bang—and it's spring. But who owns us! They do. Outside. They get the good of it all. And what did it cost back there in '67 when that Seward pulled a fast one on Russia? Seven million dollars, can you fancy that! For the most wonderful darlingest richest chunk of land in the world. Seven million dollars! I could die laughing. Why, they lay that down as first payment on a fifty-foot corner lot in New York City."

Her hearers, now taking a bedazzled glance around the unkempt little town, would wag their heads feebly, whether in exhaustion or admiration or conviction. "Sure is. Sure do. Well, that's mighty interesting. Whew!"

Ott Decker's approach was more in the Chamber of Commerce tradition. Hailing originally from California he had miraculously transferred his fealty to the Far North. His enthusiasm for this wild and remote territory was as strong, in its way, as Chris Storm's somewhat neurotic emotion or Bridie Ballantyne's hearty trumpeting. There were even those who thought he overdid it. Ott, shrewd operator that he was in the devious world of public relations, knew that the summer tourist from Kansas or Ohio or Nebraska was not interested in Alaska frustrations, resentments or politics. Personal resentment was, indeed, more likely to figure in the visitor's own comment. Standing in the midst of Gold Street he viewed its supermarket, its cafés, its dress shops, drugstores, banks, airplane travel bureaus, florist shops and bars bars bars. As he dodged its pale blue Buicks and rose-pink Fords his tone took on a peevish edge.

"It doesn't look any different from Powell Street back home."

Ott would quirk a derisive eyebrow, though his manner was hearty. "You figured Alaska would be saloons and dance halls and shooting and girls in spangled tights like in the movies?"

"Well, maybe not altogether, but when our plane stopped in Juneau, our first stop on the way up here, why, there was a place, we had a drink there, sawdust on the floor and a fella at the piano in shirt sleeves, and rough-looking characters at the bar, and you got your change in silver dollars."

"Oh, that. Sure." Ott was amiable and tolerant. "That's the new Fish and Gold saloon. It's rigged for hicks from Outside. Chicago and New York and Detroit and so on."

"You mean nobody pans gold any more, or hunts bears or lives in igloos? Or shoots up saloons?"

"Course we do. There's gold, lots of it. Like to pan some? That's part of our tourist-entertainment program. I'll drive you out to the dredge right outside of town at Moose Lake, it's the biggest gold dredge in the world. Glad to show you. And polar bears, well, depends where you are. They don't go walking down Gold Street, that's for sure. And Alaska brown bear—well, you'd have to go down to Admiralty or to Kodiak and you better be quick on your feet because they sometimes weigh two thousand pounds and stand thirteen feet high. Let's see now—shooting up saloons—well, most of 'em are cocktail bars now with that music piped in, all the hit numbers from the new Broadway musical shows. It's got so you have to elbow your way past the bobby-soxers to get to the bar. Let's see now, you said igloos. Some of the boys from Kinkaid Air Base built us a dandy snow-block igloo right there on the corner of Gold and Polaris in front of the USO Building for our annual Winter Festival. It was one of the attractions. Course it all melted down months ago."

Disillusionment on the face of the Outsider roused Ott to fresh effort. With a spacious gesture he would point toward a structure that, somehow unbelievably, rose fourteen stories high against the background of mountain and water and sky.

"How about that! Speaking of igloos—how about that! That's the Ice Palace. We call it."

2

That was the Ice Palace. Its real name was the Kennedy Building, but no one called it that. The Ice Palace. They loved it, they bragged about it. Czar Kennedy had built it as he had built most of the town's show places. On the corner of Gold and Polaris was the Miners' National Bank, Czar Kennedy, President; just across the street the Kennedy Block housed the town's largest motion-picture theater; a drugstore dispensed everything from tuna sandwiches to television sets; a hardware store; a supermarket. Solidly stituated halfway down the street stood the three-story printing plant and editorial offices of the Baranof *Daily Lode*. Czar Kennedy, President and Publisher, the masthead read.

When he had built the Ice Palace the citizens of Baranof thought this a sheer bravura gesture. Fourteen stories high, with the wilderness stretching away thousands of miles in all directions. His detractors said it would have been cheaper for him to rent himself out as a flagpole sitter, if height was what he wanted for attention. They were wrong. The Ice Palace was a paying concern from the day it opened, as was every Czar Kennedy enterprise. It was Alaska's first apartment house. People fought to live in it. Townsmen, dwelling in their frame houses and wrestling with the regional problems of heating, lighting, plumbing, water, were madly envious of Ice Palace tenants. There never was a vacancy unless a tenant accommodatingly died, rashly built a new house, or left permanently for Outside.

Circling in by plane from Barrow or Kotzebue or Nome up north; or from Juneau, Anchorage, or Fairbanks south, you could spot the

Ice Palace before the town itself came into focus. Almost at the water's edge, built of pressed glass composition blocks, it gave back the icy mountains as good as they sent, glitter for glitter—or almost as good. Time, though brief, and ruthless Arctic weather, already had smirched the walls with a patina of grit and pocked it with ice pits. Yet sometimes, when the refraction was just right, the structure took on an unearthly blue like the aquamarine tint of the vast Morgenstern glacier that lay, a giant jewel, just outside Baranof.

As though further to emphasize the incongruity of a sizable skyscraper in that tableau of snow, tundra, sea, glacier and forest, there nestled at the actual base of the edifice a weather-beaten log cabin that seemed somehow more unreal than the shining shaft soaring above it.

"I bet that Czar guy didn't build the log shanty, anyway."

Ott Decker rose happily to this. "He did, though. More than fifty years ago, and he lived in it in the old gold-rush days with his pardner Thor Storm. Pardner then, that is. There's lots of log cabins scattered around town."

"You mean people living in them?"

"Glad to. There's a housing shortage in Baranof, just like every place else. That cabin is the daddy of them all, though."

"More of a landmark now, I suppose. Nobody living in it."

"Nobody but just merely the granddaughter of old Czar Kennedy herself is living in it, that's who. Christine Storm. Chris, everybody calls her. She lives there all alone."

"Old maid?"

"Chris! Wait till you see her."

"You sound kind of—wistful."

"Damn right I am. Me and about a million other guys."

"If her grandfather owns that big new place I should think she'd live there. You said everything modern—heat, elevators, restaurant, laundry and whatnot—right in the building. No kitchens, maybe—is that it?"

"Kitchens! You ought to see them. Modern as a jet, and aluminum trimmings enough to give you snow blindness. Chris is a good cook, too. She learned it off her Grandpa Storm, I guess. The Norwegians eat good. Bridie didn't teach her much, Bridie's too quick and slapdash for cooking. Real cooking, that is."

"And this Chris lives in that beat-up old log cabin alone, huh? How old—that is—what's her age, about?"

"Let's see, old Czar's up there in the seventies, and her Grandpa Thor Storm, too. Chris? She's young. Some ways she's like a kid, and other ways she's old as her grandpas, and older than Bridie. Comes of being brought up by old people, I suppose."

"You keep talking about grandfathers. Where's the rest of her family?"

"That's all the family she's got. Just two grandfathers. Unless you count Bridie Ballantyne, and she's no more relation to Chris than she is to everybody else in town. Bridie's everybody's aunt."

"They all live together?"

"They all live separate. And they slice up Chris like that story about Solomon and the baby in the Bible."

"They don't get along, h'm? The old boys."

"They're what you'd call friendly enemies. They don't think alike about anything, except they're both crazy about Chris and crazy about Alaska. But in different ways, so they don't agree about those, either. Czar Kennedy, he just about owns Baranof, and a big chunk of Alaska, besides. Everything he touches turns to gold, he never did have to pan for it even in the old days. Czar owns the daily paper, the *Lode*, it's called. Kind of—well—conservative. Thor runs a weekly with Paul and Addie Barnett, it's called the *Northern Light*, and boy, it certainly shines into the dark corners in Alaska and Seattle and even Washington D.C. They're always battling, the two old boys, they've been battling for fifty years, folks here say who've known 'em that long."

"Tough on the girl, I should think that would be."

"Sure is. Sure was. But she had it tough from the day she was born. Thor's son married Czar's daughter, see. They're both dead. The mother died when Chris was born—no use going into that, nobody believes it anyway, only Alaskans. Her father had his scalp torn off by a bear."

"What are you giving me!"

"I don't expect you to believe it."

"Uh-huh. And this Bridie, I suppose she was spewed up by a whale, like Jonah or something."

"She was just about, at that."

"And she married both of the grandfathers, I suppose, and now she lives in a log cabin, too, all alone. That right?"

"It sure isn't. No husband now, anyway, that's the funny part of it, though they say when she came to Alaska there were about a hundred men to every woman, she could have married any one of them except Czar and Thor, and they say she was in love with both of them. It's all kind of mixed up, don't expect me to straighten it out. Anyway, you don't see Bridie living in any log cabin. The Ice Palace is quaint enough for Bridie."

"Is that what you folks call it? The Ice Palace?"

"Mostly we do. Its real name is the Kennedy Building. When it was built and finished the opening day Thor ran an editorial in the *Northern Light*. Something like this: 'Ice Palace. That could be the name of all Alaska. The people inside can see out, but the people outside can't see in, though it looks transparent.' He's a wise old boy, Thor Storm. Czar too, in another way, of course. Chris has got her hands full, managing those two grandfathers."

Nick, the proprietor of the popular Caribou Café had, appropriately enough, been responsible for the nickname by which the Kennedy Building was locally known. Nick's café handily occupied the imposing plate-glass corner at street level just next to the entrance. On the day the Kennedy Building was opened with formal festivities, and the Governor up from Juneau, Nick mischievously had arranged an arresting display in his restaurant window. Carelessly piled in a sizable heap were Alaska native stones and metals. There were glittering quartz and mica, dull green jade, chunks of mottled marble, lumps of coal. Affably mingling with these lowly members of the native geological family were stones streaked with silver, lumps flecked with gold, chunks veined with copper; a scattering of tungsten, nickel, cobalt, chrome, tin. There were even crumbs of precious platinum, Nick being a perfectionist. It all added up to an interesting miniature display of the mineral resources of Alaska. But this had not been Nick's pixy purpose.

Topping the haphazard mound was a large lettered sign, black on white. Nick's unvenerable white head had waggled in appreciation of his own humor as he outlined the letters.

STONES
Contributed by Tenants of the
ICE PALACE
As They Have
NO FURTHER USE FOR THEM

After that it never was called the Kennedy Building. The Ice Palace. No one could understand why he hadn't improved the little joke by calling it the Glass House. Newcomers assumed that Ice Palace was the building's real name.

For that matter, Ott Decker might have explained that Czar Kennedy's real name wasn't Czar; but this change had occurred half a century ago, and no one remembered it. Signing for his claim he had written his signature with a Spencerian flourish—Z. Kennedy. His Massachusetts Bible-reading parents had named the child Zebedee after the father of the apostles James and John. His school days had been tormented by the chants and horrid rhymes his schoolmates had been able to devise from its unaccustomed and, somehow, comic syllables.

In the Territory's frenetic gold-rush days newcomers were not asked personal questions. It was not considered good manners, or even healthy. But someone, glancing at the signature, had said, facetiously, "Z? What's that stand for? Zero? You sure come to the right place."

Kennedy's new-found friend, Thor Storm, had spoken up in his rather precious accent that was more British than American. "I say it stands for Czar—minus the C. Czar Alexander Second of Russia got seven million dollars for this icehouse. Let me introduce the new Czar who's going to own it if his plans come true. Gentlemen, your new ruler! Czar Kennedy the First!"

Someone in the crowd pressing around the official table in the crude land office had summed up the speaker's towering frame, the great shock of blond hair, the farseeing blue eyes of the seaman, together with the signature—Thor Storm—on the claim book's page.

"Where did you come by that la-de-da talk, Swensky?"

The blue of Thor's eyes had darkened to steel gray. "Ay yust come from Min-ne-so-ta," he enunciated. There was a note in his voice that made his questioner shrink back a little into the crowd. "Thor is my name, after another big Swensky. He was a blacksmith, among other things. Perhaps you've heard of him. He lived in a place much like this. Valhalla, it was called."

But they didn't know what he was talking about. Sometimes, after that, they used to refer to him as the blacksmith. No one remembered his prediction which, in a measure, came true. Baranof today boasted that Czar Kennedy was the only millionaire in Alaska. "That is, living in Alaska," they sometimes added, cynically. "The Big Boys in Seattle and San Francisco and Washington, they just live off it."

Through the years Czar Kennedy argued, always mildly, in that soft musical voice of his, that to be a millionaire in Alaska was impossible.

"We're lucky," he said, "if we've got a moose carcass to gnaw on and a parky to keep us from freezing. But just the same, I'd rather be a poor man in Alaska Territory than a rich man anywhere in the States."

His contemporaries—old sourdoughs now of seventy or even eighty, with decades of hard-wrung years behind them—were guileless or admiring enough to believe his canny statement. Realistic young newcomers of, say, Ott Decker's age, received this with guffaws.

"Loaded," these stated, simply. "The old coot's merely loaded with it. Who does he think he's kidding with that mashed hat and those baggy pants and that twinkle in the eye? Hell, that's no twinkle.

That's a glint, boy, same as gold." A grudging note of admiration might creep in. "At that, you've got to hand it to old Czar. He takes what you've got, but he's got what it takes, too. Most of those old sourdoughs haven't done anything for fifty years but Remember When."

The hordes of young husky construction workers; the thousands of Air-Based; the swarms of doctors, lawyers, engineers, salesmen, mechanics; all the venturesome Johnny-come-latelys were not interested in those who Remembered When. They were almost always polite and respectful to these oldsters, but definitely not interested. They thought the gold-rush days of the century's turn were small stuff. They said, look, you can make more dust in one day promoting television sets or washing machines than those poor bastards made in a year scrabbling up those hills, freezing their tootsies and chewing bacon rind and boiling their boots for soup. And for what? Gold! It's a laugh. They just about killed themselves clawing it out of the ground, and what happens! The guys in Washington stick it right back into the ground at Fort Knox. If you'd go into Kurnitz's Clothing Store today and hand Ben a twenty-dollar gold piece for a pair of pants, why, they'd shove you into the hoosegow for breaking the law.

Nowadays you rarely saw these ancient Jasons on the streets of Baranof. In the long winter days, with the thermometer at twenty—forty—sixty below zero, they snugly stayed in their log cabins listening to the radio's news and music as they serviced their guns and fishing gear in preparation for a milder day. Their energy was hoarded for the effort of keeping warm and fed. Their rifle, gleaming like platinum, was their most treasured possession. It might be the means of food for the entire winter, that moose or caribou safely frozen in the rickety lean-to off the cabin.

Occasionally, in the late spring after the ice had gone out, a few of the spryest of them actually set out for the creeks and the hills with their old simple implements of the placer miner. Some succeeded in panning a few dollars' worth of gold in the bright-flecked pebbles. As these oldsters displayed their crumbs of treasure—their tiny poke—to their more lethargic contemporaries at the Sockeye Tobacco Store, their faces took on, for a moment, the look of vitality and purpose they had worn a half century ago.

The old sporting blood still coursed sluggishly in the veins of a select group who had known the delights of the faro or blackjack tables in the early days. You might see these gregarious septuagenarians sitting in at the game of pangini that ran continuously through the black days and black nights of the Baranof winter. Their rendezvous was the back room of the old Sockeye Tobacco Store on Bering Street. There they sat around the green-baize-covered pan table, with its semicircle at one side scooped out to accommodate the dealer, like a great bite taken from the edge of a pie. Panguingui had been brought to Baranof by Tony Ferrari back in those almost mythical days of the early rush. There were those who said that it was he who first had discovered the precious metal in the creeks. The pan room was warm, smoke-dimmed, strangely quiet except for the slip-slap of the cards and an occasional cackle of triumph from some withered winner. Their faces had the wistful innocence of those who had been defeated by life. The effect of the room, with its desiccated glittering-eyed players bent over the table in that hazy air, was that of a mellow Rembrandt.

Of the less sporting among these relics you might daily, in the winter months, see a dozen at a time sitting like wax figures in the gritty lobby of the Pole Star Hotel, the maroon rep armchairs showing the imprint of their weary heads; their work-bitten hands, strangely inert now, resting loosely on the chair arms. Only their eyes moved, lively, amused. They always could spot the visitor from Outside—those brisk close-shaven businessmen just flown in from Seattle. Smart in their checked English tweeds imported from neighboring Canada, their expensive cashmere topcoats with the sharp lapels, they had office faces, these men; the elements had left no scars on their features. To the hotel clerk they said, what do you mean no room with bath, my secretary distinctly said room with bath in my wire, well, if somebody checks out remember me, will you, I'll be grateful, see what I mean.

This new world eddied around the silent old men like waves lapping a rock. Though the hotel was overheated as was every Alaska dwelling in winter, they sat in their coats and caps and mufflers and snow boots, snug now, secure, savoring comfort as only those can who have the far memory of killing cold to give them a momentary inward shiver.

From a corner of the hotel lounge a television yammered. The relaxed oldsters gazed at the antics of make-believe desperadoes whose squawking resounded in the dim room. They regarded these melodramas as a tolerant but undeceived parent views the caperings of children playing at cops and robbers. They had seen much worse than this in real life half a century ago when there was no hotel lounge, no Baranof, no anything except a cluster of tents and shacks in a wilderness of mountains and snow and ice and bitter cold sweeping down from the Arctic.

They preferred to watch the pretty young women in the commercials, so coaxing and chummy. In evening dress obviously designed for presentation at the Court of St. James's these friendly girls extolled the wonders of shining refrigerators and kitchen stoves and dishwashers; or displayed oozing cakes and pies made with Fluffier Flour; or even recommended cigarettes that magically stimulated, soothed, and built you up at the same time.

The humming new North had little time for these septuagenarians and their sagas. They had been frozen, shot at, half drowned in icy waters; beaten, cheated; clawed by wild animals; had drunk, caroused, slept with native women; stomped and yelled and fought in saloons and bawdyhouses; battled ice and snow and mosquito hordes, and heat. That they were here at all was proof of superb endurance. But who would pause to heed these ancients in a day of speed and tension? Not the young people dressed in the careless clothes of the times. Frequently you couldn't tell the men from the women, the boys from the girls. The males were genial hustlers in loud plaid shirts, tieless, the shirttail out; slacks or corduroys; sometimes even striding hatless in the smiting cold. They sped through the streets, they crowded the bars, they flashed in and out of shops and offices, they drove high-powered cars going nowhere and nowhere to go; they devoured dainties such as king crab diabolo at Nick's Caribou Café, and steaks that thick, and apple pie that flaunted a hat of ice cream. They drank coffee coffee coffee morning noon night.

"Hiyah, Pop! You're looking good!" they might yell as they rushed past.

Sometimes an oldster might pluck at a passing coat sleeve or point a wavering finger at a map on the wall of the hotel lobby.

"I walked," he would begin, looking at you like a prideful child, "I walked from here to here, all the way afoot. Year Nineteen Hunderd and One, it was. Took me sixty-three days and like to killed me. Flour rice and a bit of sugar was all. A snip of bacon, maybe. Sixty below, blisters on my feet, and frozen. I poured coal oil on the blisters if I could get it. Fella I was with boiled his boots and ate 'em. Had to. Now they make it less than an hour on the airplane."

"Uh-huh," the hustling young newcomer would say, decently polite but twitching. "Big deal those days getting around this deep freeze. Sure must have been tough going."

He would be off and out the door and into his snub-nosed baby-blue convertible at the curb.

Czar Kennedy and Thor Storm actually were of this vintage. But there the resemblance ended. Perhaps these two had been born equipped with biological luxuries more lavish than those found in the average man. Glands, or some such mysteries. Pituitaries that functioned more superbly; endocrine secretions; genes; dynamos. Whatever the superior power, these two still functioned expertly, each in his own fashion. Their names were magic in the Territory and known to many even Outside. They had been able to take in their stride this strange new frightening world from which their vintage colleagues shrank in dismay, or at which they marveled like children.

The young newcomers to Alaska neither shrank nor marveled. They took their world for granted. Seven hours to span the thousands of miles between the Atlantic and the Pacific. "Watch it, fellas." They grinned. "That'll be covered-wagon stuff. They get those jets revved up you can do it in three hours, or maybe two. Zrrrrp! Like that."

Waylaid by one of his nostalgic contemporaries, Czar Kennedy had schooled himself to the appearance of interested listener. Politic, suave, it was his business to keep the Territory quiescent, uninformed. His head a little to one side in the attitude of listening, the battered hat pushed back on the luxuriant wavy white hair, the fine eyes gently humorous and understanding, he would occasionally nod his head in agreement and utter a low wordless hum of appreciation. The professional charmer, the shrewd operator, he heard practically nothing that the garrulous oldster was saying, and cared less. He rarely even bothered to travel Outside, preferring the adulation of his kingdom to the Stateside competition in Seattle's office buildings overlooking the magnificent bay, or the buzzing low-voiced lunch tables of the Senate restaurant in Washington D.C. All this he chose to leave to the younger tougher lower-echelon Boys.

Thor Storm listened. He not only listened, he set it down for future generations. Even in her very early girlhood he had tried to impress Chris with the importance of some of these fantastic tales of Alaska, so garrulously told and considered so boring by the young.

"Just listen to them a little now and then, Christine," he counseled her. "Nobody pays any attention to their talk. Nobody hears them any more, except me—and maybe Bridie Ballantyne. But she's too flighty to get its importance. They're trying to tell you something valuable."

Pertly she would say, "I don't see why it's so important. Anyway, it's all in those books by Rex Beach and Jack London and those, and they sound kind of dated."

"The truth isn't dated. Pretty soon they'll all be gone. Me, too. And Czar. It's unbelievable that they got here at all. It isn't so much what they did. It's the result of what they did. It's like those daubings and carvings in the caves in Spain, and in the Roman crypts and the Egyptian underground tombs. They're crude, but they're history, talking. They're like the old minstrels, the storytellers. They're saying, 'Wait a minute, don't jerk away from me like that, I'm trying to tell you something you ought to know and remember for a time when I won't be here.' Someday, Christine, if we can beat off the vultures, this part of the world is going to be so important that just to say you're an Alaskan will be bragging."

Czar Kennedy had a quite different plan for her. "When you're old enough I want you to go to school Outside, Christine, the way your poor mother did. Meet people, learn the French language, travel. You won't be marrying any lunk, and die in the wilderness smeared with dead animal blood." On this one terrible subject he never had been controlled, or even, perhaps, quite sane.

Chris had a bad time trying to adjust her emotional life to the strange circumstance in which she spent her babyhood, her childhood, her girlhood. Three months with Grandpa Thor Storm, three months with Grandpa Czar Kennedy, and over again until she came of age. Other children had families—mother father sister brother.

"My family is grandfathers," she announced to her teacher on the very first day of her Alaska school life. She was six.

"I know," her teacher had said in a voice that oozed sympathy. Child psychology was not part of the curriculum. "You poor little thing, I know all about it."

"I'm not poor," Chris had declared. "Grampa Kennedy is the richest man in the world, and Grampa Storm is the smartest, so I'm not poor." There came to her mind an expression her Grampa Kennedy sometimes used to emphasize a negative. "Not," she said, triumphantly, "not by a damn sight."

Later—not too late—Chris understood. During her college years at the University of Washington, in Seattle, she had, for the first time, an opportunity to compare the world Outside with that of the lonely far-off empire Alaska; the bastion ringed by water and mountains and distances. Outside emerged a bad second. But then, by that time her friends said, not altogether jokingly, that she was neurotic about Alaska. In love with it. "Chris thinks love and life are Alaska," they said.

She could not explain—because she did not realize—that this

strange deviation of hers was the outcome of her bizarre childhood. No two men could have regarded love and life more differently than the two who had reared her. To Czar Kennedy, the child was a hostage, the one living thing saved from the tragedy of his family life; and the Territory was to him pure plunder, rich, bountiful, inexhaustible. To Thor Storm, the gentle giant of the scholarly scientific mind, the girl was a miracle, held in trust; and Alaska a place of blinding beauty and endless promise, a possible example of hope in a frantic world, if only it could be saved from the ravishment of predatory men like Czar.

Bound together by Christine, torn apart by Alaska, the two men were friends and enemies.

3

Everyone who could be stirring was out taking advantage of the hour or two of winter's lemon-colored daylight. The Gold Street office workers, the Federal Building employees, the shop clerks, skittered across the icy sidewalks for the morning coffee break at Nick's Caribou or the Bering Coffee Shop or Gabe's Sunny Nook Café. Merchants rearranged their windows and risked a brief bareheaded moment outdoors to survey their handiwork. Housewives, marketing at a brisk trot, stared resignedly at printed signs in the supermarket bins that read Steak, $2.29 a lb.; Milk, 65 cts. qt.; Eggs, $1.23 doz.; Caulifir, 81 cts.; Bread, 64 cts. loaf. They looked again at the money in their purses and thought longingly of summer when the milk and home-grown vegetables would be coming in by truck from Matanuska, or by short-trip bush plane instead of by the long costly air freight from Outside. Bundle-laden they trotted home and telephoned a neighbor. Eleven A.M. "Come on over for coffee. I made a coffeecake early this morning out of that recipe in the *Lode.* No eggs no butter no—well, sawdust mostly, I guess, but it turned out real good."

School children at their desks stared longingly out at the ice-sheathed schoolyard. It would be too dark, too dangerously cold for sliding or skating by the time school was out.

Air pilots counted on those two hours, hurtling in from Seattle with the big four-engine jobs, or from up north in the twin-engine DC-3's, or the little single-engine Cessnas or Pipers. Big or small, they usually tried to make the run before the darkness came down again; though somehow the long long nights never were quite black here with that limitless chandelier up there sparkling with a million incandescent celestial watts. In the early autumn, the late winter, and early spring nights the northern lights made a wild aerial fantasy of the skies, the fliers said it made them feel kind of crazy. Still, pilots from Kinkaid and Morgenstern Air Force Bases said they would almost rather fly by Arctic night than by snow-dazzled day. But then, they were a race apart, everyone knew they were transformed from pink-cheeked lads to supermen, once they buckled into their gear and crawled into the cockpit. They screeched through the air in jets, day or night, flinging their lives into the constellations like gods, wing-tipped.

Bridie Ballantyne, walking up Gold Street from her apartment at the Ice Palace at eleven this winter morning was dressed as you might see women garbed on Michigan Boulevard in Chicago, or Madison Avenue, New York, or Sutter in San Francisco. No great clumsy mukluks or parkas for Bridie. No one knew how she did it but there she was mincing along, a small garnet velvet hat atop the carefully coiffed steel-gray hair, her ears unprotected. A good Pribilof seal coat. White gloves. A handsome black suède bag. Coquettish black suède pumps. Her step, what with the icy streets and her own high spirits, was a sort of prance with a slight swing. Old-timers who loved her said this was a relic of the day when, a girl of eighteen, she had whisked as student nurse through the corridors of the old Seattle hospital. The evil and envious said, nurse, my foot, she was a waitress in a lunchroom on Skid Row down by the Seattle docks. Political enemies said that the swing and the prance were left over from the period of her first Baranof days when the town was a crazy new mining camp and Bridie a picture bride without a bridegroom.

Friends and opponents were stunned when, at sixty, Bridie had settled all this.

"Let 'em have it, fair and clear. I've been up to my scalp in Alaska doings for forty fifty years, politics and everything else, they've called me words you wouldn't come on even in the Bible. I wouldn't change a minute of it, not if three fairies were standing over me the way they do in the storybooks, with those sticks in their hands waving and sparks coming out."

She herself had written her life story, breezily, with perhaps an occasional assist in the grammar department from Chris Storm or from Addie and Paul Barnett, editors and reporters on Thor Storm's weekly.

The Seattle *Post-Intelligencer* had bought it, published it, and syndicated it. The digest magazine called *Look Alive* had used it in its Stranger Than Fiction department. All Alaska, Washington State, Oregon, British Columbia and the whole Northwest for that matter had read and fumed or chuckled, depending on the political and social standing of the reader.

"I guess maybe that will shut their mouths clap-clapping these fifty years past," Bridie said, quite without rancor. "It's been kind of exciting and all, being talked about and whispered about. But being they're so nosy all these years, why, I figured they should have the straight of it. So they'd know what to put on my tombstone when the time came."

With the money received from this lone literary effort she had achieved three almost lifelong wishes. She bought for herself a pair of smallish clear blue-white diamond earrings and it was said she wore them even to bed; she took a trip to Honolulu in midwinter and was, on her return, more chauvinistically Alaskan than ever, if possible.

"Hot," she said, in a kind of running travel talk. "And a little pee of rain most days just when you're out at a garden party. Liquid sunshine they call it. Summer all the time. My, I should think they'd get sick of it! Here in Baranof summer's summer and winter's winter, no mistake about it and keeps you on your toes. Hawaii they've got what they call a fruit, it's papaya, my opinion no more flavor than a rubber boot. Alaska's good enough for me, strawberries so big you have to cut them in quarters and watch not to dribble the juice."

For the third part she virtuously donated a neat sum toward the Baranof College Scholarship Fund. "For an Eskimo student," she stipulated. "One of those smart kids can take an engine or a watch or any mechanical thing apart and fix it and put it together again. Natural-born mechanics, I've seen 'em at it. Engine instinct. God knows where they came by the knack of it."

Her costume this frigid morning had been planned for the airport arrival of a group of Distinguished Visitors, to be followed by the Baranof Chamber of Commerce luncheon at Nick's Caribou Café. Now as she pranced along Gold Street she audibly sniffed the icy air as though she were drifting languorously through a balmy vale heavy with the scent of exotic bloom.

"My!" she said aloud to no one. "Smells elegant." She often talked to herself thus as people do who live alone. Everyone she passed greeted her. Hi, Bridie! . . . Miz Ballantyne! . . . See you at the luncheon?

They wore fur parkas, the hoods pulled forward so that their faces were all but obscured, but Baranof spoke to Baranof, no matter how deeply hooded in wolf. They were accustomed to seeing Bridie dressed like a *Vogue* cover, miraculously unfrosted. Younger and hardier citizens would not have dreamed of venturing out in such garb. Her keen eye recognized everyone, marked everything. Hello, Nap! Well, good morning, Zella, I hear it's a girl this time, like you hoped for. She passed Bowker's Jewelry Store window. Gus Bowker had just finished his new display and was cautiously surveying the effect from inside, his head screwed round so that he seemed to be ogling the passer-by. Bridie, not pausing in her progress, glanced swiftly at the shining show window, threw up her hands and wagged her head in a gesture conveying dazzlement. A gratified and reassured Gus removed his head from public display.

A young man in Air Force uniform, winter issue, came toward her, in town from the Base. Rashly, his head was without covering. Bridie glanced at him sharply. She saw the white blob in the center of his face. A newcomer, a rookie. "Heh, young man!" she called as he passed. "Young man! Your nose is frozen!"

He went on, heedless or perhaps unhearing. She turned to scuttle after him but he vanished into the Juke Box Stationery and Lunch, you heard the blare and squawk of the canned music as he opened the door and disappeared. Oh, well, Bridie thought, he'll find out all right when it begins to hurt in a minute. Teach him.

Always, winter and summer, when she reached the busy corner of Gold and Polaris, where the Miners' National Bank stood so solidly, she too stood solidly a moment to gaze up and down the street to the jagged sky line of the mountains at one end, to the gray water at the other, with the shining slab of the Ice Palace challenging both. She liked Baranof best in the winter. This was no unique perversity. The town had recently taken a poll. It turned out that ninety per cent of the adult population and ninety-five per cent of the school boys and girls preferred the winter months to the brief summer season.

"Just goes to prove," Bridie said. "Pioneer spirit. Pioneers like it tough or they wouldn't be pioneers."

She liked to stand there at the corner and watch the gay new traffic lights go green go red like the Christmas-tree globes in the window of Hager's Hardware Store at holiday time. Lights, snow, mountains, people, stood out sharply as though cut for a gigantic game of jigsaw.

Passing in cars or on foot her fellow townsmen were concerned a bit as they saw her waiting to be picked up by the others of the reception committee. You aim to freeze yourself into a totem, standing there? . . . Give you a lift, Bridie?

A young woman stepped briskly along the snow-ridged sidewalk, a three-year-old by the hand, a one-year-old in the gocart. The faces of all three blossomed out from the fur-bordered parka hoods, fresh and glowing and unexpected as tundra flowers.

Bridie peered down at the new-minted face almost hidden in the cart. "The new one? Look at the cut of him, would you, in that parky! The spit of his dad. And how is Augie?"

"It's a girl. And my husband isn't Augie. Lowell. I'm Mrs. Lowell Kramer."

Bridie caught this challenge deftly, she fished a name up from the swarming depths of her memory. "Who else, of course! Who else but little Lorine, as if I didn't mind the day you stepped off that plane—black winter—how long ago was it now?—four—all right, call it five years ago—and you scared he wouldn't be there to meet you from the Air Base and in another way scared he would, and there he was at the airport waiting in his uniform, and off we went to the church. And a prettier wedding I never did see, though I recall the gardenia corsage he'd ordered for you from Seattle by air was just a leeee-tle bit brown around the edges. Nipped, they were."

The girl laughed then, helplessly, half amused, half vexed. "Lowell isn't Air Force, he's a construction worker, we were married back home in Dakota and this one"—she pointed to the older child—"was born before I ever got here. I stepped off the plane, my husband had never seen him, he was so excited——"

"Oh, well, make nothing of it," Bridie said, airily, as though it had been the girl who was in error. "You're here and happy, and that's what counts." She looked sharply at the young woman. "Two, and another one coming. Three's a nice number, four is better, and Alaska wants population, those ninnies in Washington keep saying there aren't enough of us. Why, look at Oregon when it came in, and Nebraska and New Mexico and California even, not to speak of that Texas—why, twenty-eight territories with a lot less population than us got statehood but here we are——"

Bridie was off, riding her favorite subject full-tilt. The young wife thought of her marketing and her household tasks as she nodded politely, her glance distrait. The boy shook his mother's hand impatiently, the child in the cart began to whimper. Bridie broke off abruptly. "And who's a bigger ninny than me, keeping these angels here in the cold?"

A car came to a stop at the curb. Another, just behind it, halted with a screech. Windows were lowered, there was hallooing and beckoning, a girl at the wheel of the first car stuck her head out of the window. A black-eyed blonde in a white fur parka, its white wolf hood dramatically framing her face.

"Bridie! We called for you at the Ice Palace. Waited and waited and Ott went up to your room. You said you'd be in the lobby at eleven."

"Did I now, Chris! Oh, the pity of it!" The feet, in the smart black suède pumps, made nothing of the snowy distance between sidewalk and car. "I had an errand, very particular it was, and I made sure you'd pick me up here at the corner." She waved farewell to the young wife and the two children. "My love to Augie, now, and don't forget," she called, blithely.

Ott Decker emerged from the first car, he scurried round to hand Bridie in. "Oh, now, Bridie, everybody knows you can't sit still long enough to be called for. Ants in your pants."

"Mind your tongue!" Bridie commanded, teetering toward the door.

The front window of the second car was lowered. Czar Kennedy's silver head was poked out. Peering just behind it was Oscar Bogard, Mayor of Baranof.

"Someday you'll be standing here on the corner frozen stiff," the Mayor shouted, "and somebody'll put a dime in your mouth thinking you're a parking meter."

"It won't be you," retorted Bridie. "You're too stingy to meter-park, you got diplomatic immunity." Her laughter whooped out on the icy morning air.

Czar Kennedy's benevolent face, his gentle voice, chided her.

"Come on right in here where you belong, Bridie, with the old sourdoughs. You can have the whole back seat to yourself, like the queen you are."

With one gesture, Bridie's white-gloved hand rejected this courtly offer. "I'm riding with the young fry." She scrambled into the broad front seat beside Chris before Decker could assist her. "That is, if I ain't crowding." Seated, she now raised her voice to an astonishing shriek that carried to the rejected pair in the second car. "No offense, Czar, and you too, Mr. Mayor. But Bridie Ballantyne never sits at the second table." Again her whoop of laughter.

The second car now moved off into first place. As it passed smartly the two men could be seen shaking their heads in amusement or disapproval or both. "You kill me," Ott Decker remarked, inadequately, as he slid into the front seat beside the two women.

Bridie patted the head of the girl in the white parka, gave a straightening jerk to her own hat that had gone askew as she clambered in, adjusted her scarf, wrapped her seal coat about her silk-clad legs, licked her lips with a quick nervous flick of triumph, gave a little settling hunch to her shoulders, sighed with satisfaction, and took her handkerchief from her bag with a flourish that assailed the atmosphere with Parma violet—all this in a series of gestures so swift as to melt into one rhythmic sequence.

"Up front is where I like to sit," she went on, as though continuing a conversation, "so's I can see what Chris is hitting before she hits it." Suddenly she leaned forward to stare at the vehicle's pale orchid hood. "Say, whose car is this, anyway, you're driving, Chris? It sure ain't yours, unless you've bought a new one or Czar's gone wild and given you one, not likely."

"Mine," Ott Decker said plaintively. "My brand-new Thunderbird. And don't ask me why I let her drive it to the airport. Except she busted up her own. And I'm nuts about her."

Chris's voice was soft and low. Some said this was a trick she had learned from old Czar. The resentful ones said it was an affectation. She soft-pedals it, they complained, so you have to listen close, that way she makes everything she says sound important.

"Bridie Ballantyne, you know perfectly well I've never hit anything, and I've been driving since I was fifteen, haven't I!"

"Then what does Ott mean—you busted up your car!"

"Something hit me. Yesterday I was driving down past Mile Forty and a moose charged right out at me from the woods, I never saw anything so silly, I thought for a minute that I'd be out in the snow and the moose would be in the front seat, driving. It was a close thing, he damaged the radiator and broke a headlight. And my spirit, of course. I never thought a moose would hunt me."

Bridie pointed in the direction of the fast-vanishing car ahead of them. "I wish I had those two men here this minute. I got up and told them, last week's City Council meeting, I said, more moose around this winter than I've seen in fifty years, they'll be promenading down Gold Street next. Oh, no, they said, and anyway that's the wrong kind of publicity to give out about Alaska. Ott, why'n't you Chamber of Commerce people do something?"

"Do! You'll have to speak to God. It's the record cold. There's nothing in the woods for them to eat so they come out looking for handouts. You can't shoot every moose that shows its head the other side of a tree."

"That's right, protect the poor moose and the hell with the people of Baranof. You sound like one of those Absentee Big Boys in Seattle. Sometimes I think Alaska deserves what it gets—which sure is nothing."

Chris's laughter rang in the clear cold air. "Children, children! Stop fighting among yourselves. You won't have any ammunition left for the enemy."

Ott Decker reached past Bridie to place a doubled fist gently against Chris's jaw—a wooing, futile, tender gesture of his kind.

"As Secretary of the Baranof Chamber of Commerce I don't want to hear any of that enemy talk. We're all buddies from the time their plane touches down until they take off again for Outside."

"Who all's coming?" Bridie interrupted, briskly. "The General, of course, but the Base will take care of him. Besides, he isn't rightly a general any more, is he, now that he's Vice-President and Chairman of the Board, no less, of National Fish Pack Company? Seventy-five thousand a year, I hear he's pulling down. Place on Long Island, apartment at the Waldorf in New York. He a general now, anyway?"

"A general once is a general always," Ott assured her. "Flesh, fowl *or* fish."

Bridie jerked at her skirts and scuffled her feet impatiently in the way she had when she scented news. "Yes, but who? Who else? The General well and good, he's window dressing for the Seattle crowd. And Dave Husack must be coming or Czar Kennedy wouldn't be down meeting the plane. I hear Dave's gone soft in his sixties and he eats a blonde for breakfast every morning—that is, when he's away from home and that starched wife of his." Then, as a curious weight of silence fell upon the air, "Oh, Chris, I'm sorry—I didn't mean—I guess I must be going soft myself."

Ott Decker's arm slid along the back of the seat until his hand just touched Chris's shoulder. "Chris is a blonde, all right, but she sure would stick in Dave Husack's throat if he tried to swallow her."

"How did I get into this?" Chris demanded, rather waspishly for her. "I live here, don't I? And you know perfectly well who's coming, Bridie."

"Do I, now? I know Dave Husack's coming, and of course Sid Kleet. Where Dave is, there's Sid just behind, nudging him like a tugboat edging an oversized ship into harbor. Then there's General Cass Baldwin—did you say I call him General anyway, even if he's in the Fish Business now instead of the Fight Business?"

"Now, Bridie, we covered that once," Chris reminded her. "What's wrong with you this morning? I don't mind meeting Dave Husack. All that's over and done with."

"Just the same, something's afoot," Bridie persisted, musingly. "Let's see now. There's Wilbur K. Distelhorst coming too—the nerve of them in Washington! Sending just an assistant instead of the top boy. There's a fine sample of the Department of the Interior for you! I bet he's never seen a salmon, only on a platter, or a bear except in a zoo, or a stand of timber outside a movie."

"Wilbur K. Distelhorst," Chris interrupted, dreamily. "I love to say it. It's like something out of Dickens. Or Sinclair Lewis."

"Look, Chris, let me drive, will you?" Ott Decker said. "We're a little late. Can't even see Czar's car. I think I hear the plane."

"That's an old bush crate and you know it perfectly well, Ott," Bridie persisted. "Come on now. Something's afoot."

Now, for the first time, Chris tensed a little at the wheel, she risked a quick searching glance at Ott Decker's guileless face. A boyish flush suffused it as she eyed him.

"I'm a big girl now, Ott. You're nervous as a bridegroom. Are you importing some choice morsel from Outside? Object matrimony?"

Bridie yelped, "Ott!"

"No. And you damn well know why, so don't needle me, Chris."

Bridie now began to breathe heavily with the intake and exhaust of a steam pipe about to burst. "Ott Decker, if you don't tell us this minute what you're being so sneaky about——"

"All right." He threw his arms wide in a gesture of revelation. "Czar kept it under wraps. And nobody actually told me. But down at the Chamber office we put two and two together, sometimes, and it comes out five——"

"Ott Decker!" Bridie screeched.

"Young Husack's coming," he blurted. "Bayard, no less. And that girl he's going to marry—or supposed to. And he's supposed to stay six months in Alaska. The heir apparent kind of getting acquainted with his future subjects, I suppose. The old king is kind of pooped. Long live the king."

There was silence in the car. Even Bridie was momentarily speechless. Then she drew the long whistling bronchial breath of one who is about to blast. Ott Decker raised a restraining hand.

"Wait a minute. I haven't finished. Nobody knows this, Chris. Nobody but your Grandpa Thor, and Paul and Addie Barnett. And, of course, Czar's whole crowd, and they don't know Thor knows."

Chris began to laugh, not very merrily, for her. "Nobody? Well, we'll have a field day with that." She stopped, stiffened at the wheel. "But we went to press yesterday. Did they know it then? You can't unscramble a weekly. And why didn't somebody tell me?"

"They didn't know until last night. It must have been too late, they distribute this noon."

"Ott Decker! If you've known about this all along——"

"I tell you I haven't. Wouldn't I tell you, Chris! That isn't all. Young Husack's only staying a month or so now, to get the feel of Alaska in the winter. That's what they said. The feel. Then Outside till June or July, and back here and we're supposed to do the real guided tour, Barrow to Juneau, with you chaperoning, Bridie. You window dressing, Chris. Unless he marries in the meantime. But that isn't the idea. Just wait, you two."

Bridie jerked her hat forward, a characteristic gesture of utter irritation. "Wait for what? What *is* the idea! I've a mind to slap you, Ott Decker, big as you are."

"I'm the idea, I suppose," Chris said, quietly.

"Partly. But this is real old melodrama, it's like the stuff in those books I used to read out of my grandmother's bookcase when I went to visit her in Sausalito. The rich old bastard and the young district attorney and the beauteous maiden. Old-timy books left over from Theodore Roosevelt's Big Stick days. Robber Barons."

Bridie's protest now hurtled through the winter air like the warning screech of a locomotive when a cow is on the track. Ott laid a placating hand on her knee. "They're grooming young Bay for the big-time race. He is supposed to spend some time in the Territory because they aim to have him appointed Governor of Alaska. Youth, see, in the saddle." Then, as Bridie again opened her mouth, "Now wait a minute. You haven't heard the half. A couple of years is all, he resigns on some excuse, then he's back in Seattle and they run him for Congress. Then Senator. Then, by the time he's maybe forty or forty-five, he's candidate for the first President of the United States to come out of the Great Neglected Northwest Empire." He leaned forward to clear Bridie's furred expanse and stared hard at the silent girl at the wheel. "You think she'll run the White House O.K., Chris? All those lovely state dinners? And the Easter egg rolling? Couple of years now I notice they've dropped that egg rolling, it's a damn shame——"

Bridie found voice again. "Fine time to be telling us, Ott Decker. I won't forget this in a hurry. And for Chris——"

"I tell you I didn't get wind of it until half an hour ago when I was calling the Ice Palace. I found out Dave Husack wasn't staying at Czar's house this time, the way he usually does. So I got the manager's office and Goomer says they've reserved the four rooms they call the Governor's suite on the top floor, no less . . ."

"Four," Chris said, quietly. "That's a bedroom for old Dave, one for Bay, and a sitting room. And a bedroom, leave us piously hope, for her."

"I knew it!" Bridie crowed. "I had a hunch this morning early something stinking was on the fire. I just thought I'd go up and check the Ice Palace V.I.P. suite. I knew Sid Kleet alone didn't rate it, even with that Distelhorst along, and Husack generally always stays at Czar's place. The minute I laid eyes on it I smelled something funny. Sitting room, three bedrooms, dressing room in the big one, two baths, flowers in vases and the refrigerator chugging as if they had a whale in there. Whose coming rates that, I said to myself. Who gives Dave Husack flowers? I'd as soon give flowers to a Kodiak bear. The bridal suite if I ever saw it. But who's the bride, I said."

They were in sight of the airport now, a gay toy in a sparkling white setting, dotted with other tiny silver-bright toys.

"Here we are," Ott announced, foolishly. Chris's gaze was straight ahead as she guided the car toward the parking space.

"Does Grampa Kennedy know about the Ice Palace?"

"He made the arrangements."

"You knew."

"I tell you I didn't know until this morning. I had a feeling something was stewing, that's all. Old instinct left over from my newspaper days."

The warning intake of breath from Bridie. Chris laid a gently restraining hand on her arm. "Let's not get emotional."

"Look, Chris," Ott said, miserably, "I'm Chamber of Commerce Secretary. Right? My job is to go along with the people who run this town. I think the Territory's being had, but if I'm going to buck the Big Boys, why, I can resign. Czar didn't want this news around for a lot of reasons and one is that Thor's weekly went to press last night and Czar counted on a beat for this afternoon's *Lode*. He's got it."

"Thanks, chum."

Desperately, "Look, Chris, marry me and we'll get out of here. I can get the C.C. Secretary job in Topeka any day I want it."

"Indelicate!" Bridie shouted. "Asking a girl to marry you in front of a third party."

Ott hugged her as he handed her out of the car. "I'd marry you, too, if I was young enough, Bridie. But I just couldn't go your pace."

He rushed around to the other side of the car but Chris was

already making for the building. Over her shoulder she said, "I wouldn't be too sure if I were Grandpa Czar. Paul and Addie have a mukluk grapevine." A roar rent the blue. "There they are." A loudspeaker blared. The mountains hurled the sound back into the crystal air. Pan American Number Six Two Nine arriving from Seattle Gate Two . . . Arctic Clipper Number Three Seven Five for Nome Kotzebue Oogruk . . .

Ott opened the heavy door that led to the crowded waiting room. He looked at the girl and she at him, her hand touched his arm and rested there a moment. "Thanks, Ott dear."

"I could be mistaken."

"No. Grampa's never forgiven me for not marrying Bay. This is his way of punishing me. Or something. You never know what he's up to."

"How scheming can an old man get, anyway?"

"Well, Machiavelli was nearly sixty when he died. That would be, roughly, today's ninety. He did pretty well, considering that they didn't have all those steaks and spinach and B_{12} shots those days."

"Thor going to be here?"

"You know he doesn't go in for reception committees."

"Well, lean on me, will you, Chris?"

"Grandpa Storm taught me to walk alone."

"You can overdo it."

Inside the waiting room were warmth, movement, a shimmer of excitement. Modern and adequate when it was built barely six years ago, the airport now was almost obsolete. Baranof was a crossroads between Russia and the United States, between Japan and the United States, between Scandinavia and the United States, between the North Pole and the United States. The main concourse (as the publicity departments grandly phrased it) today and every day and night, V.I.P.s or no V.I.P.s, always was bursting with men and women and children and infants in arms waiting to hurl themselves into the clouds. Slim lads in Air Force uniforms. Stout colonels in mukluks and parkas. Girls with the narrow band on the third left finger, their husbands looming mammoth in wool and fur, both concentrating on a wailing goggling object in her arms. Young fry slid and yelped across the polished floor. In the lunchroom ham and eggs and waffles and steaks and coffee appeared and disappeared like props in a conjurer's trick. The loud-speaker trumpeted again.

Passengers for Point Barrow . . . Number Six Eight Nine arriving Gate Three . . . Fairbanks Anchorage Seattle leaving . . . Passengers Cordova . . . Sitka . . . Ketchikan . . . Juneau . . . Passengers for the North Pole . . .

Science had married the Wilderness and was taming the savage shrew.

Even in that crowded room it was easy to distinguish the arresting figure of Czar Kennedy. He stood tall and erect in a world of six-foot men. But it was the head that gave him distinction. Above the benevolent face your eye was caught by the spectacularly beautiful hair, wavy, abundant, vigorous. Its natural mixture of white and steel-gray imparted a silver-blue tone. Elderly Baranof matrons strove to achieve this effect at the Modish Mayde Beauty Salon. It was a standing joke. "Louella," they said, after their shampoo, "give me a nice Czar Kennedy gray-blue rinse, now."

The three late-comers made their way through the crowd toward the beacon of that distinguished head. Bridie and Ott, incorrigible greeters, halted their progress a dozen times to pat a baby's behind, to shake a parent's hand, to speak to the newsstand girl, to wave at a harried waitress rushing toward the lunchroom. Unerringly they spotted businessmen from Outside on the way to a waiting bus or taxi, and of these they cordially demanded to know how they liked Alaska. Ott darted out to the runway gate where the Big Brass stood stoically in Arctic full-dress splendor; the very best cloth, the very best leather, the very best fur, the goldenest gilt in the uniformed world.

Czar Kennedy and Oscar Bogard stood near the exit as Chris and Bridie came toward them. Ott, rushing in now, reported the plane's imminent landing.

"Well, Bridie," Czar Kennedy said gently, in indirect reproof to his granddaughter. "You would have done better to ride along with Oscar and me after all. We had time for a cup of coffee."

"I never touch the acidy stuff. Tea is my tipple, as you well know." Her high metallic voice cut through the roar of the incoming monsters outside and the outgoing humans inside. "You know what! I'd like to come down here and spend the whole day sometime. I've wanted to ever since they built the airport. Breakfast lunch and dinner at the counter, maybe a little bourbon highball toward evening, just visit around and watch the people and the planes in and out, it's better than a movie."

"Oh, now, Bridie," Ott jeered. "You trying to make out you're just a little girl from the farm? You fly all the time, you're whizzing in and out of Baranof like a bluebottle."

"Back east, when I was a little tyke," Czar mused, aloud, "we used to go down to the depot to see Number Eleven come in. It was the big city train with the Pullman cars. People who got off, or even those who looked out through the windows, were from another world. Outside. It's the same thing, planes or trains, today or yesterday."

Oscar Bogard cut short this little reminiscence. "Here's the Barnetts," he announced. His tone was less than cordial.

Chris Storm's hands were outstretched toward the approaching couple while they still were ten feet away. "Paul!" she called. "Addie!" As one would hail rescuers. The intelligent civilized faces beamed affection upon her as they made their way toward the group.

Oscar Bogard greeted this couple with an unconvincing joviality. "What're you folks doing down here! Meeting friends?"

Addie Barnett of the crisp red hair and the lively retort met this in character. "On the contrary."

Paul Barnett, tall, stooped, gangling of frame, spectacled, might have passed for a post-graduate summer college student if it were not for the slight graying at the temples. Now the myopic eyes behind the thick lenses peered down at Oscar Bogard as a microscope centers on a bug. Slow of speech, almost drawling, his utterances often took on a misleading mildness. "You haven't forgotten that Addie and I get out a weekly paper, have you, Oscar?"

"Not likely. I get more mention in one issue of your weekly than in a whole month of Czar's daily. Not better—but more."

Blandly, "It's nice to know you read us, Oscar. By the time Addie and I get through the week of being editors, reporters, linotype operators, proofreaders, compositors—and then run the paper off the press—we don't get a chance to poll the readers. How did you like Thor's editorial this week?"

Oscar's little eyes narrowed to slits. "You keep on with stuff like that against Czar, you'll lose what little advertising you got."

"That wasn't against Czar. It was about him. Facts."

"Facts! It's funny how a man who's a failure can always root up something to say against a man who's a success."

Paul Barnett seemed to consider this briefly. "Well, now, I don't know. Czar'd have a hard time rooting up anything against Thor."

"Czar!" Oscar yelled. "You talk the way you go twisting things in that column of yours."

In each weekly issue of the *Northern Light* there appeared a Thor Storm editorial and a column of astonishingly unstilted, often witty and always courageous comment called—somewhat lamely—Deep Freeze. Served up from this receptacle were odds and ends political, casual, personal, pungent. Their origin was attributed to no one in particular, but it was known that Paul and Addie Barnett, Thor Storm, and even Chris Storm contributed to the savory dish. Now you occasionally saw bits and paragraphs quoted in Stateside papers. Sometimes a Thor Storm local editorial found its way, astonishingly enough, into the editorial pages of such big city dailies as the New York *Times*, the San Francisco *Call*, the St. Louis *Post-Dispatch*, as two decades earlier the wise and witty observations of another newspaper editor, William Allen White of the little Emporia *Gazette*, had so often been nationally reprinted.

Ott Decker was herding them to the runway gates. "Come on now, folks, they'll be touching down in a second." The little group stood in the brief pale winter light, their faces turned toward the moving shining thing in the sky, brighter than the Arctic sun itself. Old and new Alaska. Czar Kennedy, Oscar Bogard, Bridie Ballantyne. Chris Storm, the Barnetts, Ott Decker.

Addie Barnett leaned close to Chris. "Have you heard about Bay Husack and the girl? I tried to get you on the telephone."

"Yes."

"Did Czar tell you!"

"No, of course not. Ott."

"Do you mind if I let Czar know that Paul and I know? Before they land? It's mean, but I can't resist it."

"Go ahead."

A little apart stood Kinkaid Air Base Big Brass. It unbent just a little in the direction of Alaska's First Citizen. "Mr. Kennedy," they said. "How are you, sir." Czar's hand went to his head in a semi-military salute. "General," he said, with a kind of sweet solemnity. "Colonel . . . Major . . ."

Now the sky monster roared toward them, it touched on tiptoe. The aluminum steps were rushed up to its shining side.

Addie Barnett raised her clear incisive voice above the tumult. "Czar, isn't it interesting that young Husack is taking over in Alaska, at last?"

A jaw muscle tightened in the old man's face. He did not turn his head. "Well, now, I wouldn't say taking over. Just getting the feel. Too bad you and Paul went to press yesterday. That's the worst of a weekly, Addie. Time. Time."

The plane door opened. Paul Barnett's quiet voice could just be heard. "As a matter of fact, we just barely made it. Addie and I worked till three this morning, setting up the story. But the paper's out and distributed by now."

"Say!" Ott Decker exclaimed, beaming. "Say! When a weekly beats a daily—that's news!"

A little cold white flame of dislike shot from beneath Czar Kennedy's eyelids.

Two plane hostesses stood in the doorway, one blonde, one brunette, coolly pretty, very smart in their blue tailored uniforms and their slim high-heeled pumps. Good-bye now! they chirped, smiling. Good-bye now good-bye now good-bye now.

The General was the first to emerge. Paul Barnett swung his camera into action. The *Lode* photographer suddenly appeared from nowhere and crouched at the foot of the stairs. General Cass Baldwin appeared the man of business now, in mufti. Somehow, minus the cap with the gold snakework, and the battle blouse and all, the profile lacked that firmness, that austerity which had been so reassuring in the wartime photographs. Rather haggard and crumpled now, the face was that of any elderly passenger who had flown across a maximum of continent with a minimum of sleep. Just behind him loomed Dave Husack, vast, opulent, cuddled in cashmere. For a moment he blotted out his shadow, but it followed him as always, for where Dave Husack stood or walked, there was Sid Kleet at his side or in his footsteps. Slight, pale, impassive, Kleet seemed negligible in contrast to the monolithic males of the Northwest—unless you looked well into his eyes. Sid Kleet, in or out of the bare shabby offices of his law firm down near the waterfront in Seattle, was a general too. But Industry, not War, was his science. He marshaled millions of dollars, not millions of men. His campaigns were mapped in law offices; over a bourbon-and-water in the libraries of private homes after dinner in Seattle and Tacoma and San Francisco; at lunch in the Senate restaurant in Washington D.C. No blueprints, no mathematics, no money figured in these meetings. Everything casual, bland, friendly. To a listener the talk might have sounded like a particularly dull collection of clichés.

"If you can see your way clear to bringing it to the attention of the House, I certainly would appreciate it, Ed."

"I'll be glad to do whatever I can, Sid. Of course, I can't guarantee anything. Naturally."

"Naturally. None of us can do more than our best, and if you can see your way clear, why . . . by the way, I see where that Tidelands bill is coming up in your bailiwick. It just might be that I could ease that a little bit by talking it over with old Woody . . ."

Down the steps, their heels clattering on the bright metal; pausing a moment for the photographers. Now the doorway framed the businesslike figure of Wilbur K. Distelhorst. Wilbur Distelhorst could look brisk even while standing still. He glanced comprehensively at the assembled welcoming committee, at the impressive Brass, at the photographers crouched at the foot of the stairs, at the fishbowl faces swimming behind the big plate-glass windows of the swarming airport waiting room. He then shook hands with the two pretty airplane hostesses and his own good-bye now good-bye now good-bye now became a bass obbligato to their soprano chirpings. He began a leisurely descent of the stairs. The effect was that of a one-man parade. You just heard his first reply to the question put to him by the *Daily Lode* reporter, "I'm here for just one reason. To learn. To learn all about your wonderful . . ." when two handsome young people appeared in the doorway; a man and a woman.

"My God, she's got on a mink coat!" Bridie Ballantyne exclaimed.

"Why not?" Chris retorted. "Wouldn't you wear one if you had it?"

"Not if I was her, I wouldn't. I'd dress plain as a post."

"It just means she's tough-fibered and honest, in her own terms," Chris said. "Out for blood and doesn't hide the switch-blade."

"I guess they're really wearing those hats this winter," Bridie concluded, mournfully, "if she is. It sure makes mine look dated."

Chris had not seen him in two years. She had not seen Dina Drake or Dave Husack or Sid Kleet in all that time. The future Mrs. Bayard Husack after all, Chris mused. Then, cattily for her, She's certainly earned it. Bay looks set and sulky, I know that look.

The Air Force closed in on the General, the committee enveloped Dave Husack, Sid Kleet, Wilbur K. Distelhorst. Somehow young Husack and the mink-coated girl stood momentarily outside this cluster. In the flurry of greetings and the brief sorting of introductions Bridie's loquacity emerged victorious. Above the murmured platitudes her hearty phrases loosely bound the group into a related bundle.

"You and Czar know each other, that's for sure . . . and Miss Christine Storm, our Miss Alaska born and bred . . . the Barnetts . . . Bogard our Mayor . . . well now, you young folks standing way out there . . . we all know you, Bay Husack, leastways your pa . . . welcome to Alaska, Miss—mmm—uh—you sure came to the right place with that nice warm mink coat . . . ?"

A shade too heartily Bayard Husack said, "Hello, Chris! Well, this is pretty wonderful it's great to see you you're looking lovely as always, here's Dina dying to see you. And Dina you've met Mrs. Ballantyne haven't you, at least you've heard me talk——"

Yes, and you're talking a little too much this minute, Chris thought, rather ill-naturedly for her. The two young women looked at each other, their hands met. The conventional smile arranged itself on their faces, they looked at each other, the tall black-haired girl whose eyes were an unexpected blue, the blond girl with the startling black eyes.

"It's wonderful to see you again. And on your home grounds. What an enchanting coat," Dina Drake said. "And the hood. If Paris could see it they'd announce the new Alaska look."

"It's a parka," rather lamely. "We pronounce it parky. Don't ask me why."

"All that white fur! It's so dramatic. Like a costume in a musical."

A poker term came to Chris's mind. You've tipped your hand early again, as usual. Well, if that's the way you want to play.

"Everybody wearing mink in Seattle, I suppose, Miss Drake," Bridie observed blandly. She never was one to bother with preliminaries.

"This?" Miss Drake glanced down at herself, absently, as though just reminded of what she was wearing. "I got this last winter in New York." In a tone that states a self-evident fact. She now removed her hat, collapsed it in some magic way, and thrust it into her coat pocket. She then drew over her head a soft mammoth mink hood which had lain draped below the neckline of the sumptous garment. The modeling of the face and the look in the eye were, perhaps, too modern and too motivated for that soft fur frame. Ott Decker, emotionally vulnerable but no fool, bustling up to herd the group indoors, peered politely at the fur-framed face. A dish, he decided, and lots of style, but she looks like the wolf in Red Ridinghood.

"Miss Drake," Bay was explaining, a bit too spaciously, no one having asked, "is Dad's second secretary. I mean Miss Gurkin wouldn't come, she's a bit vintage anyway for a jaunt like this, and of course Mother couldn't possibly, so——"

Whew! Chris thought. Elaborate. Aloud she said, politely, "And how *is* your mother, Bay?"

But Mayor Bogard was shooing everyone into the waiting room. "Any you folks like a cup of coffee here, or a little drinky or something? The luncheon's twelve-thirty but you prolly got up before breakfast ha ha!"

Distelhorst said, virtuously, never eat between meals; and patted his stomach.

Dave Husack held up a protesting palm. "They fed us every minute on that plane from the time we left Seattle. Coffee first thing, and then a big breakfast of ham and eggs and juice and fried potatoes and those sweet rolls—why don't we ever have those at home, I wonder?—and coffee coffee coffee." He talked always in a jovial roar; the nostrils of anyone within ten feet of him were pricked by the artificial woodsy leathery tobaccoy sugary costly emanation of a widely advertised toilet water called His. When he whipped one of his fine imported linen handkerchiefs out of his pocket people in confined places had been known to reel.

As he talked he revolved slowly to include the whole group, the great dull red face beaming with good humor and self-satisfaction. In the vast golden-brown cashmere topcoat he looked, as he ponderously revolved, like a miraculously trained Alaska Kodiak brown bear balancing on its hind legs.

Now his small somewhat bloodshot eyes encountered the amused gaze of Christine Storm. He had encountered that gaze before today, he had been flicked by the dart of disdain that shone behind the amusement, he resented it, he rejected it, he rejected the dark intelligent eyes and the lovely girl herself, and everything and everyone she represented—except Czar Kennedy. Without Czar Kennedy and the pattern of plans and planners that stretched, an intricate web, from west coast to east coast, Dave Husack might have had to forego the creamy-soft cashmere coat, the jaunty yacht, the cars, the luxurious office suite, the massive handsome house high on the hills of Seattle, overlooking the overpowering view of sound, straits, lakes, mountains, skies, forests.

Now he put one great fur-gloved paw on Chris's shoulder, with the other he patted her cheek. Perhaps he had even contemplated a hug, but she had stepped back just enough to elude this. "Chris!" he bellowed. "How's Alaska's Joan of Arc!"

Very low, without moving his lips, Czar Kennedy said to Mayor Bogard, "Get going."

Obediently Bogard called in the high voice of a Boy Scout leader, "Now then, folks! Let's get organized. Let's see, now. Mr. Husack, how's about you going in with——"

"What's this Mister stuff! Dave!"

"Thanks. Dave, if you'll just come this way——"

But now Ott Decker, the expert organizer, took over. He did not say well folks or now then. He had collected the baggage stubs, he had handily placed the luggage, he waved a hand toward the waiting cars.

"In, everybody! I'll break trail if you'll follow. The parade is just starting. Plenty of room, the General's gone with the Base group, he'll join us later at luncheon if they'll give him a chance. . . . Mr. Husack—Dave, that is—you're with Czar, of course, and you too, Mr. Distelhorst, and Sid Kleet, naturally. Bridie, I know Paul and Addie'll be happy to take you in. Bayard Husack and Miss—uh—in my car, I hope, if that's all right with you, it's that lavender job over there it isn't paid for yet so if you don't like the color just say the word and I'll—— Chris, in my car of course. Mayor Bogard—oh, he's already climbed in with the skookum boys."

Czar Kennedy made no move to order these arrangements, he wasted no energy on such details. Smiling gently now, his head a little to one side as though surveying a pleasing picture, he seated himself in his own good middle-class car. But then a disturbing mistake seemed to have been made. The Barnetts' shabby car already was to be seen scooting down the airport road toward town. Bridie

Ballantyne, seated amazingly between Dave Husack and Sid Kleet, was queening it in the back of Czar's car; and in some mysterious way Wilbur K. Distelhorst was snugly ensconced between Dina Drake and young Husack in Ott Decker's orchid equipage, which was on the point of leaving.

"Get out!" Czar said to the bewildered Bogard beside him. "Get out and tell that—tell Distelhorst he belongs in this car."

But when Bogard had hurriedly clambered out and had conveyed this message, standing at the Decker car window and apparently encountering good-natured but stiff resistance, he turned his head to look piteously back at Czar.

"Says he's doing fine." He floundered back to the Kennedy car.

4

Distelhorst stuck his head out of the window. He waved a blithe hand; a great grin gashed the strangely unlined middle-aged face.

"Heh, fooled you that time, Czar, and you too, Sid. Wise guys! I ride where the pretty gals are. Oops! No offense, ma'am." Noticing too late the presence of Bridie Ballantyne in the back seat beside Kleet.

Czar Kennedy waved at him, he smiled his charming smile. "Damned old goat," he muttered in one of his rare unguarded moments.

The two pretty airplane hostesses emerged from the waiting-room door and hailed a yellow taxi at the curb. Now a third figure, smart in the blue uniform of a pilot, came through the doorway.

"Ross!" Chris called to him. "Ross! Want a lift?"

The man held up a hand in greeting, he smiled. The olive skin, the white teeth in contrast, the light of recognition in his eyes gave him a look of almost startling brilliance. He hesitated a moment, then he walked swiftly to the car. He saw the passengers, he paused, uncertainly. The yellow taxi hummed past, the faces of the two pretty hostesses stared out.

Ott Decker, at the wheel, asked, "Where you in from, Ross?"

"Nome–Kotzebue–Oogruk run."

"Pile in."

Chris slid nearer Ott Decker so that there now was space for a third passenger in the wide front seat. "In! In! We've got precious freight here, and they're not used to our climate." As he entered, and the car moved off, she made the introductions expertly, over her shoulder. "Miss Drake, you've met Ross. In Seattle—remember? Mr. Distelhorst—Ross Guildenstern, as in Hamlet. Mr. Distelhorst of the Washington Department of the Interior . . . Bayard Husack of the Seattle Husacks, no less, you know him too. Ross Guildenstern is one of the pet pilots on the Arctic Circle Air Line, Mr. Distelhorst."

The bronze young man with the Nordic name removed his blue cap and turned his head toward the three in the rear seat. His vigorous hair was like another cap, black, thick, stiff. "You had us strolling around in the air there for a while, waiting for you to come in. Who was the Big Brass?"

"General, that's who," boomed Distelhorst. "Just merely General Cass Baldwin, that's all." He cleared his throat, he peered right he peered left, hunching low in the seat. "This is going to be mighty interesting. Now then. I'm here to get the feel of this country. I'd like to get a line on you young folks, it's you youngsters that will have to carry on when the torch is handed to you. That's why young Husack is here. That right, Bay?"

"Oh, on the button," young Husack said in a fatigued Harvard drawl of utter resentment.

Distelhorst plodded on, feeling freshly encouraged. "Now I know that Czar Kennedy's your grampa—isn't that it, Miss Storm? That probably answers any question I'd want to ask about you. One of the great pioneers of our day, Czar is. One of the greatest of our country."

"I've got another grandfather who's still greater," Chris said.

"Where's he?"

"Right here."

Distelhorst glanced hurriedly around as though expecting to find a concealed seventh passenger. "Oh, you mean here in Alaska. May I ask what he does that makes him so great? No offense. And what's his name?"

"His name is Storm like mine—rather, mine like his. Thor Storm.

He publishes the weekly paper, *Northern Light*. And he writes books about Alaska. The real Alaska. And he fishes."

"Fishes?" Distelhorst repeated, dazedly. "You mean he owns a cannery? Or–uh––"

An involuntary shout of laughter came simultaneously from Ott, from Chris, from Guildenstern. Contritely Chris said, "Sorry. It's just a local joke, we didn't mean–uh–my Grandfather Storm sometimes goes out in the big tenders for the salmon catch in the season. He's done it for years. That's all part of his books. And the canneries. I think you'll find the book he's doing now very interesting. You, and Mr. Kleet and General Baldwin and Dave Husack and perhaps even Miss Drake and Bay Husack. Just as local color, of course."

As though they were alone in the car Bay Husack said, "You haven't changed a bit, Chris."

Her sparkling face looked over her shoulder toward him a moment. "Not even for the worse?"

"Well," grudgingly, "perhaps just a little."

The two, one front seat one back seat, laughed together then, spontaneously, as at some old private joke. An almost indiscernible stir of resentment seemed momentarily to move Dina Drake and Ott Decker.

Wilbur Distelhorst was not a man to waste time in silence. He glanced right glanced left out of the car windows, he released a barrage of interrogation. Population . . . Industry . . . Legislature . . . Local Government . . . Baranof College enrollment . . . Fish gold timber oil food clothing daylight temperatures.

". . . one thing, I understood it would be dark all day, this time of year, why it's real bright, just how much daylight do you . . ."

Ott Decker, at the wheel, tossed the answers over his shoulder, he had answered them all a thousand times before.

"We have plenty of daylight, of course December and January are kind of dark, but the sun doesn't set until about–well, it's about noon now–it'll set about two o'clock."

Wilbur Distelhorst looked fixedly out of the window, as though considering using his influence to change all this. "Two?" he said, disapprovingly.

"Of course," Ott went on, blithely, "you know up here in the winter the sun rises in the south and sets in the south, and in the summer of course it rises in the north and sets in the north, that's when we have twenty-four hours of daylight, you'd like it then, most people from Outside——"

"Now just a minute, young man. What do you mean—rises in the north, sets in the north! Are we on another planet or something!"

"No, sir. Same planet. It's latitude or longitude, or some say it's attitude—that's our little joke—but what I've told you is a scientific fact."

"Don't you get mixed up, directions and so forth, driving or if you should be lost somewhere in these mountains? Gosh!"

"Nope. We like it this way."

"Certainly interesting. For a minute there I thought you were joking."

Chris Storm turned to look straight at Distelhorst. "Another interesting thing about Alaska is the people."

"People?"

"I think," Chris persisted, "you'll find the Alaska people interesting, too."

"Fine! Fine! Glad to hear it and delighted to meet them. Wonderful country and wonderful people and wonderful scenery. Scenery! Why, say, coming up here on the plane—of course I've been in Colorado and California and after the War I made a tour for the Government with a committee of Congressmen and Senators to look over the European situation—we flew over the Alps and a lot of others, but I want to tell you they're all just ice-cream sodas compared to these you've got here. Scare you."

"The people," Chris said again, "are even more astonishing than the mountains."

"I'm here to learn. Here to learn about this great empire of the North, its resources, its economy, its people." He now leaned forward and with one gloved forefinger prodded Ross Guildenstern in the back. "Now you, young man, in the pilot's uniform. What nationality are you—if you don't mind my asking? I've got a pretty good guess, but you tell me."

As Guildenstern turned his head Dina Drake thought, He's absolutely thrilling when he smiles. Photogenic. Pictures. "I don't mind," Ross said. "I'm an American. North American."

Distelhorst shook his head a little, but tolerantly. "Well, now, you might say the North American Indian is an American, but at the same time, why——"

"You sure might," Ott Decker agreed, forgetting for an instant his Chamber of Commerce secretarial role. A ripple of laughter—a giggle, in fact—escaped Chris.

Ross explained, pleasantly. "My mother was part Eskimo. My father was Danish. That explains the name. Guildenstern."

"You don't say! Say, that's interesting." Distelhorst took out a notebook and, somewhat handicapped by his fur-lined gloves, scribbled industriously for a moment. "Well, now, how long you been here?"

"I've been here all my life. Except during the War, of course."

"No, no. You Eskimos, I mean. How long you been here in Alaska? Way before the Russians, that's for sure. I've been reading up on Alaska, the Russian occupation and so forth, I did quite a little reading on the plane. When we bought it off of Russia people called it Seward's Folly. A smart forward-looking guy if there ever was one. We'd be in a fine fix today if Alaska was Russian. We bought the whole darned shebang," he announced, as though triumphantly producing a fascinating fact hitherto unknown, "the whole darn shebang—gold, furs, fish, timber, copper, millions of acres, twice the size of Texas, mind you, for seven million dollars. Seven million bucks, can you imagine! That was back in—let's see now——"

"Eighteen sixty-seven," Bay Husack said in a droning schoolmaster's voice.

Chris turned to look at the three in the back seat. Dina Drake registered sheer boredom. Wilbur Distelhorst's brow was contorted with the labor of ethnological research. As Bay Husack's gaze met

Chris's he closed one eye in the timeless gesture of one who privately shares a joke with another.

"That's right—'67," the questioner agreed. A persistent man, as one must be whose power is dearly gained, he was not one to let a fact escape him. "How long did you say you Eskimos been here? Way before '67, that's for sure."

His head turned slightly toward his interrogator, a gleam shot from Ross's eyes. Silent Eskimo laughter. But the profile view seemed serious; his tone was soft, courteous. "We were here before the Russians, yes. The Russians first took possession in 1729, I think. That's the date given in the history books, at least. We Eskimos were here in 1000 B.C.—or earlier."

"Yeh? That's interesting—heh, wait a minute! What d'you mean —B.C.!"

"Before Christ," Ross replied, politely.

"Who you kidding? You giving me the old tenderfoot routine? What's that you call 'em—cheechakos or something?"

"No, sir. We were North Americans before it was known as North America. Perhaps we crossed over when the Diomedes weren't islands at all, but a peninsula. Nobody knows. Of course there are artifacts and traces and so on. We've been here—well, anyway twenty-five hundred years. That we know of, I mean."

Wilbur K. Distelhorst looked sharply at the smart uniform, the lively intelligent face, the Seattle haircut, the Air Force ring on the gloveless brown hand stretched along the back of the seat behind Chris.

"Well, say, gosh!" He began to scribble again in the notebook. "This is going to make quite a report. You ever live up there, young man? I mean you ever live up there in the blubber country—you might say, the North Pole region?"

The fingers along the seat back beat a little tattoo for just a moment. The white fur hood and the dark head turned, faced each other, turned away; the hand lay quietly along the back of the seat. "Uh—not the North Pole, exactly. Of course the North Pole has become a kind of junket lately. But it's a bit rugged for everyday living —even for Eskimos."

Bay Husack interrupted. "By the way, Chris, are you people using Tommy guns on mosquitoes up here now?"

"Only when they ask for it," Chris said, sweetly, over her shoulder.

"Pardon me," Distelhorst went on, a trace of irritation in his voice. "I'd like to finish this interrogation, clear up a little research and follow through, if you'll just bear with me a minute longer. This is important. I'd like to pinpoint this. This is what I'm here for, all this long way from Washington."

"We certainly appreciate it," Ott Decker at the wheel, staring firmly ahead, his voice hearty, his tone nervous.

Ross Guildenstern went on, smoothly. "I used to live up in the northern section of Alaska, sir. Oogruk, the village is called. It's on the Bering Strait. Some of my folks still live there—cousins, and my grandmother and a brother and his wife and children. Blubber country? That's a new name for it, sir. Very amusing."

"Now you're being a little too spacious, aren't you, Ross?" Chris said, rather crossly. "Fun's fun, but without being sadistic."

"Look who's talking," Bay Husack observed from the back seat.

"What goes on here!" Distelhorst demanded, querulously.

"Sorry, sir. What was your last question? I missed it," Ross said.

"They live like Eskimos? I don't want to hurt your feelings or anything. I mean, the way you look, and all, just like any young fella. But up there, your folks, I mean, they live like Eskimos? Igloos and so on?"

Ross appeared to consider this a moment, the half-smile still lingering on the mischievous face. "I'm happy to answer any questions I can. About the blubber. Let's go back to the blubber just for a moment, shall we?"

Ott Decker made a little reproachful sound between tongue and teeth. Ross went on, equably. "Blubber isn't bad, you know. Like any fat meat or fish. Or the olive oil you use in your salad dressing. You eat salads, Mr. Distelhorst?"

"Ross!" Chris snapped.

"Igloos," he continued, with a kind of patient charm, "are out. Of course an Eskimo can build himself—I hope he still can—a temporary snow-block igloo if he's out hunting and gets stuck. He wouldn't want to freeze to death. But my family—what's left of it—up in Oogruk—and even some relatives who live up in Point Barrow where it's really rugged—you should go up there on your jaunt, sir—my folks live in a frame house in Oogruk, not bad. They have a radio and a phonograph and an outboard motor and a sewing machine and they eat steaks when they can afford them and the girls wear silk stockings and they read *Life* and the movie magazines, and they go to the movies."

"Movies!" echoed Distelhorst.

"Of course in the winter we Alaskans eat a lot of meat and fish and fat, but then, so do people in Kansas and New York and Minnesota. Now we Eskimos have got into the habit of white man's food—starch and sugar and so on. Bad for the teeth and not much cold resistance in it. Grandma clings to the old ways, good and bad; but the girls go for permanents and those ballet petticoats, or those tight pants and flats; and the boys are all in that uniform—blue jeans and black leather jacket. Crazy in the Arctic. And of course everybody—kids and grownups and everybody—they fly whenever they can afford it."

"No kidding!"

"No kidding," Ross echoed, cheerfully. "We'll soon be extinct. Unless, of course, a hydrogen-bomb war comes along."

"How's that again?"

"Eskimos don't need civilization. Your kind, I mean. We've had a kind of built-in civilization for hundreds and hundreds of years. We'd just go back—the few, if any, that were left, that is—would go back to homemade skin boats and stone weapons and hunting implements, and fur-and-skin clothing—the stuff we've used for a couple of thousand years. And maybe in another two thousand years we'd still be here, cosy as anything, waiting for a new white race to come along and discover us."

5

They were in the town now, briefly bright and sparkling.

The brand-new orchid-colored car crunched crisply over the feathery snow. Others flashed past it—red green blue pink gray cream. The new four-story Federal Building came into view, solid stone and cement, many-windowed.

"It might be any town," Distelhorst said, his tone rather flat. Then, hastily, "I mean, it's a lot more modern than I expected, everything looks up-to-date and clean as a whistle."

"It isn't, really," Chris said, perversely. "It's only snow-covered. Everybody throws everything out of doors during the winter, it's too cold to cart it away, and besides there's no proper system. Then, when summer comes it's all in the streets and in the doorways and yards—tin cans and orange peels and rags and oil drums and old boots."

"Now, Chris," Ott Decker mumbled, soothingly.

"Look! Look!" Dina came to life. Around the Polaris Street corner dashed a team of twelve huskies pulling a dog sled guided by a furclad man who alternately ran behind the sled or lightly flipped one of its runners.

Even Bay Husack was moved to utterance. The anachronistic outfit ran alongside the car, the faces of the occupants stared out at the bronze-skinned smiling man.

"My God, no!" exclaimed Distelhorst, almost reverently.

"Chris, you think of everything," Bay Husack said. "But how did you get him to time it on that split second?"

"What nonsense!" Chris retorted, briskly. "He won the dog sled races yesterday. It was the last day of the Winter Festival. You should have come in time for it. He's just showing off."

Ott Decker had slowed down. The dog sled was coming alongside now. Ross Guildenstern lowered the car window and stuck out his head. "Hi!" he called to the man on the sled runner. "I hear you won out yesterday."

"Hi!" The broad bronze face half hidden in the fur hood now flashed with the brilliance of the warm friendly smile. "Sure did."

"How much?"

"Seventy miles. Four hours, thirteen minutes, five seconds. Rough going."

"Stout fella!" Ross shouted; and closed the window. "My cousin," he explained over his shoulder to the three in the back seat. "Harry Noyakpuk. He lives up in Wiseman. Ott, drop me off at the corner of Bonanza, will you? Thanks for the lift. Thanks a lot, Chris." He turned to face the visitors, his manner his tone correct. Only the eyes still shone with glints of amusement. "Good-bye. I hope you will enjoy your visit in Alaska. Perhaps I'll have the pleasure of being your pilot some time." He opened the door, stepped out, raised a hand in farewell, was off.

Chris did not turn her head. "Does that mean you're up here to stay?"

"Relax." Bay laughed, and the sound was not merry. "Not forever. A week or two, perhaps. Now, that is. And then maybe back in the summer for a longer time."

"I'm the more tropical type," Dina said. "As you know, Chris. I wanted to go to Honolulu this month." Her speech, which had been marked by a languid elegance, now had a surprisingly common quality, as though she had been caught off guard.

They turned the final corner. The Ice Palace came into view.

"Say!" Distelhorst exclaimed, inadequately.

"Look!" Dina's voice, the elegance regained, had a note of incredulity. "A log cabin. It's a prop, of course."

Quietly Chris said, "No, there are a lot of log cabins in Baranof."

"There's even a two-story log cabin," Ott interjected, happy that the conversation had veered from the personal.

"That," Chris laughed, "always has seemed to me the last word in pioneer snobbery."

Wilbur Distelhorst was not interested in log cabins. "That there's an office building, I suppose."

Ott Decker took over in his Chamber of Commerce capacity. "That's the Kennedy Building. We call it the Ice Palace. It's an apartment house—kind of like an apartment hotel, really. We're quite petted on it, and brag a lot. Maid service, restaurant, elevators, laundromats in the basement with twenty machines. Drugstore. Supermarket. The works. It's a town under one roof. See ads."

"Say!" Distelhorst exclaimed again. "Who had the nerve to build it? Heh, wait a minute, don't tell me. Was it——?"

"That's right. Czar Kennedy. You can't miss."

"Look! There are curtains and everything in the log cabin," Dina said. "I know about apartment hotels, but nobody lives in the log cabin, do they?"

"Well—yes," Ott Decker said, soothingly. "It's been lived in by one person and another for the past fifty years or more."

"Who? Who in the world is crazy enough or poor enough to have to live in it now?"

"I am," Chris said. "At least, I do."

Every branch of the big spruce in front of the cabin was etched in light snow dry as cotton trimming on a Christmas tree. The walk was neatly shoveled. In the yard a cream-colored Malemute with a black muzzle like a mask set up a keening as they drove past.

"Alone?" Dina asked, a shade too roguishly.

"Nobody's alone much in Baranof. We're huddlers. We're company crazy. Breakfast lunch dinner. Come in tomorrow morning and I'll give you sourdough pancakes and bacon and coffee and Alaska raspberry jam and rose-hip jelly. And orange juice. And lovely coffee."

"No cream," Ott Decker added as they stopped at the Ice Palace entrance.

Chris laughed ruefully. "No cream. But lovely canned milk."

"Rose-hip?" Distelhorst's pencil still hovered over the pad. Too late now.

The yellow taxi containing the two airplane hostesses drew up just ahead of Ott's car. The girls, in their twin blue topcoats and their pert caps and smart pumps stepped out into the snow, they paid the taxi driver and picked up their little blue bags and, with an amiable smile in the direction of the world in general, scurried into the Ice Palace, and the plane company's personnel overnight quarters. They were trained, engaged and paid for being amiable, intelligent and pretty, they worked hard at it. Now, for a day, they could doff the hostess manner with the uniform, they could wrap themselves in the synthetic woolly robe and rest their tired feet in scuffs, and rinse out the pink underthings and cook their own dinner if they wanted to, with a nice dry martini at the beginning and a cigarette at the end. No trays to carry, no babies to feed, no leers to rebuff no questions to answer no mountain peaks to point out for the next twenty-four hours. Tomorrow night two other girls as like these as grapes in a cluster—friendly, pretty, intelligent—would occupy these rooms, sleep in the beds, sip martinis, relax; sit before the television or listen to the music of the radio with the other girls and the pilots in the big bright company room.

The taxi crunched away from the curb. "Here we are!" Ott announced somewhat unnecessarily. "You're putting up here, Mr. Husack—you and the lady and your father, of course. Mr. Distelhorst, sir, you're at the Pole Star Hotel. I think Mr. Husack and Mr. Kleet are stopping at Czar Kennedy's house for a moment before lunch. The luncheon's here in the banquet room off the café in about half an hour, ladies. Now let's see, I think these are yours and these are yours and these are yours and these . . ."

Now the second car drew up behind them, Bridie Ballantyne's face peered from the window. Hurriedly Ott continued. "I'll help with some of these bags and things, glad to, we don't have bellboys in Alaska except maybe Anchorage and Juneau. Chris"—he looked uncertainly at her—"Chris, you want to come along up and see if these folks are comfortable?"

She assumed her best Outside manner. "So sorry. I'll have to leave you. It's interesting—having you here. Interesting for us and for you, too, I hope."

Bayard put a hand on her arm as though to hold her a moment. "But we're going to see you at the luncheon, aren't we? And how about that breakfast invitation you dangled?"

"Breakfast!" Dina interrupted, sharply. "I'm not the breakfast type."

"Not even for sourdough pancakes?" Chris urged, sweetly. "My starter is fifteen years old, at least."

"Starter?" Dina said, without curiosity.

Ott Decker paused a moment in his battle with the bags. "Say, that sourdough starter makes Chris the leading Alaska heiress. She got it from her Grandpa Thor Storm, and he got his from an old prospector who'd been living up in the hills for twenty years, using the same starter. You know what it is, don't you, Miss Drake? Instead of yeast, a fermented mixture of flour and water that's been standing around for God knows how——"

Distelhorst now abruptly interrupted this culinary discourse. He had noticed that, although the second car was being relieved of its luggage, only Bridie Ballantyne and Oscar Bogard had descended from it.

"They putting up here, you say? Kleet and Husack?" Only Mayor Bogard was wrestling with the luggage—the handsome golden-brown leather that matched the color of Dave Husack's cashmere coat; Sid Kleet's scuffed black bag, very small, and the bulging and equally scuffed brief case which, after a beckoning hand reached out from the door, was returned quickly. Czar, benign and smiling, remained in the car. Dave Husack's ruddy face peered from the rear window. Bridie, her jaw set, eyes snapping, was plunging toward the younger group.

"That's right," Decker said. "Heh, wait a minute, Oscar. I'll give you a hand with those."

Hurriedly Chris said, "Bridie will see that you're comfortable, Dina. She's wonderful. Anything you want. Twelve-thirty, the luncheon. Don't be too late, will you." She was off toward the little log cabin. You heard the dog's shrill yapping as she approached.

"The boys say they'd a whole lot rather batch it over at Czar's place," Oscar Bogard bawled, "get some of that good Swede cooking Czar's Gus sets up."

Ott Decker's rosy face paled. "You're crazy. They can't. Anyway, the lunch. They've got to be at the lunch in half an hour. It's *for* them."

"Just a minute," Wilbur K. Distelhorst said with immense dignity. "I understood, if I'm not mistaken——"

"And for you, of course—especially for you, naturally."

Bayard Husack glanced at Dina Drake, he strode over to the car, opened the door, he thrust head and shoulders into the aperture. "Look here, Dad, what kind of kid stuff is this! If I'm going through with this charade you'll have to play along."

Dave Husack grinned, sheepishly. "We were just kidding around. Get my stuff up, will you? I hate the damn icehouse. We're just going over to Czar's house to talk a minute."

The one-dimensional parallel lines that were Sid Kleet's mouth now parted a fraction of an inch. "I'll deliver him twelve-thirty."

"Just half an hour's little talk," Czar explained, blandly, "where we won't be interrupted."

Dave's reassuring bellow confirmed this. "Sure, sure. Bay, you kids run along, we'll be there on time. Just about. Oh, God, here comes that errand boy."

Here, indeed, came Distelhorst, looking forlorn, stricken, like a little brother who, tagging along, is being deserted by the big fellows. "Heh, wait a minute now," he said. "Where you going?"

Dave Husack was all joviality. "We've just got to go over some local real-estate stuff, Disty, it would bore the pants off you."

Sid Kleet's head turned toward the disgruntled Washington emissary. Kleet's dead black eyes rarely moved. When he wished to regard an object he turned his whole head toward it, menacingly, like the barrel of a revolver that encircles the lethal load.

"You're booked in at the Pole Star," he said. "Ott Decker will drive you over, the car you came in."

At the look of outrage on Distelhorst's face Czar interposed, unctuously. "Now, Sid, Disty's probably tired, all that way from Washington yesterday, and probably wants to wash up and so forth before the lunch. So we'll drop you at the Pole Star, Disty, Oscar's about through. Just call him, will you, Dave?"

Husack poked his head out of the door. "Heh, Oscar!" he bawled. "Drop that stuff, leave them tend to it. Come on! Get going!"

Dina Drake, in the Ice Palace doorway, turned to look at the five men in the car. Four of them were grinning gleefully like mischievous urchins running away from their elders. She took a step or two toward the car. "Mr. Husack, I'll be waiting, of course, in case you have some last-minute notes." Then, primly, "Mrs. Ballantyne will go up with us. Please don't be late." It was not so much a plea as a command. Dave's big jowls sagged. Czar Kennedy gazed at the girl through the car window. A long speculative look. The car moved off.

Bridie Ballantyne hitched her hat forward and took over. A natural resilience and a half century of Alaska had conditioned her to circumstances more disconcerting than this.

"Well, now, everything's lovely so far, and here we are and up we'll go and you'll get yourselves comfortable. I know what it is, those hours on the plane, and you can see Mount McKinley even from your bathroom here, and there's a lovely little kitchen you can have a cup of tea any hour of the day or night, there's heaven for you."

"Please don't bother," Dina protested in a tone that said, oh, do run along and shut up and stop fussing and leave us alone.

A suffusion of grandeur enveloped Bridie.

"And what bother is that! Don't I live here, and have since the day it was put up! Me own apartment."

"Bridie's Queen of the Ice Palace," Ott called over his shoulder as, luggage-laden, he bumped his way through the entrance. "Come on, folks."

Bayard Husack stared after the car that was disappearing around the corner. He picked up two bags, glared down at the two handsome brass-trimmed pigskin pieces that his father had so blithely left on the sidewalk. Then, with force and precision, he kicked their plump sides so that they not only slithered toward the open door, but one of them almost managed to get through before it was nipped by the heavy panel.

"Temper temper!" said Dina. "Here, give me one of the little ones and then you can wrestle these monsters."

"Put that down, please," Bay said, between his teeth. "And go on with the others. I'll come back for those."

Booted hooded figures in fur parkas clumped along the entrance corridor lined with shops. Here was the inner entrance to Nick's Caribou Café, to the drugstore, the liquor store, the supermarket, the florist, the barbershop, a dozen units that made up this miniature market place.

Ott deposited his load in front of the closed elevator door, pressed a button, dashed out again to the sidewalk. "I've got it!" he yelled, as though this were a game; and was back with the last load of luggage. The Chamber of Commerce smile was slightly awry now, the hearty tones rang, perhaps, somewhat hollow. "Up we go! You coming along, Bridie, or you want to be dropped off at your floor?"

"Coming along of course," Bridie chirped.

The great metal door facing them slid quietly open. A spate of fur-clad figures spewed out, babies, children, men, women in parkas, almost uniform except for size. Obligingly the vast unattended elevator waited like a benign giant while the new load was crammed into its capacious maw; passengers, luggage, gocarts. It did not hurry you. Then slowly, patiently, the great door slid shut. Ott Decker pressed a button, the thing began to ascend majestically. A surprisingly large assortment of babies stared round-eyed as all the young mothers, in answer to the unasked question of Ott at the wall indicator, said in turn, "Fourth . . . Fifth please . . . Seventh . . . Eighth."

Now the four were alone in the ponderous vehicle except for three small copper-skinned boys as alike as three new-minted pennies.

Muffled in parkas of minor and mangy pelts they had gone unnoticed in the crowd. As the elevator was relieved of its burden, floor by floor, they were discovered in a corner. Their eyes were very black, their teeth very white, they pressed close together like three wary rodents. They did not look at Ott Decker, they ignored Bridie Ballantyne. Their eyes darted from Bayard Husack to Dina; from the rich golden bags stamped with Dave Husack's gold initials to the chocolate-brown of Dina's dressing case, to the startlingly chaste surfaces of Bay's aluminum luggage. Their gaze bored into Dina's mink coat, flicked down to Bay's custom-made shoes, darted up again to Dina's hood and the handbag that was the latest law in Outside accessories.

Ott Decker shook his head as he regarded them severely. "Riding again. You know what the building manager said he'd do if you kids didn't keep out of the elevators."

The boys said nothing. They did not look at him. Bridie the omniscient took over. "You the Kashak boys? No, you can't all be, you're all of a size. Not that that figures. Why'n't you at school, anyway?"

"It's lunch hour," the three said, reasonably enough, in unison.

"What do you think this is!" Ott Decker demanded, wrathfully. He turned to Bay. "You'd think this was a Coney Island concession. Up and down, up and down, you can't keep 'em out of it."

"There's only three elevators in Baranof," Bridie explained. "The new Federal Building—the kids dassen't go near it—and the *Daily Lode* office building and this. This is the easiest, always so crowded. Now you listen to me, boys"—she now underwent a surprising change of tone—"you had lunch?"

"Lunch!" Ott shouted indignantly as the vast lift bumped to a stop.

Bay Husack put a hand on the shoulder of one of the boys. "Are you an Eskimo, sonny?"

The boy's lively face became utterly impassive, he said nothing.

"No," Ott replied, "not Eskimo. They're natives."

"Aren't Eskimos natives?"

"No. Well, they're native but they're not Natives. The two don't mix."

The door slid open, any possible explanation was lost here at the top floor, for there stood a large man who loomed larger owing to his foreground pattern of very loud red-and-yellow plaid wool shirt.

He glared in triumph at the three small boys. "I knew you'd end up here. Now then—out!"

Bridie executed an astonishing about-face. "Will Goomer, if you lay a hand on these boys I'll report you to the police and the City Council."

"Look, Bridie," the man said in an aggrieved tone, "will you let me run my building and you can run the rest of the town? Out!" he shouted again to the boys. "You kids are going to walk down twelve flights of stairs and I'll be waiting in the lobby. Now out! And git!"

The three emerged, they clattered down the corridor with whoops of joy, the four adults stepped out, Will Goomer stepped in and began to hand out the luggage with all the suavity of an old retainer.

"Airplanes are everyday stuff to them, they've seen 'em all their lives, but elevators, that's new. Welcome to Baranof, folks. Hope you'll be comfortable. Anything you want here in the Ice Palace just ask for Will Goomer." The great metal door slid shut, obliterating the plaid-shirted giant.

"Here we are!" Ott announced, fatuously; began to wrestle with the luggage. Bridie swept the narrow passageway with a welcoming gesture that seemed almost to banish the dim lights, the grim painted walls, the utility cement floor, and by some magic of her own deck it with satin damask and porphyry and glittering crystal chandeliers.

"This way," she announced. "You've got the Governor's suite, no less." Her agile step made nothing of the corridor's turns. "This way, folks."

The door of the suite stood open. A big square room with a room opening off it on either side. Modern bleached furniture, chintz, red roses in a vase, a bowl of fruit wrapped in cellophane and tied at the top with a twist of scarlet.

"Why, it's quite nice!" Dina Drake said. "I mean——"

Bay Husack caught it deftly. "This is wonderful! Roughing it in Alaska. Dina, look at those roses!"

Somewhat abruptly—for her—Bridie carried on with her role as professional welcomer. "Quite nice or wonderful, either way it's the best we got, and anybody doesn't fancy what's inside, why, anyway they sure can't complain about what's outside, with old McKinley staring you in the face. Look at this folding partition thing, it folds back on itself, it's made out of one those new-fangled things—you know—plexidextry sillyfite or whatever, it folds up like velvet and there's your kitchen, your stove, your frigid, and any time you relish a nice little chop or a bit of steak your own cooking, why, downstairs is the supermarket, whatever you want, name it they've got it. Course, here in Alaska, we're partial to moose, but you've got to shoot your own, or a friend gives it to you."

"Moose!" Dina said in a kind of frigid fury. "I don't know anything about cooking." And began ostentatiously to open luggage. She did not glance at Bridie, she flung back the luggage tops, everything was embalmed in unwrinkled tissue paper that gave out an indefinite but sophisticated scent. It could be traced to nothing commonplace such as roses or carnations or violets.

"You and me, both. I'd starve if I had to eat my own cooking. Baranof folks invite me to dinner seven nights in the week. Saves my life." Bridie paused to sniff audibly. "My, that's an odd perfume. Real interesting, though, like that candy they call Turkish delight tastes, sweet, but it's got bitter almonds in it."

Ott Decker looked at her quickly, but Bridie's face was bland.

"Tie that one, Dina," Bay Husack said, grinning.

Dina Drake lifted a dress from the bag. "I wonder if you'll excuse me, Mrs. Ballantyne. I'll have to change before lunch."

Bridie made a clucking sound of dismay as she scudded toward the door. "Ott, come on. The poor child hasn't even had a chance to powder her nose, us standing here." At the door she turned and peered back at the slim arrogant girl in the suit with the artfully simple line; then at the little heap of luxuries so carelessly thrown on the couch—the soft supple handbag, the soft supple gloves, the soft supple caramel mink coat.

"All the girls will be there today," Bridie said. "The office crowd and the wives and the clubs and so on. If you want to give the Baranof girls a treat, wear what you're wearing. If they had a suit like that they'd never take it off, only to sleep. Here in Alaska we keep track of what they're wearing Outside, but we don't always get to wear it. Of course, we're a fur-bearing fur-wearing place, but that mink coat of yours—dear, it's like looking in the jewelry-store windows in Seattle. You don't think of those pieces on yourself. You just like to look at them and dream. Well, good-bye now."

Bay Husack did an unexpected thing. Unexpected, even by himself. He came over to Bridie in the doorway and he put an arm around her and kissed her on both cheeks where the sprays of finely etched wrinkles were emphasized innocently by the generous dabs of rouge. He smiled down at her.

"Pardon my display of passion, madam, but I think you're gorgeous. I've heard you were, and you are."

Bridie blushed, then, like a girl, the blue of her eyes seemed to deepen. "My, that was nice." She straightened her hat. "Who from?" For a moment there was only the sound of the tissue papers busy rustling.

"From Chris, of course, thousands of years ago, in Seattle."

"Folks, we're all due at the luncheon at twelve-thirty and it's twelve-fifteen this minute," Ott Decker announced crisply. "I'll move along and break trail for you, but don't be late now, will you? Please."

"Not for the world," Dina said, brightly, "Mr. Decker."

"Ott."

"Not for the world, Ott."

The woman bending over the open luggage and the man who came back into the room were silent while the thud of Ott's heavy boots and the chatter of Bridie's heels had ceased to sound on the corridor floor. He came to the window and stood there looking out over the white town and the icy waters and the improbable peaks.

Already, at midday, it was almost twilight, the long winter night was descending.

She came over and stood beside him. "Creepy." And shivered.

"Seattle just a few hours ago. And now we're in another world."

"Oh," she said. "Oh, the wonder of it!"

He waved toward the overwhelming spectacle outside the window. "Come on now, Dina, you can't be sneery about that!"

"Do you think she'll change her mind, after two years? I hope not, because I'm going to marry you."

"Do you want to know the truth?"

"Not as a rule. This once, maybe."

"She's in love with something else."

"Something?"

"She's in love with Alaska." He placed his arm about her shoulders, carelessly, his eyes still on the mammoth splendor outside.

"Well, I'm not, if that's any comfort to you. So if they're grooming you to be the first President of the United States to come from the great Northwest twenty years from now, don't count on settling down in Alaska with me, view or no view." She turned in the circle of the arm about her shoulder and kissed him.

"Thanks," he said. "I'll do the same for you some time. Look, do you think this necktie is serious enough? For a Chamber of Commerce luncheon, I mean."

She appeared to study it gravely. "I'd say absolutely. Marc Antony could have worn it to the funeral."

6

In Czar Kennedy's house today there on the waterfront there was comfort and even luxury, gauged by Alaska standards. There was not one single object of beauty or interest. Though he owned entire ledges of jade there was not even a chunk of the gray-green stuff as a desk paperweight. No native masks or brilliant bits of handiwork adorned the walls or shelves. No intricately carved Eskimo ivories, no paintings by Lawrence, none of the Eskimo Ahgupuk's slyly simple ink lines. The history of a thousand years in a region scarcely known to North America's mainland had been chiseled, carved, etched, painted, stitched, sculptured, on stone, skins, pottery, furs, wood. None of that nonsense for Czar.

It was not that he disliked these evidences of a crude but vital civilization. He simply was not interested in them. They had, in his scheme of things, little actual value, as property, just as, to him, the Alaska Indians and the Eskimos had little value as human beings.

He rarely openly expressed his indifference to these objects and the people who had created them. Sometimes, when a friend or a visiting V.I.P. expressed an interest in a piece of ivory or stone or intricately patterned fur, he would stare at it impassively.

"It's real interesting," he said. "All that stuff. But not around the house. That junk's for museums."

Carefully planned, as was every move he made, Czar had married the plain daughter of Einar Wendt, the Tacoma lumberman. She was older than Czar; gaunt and prim. Even her father's substantial wealth had not tempted the high-spirited lusty lads of Tacoma,

Seattle, San Francisco. She was an easy conquest for the romantic-looking, soft-talking, ambitious Kennedy. Einar Wendt himself had been early impressed with this up-and-coming young Alaskan who seemed to have a guiding hand on every promising business venture in the Territory.

"You two young people won't be living in Alaska for long," Einar Wendt had said, smiling tolerantly and regarding with prideful interest the amazingly long gray cylindrical ash that protruded from the end of his very good cigar. "Baranof's pioneer stuff, it's for young kids like you, but you're too smart to waste your time there, Zeb." He never called his son-in-law Czar, as did everyone else, even the bride. "You really belong in a city like Tacoma here, I'd like to work you into the business. Alaska's pretty rough for a girl raised the way Myrt was, and her friends are all here, all the kids she was brought up with."

Czar Kennedy raised no objection, presented no argument to the older man. He merely said, "She'll learn to like it there. There are plenty of fine people in Alaska."

"Oh, sure, sure. But twenty years from now I may want to start to kind of take it easy. If you and Myrt have been living here for, say, ten years before that, why, that's where you step in."

Czar Kennedy appeared to be considering this, modestly, amiably. The fine eyes were glowing, he ran his hand through his wavy shock of hair as was his way when under emotion. It was not the emotion of gratitude. He was thinking, "Why, you old fool, twenty years from now, if you're alive, you'll be working for me, I'll own your business and you, too, and I'll still be living in Alaska. And I'll maybe own that, too."

Czar Kennedy left the log cabin that had been his home through the years since his coming to Baranof. He and his dowered bride set up housekeeping on a grand scale for the Alaska of that day. A four-room frame house, one of the few carpenter-built houses in the town. Czar had told no one of his plans. He had said that the fine four-room house was built for the occupancy of a wealthy Seattle investor who was planning to spend a year or two between Alaska and

Seattle and wanted to feel sure of his accustomed comforts. Always secretive, he had had the furniture shipped in from Seattle, very solid. There even were sets of books, bought for prestige rather than for reading: a set of Shakespeare, red and gold; a set of Walter Scott, green and gold; Washington Irving, brown and gold, all preserved behind the glass front of the bookcase. Other volumes were on much cosier terms with the bride: *The First Violin* and *Thelma* and *Jane Eyre* and all the daring yellow-backed novels by the author known as The Duchess.

"What do you have to do to be happy in Alaska?" the somewhat apprehensive bride had asked.

"They say you have to be able to read a book," Czar had answered. "I'm too busy to read. But that's what they say."

With the years the original four-room house had burgeoned into eight rooms, the bridal furniture had been twice replaced as Czar's interests widened and his income kept pace. Now the overstuffed chairs and couches were self-descriptive, the thick brown carpets silenced the footfall, the brick-red draperies and the mammoth lamps were a background for the household's unique treasure, a Steinway grand piano, for years the only grand piano in Baranof. Now it was a commonplace object, you saw one in every night club along the Strip, with a Negro tenor or a basso posed in its curve, singing Celeste Aïda or Ol' Man River; or a cocoa-skinned stripper writhing atop it as she shed her garments scrap by scrap, to the cynical applause of the lonely lads from Kinkaid or Morgenstern Air Bases.

Myrtle Kennedy adored her handsome and successful husband and hated Alaska to the day she died. She blamed this savage country for the tragedies in her life, as well she might. Certainly her daughter, the one child of her marriage, met her sordid end because of it, and her son-in-law his hideous death. Her mental and emotional equipment were not strong enough to meet this double horror. It was not only the shock of the tragedies. Her conventional belief in the fundamental decencies of life was outraged by the very crudeness of the circumstance. Perhaps she sensed that there was something almost comic in the macabre form of this double calamity.

"I always tried to have everything nice for her," she whimpered, "and it wasn't easy, let me tell you, in this crazy wilderness. Her dresses, and trips Outside, and piano lessons—that's why we got the baby grand—and she could have married to Tacoma or Seattle or even San Francisco. But no, she had to marry Thor Storm's son, and what is he, anyway! Nobody knows, rightly. I never wrote the truth to Tacoma about the way she died, I was ashamed to. Or about him, either. Wild animals. Moose and bears. They wouldn't believe it. I heard it was in the newspapers, but I never looked. I couldn't. I don't believe it yet. Nobody would believe it. Only Alaska."

Alaska not only believed this gruesome double horror, it accepted it almost matter-of-factly. Alaska was familiar with death in violent and bizarre forms. Alaska accepted almost any human manifestation as probable and even normal. When, for example, the premature infant persisted in living. It was fantastic, it was incredible; but it was true. Baranof said that it had been Thor Storm and Bridie Ballantyne who had kept alive the faint spark in the tiny and seemingly bloodless bundle of gristle that was Christine Storm. Thor, they said in Baranof, had used some kind of hocus-pocus he'd learned up north when he used to live right there studying the Eskimos in their huts. It had been Thor who had gone up to fetch his grief-stricken son and the newborn infant, and they say one of the native women was nursing her at the breast, along with one of her own. And in Baranof, they said, there was Bridie, she certainly knew what to do, wasn't she a nurse, and came to Baranof from the Seattle hospital? —or anyway, said she did.

In Czar Kennedy's wife the shock and grief of the two tragedies took the form of melancholia.

"She won't even look at the baby . . . A girl, and they say her eyes were dark even when she was born . . . Hardly bigger than a picked chicken, and they rigged up a kind of incubator, Bridie knew how——"

The scrawny infant was brought to the Kennedy house. It was agreed that this was the natural haven for her. Certainly Thor Storm's womanless cabin was not the place. And Christopher Storm, the young widower, was numb with guilt and sorrow. He absented himself from Baranof for days at a time. "Off hunting," the town said. "Or says. Off alone. Even Thor don't know where. You'd think he'd had enough of hunting, after this. Maybe he's looking for her spirit. After all, he's one fourth Eskimo, they say. You know how the Eskimos go on about spirits."

The grapevine of gossip and conjecture spread and became a canopy that enshrouded the Kennedy house. "They say Myrtle doesn't even look at the baby . . . She acts as if it wasn't even in the house, half the time. . . . Hardly bigger than a spider and she looks like one, they say, and now they've got Bridie in. Well, she used to be a nurse in Seattle, didn't she? And here in Baranof, too, the first years. . . . They say Bridie keeps the baby's room boiling hot and feeds her from a medicine dropper. That's the second one in the family Bridie raised up. She was the one looked after Christopher Storm when Thor brought him down from up north, a baby, wrapped up in wolf skins. Nobody ever got the real story of that. They say Thor married a girl up there, her mother was Eskimo and her father was a Polish trapper and fur trader."

But Baranof accepted all this as it had, for years, accustomed itself to the fantastic contrasts of life in Alaska. On the surface there was the life of any conventional American small town. Church on Sunday, card parties, ice cream and layer cake; school, business, club meetings for men and women. Underneath all this, and surrounding it loomed a menace greater than pioneers had ever endured in the history of this dramatic America. Here Nature was the killer, like a living murderous enemy surrounding a stockade—Nature, and Distance, and Loneliness and Cold. They were lurking always, waiting to pounce on you and destroy you. Locked in by gigantic mountains and endless tundra and glaciers and snow and strangling cold in the eight months of winter; or heat and killing clouds of mosquitoes in the brief summer, those days before the coming of the airplane and the mechanized United States Army and Air Forces, actually tainted an entire population with claustrophobia. Sudden and violent death was of less news value in those days than the announcement that a shipment of beef and allegedly fresh eggs had arrived from Seattle.

The Baranof of that time accepted the fact of Christine Storm's incredible naissance, and her mother's savage confinement, and the gruesome death of her father so soon to follow. The circumstance was more dramatic than usual, perhaps. But at least, the stories and facts were known. Alaskans often disappeared and never were heard of again. Simply gone. Frozen, drowned, mangled, eaten by wild creatures, no one knew. In the household of Czar Kennedy the infant Christine owed her life, perhaps, to Bridie Ballantyne.

It was in the spring following his wife's death that Christopher Storm had gone with his friend Len Fraser on the bear-hunting trip. They were after brown Alaska bear, those monolithic creatures said to be the largest carnivorous animal on earth.

The two men, experienced hunters both, had momentarily separated. They had left their boat and gone inland. Christopher Storm must have come unexpectedly upon the monster. Perhaps, startled by the sound of humans in that wilderness, it was instinctively protecting its cubs. Alone and caught off guard, young Storm had scarcely time to raise his gun and fire. He aimed between the eyes. The monster came on, its speed was incredible. He fired again. The animal came on.

"Len!" the man called as he fled now. "Len! Len!" Christopher felt the creature upon him, he thought, This can't happen to me. With the first movement, with a gesture that was almost playful, the mammoth paw lifted the man's scalp and tore it off as a skin might be peeled from an orange. When Len, hearing the shots and the cries, crashed through the brush Christopher Storm was still conscious and even fairly articulate. Fraser picked him up and tried to carry him to the boat as best he could. They even managed to reach a nearby cabin just before he died. In a kind of muted scream, while he still was conscious, he begged of them, "Shoot me! Len, for God's sake! Shoot me!"

It was after this second horror that melancholia settled like a numbing drug over Czar Kennedy's wife. She had no interest in the infant Christine, in her husband, in her household, in the small world of Baranof. Czar took her Outside, to Tacoma. There they ministered to her with such unavailing means as science and the medical arts commanded almost a quarter of a century ago. There, briefly, she continued to live, and there she died.

Years later, when Chris, in exhibitionistic and self-conscious mood, sometimes was impelled to shock conventional society with the story of her infancy, these two gory tales of her parents' death were met with a sort of hysterical mirth. It was too macabre, too repulsive to be borne. She told it rather well. After all, a tiny infant when they died, she never had known her mother or father. It had been Bay Husack who had, for a time at least, put a stop to that form of exhibitionism.

So there was Czar Kennedy in his roomy overstuffed house on the waterfront, and there, incredibly, was the infant Christine, watched over by the indomitable, the invincible, the omniscient Bridie Ballantyne.

Now, almost a quarter of a century later, Czar lived alone in the house except for the dour servant Gus, who cooked, cleaned, drove the car when needed, expertly and with an inexplicable air of resentment. There were times when Czar did not use his house for a week, two weeks. He had an office and a small bedroom on the top floor of the Lode Building. Baranof said he took refuge there when the cold and fishy eye of Gus became too depressing.

"He's a grand gifted cook, that Gus," Bridie said. "He can make anything you want to name, elegant. I bet he could take Eskimo food, a handful of willow-bush switches and bears' feet, or an owl, and make it tasty as if a French chef had dreamed it up. But I don't know, all the time he's serving you it's like he was breathing hate down your neck. I'd rather eat at the Caribou Café, and Nick smiling and visiting table to table, you feel like the guest of honor at a banquet. It's in the Bible, says, better a meal of herbs where love is than a stalled ox and hatred. Though I must say I wouldn't care to sit down to a dinner of herbs, with or without love. Not that I'd care for a stalled ox, either."

It was to Czar's house that the three men fled—Dave Husack, Sid Kleet, and Czar himself, though the Chamber of Commerce luncheon hour gave them barely fifteen minutes of grace. They were like small boys crawling under the porch or into the woodshed to hatch their plots. The big crowded empty living room awaited them.

"What'll it be?" Czar asked. "Bourbon, Dave? Sid?"

"Well, I don't know. I had a little snort on the plane, there, before we landed down," Dave said.

"You won't get anything at the luncheon, that's for sure," Kleet warned him.

Gus was there to perform a grudging service. A bony evasive man with a curiously clay-colored skin in which were imbedded two utterly expressionless pale gray-white eyes like the eyes of a dead carp. No other house in all Alaska, perhaps, except the Governor's mansion in Juneau, boasted a manservant. If a newcomer remarked this, Baranof, quick to come to Czar's defense, said, "Somebody's got to do for Czar. All the big shots come to see him when they visit Alaska, they even come specially. He tried native help. Well, you know the way they do, come one week, get their pay, and stay away till the money's gone."

A little water on the side, Gus. No. No ice. Husack and Kleet drank, tossing the amber stuff down their throats with one quick backward jerk of the head, the gulp of water, the handkerchief at the lips, the exhaled breath. The smell of the whiskey, the scent of Husack's cologne, pricked the air. Silently the three men settled into the vast chairs. The dim midday Arctic twilight gave their faces, their motions, a strange dreamlike quality.

"We've barely got fifteen minutes," Czar said. "Gus, you come in here at twelve-thirty sharp and remind us." He had poured himself a bourbon, had carried it to his chair and placed it on the table beside him. He did not drink it. He picked up the glass now, and held it to the waning light, and put it down. "Just who's this girl, anyway?" he said. "I know who she is. But who is she?"

Dave Husack shifted his big frame in the deep chair. "Now, Czar, I told you all that, she's a smart girl, she knows the score, she knows why she's here in Baranof and all, you wouldn't think a girl looks like she does could be so smart. Her mother and Louise were school friends in Kansas City. You know. But what I want to talk about now, these few minutes, is what line do I take if they ask me for a few remarks at this luncheon?"

"You know what you say, Dave. You say what you always say."

Czar's tone was bland, but a little flame of suspicion darted from Husack's eyes. "Looka here, Czar—"

Sid Kleet's steely voice cut the tension. "That's right, Dave. Give them the old blueplate. It went down all right in Juneau." Deftly he extracted a typed sheet of paper from the brief case at his feet. "Here it is. Uh—'This vast northern empire, now a Territory struggling toward manhood among the family of the United States, will someday achieve that adult goal and will stand forth, a great state among great states—one of the greatest, in my humble opinion, if it is allowed to mature. But that time has not yet come, it should not be forced—'"

"Sounds all right," Dave agreed.

Kleet thrust it toward him. "It's as good as the day I wrote it. Better brush up on it. You should have done that on the plane."

"I needed the sleep."

"Never mind about that," Czar said, gently. "Who is that girl, exactly, Dave?"

"You know as well as I do. What in hell's got into you, Czar! All right, she's crazy about Bay, too. That's what gave me the idea. All right, she's my assistant secretary, but no hanky-panky."

"Mink coat."

"Louise's—or was. You know Etta Gurkin's getting too old for these jaunts, and crotchety, of course Etta's a crackerjack secretary when it comes to business details and so on, but the going's too rugged on trips for a woman her age, and Dina, it kind of rests the boys' eyes just to look at her, know what I mean."

"I didn't ask you for a sketch of Etta Gurkin, I've known that old battle-ax for twenty-five years. Who is this girl exactly, Dave?"

"Oh. Well." Dave Husack slumped in his chair, he took out the fine linen handkerchief and wiped his forehead. "She's no tramp. Her folks are fine people, she comes from Kansas City. Anyway, she had two years of college and then she came east to New York, she wanted to be an actress, she did some modeling, and she had a couple of little jobs in the movies—what they call an extra, I guess it was—and then she went back to modeling, fashion modeling, that is" —hastily—"I went into this very thoroughly, she got to be one of the biggest models in the Paxton Agency, they only take the best, commercial photographs and so on, she rates fifty—seventy-five—a hundred dollars an hour, she could go back there tomorrow, she's as nice and sweet a girl as you'd——"

"Married at one time, wasn't she?"

"She was. You wouldn't want a kid who——"

"Older than she looks, isn't she?"

"Well, personally, looking at her——"

A gently tolerant laugh from Czar. "Mm. Looking at her with my eyes, impersonally, the way you'd look at any strictly business proposition, not suspicious but not dazzled, either, why, what would you say? Twenty-seven, would you say? Twenty-eight, outside figure?"

Dave shrugged. "Thereabouts. She don't look over twenty-two."

"Eyes," Czar said. "Eyes." His right foot, in the shabby scuffed shoe, began to waggle now as it dangled, the right knee crossed over the left. "You fit her up with that coat and so on, Dave? That's a real nice coat."

"Say, she's the girl supposed to be marrying Bay, what do you think I'd fix her up with! One of those Eskimo parkas? We're paying her good for this, Bay don't know that. You know why she's here and she knows why, and it looks like everybody'll know why pretty soon if we don't look out. Well, Bay's consented to go through with this little hocus-pocus, set him up for Governor of Alaska and so on, so Chris will maybe change her mind about him, marry him. He's still stuck on her—if he's stuck on anybody—sometimes I wonder if he's—I swear to God—anyway, Dina's made a play for him for two three years now, the damn little bitch."

"Why, you're real touchy, Dave, a person would think you were the one supposed to be in love with the girl." At a snort from Dave, Czar raised a placating palm. "Just my little joke, boy." His hand now went to his head, he ruffled the silver plumes of his hair. "Truth is, I don't know as I really go along with this little plan."

"What's that!" Husack yelled. "Last month in Seattle——"

"I know, I know. But I'm not sure that I can see my granddaughter mixed up in a plant like this. She's difficult at times, and she's under the influence of Thor and those Barnetts, and that bunch of—uh—radicals, shall we say? But this little sight-seeing tour, with that girl supposed to drive Chris crazy with jealousy, or something. Why, say, Chris is too smart for that. That's like a movie plot in the old days before the talkies came in. Christine is headstrong and impractical and highfalutin sometimes, but she isn't dumb."

"Why, you double-crossing bastard!" Dave Husack pulled his huge bulk out of the deep-cushioned chair. A curious lavender-red flush mottled his cheeks. "I get this all set, I come up to this Godforsaken dump, I haul Bay up here, we know we can get this whole thing set so we'll have the whole Territory sewed up, from Juneau to Barrow, and from Bristol Bay to Demarcation Point. All of it. Fish and fur and oil and metals and timber."

"Got it now," Czar said, sweetly.

"We'll have it cinched for the next God knows how long. Twenty-five years. Fifty."

"I sometimes wonder why we do it," Czar mused. "You've got more money than you know what to do with, now."

"Oh, Christ's sake, Czar, who do you think you're talking to! Don't try to make with that dreamy stuff. Not with me. This is Dave Husack. Remember?"

He was breathing hard, and thumping his chest.

"Boys, boys!" said Sid Kleet.

He had quietly taken a sheaf of papers out of his brief case. He was matter-of-fact, precise, no trace of emotion of any kind marked his expression or his speech.

"Charm, gentlemen. Charm charm charm, remember. You are supposed to work it that way. When thieves fall to quarreling among themselves you know what happens. It says."

"Take it up with Czar, he's the charm department," Dave said, sulkily.

"Just please remember," Kleet continued, like a patient teacher drilling a familiar lesson into dull ears, "that this is the biggest stake yet. You've got the Northwest sewed up, you can sew up the whole country and have it in the bag. Only you've got to start now and keep going. Bay isn't important and your granddaughter isn't important. It's us. There'll be plenty of young fellows presidential timber four–eight–twelve years from now. The young guys are going in for politics nowadays, maybe they don't like the mess the country's been in since the Twenties. Anyway, they're getting younger and younger in politics, you can see for yourself. It isn't just that we're getting older so that anybody under sixty looks younger to us. They damn well *are* younger. It used to be, running for Governor or Congress or Senate, you had to have hammocks under your eyes and a couple of chins and no hair. Not any more. Now it's young and tough and hep. Look at Nixon and young Kennedy—no offense, Czar—and Meyner and that kid been Michigan Governor for God knows how long—Williams, isn't it? Even Stevenson was youngish the first run—no kid, but youngish—and he damn near made it. It's getting tougher all the time. What you want is somebody young for Front Man and us older boys to pull the strings. Young, they can take the punishment. The old ones crack up. Look at Wilson, look at Harding, look at Roosevelt, look at Ike. You take a kid like Bay, start him out Governor of Alaska, no trouble with that, then Washington State Congressman, then the Senate, he's well known by that time——"

"By that time I'll be a nice ninety-eight, if I'm alive," Czar said.

"I'll be alive!" bellowed Husack, empurpled. "I don't know about you two mealymouths, but I'll be alive."

"The way you look," Czar observed, mildly, "I'd say you're likely to fall down with a stroke this minute, Dave, if you don't watch it."

"Yes, and I'll bet you damn well would like——"

"Gentlemen! Gentlemen!" Kleet purred.

The putty-faced Gus stood in the doorway. "It is half past twelve o'clock," he said. He began to gather up the glasses as though the room were empty.

"Etta Gurkin," said Czar, musingly, as they walked toward the car. "I never believed in keeping a secretary around that long. They know too much. Get them married off—or marry them. Maybe you can't fire Etta. Maybe she's got too much on you—or something. And this girl, too."

"I've heard of old men like you, what happens to them. Their mind gets dirty."

"Gentlemen! Gentlemen!" Sid Kleet implored again.

7

Two long tables and a connecting shorter one formed the U-shaped luncheon board classic in the world of Chambers of Commerce. Nick's new Caribou Café banquet room just accommodated the guests, on this extraordinarily crowded occasion. There in the doorway, a one-woman reception committee, stood Bridie Ballantyne. Some atavistic competitive urge had compelled her to change her hat. Dina Drake, probably. The garnet velvet was now periwinkle blue. She took over in a fuss of competence.

"Well, now, it's grand to see you, you didn't show up the last luncheon, I guess it takes a general and a couple of millionaires from Outside to haul you away from the furniture business. . . . Howdy, General, glad you made it, you're at the head table of course, all the guests of honor . . . Dave, you and Czar look like the you-know-what just swallowed the canary, look out the feathers don't stick in your throat. . . . Sid, you're up at the Speakers' Table there next to Dave of course, little helping hands . . . Oh, Miss Drake dear, don't take off your mink till you're seated, the girls would miss a treat. . . . Meet Nick, he's the one in the white apron and shirt sleeves, Nick come here a minute, this is Nick, it's his Caribou Café, where you'll be eating, times you're not asked out, though that's not likely to happen here in Baranof, but don't think it's beans and moose meat at the café, let me tell you you can get champagne and steak and king crab if you've got the price."

In the stir and hubbub there was a curious lightheartedness. Alaska loved a gathering—any gathering. A stranger, however insensitive, must have detected a buoyancy, an atmosphere of youth, in this group of smartly dressed young women and sloppily dressed young men. The big room seemed to shimmer and shift with a sort of electric vibrance. Only the Big Boys at the Speakers' Table had the tired joyless faces of the terribly successful.

There was the General, resigned to the knowledge that National Fish now was his drab present and future, no matter how glittering and martial his past. There sat David Husack, his color too high for basic health, and looking the more sanguinary in contrast to the imposing silvery head and the El Greco pallor of Czar Kennedy beside him. At his left Sid Kleet, as always, gave the effect of lurking. His lethal gaze searched the crowd, passionless and coldly menacing as the eye of a Colt .38. Occasionally the slit that was his mouth parted ever so slightly, he uttered a cryptic syllable in a mutter so low that, lean though he might, Dave Husack was obliged to cup his ear in order to catch it. Wilbur Distelhorst, disgruntled and peevish, fussing, between sips of water, with a sheaf of penciled notes. Oscar Bogard, over-friendly and unwelcome as a stray puppy, moved from one to another of the seated guests of honor, his arm resting on an unreciprocal shoulder, his palm pressing an unresponsive hand.

Only Bayard Husack and Dina Drake, he with Sid Kleet at his right, she with Oscar Bogard at her left, had the look of vitality that comes of youth and beauty and curiosity. Just before entering the room she had said, "I don't care what arrangements they've made, I want you to sit next to me."

"You going to be difficult?"

"Yes."

"Why did you come to Alaska at all, if you feel that way?"

"For the ride. And because I'm mad for you. And I want to be First Lady fifteen years from now."

"You'd be ideal in the White House—you and Mrs. Abe Lincoln."

A centerpiece of fresh flowers ornamented the guest table. They had been flown in from Outside. Like the guests in whose honor they had been arranged, they, too, hurtled through the heavens, had been subjected to an altitude and environment foreign to their natural habitat. Like the human freight they had emerged intact, though slightly yellow around the edges.

A small pasteboard box stood just in front of Dina Drake's plate.

Oscar Bogard, having returned to his seat, now tapped the little box with a playful forefinger. "Something pretty for you, little lady."

She looked at the box, remotely.

"Open it," Bay said, very low. "You're supposed to wear them."

She lifted out the two exotic flowers on their pale green stem, pale golden orchids with a mink-brown lip.

"Orchids in Alaska in midwinter!" Bay said. "Well, what do you know!"

Dina scarcely lowered her voice. "I never wear flowers. I hate orchids."

Sid Kleet, of whom it was said that he could detect sounds unheard even by a canine ear, now leaned forward, shielding his tight lips with a discreet hand. Very quietly he said, "I'd pin them on if I were you—unless you hate the young man next to you, too."

She picked them up, she pinned them to her suit lapel with a single vicious jab.

The two arms of the U-shaped table missed nothing. The women seemed almost audibly to drink in Dina Drake's coat, gloves, bag, suit. They themselves were smart in wool or jersey dresses and suits, their coiffures followed the general line and style of Dina's hair, though a less expert hand had molded them. The men did not overlook Dave Husack's flamboyant and costly tie and the suit so artfully cut to conceal the threatening paunch. They noted Bay's clothes, too; the material, the lapels, the made-to-order shirt. The younger male Alaskans in the twenty-to-forty age group, whether of local stock or lately arrived, made rather a point of he-man clothes even beyond the dictates of the climate. Brown shirts, open collars; shirt-sleeved in the milder months and even in the winter, cold-hardened as they were so that the temperature of a crowded room was often, to them, unbearable.

In the eyes of these men and women, as they surveyed the guests' table, there was nothing of envy. They were enjoying this gathering, it was part of the show, until the actual speaking began they were bystanders watching a parade. Now, having seen the costumes and been refreshed by the new personalities, they began to study the faces. Perhaps, here and there, the onlookers' eyes narrowed a little.

Chris Storm, Bridie Ballantyne and Ott Decker were supposed to be present at important affairs such as this luncheon. They always avoided being trapped at the Speakers' Table. From choice they sat below the salt. They noted everything. Such comments as they made were *sotto voce*. Even Bridie managed to drop her voice to a confidential tone. Their comment was professional and without illusion. Ott Decker was seated between the two women. Chris's white fur parka was draped over the back of her chair. Her hatless head was like a golden torch lighting this end of the long table, as Czar's magnificent crown flared white at the other end of the room.

"Biggest luncheon crowd we've ever had," Ott said.

"Best show too," Bridie said, crunching a hard roll. "Look at their faces. Kind of sizing things up. I shouldn't wonder if they're beginning to get onto Dave and his crowd."

"Even the dumb ones know that Sid Kleet is Dave's hatchet man," Ott observed. "They don't know yet that Distelhorst is a Senate chore boy." He turned toward the silent girl beside him. "And how do you like Alaska, Miss—uh—Storm?" It was a familiar and timeworn dialogue between them.

"What language do they speak in Alaska! Do Alaska people live in igloos?" She glanced speculatively at the alert faces all around her. "At least they respect the General's war record even if he has swapped Mars for Mammon."

"Oh, well, no war going on just now, to speak of, that is," Bridie observed, generously. "I suppose he's got his family to keep going, same as everybody else. Where're those girls got to, anyway, with lunch, I'd like to know. Here it's quarter to one. What'll the guests think!"

Ott looked at Chris. "The crowd's puzzled about Bay Husack. They can't figure out what he's doing here. And that girl."

Bridie leaned toward Decker. "You going to eat your roll, Chris?

I'm starved, up since six and only tea and a slice of whole wheat. Do you know what I think? I don't believe that's her name at all, it sounds to me like one of those made-up names the girls have in the movies. You know—Doris Dean and June Breeze. Dina Drake me foot!"

Now it became obvious that Distelhorst, nervously engaged with pencil and paper, was signaling Ott Decker. "Excuse me girls. The Fish-and-Wildlife expert is sending out distress signals."

Immediately Bridie shifted into Decker's chair. She abandoned the well-buttered roll to concentrate on the girl beside her.

"Look, Chris, you going to actually go through with this?"

The lovely serious face sparkled now with mischief and gaiety. "I can hardly wait to see the mink coat floundering around in a ten-foot snowbank in Oogruk."

"You mean you think they'll go up there, this time of year!"

"Bay's supposed to see Alaska, isn't he? Isn't that the plot of the piece?"

Bridie turned her head toward the Speakers' Table, as though to confirm her opinion of the handsome sulky young man and the arrogant girl seated there, side by side.

"Good-looking and rich and no sissy—I don't know how you turned him down in the first place."

"Yes, you do."

"I bet there isn't a girl in the whole Northwest wouldn't grab him. If I was your own ma I wouldn't know what to advise you, looking at him now."

"Haven't I had too much advice all my life?"

"I guess you have, at that. Czar pulling you one way, Thor the other. One yelling gee, the other haw, and me yawping in between. Look what it's come to, now."

"It's silly. Like one of those old movies they're digging up on television. Handsome young millionaire, beautiful adventuress, innocent maiden, grabby old villains. It's so old-fashioned you can't believe it."

Sharply Bridie said, "Chris Storm, you've been kind of play-acting all your life, I've begun to think. Like Bay Husack said down at the airport, Alaska's Joan of Arc. Dramatizing yourself."

"Goody! Lunch!"

With a rustling sound like a flock of pheasants the Caribou Café waitresses bustled into the room, crisp and starched and tray-laden. They were young, they were hard-working, they were serious. Tucked into the breast pocket of her fresh blouse each wore a brilliantly flower-patterned handkerchief whose border burgeoned into a sunburst of color. "Parm me," they said as they deposited at each place a plateful of Chamber of Commerce provender—beef stew, dumpling, pallid string beans, a little saucer of coleslaw with a ruby fleck of red pepper nestling in its bosom. Chris began to eat her lunch with the methodical thoroughness of a young healthy woman who has eaten worse food and would again; who has breakfasted hours ago in the dark of the Alaska winter morning, who knows that it is past noontime, and that life is sustained by food.

Ott Decker had made his way to the head table, he had bent solicitously, a true Chamber of Commerce Secretary, over Wilbur Distelhorst's anguished head. "Something I can do, Commissioner?"

Distelhorst leaned back, he screwed his head around, he spoke out of a corner of his mouth, one open hand shielding his lips. "These people," he mumbled, and jerked his head a little in the direction of the luncheon throng. "They're a little different than I looked for. Would you just give me a line on the general make-up and so forth? Those good townspeople of yours."

Ott Decker looked down at the face so close to his, automatically he replied in Chamber of Commerce terms. "They're wonderful people, sir. They don't come finer than these Alaska folks."

"Yes, yes, I know. But I mean what do they do, what're they here for, what do they represent, what're they doing here in Alaska?"

Ott thought, I'd like to turn Chris and Bridie loose on him, they'd shred him. Politely he said, "Uh, didn't they brief you, sir, in Seattle or in Washington, before you came up?"

Distelhorst's head jerked round sharply as he glanced up at Decker. The bland face reassured him. "Naturally I am reasonably informed on Alaska and so forth. But as Miss Storm so ably put it, the people are interesting too. Now if you can give me just a quickie on these good folks here."

Ott Decker straightened, he looked out over the faces of the men and women. His was the middle-class commercial mind, his business was to sell, not actual commodities, but the plans and schemes and hopes of those who sold them. He was ambitious, he was sentimental, he had not quite made the football team at the University of California; shrewd enough to know that he should by now be pursuing his profession in his native California, or in Kansas City Missouri or Columbus Ohio or Terre Haute Indiana, rather than in this half-tamed half-wild northern territory. He should, he knew, be married to a pert pretty girl who enjoyed scurrying in and out of the supermarket aisles in one of those bustling conventional cities. But the magnetic North had him in its grasp; and the heady Chris had spoiled him for blander misses.

Over Ott there now swept a wave of provincial loyalty, charged with emotion. "They aren't all good, here in Alaska, or anywhere, but I'm afraid we haven't time to go into that, sir, just now. Satisfactorily, I mean. These people you see here work in banks and dry-cleaning establishments and maybe liquor stores and clothing and dress shops and television stations and construction companies, and markets and engineering outfits and hardware. Well, like any Chamber of Commerce crowd. People. Anyway, they all work. Everybody works in Alaska, men and women. Have to, to eat and live. Everything costs twice as much in Alaska, remember. That's something you don't want to forget, sir. We don't get the benefit of our own resources——"

"Parm me." A voice at Ott's elbow.

"Hiyah, Doreen!"

"Hi, Ott." Competently, she slammed the laden plate down in front of Distelhorst and moved on.

Decker bent again for a moment to Distelhorst's ear. "These waitresses, for example, are all married to, say, construction workers and bartenders and maybe clerks or salesmen, they work as waitresses to meet the high rent and food and clothes——"

"Waitresses!" snorted Wilbur K. Distelhorst. "I'm not interested in waitresses. I didn't come thousands and thousands of miles to Alaska from Washington to discuss waitresses!"

"But they're not waitresses!"

"Why, young man, you just said repeatedly——"

"They are. I mean, they're not just waitresses—though what's the matter with being a waitress I'd like to know!—I mean they're an example of all kinds of good——"

"Parm me, Mr. Decker." A great laden tray balanced just behind him proved not to have quite enough space for passage.

"Well, parm *me*," Ott said, fervently. And was away.

With the detached gaze she might have bestowed upon a blank sheet of paper, Dina Drake surveyed the homely food placed before her. She had not the remotest intention of eating it. Nick, the Caribou Café proprietor, stood in the doorway in his shirt sleeves and clean white apron. Now he clumped over to the Speakers' Table and leaned chummily over Dina's chair. He smiled his engaging smile, his eyes crinkling, his voice taking on a wooing note.

"Just try a morsel, ma'am. Trouble is, with stew, you can't fix it so it looks pretty, but Pete gets it to taste real good. Anyway, it's beef, and before it gets to your plate here in Baranof it's got to fly a few thousand miles. Here in Alaska beef's rated a delicacy."

"Never eat lunch," Dina murmured.

From her place at table Bridie Ballantyne was following every move at the Speakers' Table with the concentration of a lip reader.

"You'd think she'd mess it around with her fork, anyway. Pretend like she's eating. Say, I've been served what they call salmon in Seattle, was white as the back of your hand. But I ate it to be polite."

Now the waitresses rustled in again, with an almost mechanical economy of gesture they gathered up plates, knives, forks, and in their place substituted a saucer of some quivering gelatinous sweet and a cup of steaming coffee. The members of the Baranof Chamber of Commerce, as though their combined right arms were hung on a single hinge, reached for the coffee cup.

There was the clink of metal on glass as Mayor Bogard rose and tapped for order. The young alert faces turned toward him like a battery of lights. He spoke in the platitudes of the commanded and ungifted.

Ladies and gentlemen. Members of the Baranof Chamber of Commerce. Honored Guests. We have with us. It is my great pleasure. One who. Known to all of you. Magnificent record. War. And now . . .

The General rose, and they remembered him in the days of his command. He, too, remembered, for as he spoke, simply and somewhat haltingly, his expression was embarrassed and insecure as that of a television master of ceremonies who suddenly interrupts the flow of entertainment with a commercial plug for the sponsor's line of lipstick, cold cream and hair lacquer. The blue eyes were strained, he had taken off his bone-rimmed spectacles when he rose. The face was the life-marked, decent, placating mask of a weary man past middle age. He wished, oh, so deeply, that they would just let him stand and be introduced and sit the hell down. But he had a speech to make; he had a speech to make (or had made a speech) in Juneau, in Anchorage, in Fairbanks, now in Baranof and later, perhaps, in Nome and God knows what icy wilderness.

So. "Friends . . . this vast empire called Alaska . . . nature has indeed been lavish . . . we of the world of business and economics and others at the helm of the nation's political ship of state . . . the welfare of this magnificent Territory at heart . . ."

The closing words were momentarily lost as a jet from Kinkaid Air Base streaked past high, high in the heavens, its maniacal screech in the thin icy air taunting the man who stood there addressing the cynical guests of honor and the young attentive members of the Baranof Chamber of Commerce.

General Cass Baldwin, Vice-President and Chairman of the Board of National Fish Pack Company, sat down to respectful applause.

"Dave next, I bet," Bridie said. "Czar won't talk, he's too smart, he lets the others sluice off at the mouth. I don't know's I can sit listening to that Distelhorst."

In the dining-room doorway a little knot of people had gathered. They were quiet, polite, orderly. They stood there out of curiosity, interest, or because, late in making application, there had not been space for them at the luncheon table. Craning, Chris Storm could just glimpse Addie Barnett near the doorway, and behind her the ugly, beautiful, civilized face of Paul Barnett, his myopic eyes round and protuberant behind the thick spectacles. Chris knew that this Chamber of Commerce luncheon would be a week old before he could translate it into *Northern Light* news columns. She knew, too, that by his passion and integrity it would, miraculously, be fresh and exciting news.

Then, to her surprise, Chris caught sight of the merry face of Ross Guildenstern. Her gaze met his, her eyebrows went up in questioning. He grinned mischievously. "Why, there's Ross!" Bridie exclaimed.

"What's he doing here?" Decker snapped, disgruntled. "At a Chamber of Commerce lunch!"

"Why not? He flies a commercial plane, doesn't he?" Chris retorted. "Or maybe he's just here to see how his pupil makes out in the speaking department. That was quite a briefing he gave Mr. Distelhorst in the car."

Again Oscar Bogard stood up, again the murmur of voices died away as the clink of metal on glass called for quiet. This time Bogard's mien was not solemn and reverent. He was jovial, chummy, informal.

"Well, folks, I guess I don't have to spend any valuable time introducing our next speaker. I'd rather save the time for him. You all know what Dave Husack stands for——"

Grinning, he looked fondly at Dave and waited for the applause. Oddly, it came late, it was scattered and strangely perfunctory. In that split second of unexpected silence a woman's voice spoke crisply and unexpectedly from the crowd in the doorway.

"It isn't a patch on what Alaska's standing for."

There was a ripple of shocked but irrepressible laughter. It was plain that the remark had not been meant for the public ear.

"That was Addie Barnett," Chris whispered. "She'll feel awful."

"Paul there?" Bridie asked, craning to view the hallway. "She probably was talking to him."

"Red-haired girls," Ott Decker observed, sagely, as the burst of startled laughter died down, "are always trigger-happy."

Dave Husack stood up, an imposing figure, his high color even rosier than usual, so that a stranger might have thought that this fresh ruddy man had just emerged from a Turkish bath, a hot towel, a shave, a shampoo. He had whipped out his big sheer handkerchief, he dabbed at his forehead, the warm food-haunted room took on a woodsy scent. He spread his great arms wide. His voice was smooth, his manner folksy, his tone blandishing.

"Alaskans! Fellow Americans! Pioneers! I want to thank the little lady who made that timely little remark. If I could have chosen it as an introduction I would have—even though my good friend, your able and honored Mayor Oscar Bogard here, stated that I needed no introduction. Yes. You good and wonderful people have stood for a lot of things from a wise government and a well-intentioned group of national men of business. And you have grown impatient and fretful at times. And why? For the same reason that a strong healthy willful child is impatient at the restraints laid upon it by devoted and wise parents. A child cannot be left to govern itself until it has learned experience, wisdom; until its muscles are strong enough to carry it and its knowledge wide enough to guide it. A child cannot run until it has learned to walk. It cannot walk until it has learned to stand. Alaska has had a magnificent history of adventure and courage. The years to come may be even more magnificent. This vast northern empire, now a Territory struggling toward manhood among the family of the United States, will some day achieve that adult goal, and will stand forth, a great state among great states—one of the greatest, in my humble opinion, if it is allowed to mature. But that time should not be forced by men—yes, and women, too—who would try to use this glorious Territory for their own profit. If properly guided, however, by a benevolent and wise father——"

"But, Papa!" shouted a great resonant voice from the crowd in the doorway. "I'm over fifty years old, I know the facts of life, I want to live before you kill me with the greed you call paternalism."

"Oops! Here we go!" said Ott Decker.

"It's Grandpa Storm of course," Chris said. "I sort of hoped he wouldn't, this time." But her face was brilliant with a smile of anticipation.

Dave Husack faltered, stopped, he turned a look of outraged dignity upon Oscar Bogard. "Mr. Chairman!"

The faces of Oscar Bogard, Czar Kennedy, Dave Husack, Sid Kleet wore identical expressions of scowling resentment. They knew an old enemy. Only General Cass Baldwin and Wilbur K. Distelhorst seemed puzzled and uncomprehending.

"Dad's blood pressure," Bay Husack said to Dina.

There was a stir in the doorway. A towering figure came forward. Every head in the room swung toward him.

"Excuse me, will you, if I interrupt for just a minute? I haven't been asked to speak here today, and I'm not going to make a speech. I just want to distribute a few copies of this week's *Northern Light.*"

"Now, Thor!" Oscar Bogard remonstrated. "This is an outrage! You can't start all that again."

Under his arm Thor Storm carried a sheaf of newspapers, neatly folded. In a region of tall men his height was notable. The frame was big-boned, unburdened by fat. The hood of his parka was pushed back, its border of wolf formed a nimbus above the gold-and-silver hair, the pink cheeks, the startlingly blue eyes. It might have seemed an almost cherubic face except for the eyes. There was nothing angelic about these as, moving swiftly, he placed a neat bundle of newspapers at the end of each long table.

"Just pass these along, will you, one to a person?" His manner was genial, his tone conversational, his enunciation curiously cultivated and charming. "It won't be news to you, Dave; or you, Sid; or you, Oscar; and certainly not to you, Czar old pardner, as they used to say in those Rex Beach books. But it will be news to the rest of you Chamber of Commerce people and all Alaska. You won't find it in this afternoon's Baranof *Daily Lode*." Suddenly he stretched forward his great right arm, his forefinger pointing, he looked strangely like a prophet of old as he stood there. "Bayard Husack!" he thundered.

But this time it was Czar Kennedy who interrupted, his voice leisurely, almost purring. "Just a minute, Thor. I can have you arrested, you know, for causing a disturbance in a public place."

Thor Storm turned a beaming face toward Kennedy. "Will you do that, Czar?" His tone now was earnest to the point of entreaty. "I'd consider it a favor. Paul and Addie here would send it out A.P. and every newspaper in the United States would run it. Canada too. Do that, will you please, Czar, old pardner?"

"You're getting senile, you know," Czar observed, as though the two were engaged alone in a private bitter quarrel of long standing. "I could have you committed."

"Better yet! Better yet, pardner. What a story that would be! What testimony I could produce, what witnesses I could call, what deeds I could unfold, what secrets I could relate!"

Oscar Bogard's clashing of metal against glass as he attempted to restore order sounded like the efforts of a Swiss bell ringer. "Gentlemen! Gentlemen!" He now thwacked the table with the flat of his hand. "This is not Alaska of the Nineties! This is Alaska today." He turned his gaze away from the offender. "General, my apologies. Commissioner, please believe that this is not the way Alaskans behave. We may be a little crude and even rough in ways, but our manners——"

"Slaves!" roared Thor Storm. "Worms! Second class citizens of the greatest democracy in the world! Voteless tax-paying men and women of Alaska, and your fathers and mothers before you for sixty years. Manners! Manners! Wholesale plundering by them for another fifty years, or freedom for you! Read it! Read it! Read it!"

There was a rustling like the sound of a sudden wind rushing through the leaves of a forest as the members of the Baranof Chamber of Commerce opened the pages of the weekly *Northern Light* and began to read.

Chris Storm plucked her white parka from the back of her chair and came over to the patriarchal giant standing there, facing the room. She linked her arm through his, she looked up at him.

"Let's go now. You were wonderful, but you know the doctor said you weren't to get excited. Let's go now."

Dina Drake had been concentrating on the application of a fresh coating of lipstick, her gaze intent on her own reflection in the tiny mirror. Now she glanced up. "What's the matter? Is he crazy or something?"

"Like a fox," Bay Husack said.

8

From the beginning no two men could have been more unlike than Thor Storm and Czar Kennedy. Yet here they were in Baranof, the town to which they had come half a century ago, each bound to the other by unbreakable bonds of love and hate, of hardship shared, of common adventure, of family blood, of tragedy, and—strongest of all—by Christine Storm, their granddaughter. The intricate fabric of life that united these two septuagenarians was now of indissoluble weave, light as the dry Baranof snow, strong as the sinew of a caribou.

Together they had come to this weird wild land. They had planned and worked and fought together, each had been left wifeless and childless in young manhood, neither had remarried, each waged a silent persistent battle for the welfare—as they saw it—of the girl Christine. Each loved Alaska in his own way. Baranof had been their home for fifty years and more. They were a universe apart.

Thor Storm still lived in a log cabin as he had in his virile twenties. It boasted electricity and plumbing of a sort now, but structurally it was basically unchanged. Baranof and the whole Territory respected him, admired him, were baffled by his way of life. Here was a pattern they could not quite understand. Books. Always blatting about freedom and democracy. Well, hell, too much freedom here in Alaska if you ask me, the unknowing said. When tragedy came upon both men the town thought they would leave the North Country to go back Outside, away from the sights and sounds that had so brutally twisted their lives. They had stayed.

But Czar Kennedy—there was a man they could understand. A picturesque and romantic figure from youth to old age, he had a quiet word and a smile for everyone. To look at him, Baranof boasted, you'd think he didn't have one penny to rub against another. In appearance a composite of Shakespearian character actor, way-down-East cracker-barrel philosopher, fresh-water college professor, with, perhaps, just a dash of Mississippi River gambler. From this mixture he emerged handsome, approachable, benign, somewhat scholarly. He never read a book.

You sometimes saw him eating his breakfast at the drugstore soda counter, you'd never know he owned the building, lived in the best house in town, had that Swede Gus there could cook him anything he wanted for breakfast from fish to omelet. Sometimes he secretly paid for the breakfast of a boy or girl there at the counter, and he would vanish before they had finished their meal.

"No charge," the counterman would say to this one.

"What do you mean, no charge! You giving away this morning?"

"Party paid for your breakfast. Told me to say you're his guest this morning."

This pleased and impressed some, but it rather annoyed others. Strangely enough—or perhaps not so strangely—the least solvent were the most annoyed. It downgraded them. "What does he think this is! A Salvation Army soup kitchen! Giving out with two bits to make himself feel good?" One morning at eight o'clock Addie Barnett caught him at the coffee counter. It was *Northern Light* weekly press day, and she had been at the office since five A.M. In a spirit of pure mischief she had quietly paid the counterman for Czar's breakfast and had slipped away to station herself, unseen, behind the revolving bookrack. The counterman rather enjoyed going into the customary routine. In reverse, this time.

"No charge, Mr. Kennedy."

"How's that?" sharply.

"Party paid for your breakfast. Said you're their guest this morning."

Rarely caught off guard, Czar now was in a temper. "You can't do that. I don't like it, understand!"

"Oh? Well, *you* do it."

"That's different."

The counterman was a newcomer to Baranof. "Yeah? How do you figure that?"

Addie Barnett ran the story in next week's *Northern Light.*

The two old men had been young vital men when first they had met so casually aboard the battered argosy that dumped them on Alaska's gold-flecked sands. Tall tales of romance descriptive of vessels such as this were popular in the turn of the twentieth century. There was nothing picturesque about the rusty hulk that shoved off from Seattle toward the strait of Juan de Fuca, through days and white nights of wildly magnificent scenery.

The black-mustached gambler with the diamond shirt stud, the rugged woodsman with heart of gold and muscles of iron, the hero of the cool head and the hot passions—all the stereotypes of fiction—were missing. This boatload of adventurers headed for Alaska in derby hats and decent baggy-kneed suits and starched white collars. They were, for the most part, as unequipped as infants to battle the wilds that loomed ahead. Shoe salesmen, teachers, doctors, lawyers, small mechanics, clerks, bookkeepers, urged by the hunger for gold rather than by the spirit of adventure; farmers, some of them, weary of endless chores, poor crops, capricious weather. They were dazzled by the rainbow rumors that, four decades earlier, had lured their hardier forebears out of the eastern and midwestern States, over prairies and plains to the hills of California. Even the dozen or so women in The Business, who were on board the sour old tub, bore no resemblance to the frolicsome females of dance-hall fiction. They were deep-bosomed firm-fleshed women of almost matronly aspect. They had a look of robust health, as well they might, considering the bizarre pioneering they were to encounter. They were entering Alaska as members of the Oldest Profession. They were to become familiar enough with the sight of calloused male hands joggling mooseskin sacks filled with golden nuggets or yellow dust; pokes, these were called, and they made a pleasant sound as they were tossed, plumply, on a table or bar or bed. But eggs were a dollar each—if you could get one. A decade, two decades later—and certainly today—you were to see many of these gay girls magically transformed into wives and mothers, erring perhaps a little too much only on the side of respectability; officially presiding at club meetings, Sourdough gatherings, church-benefit suppers, arriving at these fiestas proudly bearing their contribution of a baked ham, or a meat loaf, or a devil's-food cake, or a vast plateau of oven-baked beans.

Now, on shipboard, bound for the golden shores, they were an almost touching sight in their unnautical garments; trailing skirts, vast leg-o'-mutton sleeves, ruffled jabots, flower-laden hats, veils, kid gloves. You expected to see an incongruous parasol unfurled on a sunny deck corner, and, in fact, a girl whose delicate complexion was one of her trade assets did just that one day without causing any comment.

Through bits and snatches of Bridie Ballantyne's reminiscence and chatter Chris Storm had learned much about the lively doings of these early Alaska girls. Thor and Czar had told her little of them, not so much through a prim sense of what was seemly for a teen-age grandchild, as because of the fact that the two men themselves had had as little as possible to do with the so-called dance-hall girls, either now on shipboard or later, on land. For the benefit of posterity Bridie should have talked into a tape recorder. There were no tape recorders in Baranof, so Bridie talked into the recording human ear of the eager fascinated girl, Christine.

"Men," Bridie Ballantyne said, reflectively. "Men men men. There's always been too many of them here in Alaska. In comparison, that is."

"Are there?" Chris had said, rather naïvely, at sixteen. "Are there? I'd never noticed."

"You'll notice when you get to Seattle, all right. Not that you won't always have plenty of beaux. Anywhere. But here there's never been enough women to go around, always twenty men to every woman and I guess that gave us a puffed-up notion of our importance. Not that I had an easy time of it when I came here, a girl. Easy! I thought I'd die. But the most of the men here were over-polite then, and are to this day—to the women, I mean. Those days, next to gold, and maybe food and drink, why, women were the most precious article, you might say. You're going to find men acting different, Outside. Outside it's more women than men. Any woman, those days in Alaska, who wasn't cross-eyed, pockmarked and mustached, was precious. Come to think of it, even that didn't stop Ideal Hackers. And it's a living description of Ideal."

"What a name—Ideal! Was that really her name?"

"Ida. She was one of the girls on the Line, she was so downright scrambled-looking they nicknamed her Ideal."

"That was mean."

"No, she loved it. Eyes, complexion, mustache and all, she could have had her pick of a dozen men. I heard she was bowlegged in the bargain, but lucky for her women wore long skirts those days, trailing the mud and the dust and the snow, whichever."

"What happened to her, poor thing?"

"You don't have to be weeping for Ideal. She married Hermie Hackers and settled down to housekeeping, smug as you please, and next thing you know Hermie got in with the copper crowd around 1906. Now Ideal's a widow, lives in one of those Nob Hill hotels in San Francisco, a whole suite, they say her living room's forty feet long with a view of the Golden Gate. She looks twenty years younger than she did fifty years ago. Got her eyes straightened when the money first began to pour in, got her skin peeled like a banana, got her face lifted and her mustache electrified off, I heard she even had her legs broken and reset, I wouldn't put it past her. I hear she calls Seattle the provinces. And Alaska! Well, leave us not be sordid."

"I love to hear you talk about those days," Christine said as she had a hundred times before.

"It wasn't so long ago, really, for all you're only sixteen."

Bridie gazed at the girl, thoughtfully, lovingly. "I don't know.

Sometimes I think maybe you've been too much with us old ones—Czar and Thor and me, one pulling you one way, one heaving another direction, it's a wonder your arms and legs aren't out of joint, let alone your head."

"What's wrong with me!" the girl demanded, gaily. "I may not turn out to be the *femme fatale* that Ideal Hackers was but I'm not so awful, am I?"

"Don't be fishing for compliments, you won't get them from me. You'll have to work a little harder for them in Seattle, too, so you might as well get used to it. Competition there, you'll find."

"Darling Bridie, it's too late for you to try to break me down. You three have been working like slaves to build me up ever since I was born."

"It's terrible any more how pleased you are with yourself, these days. Still and all you've come through these years pretty well, considering you've been reared by three old things, and all of Baranof and most of Alaska. It's a wonder you didn't turn out unbearable. Next thing you'll be what Thor calls a rounded character. I hope not. Everybody ought to have anyway one slab side."

The three had given her all they had. From Thor she had absorbed a knowledge of the humanities; the habit of reading, a feeling for nature and for history. From him, too, she had learned to use her mind and her muscles; practical things such as cooking, and how to handle a gun; later, how to set a stick of type in the gritty little print shop of the *Northern Light*.

Czar, in benevolently practical terms—or so it seemed—stressed the value of money, of power, of position, of security. To Christine he imparted surprisingly cynical advice.

"Making friends of people like those will never get you anywhere." He might be speaking of Paul and Addie Barnett, or Ott Decker, or the young half-breed Eskimo, Ross Guildenstern. He might have been tempted to include Thor and Bridie, but he was smart enough not to risk that.

"I don't want them to get me anywhere. I just love them."

"That's a childish way to talk."

"I don't choose friends," she said, very grand, "for what they can do for me."

He could have said, If it weren't for me you'd be nobody, if it weren't for my money and my connections and my brains you'd be behind the counter in the Five-and-Dime at best. But he was too canny for that. He had his plans for her, as clear-cut as the blueprints by which he had achieved the Kennedy Block, the Baranof *Daily Lode,* the Ice Palace.

"You're going to meet people who are people. Not riffraff nobody knows about. You know some of them already. Dave Husack and his wife. And Sid Kleet. You'll meet the cream." Then, mildly, almost as an afterthought, "And young people, like Dave's son Bay."

She laughed then, and came over to him and hugged him, her fresh young cheek against the lined one. "You're an old-fashioned darling. You're not trying to marry off your granddaughter to the Seattle rich and mighty, are you, Gramp?"

"He can have his pick of any girl in Seattle. Or New York or Washington, for that matter. You'll be lucky if he takes you to the drugstore for a Coke."

"I don't like Cokes," Chris retorted, somewhat maliciously.

Curiously enough, it was from Bridie as well as from Thor that the girl had got her sense of history, her feeling for background, for beginnings. Few young people had it, but then, few girls, as Bridie succinctly put it, had three old crocks instead of a young father and mother to bring her up. It was from Bridie, too, as well as from Thor, that she had got a sense of comradeship with the world. Perhaps the very remoteness and aloneness of the land and its people had somehow, paradoxically, been responsible for this.

Every matron in Baranof attempted to have a hand in the girl's upbringing; and certainly every unattached widow or spinster, with an eye out for the widowered Thor or Czar, yearned over her. But it was Bridie who took over, Bridie was for Chris her Juliet's Nurse, social guide and fashion mentor. It was Bridie who said, "I don't care what the other kids are doing, you'll wear your fur parky as long as it's zero. Now don't make me have to tell your grampas."

Later, as Chris approached young womanhood, Bridie brought her taste in dress to bear on the girl's problems. "Your coloring, yellow hair and black eyes, you can wear anything, I suppose; only can you? Because what goes with your hair would fight your eyes. The thing that saves you is your complexion. By rights you ought to be sallow, but you've got Thor's pink, isn't it lovely now! You're a blonde and a brunette and whatever they name in between. Blue is a good color for you, you can wear pink, too, and green and even yellow though I wouldn't advise it, hair or no hair. If you're sunburned your black eyes will make you look native. And if you're too pink and white your yellow hair will kind of wash out. You've got your work cut out for you the rest of your life, Chris, dressing."

Perhaps if all historical data of the past half century in the Alaska Territory had been lost, swept from memory and from record, leaving Thor Storm, Czar Kennedy, Christine Storm, and this Bridie Ballantyne only, there might still have emerged from these informal records a fairly comprehensive history of the manners and mores and events of the time and place.

Occasionally, in her childhood, Chris had burst into rebellion against the three middle-aged guardians of her life. But when she rejected them she had only herself to fall back on—or one of the three against the other two.

She had been a small girl when first a playmate in the course of a squabble had confronted her with the ultimate threat. "I'll tell my mother on you."

"I'll tell my Grampa Thor on you, then."

"Pooh, who's afraid of him!"

"I'll tell Grampa Czar."

"Nobody's afraid of grampas."

"I'll," summoning her last defense, "I'll tell Bridie."

"She ain't your mother. She ain't anybody's mother. You haven't got a father or a mother or anything."

Shocked, Chris rallied all her forces, the black eyes glaring, the pink cheeks scarlet. "Is that so! I've got Grampa Thor and Grampa

Czar, they're better than anybody, they're better than anybody's mother, and I've got Bridie. And Alaska. I've got Alaska."

"Alaska?" Puzzled.

"Grampa Thor says Alaska is better than any place in the world, and I'm Alaska history."

Stunned, the other regarded a moment the wild-eyed infuriated little figure of her antagonist. Then, "You're crazy," she announced, decisively, and ran home.

In her childhood she was a question-asker, as were most children of her age, but in her case the custom burgeoned into a habit that sometimes irritated Bridie and enraged Czar. Thor encouraged it. "When you don't know a thing—ask. I'll always answer if I can."

She had been fascinated by the story of Bridie's arrival in Baranof so many years ago. At twelve, through a series of questions, Chris dug to the core of this situation.

"That place where you nursed the ladies that were sick with smallpox—why was it called the All Nations?"

"The people who lived there came from different countries, I guess. Or claimed they did."

"You said they were all ladies living at the All Nations house."

"Yes. Yes, they were."

"Why? Was it a boardinghouse just for ladies?"

"Kind of."

"Were they married and did they have children?"

"Well, no. No, they didn't. Weren't."

"Why not?"

"You ask too many questions for a little girl."

"That's what you say when it's something you don't want to answer. I'll ask Grampa Thor."

"No. No, I wouldn't do that. He's busy."

"He says he's never too busy to answer my questions."

"There's things you're not old enough to understand."

"If they weren't married and didn't have husbands did they work to earn money?"

"In a way. Now run along and don't bother me, can't you see I'm busy! Children your age have lots of time to learn things later."

"Did they earn money at the All Nations place?"

Instinct taught Bridie certain therapeutic methods that, a quarter of a century later, psychiatrists were to put into general use. "They lived there and kept people company—lonely people—men who hadn't got their families with them, their wives and children and so on, and were working the creeks for gold, those days."

"Did they love them?"

"Did who love who?"

"Did the ladies at the All Nations love the men who were lonely."

Bridie started as though some one had jolted the chair in which she was sitting. After a moment she said, quietly, "In a way."

"Well, if they loved them why didn't they marry them?"

"Sometimes they did."

"If they didn't marry them did they pay them for loving them? Is that the reason they earned money?"

"Yes. And that's just about enough from you. Who do you think you are, a schoolteacher or something, questions questions questions. Stop it, I say, unless you want the back of my hand."

"When I grow up nobody will have to pay me for loving them. I'll love them for nothing."

To compensate, the three saw to it that her parka was of the finest pelts, its hood faced with wolf; her dresses, often as not, ordered from Seattle. Bridie, through the years, had achieved a great reputation for style. Fond Baranof said that Bridie Ballantyne was the Ten Best-Dressed Women in Alaska. Best-Dressed Member of the City Council. Best-Dressed Alaska Public Relations. Best-Dressed—uh—Mature Type. Best-Dressed Candidate for the Legislature. Best-Dressed Alaska Pioneer and Sourdough. And so on.

Even in her later years Bridie's neatness never was besmirched like the food-stained bosoms of the elderly whose spots were decked with an unavailing façade of chains, beads and brooches. "There never was a diamond big enough to cover a grease spot," she said in one of her sententious moments. "Even if you can't see the spot you kind of know it's there."

"Neat," Bridie counseled the girl. "That's all there is to it. I learned that when I was student nurse in the Old Country, and in Seattle. You know the way young nurses always look pretty. Specially to men's way of thinking. Half the time they're plain as posts, but you get white or blue-and-white up under the face, and put plenty of starch in it so it rustles and smells fresh, and a broad stiff apron band that makes the waist look tiny, why, you'd give off the effect of spring flowers in a paper frill. Neat does it, before style or richness, to my way of thinking."

So now, when Bridie said, "That dress is tacky," Chris discarded it. When Czar said, "That boy acts all right, but he'll never amount to anything," she was likely to defend him, though doubting her own sense of values. Thor said, "Read that, and you'll know Thomas Jefferson was a greater man than Alexander Hamilton, and always will be. He thought of the United States in terms of people, not as an example of the capitalistic system. They were both right, but people are more important than any system." She won the negative side of the Baranof College Forum debate on "Would Hamilton Have Been a Better President Than Jefferson?"

It spoke well for the three, and for Christine's disposition and strength of character, that she did not emerge as an insufferable example of overconfidence. She had been president of her class at Baranof; voted the most popular girl on the campus; best-dressed co-ed (she wore clothes identical in style with those of the other girls, but the effect was, somehow, distinctive); the recipient of a half-dozen invitations to every social or athletic affair from ice hockey to the annual prom.

Frequently, in the course of growing up, she deliberately or involuntarily acted against the judgment or the wishes of one or two or even all three of her mentors. "Trial and error method," Thor said, when such behavior came up for discussion. "Leave her alone. She'll learn that way."

9

Of all the passengers on the scabrous vessel that had shoved off from Seattle, Alaska-bound, probably the only two who had themselves in hand, who knew the plan they definitely would follow, once ashore, were the Norwegian Thor Storm and the New Englander Zebedee Kennedy, whose far background was Scotch-Irish. These two had not been dazzled by mad stories of gold lying like pebbles strewing the Bering Sea shores at Nome, or the creeks of Baranof; or forming chunks in the Fairbanks or Juneau lodes.

They had come together on deck one evening after the greasy supper. The other passengers were swarming inside the ship's shabby saloon, drinking, shouting, stamping to the whine of harmonicas or intent on the shuffle and slapslap of grimy playing cards. There the air was malodorous with smoke, food fumes, unwashed bodies and the acrid smell of unspoken fear and apprehension, the effluvia one encounters in courtrooms, in stockades.

Separately the two men had sought clean air and quiet on deck. Each had marked the other before meeting. They were set apart from the rest in bearing, in the light of intelligent purpose that was reflected in their faces. They wore a confident and resolved expression, quite different from the nervously grimacing features and the feverishly glittering eyes of the other men. Each had recognized in the other the unusual, the purposeful. The man who was to be known as Czar Kennedy saw with the shrewd eyes of the born trader, the canny commercial opportunist. Thor Storm looked out at the world through the eyes of the natural student of the humanities, his gaze colored—and perhaps handicapped—by love, compassion and curiosity toward the human race.

Both were tall men, but Thor Storm towered above Kennedy, his was the physique of a giant, but without the giant's usual pinhead. Kennedy, slighter in build, seemed almost fragile beside him. The casual observer would have mistaken Kennedy for the scholar, the thinker, with those curiously dreamy long-lashed eyes, the leonine upper head that contradicted the square punishing jaw. The thick crown of black hair was worn longer than ordinarily, and it had a natural wave. In later years, as he turned into his fifties, and the wavy black locks were powdered with white at the temples and the forelock, he took on an almost poetic look, with a touch of the ham actor.

Thor Storm, with those great shoulders, the merry eyes, the pink cheeks, the yellow hair that seemed almost to sparkle, appeared the man of physical action and material mind. Nature had played a trick on both these men, and on the world in which they functioned.

Now the two young strangers stood at the boat rail, mysteriously drawn together by a magnetic force that was to bind them for life. They seemed to be gazing at the almost shockingly magnificent view of water and snow-capped mountains and sunlit north night sky. Each saw the other out of the corner of the eye. Kennedy's coat collar was turned up against the fresh wind that even in midsummer tasted of the snowcaps.

He, the charmer, spoke first, he flung an arm in exposition of the splendors before them. "I bet you never saw anything like that before in broad daylight at ten o'clock at night."

"Great mountains like these, no. But daylight at night, yes."

"How's that?"

"I was born in the North Country."

"You mean here!"

"No. Not here."

Piqued, Kennedy pressed on. "I suppose you're hell-bent for gold, like the rest of those fools in there?" He jerked a thumb in the direction of the lights, the shouts, the music. As the man did not reply at once to this blunt question Kennedy added, hastily, "No offense meant. They seem a poor lot, those in there."

"Perhaps not as lacking as they seem. They must have courage of a sort, or they wouldn't be here. I suppose you could say that of any pioneer."

"Call these fellers pioneers!"

"Why not! They're dissatisfied and want something better—freedom or land or peace or money. The early ones crossed the sea to Massachusetts or Virginia, the later ones crossed the continent to California or Oregon. They started because they were dissatisfied or curious or ambitious or adventurous. The frightened and the cautious stayed behind, even if they were dissatisfied. And they let the world roll over them. We're all different in the same way—you and I and those men—and even those women, too—or we wouldn't be here."

"Don't lump me in with that parcel. They're after gold. You get bit by that craze it isn't courage drives you. It's a kind of"—he searched for the word—"a kind of frenzy takes hold of you. Now, you don't look like that, wild-eyed."

"No, I'm not after gold." Again the silence.

"What then?" Persistence was a trait that later contributed much to Czar's success.

Thor Storm looked down at the water churning below, and then up at the Northern sky so strangely bright above them at this night hour. "New strange people. New adventure. New discovery. Like my ancestors who discovered America."

"You don't look like an Italian, or talk like one."

"I was born in Norway. My people for cen—all my people have been Norwegian."

"Well, say, Columbus discovered America, any kid knows that. He was Italian."

"The Norsemen touched here long before Columbus. And the Eskimos were here before that. But it doesn't matter. If you think those men in the saloon are fools I suppose you're not looking for gold, either." His accent was almost pure Oxford English.

This unconscious elegance of speech irritated Kennedy into a boasting loquacity unusual in his canny pattern of behavior. "Not me! I'm too smart for that. Let them freeze in the wilderness and starve and scratch for a few crumbs of gold. What's gold, anyway!"

Thor Storm turned to look at this man, then, deliberately. He smiled a little. "Gold is a soft metal chemically formed in the earth. It isn't as beautiful as quartz or common mica or even copper. But there's less of it and it's more difficult to find, and nations have made it the medium of exchange. If they decided on coal, for example, or oyster shells, or coral, then those would have been precious. Like wampum used by the North American Indians."

"You sound like a smart fella," Kennedy said, grudgingly.

"No, I'm not what you would call smart. I'm only intelligent."

"Well, I am. I'm smart." Curiously, there now was no note of boasting in his voice. It was said as a simple statement of fact. "I'm headed for the camp they call Baranof. They say that's the place with a future. Not like Nome, they'd skin you alive and throw your bones into the Bering Sea. Baranof I hear they've put up wooden houses and a land office and a bank and there's talk of running a railroad from there to the coast. I know where I'm headed in, but I don't make any sense out of what you said—new people—new discovery. Where's the money in that?"

"No money."

"Then I can't figure it. You one of those scientific fellas looking for the North Pole?"

"No."

Zebedee Kennedy was angry now, his hands gripped the rail, he spoke very quietly as always when he was at high emotional pitch. "You murdered somebody?"

Thor Storm laughed then, a great rich rollicking laugh that boomed on the clear air and echoed from the menacing white-capped mountains. He put a hand on Kennedy's shoulder—an incongruous hand for a man of his build—long-fingered, sensitive, the hand of generations of aristocrats.

"No, I am not a murderer running from justice. I'm here because there's never been anything like this since the world was made. Men have roamed the world through the centuries for plunder and for land and for adventure. Europe and Asia and Africa and America North and South. Just a few years ago Oregon and Washington and California. But those were warm and lovely lands. Sun and rich valleys. But this! This is as it was when the world began, when it was just made. It is like being at the beginning of the world. You wait. You'll see."

"Say, *you* wait a minute, will you! Just a minute. I'm not figuring on any place that's like the beginning of the world. I'm going to fetch up in a town. A town with a future."

"The future there can be anything you want to make it. It can be a model for civilization. There is Alaska, raw as the day the world was born. The Russians have been there maybe a hundred years or so, but they haven't made a mark. It's as if the world had just been finished, and we're in on it the day after Creation. Like gods. It's all there, waiting for the work of our hands"—he hesitated a moment then finished, almost shyly—"and our spirits."

Now there was something of distrust and disappointment in the narrow look with which Kennedy regarded his deck companion. "Your collar's turned the right way, but you sure talk like a preacher."

A quarter of a century later they could laugh about it, ruefully. A hundred times Kennedy had said, almost nostalgically, "Do you recall that night out on deck? A pair of babes, for all we knew what we were up against. Even you, with all your books."

"We were better off than the others," Thor reflected. "We didn't just stay in Alaska because we had nothing we wanted to go back to. We were both crazy about it in a queer way. And we were both doing what we had come to do."

Prophetically, even on the battered old boat, Thor Storm had known that everything in those next decades in Alaska would be larger than life, out of drawing, fantastic, so that the reasoning mind rejected it while actually living it.

He had tried to convey something of this to his fellow passenger.

But Kennedy, a realist, was not possessed of imagination. He was merely, as he said, smart, with an almost prescient sense of material values.

"This whole thing," Thor now persisted, and swept the air with one great arm that included the ship, its passengers, the overpowering mountains, the sea, the endless sky and the singularly vital air, "this whole thing is ridiculous."

Kennedy stared at him, suspecting a joke he did not understand. "How d'you mean?"

"It's ridiculous to happen in a civilized country like the United States in the twentieth century. People rushing in and grabbing whatever they want. For two hundred—three hundred—five hundred years or nearly—this continent has been ravaged, it's a wonder it has survived. But it has. Now they're swarming into this wilderness like the Spaniards into Mexico, like the forty-niners into California, like the Sooners into Oklahoma. It's the last of it, I think. There can be no more unless someone discovers a new continent, or the day comes when we can somehow reach the other planets."

"Looks like you know an awful lot about this country, and all—about the United States, I mean—that is, for a foreigner."

"Everyone in the United States is a foreigner, or the son or grandson or great-grandson or great-great-grandson of a foreigner. Everyone except the red Indians, and, in Alaska, the Eskimos. All the others are foreigners."

"Say," Kennedy drawled, amused, "you go to calling those men in there foreigners to their faces, why, you're liable to get yourself into a hell of a brannigan, puny-looking as they are."

"I'm glad you don't underestimate them entirely."

Scoffing though he appeared, Kennedy had been listening. The veiled eyes were lifted now to Thor's earnest face. "Well, anyway, I know that each of us alone is bigger than any two of them in there, together. And not only size. I've been thinking that, smart as I am, and you with your special education, why, we might think of working together, like. Maybe not pardners, exactly. But working together."

"What makes you think I've had a special education?"

"The way you talk. I've heard Boston talk, and New York, too, but you don't talk like an American, or a Swensky either, even if you are. It's more what they call an English accent, isn't it? Special."

"My t—that is, I had an English teacher, perhaps I imitated him." He had almost said, My tutor was an Oxford man. He led the subject away from himself. "So here we are on our way to Alaska, you and I, with these other men. What makes you feel you are smarter than they? Probably you are. But why do you think so?"

"Because they're going to work themselves to the bone scratching crumbs of gold out of the ground, and I'm going to get it away from them, in comfort, by selling them the thing they'll need and want. Not little piddling things. Big. They'll need boats to get up the rivers —sizable boats, I mean—and I'm going to get hold of a boat and maybe run it. My folks back east were seafaring men. These ninnies yelling their lungs out in there"—he jerked his head toward the crowded saloon—"they'll have to have places to live in, wagons for hauling, I bet there isn't a horse in all Alaska. I've already got connections in Seattle. Let those poor suckers in there dig the gold. I'll get it without digging. I know ways. Lots of ways I'm not talking about."

The fair-haired giant looked at him then long and steadily. "Women? I hear they're scarce, too, up there. Scarcer than almost anything else needed. These girls on board were congratulating themselves."

"I'm no pimp. I'll make my pile and get out, but I'll make it fair and square enough. Everything legal."

Everything legal. Years later Thor Storm sometimes recalled this phrase with wry amusement. And, he told himself, it was. Even if Czar and the Big Boys had to make the law themselves and lobby it through Congress under their own steam.

Now, standing there at the ship's rail, he said, "I see. It sounds a practical scheme."

"Damn right it's practical. I'm not just going it blind."

"You say you'll make your pile and get out. If it's money you're after—and nothing else—I wouldn't get out too soon. Nobody knows yet what there is in this Alaska. It may be as big as all Europe. It's like a seventh continent. I'd say that gold is the least important product they'll take out of it. There are precious and valuable things in Alaska—furs and metals and coal and timber. And fish."

"Fish." Kennedy's tone was contemptuous.

But Storm was paying little attention to the man beside him, he seemed to be ruminating aloud. "Of course Bering was a Dane, though the Russians financed his voyage. What a voyage, poor man. But Steller, the botanist, the ornithologist—he was the first white man actually to set foot in Alaska. Did you know that? Most people don't."

"No, can't say I did," Kennedy replied because it seemed expected of him. The fella was kind of cracked, after all.

"It's true. He was nine months on Bering Island, for example, and of course he was on Kayak, too, and Kagal."

"Course," Kennedy conceded, politely.

"Do you know," Storm continued, absorbed in his topic, "how Steller proved that Alaska was part of America, part of the North American continent!"

"Can't say I do, exactly." He wished himself out of it by now, casting an almost wistful eye toward the noisy saloon. "How was that?"

"The bluejay."

"How's that again?"

"The bluejay. Steller knew that the eastern bluejay and the western bluejay were to be found nowhere but in the Western Hemisphere. And he actually saw one and shot it and examined it. It's in his diary and there is his magnificent book *De Bestis Marinis* published in 1751. What wonders that book revealed! Would you believe that until that time the world actually never had heard of the sea otter, the sea lion, and the fur seal!"

"That a fact!"

"That news alone brought the Russian fur hunters in droves to Alaska. Sealskin. Otter. Money. Money. But then, the sea cow! That was the real Steller triumph. What about the sea cow!"

"Yeh. Sure. The sea cow." Kennedy shook his head placatingly. The feller was crazy as a coot. He began to edge toward the saloon and safety.

"But that's all in the past," Storm went on, his tone regretful. "They're almost mythical animals now, except the fur seal. Man's greed destroyed these magnificent and valuable creatures years ago."

"Damn shame. Well, kind of chilly out here, guess I'll—"

"And now the real gold in Alaska—do you know where that is?"

Kennedy had turned away. But something in the man's earnest face and manner cautioned him to wait and hear. "Where's that at?"

"The rivers. The inlets. The bays. There are millions and millions there, waiting to be discovered." His words were exciting but his tone was quiet, thoughtful.

Zebedee Kennedy was thoughtful now, too. He had turned back to the giant. "Gold in the rivers, huh? Anybody knows that. Rivers and creeks. This feller Steller write something special about that, did he? In his book—*De* Something?"

"Not gold. Fish."

"Fish!" Kennedy yelled, in disappointment and anger. "That's the dumbest joke I ever did hear. I don't need any dumb Swede to tell me there's fish in Alaska."

Storm seemed not to have heard. "Millions of fish," he repeated, musingly. "Salmon. Millions and millions of salmon, enough to supply the world. For years and years and years. And timber. And coal. And metals. Those are the things to make Alaska a place of permanent value. Long after this little gold rush, as they call it, is over, those still will be there. Basic industries to make an empire out of a wilderness."

Kennedy thought (with one small part of his quick mind only) that this fellow sounded like one of those Fourth of July orators back home. But he no longer felt chilly. He stared hard into the man's face, his own face tense. He tried to be casual. "Yeah? What else besides?"

"Land, I suppose. Town land in a new world like this."

"Take a lot of money—fish canneries, timbering, real estate."

"I don't know about that part of it. I only know what I know. You said you had—what was that word?—connections—you said you had important connections in Seattle. Perhaps they would furnish the money."

Kennedy coughed a little preliminary cough. "We been standing here, gabbing, I didn't even tell you my name. Kennedy is my name —Z. Kennedy. Stands for Zebedee, out of the Bible. Zeb, everybody calls me. Pardon me being blunt, but I don't make you out, exactly. You talk like you know what you're talking about, you can see you're a man of education and so on. Next minute you're an explorer like Columbus or the Vikings. I only went through sixth grade but I know about the Vikings, a little anyway. You got the yellow hair, but you're lacking the helmet and spear and so on. I don't believe I got your name, sir."

"My name is Storm. Thor Storm. Thor after one of the Vikings, you know. Remember?"

"Pleased to make your acquaintance." His right arm extended, the two men clasped hands. "You sure appear to know a lot about Alaska."

"It isn't what I know. That isn't much. It's what I feel. This can be Valhalla. We can be gods."

Kennedy began to look uncomfortable again. "Well, I don't know's I want to be any god, exactly. I just figure to make my pile and get out."

"No. No, you mustn't do that. You must stay and make this a proud place. It's a proud place already—the native Indians and the Eskimos."

"Now wait a minute. They're nothing but savages. Dirty savages."

"The Eskimos are a civilized and resourceful people. They do not fight wars, they don't kill one another. They share."

"Civilized!"

"Well, perhaps not in our way. In their own way. And how civilized are we, after all?"

Kennedy now laughed, disarmingly, his manner was open and

friendly, his eyes were cautious, speculative. "That's what I always say. Uh, by the way, for all our talking here, and it's been darn interesting to hear you go on, I don't know yet what you do. For a living, I mean. What's your line of work? Back home, I mean."

"I fish." Then, at the look of blank disappointment amounting almost to shock in the other man's face, he added, "I come of sea people. Like yourself. And chiefly I study about people and places, their background and their life today because of that background. And then I write about them."

"Write! Books, you mean!"

"I've written one. Nobody much read it, the first one. I hope to write another someday."

"Write about this, you mean? Alaska and so on? The gold rush?"

"That's only a small part of it. An incident, really. Now, the Eskimos——"

But this was too much. Huffily, and with haste, Kennedy began to backtrack. "Books and Eskimos, they're not in my line. What you said about millions of salmon in the rivers—and coal—and metals—and so on—that's different. That's likely to be important. If you know, that is." Craftily he tried to gauge this man whose inner quality eluded him. And was this man a babbling fool, with his books and his Vikings and his fish, or did he know? If he actually could prove this knowledge, then what was the basis of the future relation between the two?

Quite simply Storm said, "I know this region, though I never have seen it."

Suspiciously, "How's that?"

"There are records and early histories, there are scientific books in the libraries and archives of many cities—Copenhagen and St. Petersburg and New York and others."

"You've seen those!"

"Yes."

"When?"

"When I was sixteen—eighteen—twenty—all my life."

"You must have had money to travel and jaunt around like that.

Archives." To this the man said nothing. Kennedy's face hardened. "I want to know just where I stand," he said. It was to become a business slogan with him, a safety catch used through future decades in all the preliminaries to his plans and schemings. "I want to know just where I stand. I take it you'll want your share of anything comes out of this. If we go in business together, that is." Hastily added.

"Business?" Thor Storm shook his head, a look of amusement lighting his face. "Business is not for me. I know nothing of business."

"But you just said. Damn it, you said you knew where things could be found."

"I do. I can tell you. I can tell anybody."

"No!" Kennedy yelled. "Me! Tell me!"

Thoughtfully, and—to Kennedy, maddeningly—he presented his terms. "All these things—all the riches of this great rich Alaska region—must be put to the good of the region itself. Not like the history of other parts of the United States in the old days. They grabbed and they schemed and they kept it for themselves—the land and the metals and the forests and the streams. This time, the last of the free land, it must be for the good of the people. All of them."

Kennedy stared at the man Thor Storm, at the guileless face, the quiet eyes. Something in their gaze caused him to shift his own eyes. He laughed, then, a little short bark of discomfiture which he hastily tried to change into a cough. "Well, sure. That's the way to look at it." Desperately now he persisted. "We could make a go of it together. After all, you have to use money, same as everybody. Like you said, it's the medium of exchange. I don't want to lose track of you. Where you heading in, exactly?"

"Baranof, like you. As a base, at least. Then out from there, up and back and around, as far as I can go."

"Baranof." Zeb Kennedy let out a great breath, smiling. His shoulders that had been hunched and tensed, relaxed. "Now, about that fish and coal and timber and metals and so on? Fish and coal alone, they add up to food and fuel. Everybody needs food and fuel, everywhere."

"And friends," Thor added. His smile, for the first time, was quizzically amused. He put forward his great hand. "Luck to you," he said. "And hoping you will make that pile—as you say—whether boats or houses or gold or fish. But for the common good. That is the only share I want in it."

It was the beginning of their half century of friendship and enmity.

10

Bridie Ballantyne had been the first picture bride to come to Baranof. Perhaps this was because Baranof, from the beginning, had taken on a definitely solid aspect. Other settlements —Nome, Ketchikan, even Juneau—had had a wilder history. It was as though Baranof, and Baranof's early sourdoughs, sensed that this was to develop into a substantial town.

Her coming had been the result of a joke fundamentally more stupid and rough than actually cruel. The men who had perpetrated it belonged to a lesser layer of the town's citizenry in those early days. Drunk when the joke was devised, they were mildly resentful of the already successful Czar Kennedy. Probably they never would have conceived this jest if both Czar and Thor had not, each in his own way, been unique.

"Who does he think he is!" a prospector might say, after his fourth drink. "Keeping to himself, so high and mighty. We're not good enough for him. Even the girls ain't good enough for him. Him and that big Swede, too. Who do they think they are, anyway!"

"You're just sore because your claim dribbled out on you," a more reasoning one would say. "Why don't you do like Czar does? Use your head."

"Czar Kennedy, he uses everybody's head," the disgruntled one announced with a flash of drunken clarity. "Everybody he meets, he picks their brains, quiet and smooth as a cobra."

"Cobras don't pick brains. Leastways, if they did they'd have a sorry meal off yours."

"Oh, so that's the way it is! You're in Czar's pay, the way a lot of them are."

"I'm in nobody's pay. I work my own claim."

"Yeah? Well, maybe I'm smarter than he is, some ways. Or you, either."

If Thor Storm and Czar Kennedy had been philanderers, or even fairly steady patrons of those early-day saloons and Line houses, lonely when alone, driven to the false comfort of drink or the fleeting solace of the town women when oppressed, Bridie Ballantyne never would have known Alaska, much less become one of its most respected citizens.

Czar and Thor took a drink now and then at the bar of the Rocker Saloon or the Poke of Gold. But it was known that they were not drinkers. They were polite and friendly toward the girls, they knew the women in the little close-huddled log cabins on the Old Creek Road. But no woman claimed them, the two stood apart. Both, to the other citizens of the haphazard town, came and went mysteriously.

Baranof admired the two men, sometimes grudgingly. They sensed that in each there was something distinctive. "Not stuck up, though. I mean they don't exactly act like they think they're smarter than other people." Then, wryly, "Say! But they are, at that!"

Confined as the Baranovians were by barriers of mountains, water, trackless tundra and killing cold, everybody's business was everybody's business. News traveled by what was called the mukluk grapevine. Mukluks are Eskimo boots of soft strong mooseskins, or caribou. News, then, that travels on foot, silently.

They say they say they say. They tried to extract news of Czar from Thor, and to verify Thor's puzzling pattern of life through Czar. Each was loyal to the other, though by now their differences were many and acute. Each pursued his own way of life and process of thinking. The men were in direct antithesis.

That crazy Swensky he goes off alone with his dog team up to the Eskimo villages, they say he learned to talk Eskimo, he writes pieces about them, they say when he's up there he lives right in with them, dirt and all and eats the stinking stuff they eat, raw. Summers back here he goes out in the salmon season with the boat crews that bring in the big catch for the canneries, July and August. They say he works like that, summers, so he can do his writing, winters, real scientific writing. He'll talk to you about it, if you come right out and ask him, but for all he's so good-natured and all, why, you feel he's kind of studying you, he kind of studies everybody, friendly, mind you, but there's a look in his eyes like he isn't only listening to you, he's storing away what he hears. Somebody said he married one of those half-breed Eskimo girls but he isn't as big a fool as that, I mean he's kind of crazy but he's no fool. Leastways, he ain't as crazy as all that. Any Eskimo will lend you his wife, anybody knows that, if that's what you want.

Thor Storm had been absent from Baranof for more than a year. Isador Raffsky, the fur trader from Oogruk, came down with the news. Authentic news.

"The missionary minister of the Presbyterian mission up near Kotzebue married them in a regular church ceremony, right in the Mission Church. A year ago, almost. The baby has black hair and blue eyes. A boy. Christopher Storm his name is."

"So the girls around here weren't good enough for him," the boys jeered. "He had to be choosy and get him a real select Eskimo squaw. Say, I always knew he was nutty, but I sure didn't think he was really crazy like that. Next thing he'll be bringing her here, I suppose, and expecting our womenfolks to call."

With a great show of casualness a questioner would approach Thor.

"Haven't seen you for a coon's age, Thor. You been away?"

"Yes."

"Far?"

"Any place is far in Alaska, isn't it?"

"I see Czar's made another trip to Seattle and back. Way he goes Outside, you'd think it was across the street. What's he do so much in Seattle?"

"Business, I suppose. He's a man of business, Czar."

"There was a fella here to see him last month, you were gone that time, too. Must have been one of those Seattle or San Francisco millionaires, he had a coat was fur-lined, and cloth on the outside, I guess the Eskimos aren't so dumb after all, that's the way they fix their parkys. Anyway, one of the boys saw it, says it was mink from collar to hem, inside, mind you! And a gold watch chain this thick, you'd think he was the one had struck Bonanza Creek. Know who he was?"

"No. Who?"

"I'm not telling you, I'm asking you."

"I don't know."

"They say it isn't all business strictly with Czar, those trips Outside. I notice he don't have much to say to the nice girls here in town, or the other kind either. They say he goes around with high-class society in Seattle and they say he's making up to Einar Wendt's daughter, the Tacoma lumberman. Lumber king, some call him. They say she's real plain-featured. And no chicken. Still and all, I guess Czar knows what he's after, he usually does. Like the fella says, you can't sometimes see the woods for the trees. They say he's fixing to marry her. Is that right?"

"It sounds a practical plan."

"Czar's practical, that's sure. Still and all, no daughter of Einar Wendt is going to come to Alaska to live. Czar'll have to settle down in Tacoma, for all he says Alaska is the only place for him."

In Czar's presence, one of the men essayed a mild joke about this rumored courtship. Czar did not openly resent this, his face remained impassive, perhaps the cold blue-gray eyes became a degree more icy behind the screen of the long black lashes. A little later the joker found himself somehow in trouble. He had difficulty with his credit at the store. Big Lena, at the Nugget, treated him coldly, finally refused to have anything to do with him. Then an inexplicable dispute arose concerning his claim on Heekarree Creek.

There was no proof that Czar had had anything to do with all this. But the disgruntled joker decided for himself. Two or three friends were told of his little plan—just enough to carry it through. Sober, they never would have started it. Once started, it carried itself to the finish. When, terrified by their own success, they tried to stop it, it was too late.

They placed an advertisement in the Seattle *Post.*

PICTURE BRIDE

> Will exchange letters and photos with young respectable single lady of good appearance who can stand up to adventure and maybe roughing it in Alaska with young gentleman of steady habits who wants a lifetime partner to share his poke of gold. No shady characters or fly-by-nights need apply. Object matrimony. Send photo. Life in Alaska healthy and has got a fine future. Address: P.O. Box 19, Baranof, Alaska.

They had a dozen replies, but they decided on Bridie's because hers was the briefest, the plainest. Her letter was literate enough, but there was about it a simplicity that the jokers mistook for ignorance.

She had been six months now in the United States; the vast overpowering size of it had filled her with pangs of loneliness and even fright, courageous as she was by nature. More in a spirit of fun and adventure than any serious intention she had answered the advertisement. There had come back by the return boat a photograph of the unknown Box 19. Czar Thor, it said his name was. Queer enough name, Bridie thought. But the photograph banished any criticism of the name. The handsome, almost spiritual, face; the magnificent eyes, the wavy hair, won the girl's heart. This was romance. This was the Ameriky she had dreamed of when she had carried the heavy-laden trays in noisome hospital corridors.

She sent her photograph then, and a second letter. Looking at her picture—the honest eyes gazing straight out at you from the decent purposeful face—and reading her simple, self-reliant letter—the pranksters found the situation less hilarious than they had expected. They had meant to show the picture, the advertisement, and the letters to Czar just to kid him a little in the presence of the boys and girls if they could catch him, some evening, at the Rocker or the Poke. But it didn't seem so funny now, and anyway Czar had gone on one of his sudden trips Outside. Bridie's last letter created panic. She was coming. By the time this letter was received she would have left.

In a handwriting that was dashing in a childlike way, she stated her facts. ". . . from Ireland to the hospital in Lancashire, and there I got my training and then to America and my cousin in this Seattle. . . . I thought I never would see the end of the way, days it was to cross this big land . . . job in the hospital here in Seattle but the training is different to what we get in the old country . . . this Alaska you hear nothing else these days only Alaska, it sounds a fine big place and I was always one for adventuring and new sights. . . ."

"God Almighty!" The joker who was reading this letter looked up at his fellow conspirators. "This one's coming. She's left. Boys, I'm getting out of here until this blows over. I'm going out to the creek and stay. Anyway, thank God, Czar ain't here but he'll be back maybe even by the time she . . . look, I'm getting the hell out of here for a spell, anyway. Right now."

Bridie Ballantyne took the small sum she had somehow hoarded—the great heavy American silver dollars that, big and shining though they were, still seemed to buy so little in this hugeous west place Indian-named Seattle—pagan Indian images mind you, to be had in the shops down by the river.

It was a staggering journey by boat, by train, by boat again. When first she had come to Seattle some of her old-world rosy coloring still bloomed in her cheeks. But before she left for Alaska, what with the hospital work, the preparations for the journey, and a clutch of doubt and fear at her vitals, she looked quite gray-faced as she came aboard.

The suit she had managed to buy for the journey was just the latest thing in Seattle, a long flaring skirt very grand, with three spaced rows of satin banding from the knees to the hem. The bodice had the new leg-o'-mutton sleeves and a high ruched collar. There was a jacket too, mind you, of the same stuff as the dress, and its sleeves were even bigger than the bodice sleeves, as they had better be. Topping this splendor was an ulster with a good collar, it buttoned right up to the throat, warm brown-and-gray woolen stuff, no shoddy for Bridie Ballantyne; and her hat was a broad-brimmed sailor sporting not a mere wing but an entire bird nesting in a sort of copse of flowers and shrubbery. Even in that day Bridie knew what the well-dressed woman was wearing. Her mother, back home in Ireland, had been a seamstress.

In the dour Lancashire hospital of her student training days, before ever she had set foot on the New World, she had bolstered her energy, her spirits, by singing a familiar song as she scrubbed and swabbed and emptied slops. Thousands of immigrant boys and girls before her had sung it in anticipation.

Adieu unto your Liffey Banks,
Your Mourne Waters wide,
I'm sailing for Ameriky,
Whatever may betide.

Whatever may betide. Well, good or bad, it was too late now, she told herself as, days later, she stepped off the boat. There was no one to meet her, scan the faces though she would. She clambered up the refuse-strewn beach to the main street of the town, a street of log cabins and tents. She stood a panic-stricken moment staring at mountains and water and sky. Seattle had accustomed her to the impact of lavish panoramas, but compared to this, Seattle was cosy. She lowered her gaze from the vast vision to the nearer sights. Sordid dwellings, dirt, bearded men. She never had seen a human settlement such as this.

Up the travesty of a street there was a log house outside of which an American flag hung limply from a pole, for there was no wind. The sun was warm yet the air was cool and heady. The American flag, well, then that place must be right enough. People seemed to be coming in and out, a group of men in good cloth suits and derby hats stood outside, talking with serious faces, like men of business and property, not roughs. She left her luggage there on the beach—the two old-country valises that held everything she possessed, including her nurse's uniforms. She clutched to one side a handful of skirt and petticoat to lift them out of the mud, but not so high as to show her ankles—she knew what was right and proper; and mud would dry and could be brushed off with a whisk. She was reassured, as she plodded along, that everything—ulster, hat, gloves, high-buttoned shoes—all were as they should be.

When she reached the place with the flag she hesitated. The men looked at her with interest, they seemed still to be discussing a topic of real importance and now it seemed to her that she herself was, incredibly enough, a possible part of this discussion. Their glances were respectful enough and they held not only interest but conjecture. As Bridie stood, hesitating, uncertain, one of the men—an older man with a settled look about him, and some gray in his mustache—came toward her.

"Are you the nurse, ma'am?" he asked.

Falteringly, "Yes, I'm a—I'm the nurse."

The man's face cleared, he seemed almost to beam. Panic-stricken, she thought, But that can't be him, he doesn't look like the picture, so old-looking, surely that can't be him. The man turned to the others, he waved a triumphant hand. "Here she is, boys!" he shouted. "Here's the nurse."

The other faces beamed, then. "What difference does it make," she asked, almost resentfully, "that I'm a nurse?"

The older man laughed at this, a little ruefully. "We'd about given up, and that's a fact. We tried nearby first, Fairbanks and Nome, if you can call that nearby, but it got so we figured nobody would come, Seattle or anywhere, though we tried. Nobody would come on account it was smallpox."

"Smallpox!"

"Seven of them down with it now, two new ones at the All Nations, and Ideal at the Lucky Streak, her face's a sight they say, like a red raspberry patch, and fever." Now he looked at her as though for the first time, doubtfully. "You look young," he said, "for a nurse.

Doctor's off up north. But I bet you know what to do for smallpox, first off."

"Balsam of Peru lotion," she replied, automatically. "Balsam of Peru lotion. Apply to pustules. For relief."

"Sure thing!" the man agreed, triumphantly. "That's the stuff. The girls don't want no men around—for a change. Not," hastily, "that we're scared."

"Ya-a-ah!" jeered someone in the group.

"Well, maybe you are, but Thor ain't," the man retorted. "Thor went and fixed them some tea and tried to help, didn't you, Thor?"

"Thor!" Bridie repeated, stiff-lipped. She looked up at a giant of a man who now stepped forward from the crowd—a man well over six feet tall with a short golden beard and eyes that were different from the other men's eyes, serious but friendly, too, and smiling.

"Where is your luggage, miss?" he said. His words and voice were different, too, something like that London doctor who had been head of the Lancashire hospital.

Gazing at him Bridie gasped, "Are you English! You didn't say you were English."

"Heh, Swensky! Heh, Thor!" a voice called. "You an English swell?"

Heedless of this, still gently smiling, the big man looked down at her. "I'll fetch your luggage if you'll point it out to me. Possibly there may be a room for you at Mrs. Belcher's boardinghouse, a respectable place, I can assure you of that. But I'm not sure she'd want you there after you've seen your patients. After all, Mrs. Belcher has two small children, it might be a risky thing——"

"Oh, no, no!" she cried. "It's a mistake!"

Soothingly, he went on, "If Mrs. Belcher objects, you can stay in my cabin and I'll move in with someone else until it's over. Czar's moved out, anyway, it will be quite all right."

Desperately, she cried, "But you're not him! His name is Czar—wait a minute"—she groped in her reticule for the photograph and fished it out, her hands shaking—"Czar Thor, his name is. Mr. Czar

Thor, Box 19, Baranof, Alaska. I came to see him. They called you Thor, but you're not him!"

The big man took the photograph from her and gazed at it in silence. He looked down at the girl's face upturned to his—the plain, fresh decent face upturned to him. One of the other men had peered over his shoulder.

"Kennedy!" the man yelled. "It's Czar Kennedy!" Then he, too, stared at her. "Why, say, miss, Czar's left for Seattle and Tacoma to be married. He left on the boat last week. He's married by now."

Years later, when Christine was a woman and the mother of children, Bridie still found herself answering the questions questions questions put to her by this insatiable lover of the always mysterious Alaska. Bridie could answer the questions freely and frankly now and she had miraculously retained, old as she was, the astringency, the piquancy of her verbiage. She loved to hear the ripple of Christine's sudden laughter when the answer to a question was more than ordinarily pungent.

"I'll never forget that first day. Come, like a ninny, to marry a man who'd never heard of me, and finding myself nursing a bunch of girls down with smallpox in a House. Not one of them died, I'll say that for myself, but then they were a husky bunch, they had to be to stand this climate then, no conveniences. Conveniences! Well, we won't go into that. A gold-rush camp, rough as a bear's den. They were kind of like children, those girls. Their minds, I mean. Dull-thinking, most of them. They'd sit in their wrappers, afternoons, in the back yard, fenced in, it was, wearing Mother Hubbard wrappers, there was a hammock I remember, slung between two posts. They'd wash their hair and fluff it out in the sun, summers. And the waiter—he was a Negro fella—he brought them beer and sandwiches on a tray, and they talked and laughed and read those yellow-back paper novels or the little newspaper, maybe, it was about the size of a handbill. Sometimes they played games, like little girls. I've seen 'em play jacks, even, on the back steps, and fight over the little rubber ball."

"An easy life—for that day."

"A hard life."

"Bridie darling, don't be offended—but were you ever—after all, you'd been tricked into coming to Baranof—were you ever tempted to give up and go into one of the——"

"I was a nurse," Bridie said, simply.

"I never could understand why you didn't marry either Grampa Thor or Grampa Czar—anyway, after both my grandmothers died or whatever it was. At least, I suppose Grampa Thor's wife died, too. My other grandmother. Doesn't it sound mixed up! But anyway, why didn't you? I've seen those pictures of you, you were young and—and fresh—and your eyes looked out so straight and honest and direct."

"That was it, I guess. Straight and honest and direct. I don't mean to sound crabby. Truth was, I was in love with both of them, it sounds crazy, but it isn't. They weren't in love with me. There I was, looking after you when your ma died that awful death, nursing everybody, and I was in the house, either Czar's house or Thor's, day in day out, crackling around all starched and bossy and independent. Everything plain and aboveboard, like you say. I was like a loaf of bread in the house. There's always a loaf of bread in any house, poor or rich, there it is, if it's only half a loaf or a bit of the heel, it's bread, you don't get excited about it, you take it for granted. That was me."

"But Mrs.—Mrs. Ballantyne. Of course now everybody calls you Bridie, but you must have married somebody."

"I did. Hardly anybody knows that. I was discouraged, I guess, about Czar and Thor. Czar was looking higher than me, and Thor was in the clouds, he had to be democratic, he was hell-bent on being democratic, he had to be more democratic than the usual run, so he married as much outside of his own line as Czar had outside of his—but in what they call reverse. I was married one week to a fellow from Nome, I'd put by a bit of money, nursing, and he skipped out with it. It was pretty hard to skip out anywhere in Alaska those days, there was nothing to skip in or on except by dog sled or boat. So maybe the varmints got him, I never heard. I just kept my name

Ballantyne and left it at that. Chris, I've almost forgotten how he looked. Isn't that awful!"

"You're wonderful, Bridie darling. You're as vital and wonderful today as you were then."

"I'm an old woman. I'm not talking in complaint. I've had a fine ride of it, the people and the scenery every inch of the way. The world owes me nothing. Now I'm an old old woman, and not really needed."

"Don't say that. We all need you. I need you, the children need you. Everybody——"

"Nope. Not so. Who cares about the old, really? Well, I'll tell you, Chris dearie. Nobody. They say they care, they say ain't she wonderful now, my, she's young for her age, look at the way she gets around, her mind is clear as a bell! But they don't really care and why should they? It's only natural. I say to myself, I say, you've had your nice ride, you're old, the new models come along, the old ones only block traffic on Gold Street, they have to pull over to the side to let the new ones go by, the fast ones, the big bright-colored blue-paint jobs."

"Addie Barnett was saying only yesterday she never saw any-one——"

"I know, I know. Addie's a fine girl. I'm not complaining. Only I want you to know I'm old—but not foolish."

11

"My family tree," Christine Storm, much later, explained to bewildered Outsiders, "is a forest. I don't expect visitors to grope their way through it. I often get lost, myself."

By the time she was twelve, she had pieced together the intricate pattern of her brief life, and that of the three adults—Czar, Thor, and Bridie—who governed it. Thor Storm never had stunted the growth of her curiosity.

One of the results of this encyclopedic plan was that, at sixteen, she knew as much (and possibly more) about Alaska's politics, people, prospects, resources and injustices as any Seattle, San Francisco, New York or Washington absentee millionaire.

Why Why Why? she asked, at twelve. What what what? Czar Kennedy turned her off with a grandfatherly, "Because I say so, that's why." Sometimes she would repeat to Bridie bits and pieces of conversation remembered from Thor's Bergsonian philosophy or Czar's blandly material view of life.

Bridie would discount this, briskly. "Pay them no mind, child dear. They're not talking to you. They're talking to each other through you, like a jealous couple. In a way, you're the wife of both of them, and I'm their widow. No, forget about that, Chris child dear, forget I said that, I was gabbing. Just forget that now. They love you and that's all that matters, so just let the talk flow off your little shoulders like a cape, like an easy garment, warm and light, as it's meant to be, I'm sure."

A merry child she was at twelve, yet thoughtful; lighthearted and strangely serene, like her grandfather Thor; somewhat zany, yet worldly, like Bridie Ballantyne, her duenna, nurse, mother, all in one; canny, too, like Czar, but without his hard shrewdness.

"Real streak of Eskimo in her, too," Baranof said, but fondly, "on her father's side—anyway, that is, if it's true that old Thor married an Eskimo half-breed girl up there near Barrow, years ago, and they had this son he brought down here alone to Baranof one day, calm as you please, no one knew if the girl had died or left him, or what. Nobody ever saw the mother but the baby grew up here, he married Czar's daughter, he was Christine's father. Yes, it does sound mixed up, I suppose, to you, but not to us old Alaska sourdoughs it doesn't. Nothing surprises us, nothing mixes us up—cold, heat—blond, dark—rich, poor—old, young—good, bad—we take it as it comes. Maybe we're more civilized than they are Outside."

By the time she was twelve or thirteen nothing surprised Christine, nothing shocked her. At that age she said to Thor, "Everybody died, didn't they?"

"Not everybody, Christine."

"My father and my mother and my Gramma Kennedy and Gramma Ewok. That's everybody but you and Grampa Czar and Bridie. Why?"

"I don't know. Life here is rougher, in some ways, and harder, than in other places."

"Outside, you mean?"

"Yes."

"But it's nicer too, isn't it?"

"I think so."

"I do, too." She had been nowhere. "But if it's rougher and harder why did you and Grampa Czar come? And then stay here?"

"You know all about that as well as I do. You know we came on the same ship. Czar came to earn his living and get rich if he could, which is a fair and legitimate ambition. I came to study Alaska, in a way, and I thought it would give me a feeling of freedom, and it did. I did my work and Czar did his. So we've both lived the life we wanted to live. We've lived history. Anybody who lives even a year in Alaska is history."

From the vantage of her grade-school knowledge Christine disputed this statement. "You have to be dead to be history. History is war. And long journeys to places like the Pilgrim Fathers. In history you wear different clothes and do brave things or bad things, and anyway you're always dead if you're history. At the end, I mean."

Thor might have retorted flippantly, "Aren't we all!" But he cared too much for that. He cared too much about the child Christine; and about Alaska. To him they were not merely a beloved human being and a region at once familiar, dear, and awesome. They were symbols of the future of the human race.

"History is just people, Christine. History isn't only yesterday. It's today. We're making history right now, this minute, here in Alaska. There is no history without people, any more than there is sound without hearing. If a great tree falls in the forest and there is no one there to hear it, it falls without sound—no, forget that, it will only confuse you. What I am trying to say, child, is that for about three quarters of a century now—ever since 1867—Alaska has been a living example of United States history. And you are part of it. You are history."

The child stared at him. "Me! This minute!"

"This minute. You."

"Are you history, too?"

"I am. And so is your Grandpa Czar. And Bridie."

"Well, my teacher didn't say so."

"Then you tell her. Those people who came to Virginia and Massachusetts and California and Oregon a hundred years ago, or two hundred or three, are history, but they didn't know it then. Alaska is history made while you wait. People who live through such things and stay with it, and their children, and their grandchildren——"

"Like me?"

"Yes, like you, Christine. Those people have what is called the *élan vital.*"

"What does that mean?"

"I was going to tell you. It means a vital drive, a strong life force. Enthusiasm. Vigor. They endure, they last, in spite of everything—hardships, and enemies, and hunger, and fear. It's a wonderful thing to have, it's the most valuable quality you can possess. Whole nations have it. The English people have it, and the Norwegians. Perhaps a few besides. The Jews, too. They've persisted these thousands of years in spite of incredible horrors. It is a quality that can't be taught, it can't be commanded. It must spring from within. The United States has had it for centuries. Boiled down, the essence of it is the will to keep your spirit and independence even at the cost of your life. But now things are too easy, too lavish, too rich in the United States, we've grown soft and careless. The vital drive has weakened, we let others act for us, they think for us, even play our games for us. The drive now isn't much more than a mechanical thing at the wheel of a big shiny automobile. We're losing it. It may already be lost."

"Alaska too? Is it lost in Alaska too?"

He stared at her. His great arm gathered her to him, he held her close. "I was thinking aloud, Christine. Well, Alaska. Yes, Alaska still has the *élan vital,* perhaps it isn't only because of climate and struggle, perhaps it isn't even because we've always been so remote from the rest of the world. It may be that the pioneer stock is still running strong in our veins, first and second generation still. Even the new ones, the late-comers, who leave their homes for money or freedom or adventure, like all pioneers. It takes a vital drive to do that, and that doesn't wear out for a few generations. Perhaps someday soon there'll be thousands of miles of roads in Alaska, as there are in the states of the United States. Or the sky will be humming with planes all the way from Ketchikan clear up to Point Barrow. But in Alaska now we're still far away from the rest of the world."

"Grampa Czar says we aren't. He says pretty soon no place will be far away from any place. He says Russia is right up there"—excitedly she pointed in the direction that might be north—"he says any minute look out bingo!"

He took her small hand in his great one, the steady blue eyes looked down into her glowing black ones.

"Don't you worry about that, never mind about all that, little Christine. What were we saying before?"

"History. I'm history, you said."

"Oh, yes. Well, that's important just now. Being history. There are even men alive today who can remember when this land was Russian land, before it became part of the United States. One old man even claims he was there when it happened. He lives in the Old Pioneers' Home in Sitka now. Of course there's no record to prove it. He was born in Sitka, it was called New Archangel then, it was the capital of Russian America."

"I know that," she interrupted, pertly. "That's in our history book about Alaska, but that's long ago."

"Not so long, if a man remembers it. I don't say that I believe him, but it could be true. He was just a boy."

"Why don't you believe him?"

"That was–let's see–the date was 1867–about eighty years ago, the old fellow's almost a hundred–well, it could be, certainly. But maybe he just read about it, or heard someone tell of it. It was very dramatic, the day they took down the Russian flag and ran up the American flag. But no very old man would be likely to remember it the way he tells it. I've heard him."

"How does he tell it?"

"He says he remembers the soldiers lined up in the Russian settlement. The United States had bought all of Alaska for seven million dollars. Imagine that!" But at the look of incomprehension on her face he interrupted himself contritely. "That doesn't mean much to a little girl. But it's interesting to know that most of the people of the United States were very angry at a man named Seward because he was the man who advised them to buy it. And now we know he was right, it's worth a hundred times that, and more. So that wasn't such a bad bargain, was it?"

"Go on. The soldiers were lined up——"

"Oh. Well, there were the Russian soldiers on one side, and the American troops in blue uniforms lined up on the other side."

"The other side of what?"

"Of the flagpole, with the Russian flag flying at the top of it, ninety feet up in the air. The Russian flag had a double golden eagle on it, it was called the Imperial Flag of Russia then. There was an ocean breeze up there on the hill where they all stood, and the flag was very pretty, waving and snapping in the wind. They were in front of the house of the Russian Governor, Prince Maksoutoff. The Russian officers wore uniforms of scarlet with gold braid. There was a salute from the artillery of the Russians and then a salute from the artillery of the Americans, all very dramatic, as you might imagine. And then very slowly they began to lower the Russian ensign—"

"What's an ensign?"

"Flag. They began to lower the Russian flag and it fouled in the halyards"—he caught the question before it was uttered—"that means the flag got caught and snarled in the ropes that were pulling it down. This man says he really saw this. So they sent an American sailor up the pole to loosen it, but he couldn't work it loose, and there were all those people with their faces turned up toward him, looking at him and the flag. He couldn't work it loose and he was sort of desperate then, and nervous, so he tore it down and threw it and it landed on the heads of the Russian soldiers. That was bad."

"Why was it?"

"Because the flag of a country isn't just a piece of cloth, it's the sign of the country, the emblem, it's something you treat with great respect and honor. Well, then, the Russian flag came down, and the Stars and Stripes—the United States flag—went up, and the cannon boomed, and they made speeches, first the Russian officers and then the United States officers, and then everybody cheered except one person, and they say she cried as if her heart would break when the Russian flag was lowered and the land that her husband had worked for and believed in passed from the rule of the Czar of Russia to the rule of the United States."

"To Grandpa Czar?"

Startled, "No." But then he laughed a little, ruefully.

"Who was the one who cried as if her heart would break? And did it?"

"Her name was Princess Maksoutoff, and she was the wife of the Russian Governor, and they left Alaska then, forever, and went back to Russia. No, it didn't break, it seldom does," he said, contritely. He thought he must be more careful in his figures of speech, with the child.

"Was she a young and beautiful princess?"

"All princesses are young and beautiful," Thor Storm said, gently, remembering the gaunt and long-toothed princesses of Scandinavia; and remembering his own childhood and youth, so incredibly unlike his life here in the past half century.

Shuttled back and forth from the cushioned comfort of Czar's house to Thor's neat little log cabin—three months with Czar, three months with Thor—even an adult might have been shredded by this split existence. That Chris survived as a whole human being—though scarred—was miraculous. Oddly, she was happier in the three-room shack at the water's edge than in Czar's ample house with its bouncy mattresses, its thick carpets, its plate-glass windows. Through the protective panes she could see the splendid panorama of sky and water and mountains, yet here the child never had the feeling of security, of belonging. The world looked unreal and distant, somehow, viewed through all that glass. At Thor's cabin the mountains and the water and the land were part of her daily life, she did not view them merely; she partook of them. Together she and Thor trudged the hills, fished the waters, slogged through the tundra gathering the delicate low-growing wild flowers, picking the low-bush wild cranberries for jelly. There were blueberries, too, and salmon berries. Thor held forth in terms of philosophy and economics and history. She was too young to understand it all, but much of this must have stuck in her memory and been preserved in her emotional storehouse. Years later she brought it forth, undimmed, like golden coins retrieved from a buried treasure chest. Not only Thor, but often Czar and Bridie, spoke to her in adult terms, and though she often was confused by this she thrived on their competitive affection.

At mealtime Czar, pointing with a knife or fork, would say, "Eat that lettuce, it costs a fortune, lettuce does." Or cabbage or beans or any green growing thing. "Freighted all the way from Seattle, and that costs plenty, I can tell you."

"Then let's not have it any more," Chris suggested, brightly. "I don't like it anyway."

"Like it or not, you'll eat it, young lady!"

"Why do I have to?"

"Because I say so."

Thor made a sort of game of his lessons in food values. "Nature has a wonderful way of taking care of you, if you'll only heed her. Take salmon."

"Ugh! The natives eat it all the time, you can smell it even when they walk past you down the street."

"Salmon is a cold-water cold-climate fish. It's fat. And fat is fuel that protects you from the cold. Up north, in Barrow and Oogruk and Kotzebue and all the villages, the Eskimos eat seal oil and whale blubber—don't make a face, it isn't bad, with berries and so on—and that keeps them warm. Keeps them alive. People here in Baranof, though, don't eat enough green stuff. Meat and potatoes and sweet stuff, that isn't good enough. Remember to eat green things when you're with—when you're not with me."

"Why?"

"Because they'll make your hair curly and your cheeks pink and your eyes bright. And that means you're healthy. There are elements in them that keep you well. Vitamins they're called."

As a sort of game they scoured the countryside for their own greens. "The Eskimos," he told her, storybook fashion, "go out and hunt for green stuff as though they were hunting for meat or fish or furs. There's sourah, that's the yellow stuff inside the pussy willow, they call it willow meat. And there's wild chard, and there's a plant they call asakluk, it grows in sandy places. And lots of others. They pick them and wash them and store them for the winter in a seal poke."

"Seal——?"

"Someday I'll teach you how to make a seal poke. It's quite a trick. Now, let's go out and see what we can find. Greens or berries that are good to eat."

No such fancies spangled her months with Czar Kennedy. She lived in the finest house in Baranof, she wore dresses bought in Seattle, she ate the best the town afforded. On one of his rare trips to Seattle Czar even took Christine with him. In her early girlhood this journey was by no means the casual fling through the firmament that—thanks to the airplane—was to bring the mainland a mere handful of hours away from distant Arctic shores.

Most Alaskans did not dream of staying at the Olympic Hotel when they visited Seattle, that first Outside stop. It was too grand, too costly. They chose one of the small side-street hotels where they knew they would encounter fellow territorials whose tastes and pocketbooks matched their own. With or without Christine, Czar stayed at the Olympic. The hotel staff knew him, there always was a room for him, no matter how many national business conventions might be crowding the lobby, the halls, the restaurants. Long ago the room clerks, bellhops, waiters had learned not to be deceived by the baggy clothes, the battered old hat above the ascetic face, the veiled eyes. Bridie Ballantyne, provoked perhaps by some fresh evidence of ruthlessness, had said with characteristic acumen, "That face of Czar's, and the look of it, it's like you were looking at one of those paintings of the prophets, mild and understanding everything, and forgiving. Then all of a sudden he looks at you, you notice his eyes, and they're like that FBI man was here once during the War. Cold steel."

This glimpse of the Northwest metropolis had dazzled the child, and puzzled her. Like an Alice in Wonderland she stared, confused and sometimes unbelieving, at the hotel's luxurious appointments, at the wide streets, the amazing hills, the shopwindows, the handsome houses, the cloud-crowned office buildings.

"Baranof doesn't look like this," the child said. "Why doesn't it?"

"No money."

"Then why doesn't Seattle give them some money?"

He stared at her, startled. He had been hearing this question lately, from other sources. Then he laughed. "No, that wouldn't do. That's the wrong way round."

Not wishing to leave her alone in the hotel, or on the street, he took her with him when he had a business conference in this office or that, with Dave Husack or Sid Kleet or any one of a half dozen other Northwest nabobs.

"Now you sit here," Czar would say as they entered the outer reception room of one of these luxury office suites, "and read a book or look at these folders with all these pictures in them, I won't be long."

"I want to come in with you."

"You can't. We've got business to talk about."

"I won't stay here. I want to come in there with you. I'll be quiet."

Sunk in the depths of a vast leather armchair, a book in her lap, the child was so quiet that the men actually forgot her presence. This room, in whatever building (with the exception of Sid Kleet's bare and gritty office) always was baronial. Invariably its many windows looked out upon Seattle's glorious bay and mountains. The ceiling was high, the room vast, the walls mahogany- or oak-paneled. The visitor trod on the ruby and sapphire, emerald and topaz of an oriental carpet. Paintings of ships and mountains and waters seemed to reflect the view one saw through the windows. Models of ships stood on the mantel shelf. The fireplace was cavernous, the desk a plateau, the leather-upholstered chairs gigantic. The child sat quietly, quietly, every object in the luxurious room, every color, storing itself in her memory. She heard every word the men said. It did not interest her, she understood none of it, she merely retained it. She was like a reservoir into which every fluid thing from trickle to torrent finds its way. She liked the scent of the cigars the men smoked, sitting well back in their chairs, their legs spread comfortably, their eyes approving the long lavender-gray ash that clung so tenaciously in proof of the costliness of the oily brown cylinder. They talked quietly, leisurely, one would have thought, from their manner, that their subject was, perhaps, philanthropy.

"Thing to do is put pressure on him, give him the screws."

"Lubbock says he wants to see the situation from every angle before he makes his report."

"Lubbock wouldn't know a salmon from a herring if he ate it."

Sid Kleet's dry nasal voice. "Gentlemen, I would like you to give me authority to by-pass fisheries commissioners and directors and little stuff like that."

"What have you in mind, Sid?" It was Czar's question, his tone one of mild interrogation. He knew the answer, he wanted it stated in words uttered by the group's legal representative.

"Go over their heads," Kleet barked.

"To who?"

"You damn well know to who. Cabinet Member. Senator. They'll get action."

"What'll you do with Lubbock?"

"Same as we did with Diener. Get him."

"Yeh, but how about old Storm?" Dave Husack demanded. His voice, booming from that barrel chest had the effect of a bellow in the quiet, almost somnolent, room. Czar waved a cautioning hand toward the child.

Very early in her childhood Bridie had impressed upon her the vileness of tattling. "Now don't you go tattling to Czar about Thor, or Thor about Czar. You got anything about either of your Grampas, why, just come and tell me."

"Wouldn't that be tattling?"

"No. I'd be a kind of a judge, like Judge Gannon here, I'd think about it, not leaning to one or the other, and then decide about it and try to fix whatever is wrong. I'd do the best I could for all three."

As Chris's keen mind missed practically nothing, and as she had almost total recall, the plums that fell into Bridie's lap were rich and juicy. This office conference, for example, conveyed quite innocently in Christine's childish terms, sent Bridie scurrying to the office of the

Northern Light. She was discreet, she did not give her source, she merely hinted.

"We'll be able to block that plan," Addie Barnett said. "We'll merely print it in full."

"Each one," Paul Barnett observed, "will think the other blabbed. And they'll all probably blame old Einar."

Thor said, almost sadly, "It's like that old cartoon of Nast's—the famous one—of the circle of political thieves each pointing to the man next him and saying, 'He did it.' They're old-fashioned plunderers, but it still seems to work."

Now, in the big luxurious Seattle office, as Czar cautiously indicated the child at the far end of the room, some atavistic instinct told Christine to shut her eyes. The men saw the golden head, snuggled in the engulfing depths of the vast chair by the window, touchingly cushioned against the plump tufted leather. She was breathing lightly, regularly, the innocent half-smile of pleasant dreams curving the lovely lips.

Czar relaxed. "She's asleep."

Dave Husack did not relish this cosy interlude in the battle of big business. "You shouldn't of brought her here in the first place."

Czar's tone was mild, paternal. "Never you mind, Dave, about what I should or shouldn't do. Though it's real thoughtful of you toward the child. I make it a rule never to go any place I couldn't bring her to if I was so minded." His eyes were cobalt.

"How's that again about who was it?" old Einar Wendt asked. Czar's father-in-law, he was over eighty now, tough as a tree, he had come to Seattle from Tacoma for this meeting, he wanted to get on with it and go home. He cupped his right ear with his hand, he spoke in the high monotonous voice of the deaf.

"Storm!" Husack bellowed. "Thor Storm, you know him, the old crackpot who runs that paper."

"What about him?"

"He's raising a stink, that's what. Papers outside are copying his stuff, he's been running articles and editorials and so on, he's got a column full of snide remarks about me and Kleet and the whole cannery crowd. He comes right out with names in Washington, right in the government, it's libel, we could sue him for a million dollars only the poor old moosehead——"

"No libel suits," Sid Kleet snapped. "Too much publicity in libel suits. There's other ways."

"Such as what?" Mort Caswell demanded. The Caswells were Ships, this Mort was Ships and old Mortimer had been Ships, and old old Mortimer, and old old old Mortimer in the days of the Yankee Clippers long before his descendants had transferred their sea heritage from the Atlantic to the Pacific. It was said that the first Mort of the New England line had run slave ships, and now young Mort ran slave ships of a sort, though legitimately. The Caswell Clipper North Coast Line made sure of that. Cannery workers from the mainland for two or three frantic summer months—thousands of cannery workers shipped to Alaska, shipped back home again to California, to Washington State, to Oregon, their summer wages, unspent, bursting their pockets. Young Mort and any surviving old Morts were no fools, they realized that planes, rather than ships, would now be the means of transporting the cannery workers and every other passenger Alaska-bound. So now the Caswell Clipper Air Line was about to add its glint to the spangled Arctic skies. This massive mahogany office in whose great chair Chris now sat so comfortably cuddled was, in fact, the Caswell office; and young Mort (fortyish) and young young Mort (twentyish) each would one day soon fly his own small pleasure plane and have only a somewhat remote loyalty for the ship models which now sailed the mantel shelf and the walls.

"Such as what?" Mort Caswell asked of Kleet. He was bored with these Old Boys, he had been bossed by the Old Boys of the long Caswell line for years and years, he had a club date for lunch and golf.

"When the lifeblood stops flowing to your heart, what happens?" Kleet asked the group in general.

The older men shrank back in their chairs as though Mort had thrown a live snake in their midst.

"I bite," young Mort said, rather contemptuously. "And I'll save time by answering. The heart stops beating and you die. R-r-right?"

Sid Kleet scarcely unclenched his teeth to say, "Right." He turned his malevolent glance away from the younger man, toward the oldsters, a gesture of ignoring a child. "So what is the lifeblood of a newspaper? Advertising. And when the advertising stops, what happens? The newspaper dies. So, gentlemen, if we tactfully convey to the Baranof businessmen, and so forth, that they'd better quit all advertising in Storm's weekly *Northern Light* and confine it to the *Daily Lode,* or else their business might fall off, why, in practically no time that stink you spoke about, Dave, will kind of evaporate away."

"No," said Czar Kennedy, mildly. He had been sitting motionless; not smoking, not waggling a foot as the others did, or tapping the arm of a chair with nervous fingers, or crossing and uncrossing his knees. "No." Quietly.

"What's the objection?"

Czar had kept his battered soft hat on, as he frequently did indoors. Pushed back from his brow it had the effect of a rather rowdy halo. Now as he gazed dreamily into space, a half-smile on his benevolent face, the silvery hair glinting in the sunlight of the many-windowed room, he was one of the kindlier prophets of the Bible, in store clothes.

"No objection, Sid boy—that is, no objection to the plan as a plan. It's a clever idea, well thought-out, and workable, I'd say. But I believe in competition. Now, you say advertising is the lifeblood of the newspaper publishing business, and so it is. But competition makes a horse race, as the fella says. I've always been a great believer in competition. Thor moves out with his weekly, why, some other fella moves in with a weekly, some new crackpot, young, the woods seem to be full of them lately, maybe he'd be hard to handle. Now, Thor, we know his gait and speed and conformation and staying power. But you get a dark horse in there, he's anybody's guess. So I say, let sleeping dogs lie."

"But he ain't sleeping!" Dave Husack yelled.

Mortimer Caswell, in a *sotto voce* sneer, murmured, "You're mixing your metaphor." But no one heard him.

"You mean you won't go along with this?" Dave Husack demanded of Czar.

"Not for the present," Czar said, gently. "Not for the present, Dave boy."

Einar Wendt, whose chin had been sunk on his chest, raised his head now and smiled amiably upon the group like a child just awakened from sleep. Indeed the crumpled ancient face was like that of an old old baby. But the eyes were shrewd and crafty. His mouth formed an O before he began to speak, as though in warning. He said everything—or almost everything—twice.

"Know what I think?" he piped in that high thin voice, "I think Czar's a little bit scared of Thor, a little bit scared. And I think he can't get over the feeling that he and Thor used to be pardners in a way. And then there's the family, there's Czar's girl married to Thor's boy—or was. You can't loosen ties like that, not so easy. It killed my daughter, marrying into that family, but Czar goes his own way, nothing can turn him aside, nothing can turn him aside."

Czar wagged his head from side to side, as though in admiration for a child—or in sympathy for senility. "Einar, you're a great old guy. Yessir, you'll always be yourself, no matter how old you get."

Mort Caswell now shuffled the papers on his desk, he pushed back his chair and leaned forward, half rising. "Well, gentlemen, I don't believe there's anything more just now, we'll be meeting again tomorrow, I hate to be the one to break this up, but I have a business luncheon appointment at one——"

Dave Husack stood up, a towering figure. "Anyway, that advertising idea is kid stuff." Belligerently he turned his empurpled face toward Sid Kleet. "Tell Baranof businessmen to take their advertising away from Storm and they'll feel he's getting a tough deal, they'll stick by him, that's the way those crazy Alaska people do. There's other ways, better. When the time comes, stop his print paper supply. He gets his paper from Canada, don't he? We can stop it altogether or if we can't do that we can make it so they'll have to route it to him to Seattle and then all the way across from Seattle to Baranof, he won't be able to afford that, nobody could. And his printers. Get after them through the union and no printer will work for him, wouldn't dare to, or linotyper either. You can't get out a newspaper without print paper and printers and linotype operators, can you! So there you are, boys, and what d'you say lunch?"

Three now were standing. Only Czar remained seated, his hands clasped easily in his lap, his face tilted up toward the others.

"Thor Storm," he said, as though ruminating, "has got a young fella there in the *Northern Light*, working for him, he's got a little bit of money in the paper, too. Barnett, his name is. Paul Barnett. He's a Harvard boy, no less, but smart, you've got to hand it to him. Real smart."

"What's that got to do with it?" Sid Kleet snapped. He rarely allowed himself to show irritation, but Dave Husack had offended him deeply, he was impelled to strike out at someone, anyone.

"Nothing. Maybe nothing. Only, when you talk about taking away the *Northern Light's* advertising and stopping the print paper and so on, why, you don't know Thor and you don't know Barnett. Paul and Thor both can set up a paper by hand if they have to, and they're both licensed linotype operators, and they can run the press and do the leg work getting the news, they could double as the office cat if they had to. They're no friends of mine, but I'm telling you, just in case. And Thor? Boys, Thor would get that weekly out, believe me when I say it, if he had to print it on toilet paper with a lead pencil."

He rose leisurely and walked the length of the great room to where the child sat. He placed a hand tenderly on her shoulder. "Christine. Christine child."

She opened her eyes, she looked up at him. "Grampa Czar, I'm hungry."

"Well, sure. So am I. We'll go back to the hotel and we'll have a fine lunch. Rock crab and ice cream."

She jumped from the chair, shook herself like a puppy. "I don't want to have lunch at the hotel, I'm tired of the old hotel, I want to have lunch down by the water at that place where the vegetables are all spread out, like a garden. And the Japanese sprinkle them with watering cans. And we can eat those little tiny shrimps out of a paper bag."

She was startled by the whoop of laughter from the men. "Czar, you sure picked yourself a girl won't break you," Dave Husack shouted.

Her hand in Czar's they walked down to the waterfront, and to the color and sound and delicious smells of mingled fruits and vegetables and berries and coffee and crullers and cheese and fish and apple pie and flowers of the Farmers' Market.

"I didn't like those men," she said. "Where we were."

"Why not?"

Something warned her not to reveal what she had heard. "They aren't like the people in Baranof."

Triumphantly he said, "That's just it. That's why I brought you along with me to Seattle. I want you to get used to the way people act Outside. When you get older you're going to school Outside. Here, maybe. And you'll meet people who are somebody, the way your Grandma Kennedy was, and your mother, too, before she married that—that mongrel."

She sprang to the defense of the father she never had known. "My father was Grampa Thor's son and my mother was married to him and I am their daughter and I was born in a caribou—"

"Stop that! Never mind about that!" Czar shouted in a rare display of emotion. "I don't want you to talk about that, understand me!"

"Why?"

"Because I say so."

"I told that Mrs. Husack about it that day you left me at her house and I had tea with her and her friends and one of them said it was—wait a minute—that lady said ma-cabber. Oh, what a ma-cabber story! What's that? And they all stared at me."

"Then don't talk so much. Now you listen to me, Christine. By the time you're eighteen I'll about own Baranof and a good chunk of the rest of the Territory besides, and these people here will be eating out of my hand. You're going to come into money someday. Big money. People are going to try to take it away from you, but you'll be too smart for them. I want you to know what it's good for and how to handle it."

"I know what it's good for and how to handle it, too," the child announced, with pride. "When I go to the Nugget Drugstore for a chocolate nut bar I give the man ten cents and then he gives me a chocolate bar."

"Oh, my God! Chocolate bars!" But then he reflected aloud, cannily. "Well, thank God, everything'll be in trust."

12

From the hill which was the campus of Baranof College you beheld a view to send the soul soaring if (Baranof realists said) it hadn't been too cold to stand there in the winter; and too mosquito-infested in the summer. From October to April the land, snow-blanketed, sloped away to the river, the great inlet, the mountains. Mount McKinley, king of them all, could be seen for a hundred miles in all directions, and during the brief summer, when the white world changed miraculously to green, he sometimes donned his rare ruby and diamond crown for all to behold. Lovers strolled the roads and paths of the college hill, or sat stifling in their cars, the windows shut tight against the winged stingers. Students taking the summer courses said, "Look! You can see old McKinley as plain as the Ice Palace, almost."

"How about a movie? Want to go to a movie?"

For throughout the summer months here in Baranof it was daylight all day, it was daylight all night, and sunshine is not favored of lovers. The young moderns preferred the kind gloom of the little bars and the motion-picture theaters and the cloistered privacy of a high-backed bench in a coffee shop.

Ivied walls and cloistered halls and Gothic façades of stone were not characteristic of Baranof College. No gargoyles leered down at the students. Still, the buildings on the hill began to form quite an impressive group. Between two World Wars they had somehow grown to a dozen solid forthright structures whose doorway inscriptions read: School of Mines; School of Engineering; Chemistry and

Metallurgy, Business Administration, Agriculture, Geophysics, Home Economics, Arts and Letters. Here, in this sturdy little power plant of learning Alaska youth of incredibly varied background—Scandinavian, German, Polish, Eskimo, Russian, Indian, Negro, American, Canadian—gained knowledge of botany, zoology, political science, history, business, music, anthropology, genetics. Young people in sweaters and ski pants and mukluks trudged the hill and swarmed the classrooms. They studied and skated and skied and danced and courted and parted and married and graduated and found jobs. They behaved like college students.

There was no building called the Kennedy Building in the group on college hill. It was not that Czar Kennedy was opposed to formal education. He believed in it, he had publicly said so many times. Simply, he knew there was no money in it for Kennedy enterprises. Education for learning's sake was not a good investment.

"College education is a fine thing," Czar said. "For certain professions, that is. Medicine, law, and so on. I don't recall that Edison or Ford or Rockefeller had a college education." Modestly, he did not include his own name.

They came to him, singly and as committees. Thor Storm argued with him, and Bridie Ballantyne argued, and Dr. Glenn Shields and —in later years—the Paul Barnetts, and Matt Berg of the town's one bookstore, and assorted mothers and fathers of small children who, in ten or twelve years, would be of college age. "Maybe," these said, "if we could get private donations and benefactions in wills, and so forth—not that we expect anyone to die—goodness no!—but if we make a start maybe the government would grant Alaska some kind of appropriation the way they do for other—that is, for states."

"Well, now, that sounds like a wonderful idea"—then, as his hearers brightened—"someday in the future. Just now a college in Alaska would be a failure. Take here in Baranof, for example. If people want higher education for their boys and girls, why, they can send them Outside. Broaden them. Give them a picture of life outside the confines of the Territory."

Thor had said, "Who can afford that? You can. But who else?"

"Now Thor," Czar chided him, smiling tolerantly. "You've been in Alaska as long as I have. Do you honestly claim that there are enough college-inclined young people in Baranof to justify a college here?"

"Who's talking about Baranof only! They'd come from every part of the Territory, north as far as Barrow, south to Ketchikan, boys and girls, white and Native and Eskimo."

Czar was silent a moment. It was his way of controlling anger. He had trained himself to wait until the seething had subsided, giving meanwhile the appearance of deep thought as he tapped his cheek with a pencil or gazed through the window at the sky. "Mm, tell you what, Thor. I haven't exactly figured it all out. Dollars and cents, I mean. But I'd be glad to do that, and then I'll go over the figures with you and your committee."

"What figures?"

"The cost of living in Alaska against the cost of living Outside. Even in a big city like, say, Seattle or San Francisco or Los Angeles even, or Portland. Any one of those college towns a kid could live cheaper than here in Baranof, supposing that they came here from other Alaska towns, like you say, such as Nome or Fairbanks or Juneau or off in Sitka or in Valdez. They could go to a real college Outside cheaper, and get a taste of Outside life in the bargain, that's an education in itself. Even with the cost of their transportation and board thrown in, it would be cheaper. Look at what food costs here, and clothes and rent. They'd be fools to come here to a little jerkwater home institute called a college. And your Eskimos and Natives that are going to make students—I don't want to be impolite to an old pardner, and laugh in your face." Which he now proceeded to do, but gently.

This was years ago, and the straggling little town certainly seemed to justify Czar's pessimism. Yet somehow a building or two was added to the rather ramshackle one on the hill. And another. And another.

Curiously enough, Czar Kennedy had not counted on the resilience and the love of adventure that youth had now, as it had had when he himself was a young ambitious man on his way to the North

Country. And he had not counted on the effect of the Mad House Painter of Austria. The little college staggered to its feet like an infant learning to walk. Then the swarms of little yellow men swooped down on the Aleutian Islands and took them handily. And then the young American boys came in, thousands of them, and took them back, and thousands of them died doing it. And then the United States Army Bases sprang up, and the crystal Alaska air was torn by the screeching and thundering of fighter and bomber planes. Now young men wrapped in white like pranksters on Halloween stepped forward to the open doorway of a plane high in the sky, and at a given word they stepped out into nothing, knowing that life depended on the jerking of a cord that might whimsically refuse to respond to the pull. Like great snowflakes they drifted down out of the sky and the ghostly figures found protective coloration with the billions of other actual snowflakes that blanketed the Alaska landscape. Beneath the white covering they bore lethal weapons that were no part of a prankster's equipment, and in their heads was knowledge of how one might survive for a brief time on a terrain which ordinarily did not predicate human survival.

One would have thought that experiences such as this would have bred in these men a deep distaste for the wild relentless North Country. A curious thing happened. Scores of them who had frozen and sweated in the numbing cold and the clammy heat of the Arctic mountains and tundras and forests and waters now, with their GI college rights in their pockets, elected to come back to the Territory to gain an education at Baranof College. School of Mines, they said. One of the best in the whole country. Engineering. Agriculture. And —I don't know—it's a kind of a free feeling. What I like, there's nothing coming *at* you, know what I mean? It's busy, but it's quiet. No dodging. The fishing is great. And hunting! Boy, is this the happy hunting ground! Moose. And bear! Browns thirteen feet high on their hind legs. And polar bears, their hide would cover the whole floor of this room. I'm going to get me a bear if it's the last thing I do— and it ain't going to be the last.

They came, unbelievably, from California, and from Oregon and

Nebraska and Illinois and the Carolinas. They never talked of the War, you would not have known they had been snowflakes, if you had not seen in their young faces certain deeply etched lines which ordinarily are found only in old faces.

They added fresh life to the town of Baranof. Some of them stayed and became Alaskans and bred Alaskans. Army bases ringed the town. Gay-hued private cars and drab army cars and trucks swarmed the pavements, and pretty young mothers and vigorous young men and perambulators and strollers and toddlers imparted to Gold Street a virility that hit you with the impact of a blow.

Perhaps Bridie's maternalism stemmed from those days when she, a young, frightened, homesick girl, had come to Baranof, alone and lonely. She knew and understood about some of those men—scarcely more than boys—surrounded by thousands at close quarters at Morgenstern or Kinkaid Air Bases, who knew loneliness such as only a mechanized society can produce. On leave they washed, shaved, dressed with extra care; boots were shined, uniform brushed. They lounged around Baranof's Gold Street, they dropped in at the juke box joints, they slipped coins in the slot to be lulled or soothed by the tranquilizer; artificial music. A mechanical sound hammered out "You're a Livin' Doll," or the whining self-pitying ballads of the day —why did you leave me . . . was it to grieve me . . . you in my arms . . . you have those charms. They sat in the USO big room listlessly reading an Outside newspaper a week old. The colored boys huddled in a corner watching TV. You rarely saw them standing on a street corner, these boys, surveying a passing Alaska world in the dim cold, calling out an unconvincing and unconvinced "Hello, Gorgeous!" to a bearlike female figure so muffled in hood, parka, mukluks, mittens, that it was impossible to tell whether she was fifteen or fifty.

Air Base Brass did not mingle with the ground, or very rarely. You did not see Air wives shopping in Baranof. They lived an intensely concentrated social life on the vast base, as did their martial male mates. The women belonged to clubs on the Bases, they attended teas, cocktail parties, dances, movies. Their children went to Base schools.

As Bridie put it, somewhat sniffily for her, "Air doesn't mingle with us peasants. But those kids—those boys around—they kill me. The look on them."

The girls began to arrive from everywhere. Again they were following the men into Alaska, but they were not at all like those girls who had come at the turn of the century. They looked terribly young in the inadequate pale blue coat and the little high-heeled pumps, hatless, the pretty dress belling out over the bouffant nylon petticoat, as they stepped off the plane into the icy airport.

No one in Baranof quite knew how Bridie Ballantyne had become unofficial welcomer, chaperone, witness, arranger and matron of honor for all these girls who, suddenly prim and apprehensive, descended out of the air into the waiting arms of an equally stiff apprehensive young man in Air Force uniform or in parka and mukluks.

Everyone in Baranof knew Bridie, so perhaps, in the beginning, one of the Air Force men or one of the construction workers or one of the Baranof College students had said to her, meeting her on the street or in the USO, "Uh, Mrs. Ballantyne, I'm going to be married day after tomorrow, I thought you'd like to know, you been mighty nice to me getting me acquainted round, and so on. I'm having some trouble getting her a place to stay overnight, she's coming in on the noon plane from Seattle tomorrow."

The girl on the plane had kept her hair in pins until the last possible moment and had then rushed to the lavatory to unpin the curls that sprang in lovely tendrils to frame the flushed or pale face; the eyes wide with sudden doubt, the heart hammering so that it was hard to tell which was heartbeat and which the throbbing of the great plane's engines. She put her hand to her breast where his Air Force ring hung suspended by a slender gold chain. There had been young men on the plane, and these had eyed her with interest and speculation and longing, but now they relinquished their fantasies. Her face was pressed against the window; as the plane taxied in, her eyes searched the figures at the airport gate. There he was, and beside him and speaking to him was a white-haired woman who looked a little like her mother, only more smartly dressed. The eager young men in the plane said, one to another, give it up, boy. She's fetched.

There had arrived dozens—scores—hundreds of these in Baranof in the past few years. Addie Barnett had been one of them, and Paul Barnett had been the man at the gate, peering nearsightedly at the figures spilling from the plane's maw.

And now Bridie met the plane whenever asked. It cut fearfully into her busy day. No one quite knew why she did it. Bridie knew, and perhaps Thor Storm. He once said to her, "It's because of the way you came to Alaska that day, isn't it, Bridie?"

"I guess *so*," she admitted, and closed her eyes for a moment as she remembered the girl in the picture hat and the long sweeping skirt who had clambered up the beach in response to a cruel joke. "Maybe *so*. I want them to feel they're doing something serious. And for life. Not just flying up here in a plane, like for a college stunt or something. I can't make out whether they're younger than brides used to be or I'm just getting older. Little of both, maybe. In crazy times, like now, people always seem to get married younger. War times, and after wars, when folks are scared and nervous. They want company, I suppose, and can you blame them! Somebody they can hang on to, and talk to, and love. And be loved by."

The thing grew so that it became one of her many projects and, urged by Thor Storm and the Barnetts, the town finally voted her a tiny salary for the work. Most of this dribbled away to the young couples, though they scarcely noticed it. A wedding cake bought by Bridie at the Sweet Tooth Bakery; a bunch of somewhat frost-shocked flowers for the altar; a prayer book for the girl; a festive boutonniere for the bashful bridegroom.

Now she had an impromptu sort of office in a remote corner of the Ice Palace lobby. No one quite knew how she had come by it. Even the superintendent was mystified, and it was known that Czar Kennedy had refrained from ousting her only because Bridie's position in the town's affection had somehow mysteriously become more solidly established than his own.

In the beginning he had demanded of the Ice Palace staff, then of the tenants, and finally of the City Council, "What's she doing there? Running a soup kitchen or a First Aid to the Lovelorn or something! Next thing they'll be sleeping in the lobby and the Ice Palace will be a flophouse. I want her out of there."

But she stayed. Her desk was a ramshackle affair salvaged when the Miners' National Bank next door went in for modern decoration. Daily Bridie sat at this desk for hours, while over its time-scarred top passed such tales of romance, failure, nostalgia, love unrequited, love fulfilled, hopes, despair, as would have staggered any recipient less sturdy than Bridie. Aside from a disorderly clutter of papers, pamphlets, scribbled notes, plane-and-railroad timetables, the desk's surface was likely to hold a vase of drooping flowers or a brown-edged corsage bouquet left over from last night's club dinner; a chocolate cake contributed by a women's-club cake sale; a pair of hand-sewn mukluks, palpably an offering (she wouldn't have worn them caught in a ten-foot blizzard on a mountaintop); half a cup of cold gray tea; newspaper clippings; a photograph of the latest Air Force bride and bridegroom. That same photograph—at least, it looked the same, though the boy and girl were always a different boy and girl—was tacked or taped all over the walls of the cluttered corner.

Inevitably Chris Storm was drawn into this haphazard project. She found herself repeatedly acting the role of bridesmaid at the wedding of two people she never before had laid eyes on. The pattern of the weddings almost always was the same. Bridie conferred with the scared and inarticulate young bridegroom. He sat in her makeshift office, his young face serious and strained. He had been confronted, stunningly, with the fact that the girl from North Dakota or Michigan or Alabama was coming up to Alaska to live with him forever after, amen. This he had asked her to do, but now, confronted with the reality, his mind rejected fact. Whoever he was, he thought of the other young men like himself—at the Air Base or on the Construction Job or a student at Baranof College—married now, living in a crowded company house or a two-room rental or even a trailer, the girl seemed forever to be doing the washing and wheeling the baby and complaining about the cost of food and looking shapeless with the next baby coming. Gone, he realized in a desperately quiet panic, were the hours when you could lie on your bunk, reading and smoking or just looking up at the ceiling, or sleeping; the nights down on the Strip, close to one of the girls, or listening to Gamboge, that yellow boy entertainer, who sang fit to bust your heart.

"Now," Bridie would say, and he tried to listen as he sat there at her desk side, "now you want to get her a nice corsage, I'd say one orchid is better than a whole bunch of other flowers, they just love 'em. I'll order it for you if you want me to."

"Say, I wish you would, ma'am."

"Seven dollars at Gresen's Florists, Matty'll fix it up for me with ribbon to match, and fern and all, it looks like a million dollars. You got the ring?"

He looked stricken. "Gosh, no! I forgot. I'll get it now."

"That's all right. Wait till she gets here. They love to pick their own wedding ring. Besides, size."

Chris was sixteen when first she found herself taking part in these somewhat touching festivities. Usually the bride arrived in Alaska unaccompanied, and the bridegroom, himself a comparative newcomer, had no backlog of young feminine relatives or friends sturdy enough to act as attendant on the flustered girl. Certainly his local girls were more likely to be resentful toward the occasion, rather than helpful.

"Snort McHugh told me you're going to be married."

"Uh, yeah."

"When?"

"Well, she's coming on the noon plane Tuesday, we're planning for that afternoon, or Wednesday morning if I can find a place for her to stay Tuesday night."

"That's lovely. Specially as you never even told me you were engaged."

"We weren't—that is, exactly. I didn't think she'd ever make it here. So far, and all. And different. And her folks aren't crazy about the idea. She just took off and came. Or will."

"That's just lovely. Congratulations."

"Well, thanks. Say, I suppose you wouldn't—an old friend and all —I suppose you wouldn't want to act as b—uh, no."

"Thanks awfully. Tuesday is all jammed up. I'm going off skiing with a boy friend, and I've got a dinner date that evening, and then another friend has asked me to get together with the bunch at his place——"

Bridie herself always was willing to act as temporary mother of the bride, chaperon or matron of honor. But she felt that a young girl should be in attendance. "Gray hair is kind of grim," she said, "I mean, at the altar. A young face is what you want, not one that looks like a warning."

Chris's first wedding was that of Paul Barnett and Addie. Addie was twenty-six when she arrived in Baranof for her wedding, and to the seventeen-year-old Christine she seemed middle-aged, or almost. A college girl. Majored in journalism, had run the college paper, and had even had a year of general reporting on a Boston daily.

Chris knew about newspaper offices. Since her childhood she had had the freedom of the grubby little composing room, editorial office and print shop of Thor Storm's *Northern Light*. The big building which housed Czar Kennedy's *Daily Lode* was a different matter. Czar did not want his granddaughter running about that humming hive. "A newspaper office is no place for little girls," he said. "You get caught in one those rollers, or a belt or something."

"I don't go there. I like the front office where they come in with the news, somebody killed or something, and they sit down and rattle it off fast, it's exciting. I think a daily paper is more exciting than a weekly, I wish Grampa Thor's was a daily, too. And I like the linotype machines, the way that arm reaches over, and takes a handful of type, and drops it, just like a human being, almost."

"You just keep away from there, Christine, hear me."

So she spent hours, ink-smeared and happy, in the dim dusty little shop of the *Northern Light*, listening to shoptalk, hearing almost heedlessly the news, the politics, the sociological problems, the social life, the scandals and tragedies and merriments of the region. Some of this she did not understand, but much of it stayed in her mind, and as she grew older she was, unconsciously, a modern gold mine of Alaska riches.

In time Thor Storm's weekly *Northern Light* actually was to exceed in circulation Czar Kennedy's *Daily Lode*. This was due to Addie Barnett. This dynamic redheaded girl was gifted with a natural sense of news gathering and news dispensing as other women might possess a talent for acting or singing or cooking or designing or buying or selling or painting. It was at the Barnett wedding that Christine Storm met Ross Guildenstern for the first time. It was spring and the long days and the white nights had already begun in Baranof. The little wedding party had assembled to meet the incoming bride. It might have been considered a rather odd little wedding party in any place but Alaska, which was so much less provincial than, say, New York or London or Los Angeles. Besides the bridegroom there was Bridie Ballantyne, matron of honor; Thor Storm (Barnett's boss); Christine Storm, bridesmaid; Ross Guildenstern, groomsman.

Chris looked at the young half-breed Eskimo without designating him as a young half-breed Eskimo. She merely thought that he was enormously attractive and she thought that this might be only in contrast with the other males of the wedding party. Paul Barnett, tall, loose-jointed, long-jawed, spectacled. Grampa Thor Storm, an impressive human being, but an ancient in the eyes of the girl of seventeen.

When the energetic red-haired Addie descended the plane steps and came toward the waiting group Chris thought her rather plain and old for a bride. Then Addie had smiled and had called out, even before she reached the waiting bridegroom, "I never saw anything so dazzling in my life!"

"Who? Me?" Paul Barnett asked.

"Certainly not. The scenery between Juneau and here." She stood looking up at him a moment, he down at her, with a sudden terrible shyness. Then she stood on tiptoe, he bent to her, his arms went round her.

"Scenery!" Bridie said. "Well, that's more like it."

The young bride seemed to find nothing extraordinary in the wedding attendants; the elderly man and woman, the girl of seventeen, the handsome olive-skinned young man. An hour later she was Mrs. Paul Barnett, properly married in church by the Reverend (Flying Missionary) Mead Haskell; a vase of flowers at the altar, organ music, bridal bouquet. The little group had scarcely reached the vestibule when Addie said, "I'd like to see the *Northern Light* office."

"Not now, for the love of heaven, girl!" Bridie, the romantic, was outraged. "We're having the wedding lunch at Nick's Caribou, Thor here is giving it, wine and all."

"Afterward then?"

Gently Thor said, "Yes. Perhaps lunch first would be the thing. And then the office. Don't expect anything like your Boston plant. This is a small-town weekly. And an Alaska small-town weekly."

Christine thought this was not at all the way a new bride should behave, but the bridegroom was grinning and shaking his head waggishly.

"Remember what I told you yesterday, Thor? I said you and I would be lucky if we could keep our jobs after Addie came in."

It was not that Addie Barnett lacked the qualities of warmth and affection. Paul Barnett knew this, and the others soon learned it. She became a fond and capable wife and mother, but she was a born newspaper woman, as in love with her profession as a stage-struck actress with hers. She was inquisitive about every manifestation in life; brash, courageous, alert; she had the gift of making anything—a Sourdough gathering, a women's church sodality cake sale—seem an interesting event. She had what is tritely called a nose for news. Baranof was to find this irritating or amusing, depending on person and circumstance. Before the day was finished Addie knew almost as much about Baranof as many others who had lived a full year there. The red hair seemed to send out sparks, the face, plain in repose, was brilliant with animation.

On the drive from the church to the restaurant she sat between her husband and the Reverend Mead Haskell.

"Just Mr. Haskell," he said, in answer to her first question. "Or Mead. We don't do much about titles and forms and ceremony in Alaska. I suppose it's because everybody's working so hard, and there's a kind of all-in-it-together feeling."

"Aren't you young to be minister—pastor—anyway, head of a church like that?"

"I'm only an assistant—and a part-time assistant, at that. I'm a missionary. I fly back and forth between the Eskimo villages."

Now she turned to look at him more closely. Intelligent compassionate eyes, rather good-looking in a conventional way. He might have been mistaken for an advertising man, an insurance salesman, a lively young merchant.

Paul patted her knee proprietorially. "No, he isn't called the Flying Parson. Up here they're just about all flying parsons—the Catholic priests and the Protestant ministers and the missionaries. Mead used to be Air during the war. Now he buzzes all around the Arctic in a little Piper Pacer, carrying nurses and women missionaries and medicine and phonograph records and stuff."

Even Addie appeared momentarily unable to digest this. "Phonograph records?" she repeated.

"I try to teach the young Eskimos something beside God and religion," Mead explained, matter-of-factly. "Their taste in music is awful, like most kids'. The boys buy those old twenty-five-cent records. They like hillbilly tunes. That dismal nasal whining, over and over, seems to fascinate them. It's soothing, I suppose, in that ice-locked world. And the really cheap stuff. Lyrics. 'I told you I loved you in twenty-two bars. Now you can buy your own beer.' Sometimes I get so fed up with it I yank the record off the spindle and take it outside and spin it whirling and flipping and skipping across the snow and ice the way you'd skip a flat stone across a pond. I suppose I shouldn't do it. I bring them good records." He seemed to be brooding about this. Then he glanced up, peered out. The Ice Palace. "Here we are. There's Nick in the window."

Nick had arranged a corner in the vast private banquet room. "It looks like a barn in here, one table. But you don't want 'em all crowding in on you, day like this." He turned his back a moment. There was the unmistakable pop of a champagne cork. "On me." He held the smoking bottle aloft for a moment. "Bollinger '47. The bride and groom!"

"Now, Nick," Thor remonstrated. "You know this is my party."

"That's right. The champagne's just so I get in good with the press." And vanished.

"I'm going to like it here in Alaska," Addie said. She looked around the table. "I like it already."

"Wait," Ross Guildenstern said, "until the Eskimos boil you in seal oil, and the polar bears gobble you up, and the snow is over the rooftop, and there's nothing to eat but caviar and champagne and Persian melon and tenderloin of beef."

"Are all Eskimo men as handsome as you are?" Addie asked.

"My bride," Paul Barnett said, plaintively, "on her wedding day."

The others laughed, but Ross said, gravely, "Wait till you see me in my pilot's uniform. Kill you."

It was then that Chris, delighted, said, "I didn't know you were a pilot, Mr. Guildenstern." Suddenly she felt very adult and worldly. Her first glass of champagne, her first wedding party.

"I only fly a freight crate. Maybe some day they'll give me a passenger plane."

"Why not now?" Addie demanded, in character.

He shrugged. "Eskimo, I guess."

"Nuts," said the Reverend Haskell. "You flew in the war when you were about five years old, or thereabouts."

"That's different."

"But Guildenstern?" Addie pressed on.

"My father was Danish. But no relation to the gentleman you've met in the book."

"Who knows?" Thor said, musingly.

On Ross Guildenstern's left temple, just below the hairline, there was a scar, it showed a thin white tracing against the darker skin.

Chris looked at it, fascinated, she felt an impulse to touch it, a strange impulse which was followed by a still stranger and more pervasive feeling. She must remember to ask her grandfather or perhaps Paul Barnett about that scar.

Addie Barnett saved her the trouble. "Is that scar on your temple a war memento?"

"Not really."

Mead Haskell took over. "He's war shy." He glanced round the table. "Tell them the story, Ross."

But Guildenstern shook his head. "No old soldier's reminiscences. They went out with the Civil War."

Paul Barnett said, "Mead, tell them about the time Father Gilhooley was caught up there." Then he and Mead began to laugh in the annoying way people have who know the joke.

Thor Storm said, "If it's as funny as that, out with it. A little laughter at a bridal party is a fine thing."

"That one!" Ross jibed. "Some version of it in every country in every language in World War II."

Mead Haskell looked injured. "It really happened. But it's grown kind of apocryphal, all the way from the South Pacific to Iceland. Well, this Father Gilhooley—you know him, Thor, he used to be up in Atkasuk—he's a young missionary flying a little Piper and he hasn't logged a million miles by a long shot. But he's learning fast, kind of an eager beaver, and he gets up to Oogruk with the nurse he's carrying and the runway is socked in. He can't come down, there's no place to go, there's no airstrip near. He calls down:

" 'I've got to come in.'

" 'Stay up. You can't come in,' Ground Control says.

" 'I've only got gas for another ten minutes.'

" 'Stay up.'

" 'I've got a nurse with me.'

" 'Stay up.'

" 'My engine's coughing.'

" 'Can't come in.'

" 'God's sake what'll I do!'

"'Repeat after me: Yisgaddal v'yiskaddash sh'meh rabbo, b'olmo d'vro kir'useh v'yamlich malchuseh, b'chayechon uv'yomechon uv'chayeh d'chol bes yisroel—'"

Mead Haskell broke off into helpless laughter in which Ross joined. The others wore the resentful expression of the uncomprehending.

"Very funny and all, I don't doubt," Bridie said, crisply. "But maybe if we knew what it meant it would seem funnier."

Contritely, Haskell and Ross became suddenly almost solemn. "Sorry. You see, Ground Control was a Jewish boy, and what he sent up to Father Gilhooley to repeat after him was the Hebrew Prayer for the Dead."

The faces of the others remained thoughtful. Christine was frowning. "Did he—did they die?"

"I don't think so. That was two years ago, and I saw Father Gilhooley last week up in Kotzebue."

Ross Guildenstern said, "Your story's a flop, Mead. You just won't learn."

"Tell yours," Mead urged. "At least it isn't supposed to be funny."

But he would not. Christine heard it later and remembered it always. So did the others, including Addie. But by that time World War stories were not even back-page news.

It looked almost like a toy, a silver and scarlet toy, standing there on the runway, if any unknowing eye had seen it. But it was Alaska winter night. There in the tiny cockpit Ross Guildenstern took it up thirty-two thousand feet, at which point the plexiglass top blew off as completely as you would chip the top off a soft-boiled egg. With it went his oxygen and the headpiece that was his only connection with the mechanical reception of the world below him and perhaps around him in the air. But almost before that thought could form he had lost consciousness in the rarified atmosphere. Consciousness returned as the plane nose-dived toward the earth. Instinctively he knew he must pull the ship up again into the comparative safety of the faraway sky. The toy was not planned for cruising in a low altitude, the fuel would not last down there. He was safe as long as he could stay high, high.

He pulled the plane up. Up. Get her up get her up get her up. There. Twenty-five thousand. Now again he lost consciousness. Again he awoke as the plane dived. Now, miraculously, below him in darkness, was the almost imperceptible suggestion of what might be Kinkaid Field. No headphone. No connection. Well, there was Kinkaid below him, if it really was Kinkaid and a goddamned miracle anyway even if he couldn't set the ship down. No chance of setting it down, they must hear him down there, they couldn't get to him, he might put her down on top of the General's house for all he knew, right down on Old Bull's head in bed with that wife of his, they must look funny in bed, at that. Helpless he looked down at what might be Kinkaid Field, no gas; helpless, the unseen faces must be turned up toward him, up there dead or alive in the little silver and scarlet toy that was dropping so swiftly toward the earth.

In the small hut near the runway, Ground Approval Control repeated, "You're too low! You're too low!" though Ross could not hear him. Ground Control forced himself to resist the impulse to crouch and hug the floor as the toy seemed to skim the hair of his head.

Ross came down almost gently, he put the plane down on the field in the darkness and they came running toward him and then the blackness came down over him again, he was a bundle, limp but living, as they lifted his body in the clumsy straps and trappings, the face battered and bloody. Nice work, they said to the unconscious form. Nothing like a little fresh air while you're working, they said. A month later he was out of the hospital and flying another dainty silver and scarlet toy.

13

Now the real battle for Christine began. She was seventeen; no longer a child, not yet a woman.

"Washington State University is the place for her," Czar said. "I don't want her to go east to school, the way my—the way her mother did. No good came of that, that's sure. Seattle, I can keep an eye on her, I'll go see her, she can come home holidays."

"What's wrong with Baranof College!" Thor argued. "We've got a course there in the humanities that Washington can't touch. And political science and modern history and racial——"

"That settles it! What am I supposed to do? Stand there while you make a long-faced Commie out of my Christine! She's going to Seattle. She's going to mix with her equals."

Bridie, distracted as a hen whose lone chick is being swooped upon by hawks, now entered the fray. "Why don't you let the child decide for herself? Seventeen years old, she's got a mind of her own."

"She hasn't had the experience to decide a thing as important as this," Czar said.

"But she's experienced enough to live in Seattle alone?"

"She won't be alone. Mrs. Husack and Dave and the Caswells and Kleet and that whole crowd will be looking after her."

"I was afraid of that," Thor said.

Bridie, fuming, burst into the battle again. "You two talk about Chris, you'd think she was a slave or idiot or something. I've always asked her opinion and let her try and decide—so have you, Thor,

I'll say that for you—about anything she could. I always said, which do you like, the pink or the blue. You two aren't thinking of her, you're thinking of yourselves."

Czar turned his wintry gaze upon her. "You don't understand, Bridie."

"Understand! I've understood for seventeen years and more ever since I fed her with a medicine dropper. And I suppose Bridie Ballantyne hasn't understood you these years and years, and Thor, too. I understand wolves trying to tear a lamb to pieces when I see 'em."

Czar shook his head, gently. "Hysterical." He turned away from her, he looked only at Thor, it was as though the two men were alone in the room, battle-locked. "Christine is going to the university in Seattle, by the time she's finished there she'll be twenty-one, a woman grown, she'll know how to behave in decent society. Louise Husack will be more like a mother than a chaperone, she says her house will be Christine's second home. You might as well know I sent Christine's application to the university three years ago."

Thor stood up now, the towering frame seemed to take on even greater dimensions, the blue eyes turned strangely dark, but the rosy face was mild, the tone reasoning.

"I'm as much Christine's guardian as you are. You know that. Until she comes of age. After that she'll be on her own. She's adult even now, in her thinking. She mustn't be bullied or tricked to do anything without her consent."

"She's going to Seattle and civilization."

"Only if she wants to. And I think Alaska is civilized."

"She's going around with a lot of mongrels here. And people too old for her. Radicals, to put it in flattering terms. That Guildenstern, I hear he's been taking some kind of GI course at Baranof, and flying a bush crate."

"That young man," Thor said, "could make a plane singlehanded if he had to, out of oil drums and a Model T Ford."

"They're all natural-born mechanics, those monkeys, I'll say that for them, I don't know where they get it and I don't want to know.

But that's not saying I'm going to allow my granddaughter to run around with one of them."

Cheerfully Thor chided him. "Now now, Czar, are you pretending you've forgotten Christine is part Eskimo herself?"

Always ivory pale, Czar's skin now took on a curious clay color like the waxen skin of the dead. His voice was low, monotonous, too controlled, as though it might have risen to a scream if he were to unleash it for only a moment. "I know that my daughter married your son. I suppose he was your son. I wish she had died first."

Bridie had often been witness to scenes between these two high-powered men, but early in this encounter she had sensed a feeling stronger, more passionate, than ever before. She once had seen a crude local painting of two moose bulls horn-locked in battle. She thought of this now.

Bridie flung out her arm then, as though she had been physically struck. "You can't say that in front of me, Czar Kennedy, and go free of it. You're wishing Chris herself dead when you say that, or never born at all. Shame to you!"

Czar ignored her. He was looking at Thor as one would stare, remotely, at a stranger. "I don't know who you are. And I'm going to find out. Fifty years, and I don't know anything about you. Nobody in Alaska does."

"There's nothing to know, Czar. Nothing of any importance to you or to me or to Christine."

"Uh-huh. That's why you've kept your life a secret? With your books and your wanderings and always yelling about freedom, and living in a log cabin like a pauper. I'll tell you what I think. You're a criminal. I've thought so ever since I first saw you. You'll have no rights to Christine, I'm damn sure of that. You'll be on your way out of Alaska—let alone Baranof. I'll spend all the money it takes. I'll make it my business to find out."

"I wouldn't do that if I were you, Czar."

"I bet you wouldn't. Everybody knows me, knows where I came from, and my father's name and my mother's, and their fathers' and mothers' names, like any decent American family. Time I'm through,

I'll bet I'll find out Christine has got a double taint on her, father *and* grandfather."

Addlepated though she might seem at times, Bridie Ballantyne, in a crisis, represented pure reasoning. "That case, I'd think you'd be better off, and Chris too, letting it lay. Unless you want to make a martyr out of her. Spite, if I ever saw it, Czar Kennedy. Pure mean spite. Spreading things around people shouldn't know, and none of their business. If I was to spread around what I know about Baranof folks the town would look like a cops-and-robbers movie. And that includes you, Czar Kennedy. Maybe people know who you are, but do they know what you are? I do. And Thor does."

Thor smiled down on her, his pink face radiating pleased surprise. "What have you been reading, Bridie?"

"You know I don't get time to read. I've just been listening to you for years and years, and Chris ever since she was old enough to make sense out of what you've told her."

Czar got to his feet then, he pointed a finger, his arm outstretched, like an accuser in an old-fashioned melodrama. "That's it! He's poisoned the child with his crazy talk. Anti-American through and through."

"Know what I think?" Bridie demanded, crisply. "I think you ain't well, Czar. Putting it politely, that is."

He stared at Bridie with a cold and baleful eye. "Keep out of this. You've got nothing to do with this. This is between Thor and me."

"That's right," Bridie agreed, with awful affability. "I only brought the child up and kept her alive when——"

"Let's go now, Bridie," Thor suggested, quietly.

"Running out, eh? Scared." Czar sat down now, he seemed suddenly relaxed as though his suspicions were at last justified. "I'm just doing this to protect Christine."

"Not for your own satisfaction?" Thor's tone was quizzical, but the blue eyes were serious.

"You must have taken me for a poor fool all this time. Why, years ago, when we first got here, they'd take pictures of the crowd of us somewhere, one of the boys had struck it rich, maybe, or there was a jamboree of some kind, citizens of Baranof and so on. You always slunk away before the camera snapped. No man hides out unless he's got a good reason for not wanting his face where it can be seen and traced."

"And let me tell you," Thor remarked, cheerfully, "slunking and hiding is a difficult feat for a man who is six feet four."

Bridie tactlessly and involuntarily giggled at this. A grayish film seemed to come down over Czar Kennedy's eyes.

"I'll get detectives. Private detectives. They'll trace you right back if it takes years."

The ruddy giant shook his head sadly. "I wish I could make you understand why you want to destroy me. I know. Your hatred is understandable to me."

"I don't hate you. Though I know if it wasn't for you my wife would likely be alive today, and my daughter, too, and I'd probably have other grandchildren for my old age."

"That's not the reason. It goes deeper than that. You can't forgive me for having shown you the way to success. You want to believe you started yourself, as everyone else believes. Can't you ever forget that I showed you the way? Even if it turned out that you made it a destructive way for Alaska?"

Lines of hatred carved themselves on Czar's face, they curved from his nostrils to his lips, they were imbedded between his eyes. "You're just evading the issue. I only know you're not a fit person to have any guidance of my granddaughter. Bridie, here, that's different. I know about her, I went to the trouble of looking up her past, she was a decent enough girl, her family in Ireland were decent people, she trained and nursed in a hospital in England, like she said, she nursed in Seattle, she came here and took care of those girls with the smallpox—well, she was only doing her work, after that she conducted herself in this town in a decent——"

"You'll stop right there, Czar Kennedy, sitting there and acting like you're God! You with your banks and your newspaper and your buildings and your money. And your Outside crowd. I'm a decent person, is it! Well, *you* ain't."

Mildly, Thor interrupted Bridie's tirade. "Why this sudden change, Czar? We've shared Christine's upbringing, with Bridie as ballast, all through her childhood."

"It doesn't matter so much what you tell a child. A child's way of life isn't so important. She's a young lady now——"

"Oh, Czar, Czar! Once you've baked a cake, you know, you can't take the eggs or the milk out of it or the flour or the butter or the spice. They're baked in, they're ingredients of the whole, they're in forever, until the actual thing itself is destroyed. Human beings are like that, too. Everything that goes in stays in. Christine is almost baked by this time, there's only the icing to put on, plain or fancy."

"Oh, I'm sick of you and your talk, Storm, for years and years and years. Now listen. I'm going to make it impossible for you to have anything to say about my daughter's child. I'll tell you now, frankly, I've been getting a line on you, they got as far as Minnesota and then it quit. But they're working on it. No matter how far and how long and how much money it takes."

Thor nodded reminiscently as though surveying with pleasure a serene past. "Yes, I came to Minnesota and I worked in the wheat fields and in the woods, lumbering, with all the other Swenskys, as they called us—Norwegians like myself, and Danes and Swedes. All Scandinavians were Swenskys in America, I found. It wasn't a bad life for a young fellow. Everything was big—the lakes and the hills and the fields and the forests. But I hadn't come to America just for that, so I started across country, across this enormous land, from the North to the East, to Midwest, to West, to Northwest. A fine journey. I had been in the countries of Europe, many of them. But this took my breath away, I had hoped it would be like this, and it was. Then I heard about this new Alaska land. Alaska was what I wanted, a new world not yet begun, or scarcely. That's how we met. And well met, Czar, no matter what you say. It brought us Christine."

"No travel talks, please. Anyway, I know all that. They got that for me."

"It must have been disappointing. Just another big Swensky in a place full of big Swenskys."

"I'll find out. I'll find out. And when I do I won't have to sit and listen to you. My life is an open book."

"Dull reading, too," Thor said, as though to himself. "In spite of all you've managed, a monotonous life. Power is all you've wanted. It's like a disease that has crippled you all your life."

Suddenly Czar, the low-voiced, the self-contained, began to shout. "You leave my grandchild alone, Storm. I'm warning you. Next week I've got a man going over to Norway, he'll track you, fifty years is nothing to him."

Bridie, the erstwhile nurse, looked at him and saw danger in the face, now flushed, that habitually was so colorless. "Now Czar, you'll be sick, a man of your age. A stroke, if you're not careful."

He glared at her. "Get out of this, Bridie. What are you doing here, anyway! This is between the two of us."

Thor had been silent, his clear blue eyes fixed on Czar, speculatively. It was a look that Czar translated into defeat as Thor said, "You win, Czar. You can save yourself all that money for detectives and travel. They'll trace me easily enough, over there."

"Aha!" Czar gloated, like a villain in an old-time play. But now he seemed again suddenly benign, the beatific mask slipped down, a fine glaze, over his face. "Come to your senses, h'm?"

Bridie was not accustomed to the role of listener. "Thor, don't say something you'll be sorry for. Alaska's full of people who want to let their past life stay in the past. The world everywhere is full of people like that. What of it! It's what you are now, counts."

But Thor did not heed her. "I'll make a bargain with you, Czar. If I tell you the truth about myself—and you can prove it easily—will you credit ten thousand dollars to Christine's account in the Miners' National Bank?"

"Take me for a fool!"

"It costs money to send men to Copenhagen and London and Paris and Stockholm and Oslo and New York. Salaries and ships and planes and trains and hotels and all that goes with these. Much cheaper to give it to Christine and let me tell you now. Besides all the trouble."

"How will I know you're telling the truth?"

"You will know. From past experience." He laughed then as at a little private joke. "But I warn you it will sound ridiculous."

"How do you mean—ridiculous." He was suspicious at once. This was not a word he had expected. "Look here, I don't want Bridie around in this."

But Bridie grasped the arms of her chair, she dug her heels into the heavy carpet, braced for the worst. "Don't think you can make me go. Never. You'll have to carry me out, the two of you. I'll screech murder every inch of the way, they'll hear me from this to the top of the Ice Palace."

Thor laid a hand reassuringly on her shoulder. "Stay then, Bridie. But I must have a promise from you, too." He glanced at Czar. "For that matter, another promise from you."

"No, you don't! And I'm not so sure about the first. I hand ten thousand dollars over to Chris. What for? She isn't of age, what do you do? Get it away from her?"

"If it was money I wanted I could have had plenty of it these past years. More than even you have piled up. I want Christine to have a little of her own. It's a risky world for a penniless woman and she can't depend on you. She may not want to live the life you want for her. Then you'll punish her."

"You talk too much, like most old men. Gab gab gab."

"I'll make it brief as possible. You'll write a check now, made out to Christine for ten thousand dollars. Bridie will hold the check until I've said what I have to say. If either one of you—or both of you—feels that I'm a possible disgrace to Christine——"

"—then I'll be sole guardian," Czar finished for him.

Thor considered this a moment, in silence. "Yes. With this second provision: Neither of you will ever speak of what I'm going to tell you, to Christine or to anyone else." He smiled genially at the palpitating Bridie. "That's going to be harder for you than for Czar, here." He waited a moment. "Promise."

"I promise." She raised her right hand, dramatically. "Oh, Thor, I hope it's nothing too bad, though who's free of black moments?

I always say, if everybody had killed the person they've said, one time or another, they'd like to kill, why, the world would be depopulated by now."

Czar had taken a slim little checkbook from an inner pocket, his pen from another. He wrote swiftly, he tore out the check. Before he could rise, Bridie had whisked across the room to snatch it. Almost menacingly Czar warned her. "None of your tricks, Bridie Ballantyne. I'm not above taking it from you by force." He looked at Thor. "I'll promise, but it's for Christine."

Bridie began to giggle again, what with nervousness and an overwhelming Irish sense of the ridiculous. "It's as good as a play, but I feel foolish."

"So do I," Thor said, very low, as though to himself.

"Stop mumbling! Get it out! Unless you're making a fool of both of us."

"No. No, I'm not. The truth is, Czar, I come of a stock and class that would be called old-fashioned now, here in modern American Alaska. I come of the Scandinavian nobility–Norwegian as you know–but the Norwegian royal family is all mixed up in its history and its politics with the Swedish nobility, and the Danish especially."

"Nobility?" Czar repeated the word, dully, as though not quite hearing. He did not, in fact, understand what Thor was trying to tell him. "What d'you mean–nobility?"

"I was nowhere in line for the crown, I don't mean that. But I was a student, I wanted only to study and know. Everyone knew that Oscar would resign in time——"

"Oscar?" Czar said, almost feebly.

"The King. But of course he wasn't a Norwegian, he was a Dane, and then when he gave up the crown in 1906, Haakon came in–another Dane–he had been Prince Charles of Denmark, as you know——"

"Well, sure," Bridie gasped.

"–and his wife, Queen Maud, was English, the youngest daughter of Edward of England. By that time I had gone, and well out of it. I was to have married a Danish——"

"—princess!" Bridie yelped.

"I don't believe a word of it," Czar said, slowly. "I don't believe a damned lying word of this stuff. Ridiculous, you said. And ridiculous it is."

Simply, Thor said, "My papers are in the bank box in Seattle. They've been there for years and years, since the day you and I met on the boat that brought us here. You can see them. I want you to." Smiling, he turned to Bridie. "No, Bridie, my dear, she wasn't a princess, though she's a princess now, if she's still alive, which I think she isn't. A nice girl, I remember, though a shade dull, and rather long in the tooth."

Bridie drew herself up, she seemed to gain inches in stature, she looked about her from heights not attainable by the herd.

"All these years," she said, in a voice of awed wonder, "all these years here I've been a lady in waiting to royalty and didn't know it."

"I'm sorry to spoil your dream, Bridie, but that isn't quite so. All the aunts and uncles and cousins would have had to be killed or removed before the political hand could fall upon me. I was hardly more than a boy—a student—but I always disliked form and ceremony and fuss—though there was little of it all at that democratic court. They're more democratic, really, than we are here in the United States. I was proud of them in this last war. What courage, what dignity, when the country was occupied and over-run. I sometimes thought they might all be destroyed; and the cities. When I heard what the barbarians did to Holland. Well, I was out of it half a century before that. Every now and then some young rebel beats his wings against the golden bars. Usually it doesn't turn out quite right. Take that young King of England—young enough, at least—when he rebelled. But it didn't help. He only exchanged a golden prison for a shabby brass one."

"If all this fairy-tale bunk is true, how is it they haven't been after you all these years?"

"I wasn't important enough. If I were to go back now, no one would remember me, or care."

"That girl—what became of that girl you didn't marry?" Bridie, the romantic.

"She married someone else, I once came on a magazine picture of her taken with the family. They all looked alike, those girls, but I recognized her, she hadn't changed so much. An old lady, very thin and spare, she looked just as she used to, not even much older, though half a century had gone by. She sat straight as a stick in her good satin dress and her good rope of pearls and her long jaw and her nice eyes, as though some one had etched some wrinkles with a pencil on her face, the young severe girl in her strait jacket of court convention hadn't changed, really."

Almost—but not quite defeated, Czar put a last question, foolishly. "If it's true—and I don't swallow it by a damn sight—what do you want here? What are you doing here? What have you got out of it!"

"I've lived the life I wanted to live. I've earned my living as you know, fishing in the summer season, trapping in the winter, I've studied the people, I've read and learned. And I started the little weekly paper. And I've written. In another three years Christine will be twenty. Twenty! I was twenty only yesterday. I've seen this great icy treasure land plundered and almost wrecked by men like you, Czar. It's an anachronism in this day and age, it's like a story you've read out of the past. But I've put it all down, day after day, year after year, everything, all of it. The Eskimos, the Russians, the traders, the Hudson's Bay crowd, the New England shipowners, this place they called Seward's Folly and Seward's Icebox when it became part of this country. And then Congress after Congress and Administration after Administration that would allow no settler to take title to land, or clear a bit of wilderness land and claim it. And the plunderers, the robbers with their lobbies in Washington. I've got it all down now—or almost all. Maybe no one will ever read it. The history of this Alaska, locked in her ice palace, with Outsiders holding the golden key."

Czar stood up, his hands in his pockets, he began to pace the room, he threw a glance over his shoulder at Thor, as though to catch him unawares. Suddenly, "Christine know this? Any of it?"

"No, no! I told you that. That's the bargain."

"What would her—uh—her title be?"

"Nothing."

"She's the daughter of a fella whose father is supposed to be a—well, anyway, was——"

"You see how foolish it sounds! Counts are passé and barons and kings and queens and princesses. Even bogus kings like you and that great noisy Husack and little Kleet who is like a jackal at one of the twelfth-century courts—even you are passing. By the time Christine is a woman and has children of her own you and all your kind will be as mythical as old-fashioned royalty. I hope."

But Czar was not listening, he was pursuing his own thoughts. Almost wistfully he mused aloud. "I'd have liked Christine to be a—what was it?—a——"

"She isn't. If you repeat any of this I'll deny it. I'll deny it as a joke. Old Thor, the Swensky. Thor, the blacksmith. What a snob you are, Czar! You build banks and movie houses and high buildings. You pretend to be plain and simple. You love power and position."

"You two," Bridie commanded, emerging from her daze, "stop calling each other names and get practical. It was Chris's schooling started this, so let's go back to it." She eyed Czar craftily. "I'm holding this check for ten thousand, made out to Chris. I guess you don't think what Thor's been telling us is a disgrace, exactly. Well, then?"

"Let's have her in," Thor said, "and done with it. It's her education, it's her life, no three old people should make this decision for her."

"Now?"

"Now."

"Where is she?" Czar demanded, irritably.

Bridie, very brisk now, was already at the telephone. "Down at the *Northern Light*, probably, waiting for the breakup news to come in. She and her crowd got together made a pool, five dollars apiece,

Chris bet on the ice would break up May third, it's been such an unusual winter."

"Oh, stop clacking and get her," Czar said. "I want this settled now. Today."

"Neurotic behavior," Thor observed; and strolled over to the glass-fronted bookcase where he stood surveying the titles, a look of unbelief on his face.

"No," Bridie was saying, at the telephone. "No, nobody's sick. I tell you, Chris, they ain't. It's just important, something's got to be settled. No, now. Right now. I don't care if you might win a hundred thousand dollars in the ice breakup, anyway it's always won by some construction worker nobody ever heard of. Well, you get yourself over here, your Grandpas say."

Bridie hung up. "She's coming." She held at arm's length the check in her hand. "What you boys want to do with this? One of you put it in the bank, for Chris? Or what?"

"You do it," Czar snapped. "But it's not to be used till she's twenty-one. Interest till then. And she's not to know."

"Pooh! A lot of fuss over a bit of money like that. Your friends spend that for a nice little car, in the States."

She began to bustle needlessly about the room, straightening a window shade already straight, plumping a cushion, adjusting a lamp shade. Thor had resignedly taken a book from the shelf and was seated reading, his steel-rimmed spectacles slipped halfway down his nose. Czar, at his desk, jotted down figures on a scrap of old envelope. When a car stopped abruptly with a snort of engine and a squeal of brakes, the three stayed as they were, frozen in attitude, like figures in a children's game of statue.

Four heads could be discerned at the car windows. "Unless it's something serious make it snappy," a voice called. "We'll wait."

When the girl came in with a rush she looked apprehensively from one to the other. "What's the matter! What happened!"

Czar put down his pen, Thor closed his book, Bridie came over to her and plucked at her parka. The girl shrugged away from her, her eyes were wide with alarm.

"Nothing. Nothing," Czar said, smoothly.

"What is it? Come on! I'm braced for it. Something dreadful has happened." The three looked a little foolish now that they were confronted with the lovely anguished face.

Mischievously Thor explained, "Czar here wants to discuss some plans for your education."

She stared. She repeated the word. "You mean nobody's sick, and you're not killing each other, and the house hasn't burned down?" She looked so terribly young and vulnerable; they felt so old and foolish.

"Well," Czar began, sheepishly, "we felt the time has come to decide about your education. The three of us, that is."

"That's all? You mean that's all?"

Thor sat smiling at her over his spectacles. Czar said, "All!" somewhat feebly. There was a moment of awkward silence before Bridie bustled into jumbled speech. "Three people trying to do their best for you, wanting you to get the education they didn't have"—then, hastily, eying Thor—"anyway, two of us. And all you can say is all. Czar says Washington State, Thor says Baranof——"

Chris cut in like a whiplash. "And you've brought me here, scared numb, to talk about education when the breakup is due any minute, you can hear the ice groaning—of course my bet wasn't until next week—but it may freeze again and if the ice starts moving and the tripod starts wiggling they'll get the flash first thing at the *Northern Light*——"

A horn sounded outside—not loudly, not impertinently, just a small questioning squawk.

"—and besides, I've decided about my education long ago, so why did you have to bring it up just today?"

"We realize," Czar said, heavily deliberate, "that the annual ice breakup is more important to you than any four years of college, no matter where. . . . Still, the ice break comes every year at about this time, and you'll only be eighteen once—unless I'm mistaken."

She melted then, she became their child again for a moment, she looked at them and her young face that had been hard with resentment mirrored a pang of understanding and compassion. In a little rush she kissed Bridie, she kissed the protesting Czar, she kissed Thor, her fresh cheek pressed a moment against their unresilient skin.

"I decided long ago. I'm going to Baranof two years and then to Washington State two years. I put in my applications long ago, Ross told me you have to, with all those GI rights——"

Czar turned a baleful eye on Thor. "See what I mean?"

"—and anyway, Addie Barnett says——"

The horn sounded again outside, a querulous pip-pip.

"They're waiting for me. Oh, how you scared me, you bad darlings!" She was out of the room, she was outside, they could hear her calling as she ran. "I'm coming! Nothing. Not a thing. They just——"

"Learn you, I hope," Bridie said to the two silent men. "She's grown up."

14

Later Baranof boasted that Chris Storm could pilot a float plane, drive a car, mush a team of nine huskies, paddle a skin boat, handle an outboard motor, cut up a seal with an ulu and mix the best sourdough pancakes in Baranof. Only this last accomplishment made her the envy of the town's more solid citizens. She had inherited her sourdough starter from Thor, who had originally come by it from a prospector on one of his Far North journeys. Melting, feather-light, delectable, the golden circlets were a more potent asset than all of Christine's more spectacular activities. She had shot a polar bear, helped pull in a beluga white whale, caught king salmon. She could knit and wear a sweater expertly. In her second and last Baranof College year Chris appeared at the final big dance in a slinky black strapless dress. The effect, with all that *blondeur,* was devastating. All the other girls were in bouffant pink or blue or white. Anyone less fundamentally liked than Chris would not have had a female friend left by midnight. Most of the male population of Baranof would have been more or less in love with her if they had not been—again more or less—afraid of her. She did too many things too well. Biceps-flexers and six-footers were most easily discouraged.

Thor said, "Self-reliance, Christine, that's the important thing in Alaska. In life. I want you to be able to do all the things an Alaskan may have to do, one place or another."

Czar, fuming, protested. "Is he trying to make one of those all-around female athletes out of you like that woman shot-putter?

How's it happen they haven't got you playing fullback on the Baranof football team!"

Bridie's objection was more practical and pungent. "I never yet saw a woman could catch a husband because she could do everything better than he could. It isn't nature. Breaks them down to see a girl outsmart them."

"I don't want to catch a husband. Anyway, not for years and years and years. And he'll come without catching."

"The way you girls dress nowadays, I guess the men think they don't have to marry you. Those shorts in the summer, nothing on you from here down. And in the winter, at the dances, nothing covering you from here up. Reminds me of a joke the nurses used to tell in the hospital when they were washing the patients, they—no, I guess not. Anyway, all I know is, if the girls in the Last Chance and the Poke and the All Nations when I first came to Baranof, a shanty town—if they'd worn that kind of getup, why, the men would've taken off their coats to cover them; or run them out of town. An ankle-length skirt on the street was considered fast."

"Do you think that was good?"

"Well, no, I don't. Not now. Things change. The way girls dress now is better. Healthier, I mean. Necks free, legs free, waist free, you can breathe right. But there's always the chance of overdoing a good thing. That's the trouble."

"The trouble is I've got three parents. You don't like this, Grampa Czar doesn't like that, Grampa Thor likes something else. Why? I don't try to do anything other people don't do."

"Yes, but you do them all, and better. Next thing you know, you won't have a friend speak to you, boy or girl. Miss Perfect."

"I'll try to flunk my exams for you, Bridie darling. Anyway, I can always count on you, can't I?"

"Maybe so." She tried to make it sound grudging.

"There I'll be, like the girl in those nasty ads, always a bridesmaid, never a bride. Won't it be wonderful!"

The two old men had solemnly shaken hands on their pact as they had clasped hands in their first agreement many years before. There was something fantastic about their unspoken understanding that two years of this vital girl's life would belong to Thor, two years to Czar. But Christine went blithely on, living the carefree existence she always had known, strangely unspoiled by the omnipresent and omniscient Thor and Czar and Bridie. Do this. Do that. We're here to protect you.

Each old man was, in his own way, fanatic. Czar's plans for Chris were drawn up complete in his mind, a mental blueprint. Thor sensed this, he had two years in which to circumvent these plans. He could not reason with Czar, he could not ethically explain to Christine, he had no one to whom he could confide his apprehensions except Bridie; and he knew she would not wholly understand.

"I'd like you to understand how I feel about Christine's education these next two years, Bridie. I'm not planning to change her. I want her to grow. I want her to emerge free just as I want to see Alaska emerge free. I'm afraid Czar thinks of her as being expendable just as Alaska is expendable to him. Do you see what I mean? He gave Alaska movies and shops and newspapers and high buildings, all with his name on them. His brand. So he'll give her clothes, Outside travel, parties, piano, television, Husacks, Caswells, luxury. To use her as he uses the lobbies in Washington."

"Now, Thor, fair's fair. Czar loves Chris as much as you do. He's loaded with money. It's only natural he wants to give her pretty things, a young girl, his only grandchild."

"Bridie, Bridie, that isn't what I mean!"

Alaska, too, went blithely about its business of life, now surrounded in the air, on the ground, under the ground, on the sea, under the sea, and on the mountaintops by the most modern and appalling machinery of war, against war, and for war. Armies, planes, radar, directed missiles, rays, spotters. Alaska lived like a prankish boy smoking a cigarette in an arsenal.

Christine's childhood years of close association with the three who were thrice her age had established a fundamental pattern of thinking and doing. She took part in the social life of the college and the town, but there was some complaint among the more amorous young men and the frivolous young women.

"Chris is fun," they said, the one to the other. "She can do anything. But then she sounds off about politics and territorial rights and absentee owners and stuff. I'm interested in all that gunk too, of course. Who isn't! But does she get steamed up about it! You'd think she was addressing Congress or something."

In her spare hours Chris was likely to be seen drifting in and out of the *Daily Lode* city room, or happily ensconced at a desk in the *Northern Light* office, reading proof or typing a column of college news. Best of all, she liked the evenings spent at the Barnetts'.

Housing shortage—that condition which, since the end of World War II, had taken on the proportions of an epidemic—was an old story in Baranof. Since the early Nineties, when the first tent of the first prospectors was tipsily pitched on the beach, Baranof had outgrown its shelter. Construction workers poured in; government workers, civil, professional, business. They sent for wives and children and these swarmed off the planes and adapted themselves, cheerfully or complainingly, to a fantastic new way of life. The DEW Line—the magic Distant Early Warning of a sinister something that might any moment come through the air—began to weave its web across a frozen waste that never before had known the foot of man. Robots in heavy boots and wool-lined jackets and carrying metal boxes of their precious tools clumped down the plane stairs. "Five hundred a week, and grub," they had argued with their protesting wives back home. "Five hundred a week for Cri's sake, for six months! And when I get back we can build us a house right here and live in it the rest of our lives, and a yard for the kids. It's only six months. A year at the most. Suppose it was a war! You'd get along without me. You'd have to."

The terrible loneliness of distant places sometimes was too much for them. The curious lack of pressure, the strange, almost hypnotic power of the climate and the magnetic air, wooed others. For some, the boundless fishing and hunting made a male paradise. They sent for wives and children; or they married local girls, they became

Alaskans. Then there always were those who, seized with the claustrophobia familiar to the region, bound to any one of a score of towns ringed by towering mountains, vast waters, morasses of tundra, wastes of snow and ice, went berserk. These crowded the courtrooms, filled the jails.

Anything with four walls and a roof, in which a man could stand upright, was a dwelling.

Paul and Addie Barnett lived in an abandoned saloon. It had been a relic of Baranof's early gold-rush days. In two years Addie had transformed the battered boarded-up structure into one of the most attractive dwellings in town, and certainly the most popular. Before his marriage Paul's bachelor quarters had been one grubby room at the rear of the *Northern Light* print shop. A cot-bed, a chair, a lopsided chest of drawers, a shelf for books (they had overflowed onto the floor) and such flotsam and jetsam as might wash up from the front office; galley proofs, a pile of old Outside newspapers, a spirit lamp, a coffeepot; a gun, a fishing rod—standard Alaska equipment, these—though Paul was not inclined toward sports.

Before Addie's arrival Paul had desperately tried to find a house or part of a house or two rooms somewhere, anywhere. The Ice Palace was an unattainable dream. Defeated, he had attempted to lighten the grimness of his little room. Bridie and Christine took over. They hung curtains. With a cover and gay cushions they tried to transform the bed into what they termed a studio couch. Paul, with Addie's red hair in mind, fondly painted the walls the clear blue she loved. Linoleum now covered the gritty floor, a blue cotton rug in front of the couch broke the bareness of the room. Finally, on the day of her arrival as though in desperation to convince himself that this now was a home fit for a bride, Paul had bought and hung a somewhat grim local painting of mountains, ice, and snow, and had arranged a bowl of flowers on the precariously slanting chest of drawers.

In Boston, Addie had had a smart little two-room apartment on the top floor of an old remodeled mansion facing the Charles. Her more solvent beaux, her editors, her old Boston family friends and an occasional lavish newspaper interviewee had accustomed her to the dim cosiness of the Ritz bar and the delectable cuisine of the stately pillared Ritz dining room facing the Public Garden; or to the succulent broiled lobster at Locke-Ober's, the scarlet shells and claws gleaming in contrast with the smoke-blackened oak walls.

After the wedding, Addie and Paul, his arm about her, had stood in the doorway surveying this wistful little makeshift dwelling. For the tenth time, Paul repeated the plaintive facts.

"Now you know why I kept writing you not to come, though I wanted you so. I wanted to get a decent home for you, first. There isn't a house in town. Not a shack, even. The week before you came I began to think about how I could murder a whole family—any family living in any house—without being caught at it. Oh, God, look at the slant of that chest!"

"It's perfect," Addie said in a tone that would have convinced anyone who was not looking at the room. And at that moment the big press out front began to run off the weekly edition, thump thump thump thump, shaking the whole rickety building. They looked at each other, grinning, then they broke into hysterical laughter, leaning on each other for support or perhaps solace, their arms tight about each other.

They settled down in Baranof without a honeymoon. Perhaps settling down was scarcely the term to apply to the newly wed Addie. She was, some thought, a shade too bossy for a bride. She called him Barnett, for example. Not Paul, but Barnett. When she did this he looked bemused with adoration, as though she had addressed him with some fragrant endearment distilled from the very essence of love.

"Look, Barnett," she said now. "I've traveled across the entire United States from coast to coast, and then across all this water, whatever it's called, to get to you. And I've got. Here I am. Honeymoon or no honeymoon, I want to stay and catch my breath. I don't want to start to go back Outside where I just came from."

"Start to go back Outside where I just came from," he repeated, his head critically cocked. "What sentence construction for a Radcliffe girl!"

"Someday we'll have a honeymoon. We'll go to California or Honolulu or Greece or Italy. Just now, Barnett darling, can we afford a house or something—if we can find it?"

"I'm not—we're not poor. Of course nobody's rich in Alaska. Except, perhaps, Czar Kennedy. It's just that everything costs three times as much as it does anywhere else. Everything goes out of Alaska, and nothing stays in. Including money. Nobody can save any money—that is—money."

"I know. You've written me so much about it, and of course I've read all the editorials and articles in the *Northern Light*. But I want you to talk to me about it. Because we're going to work on it, aren't we? And on getting a house. A house in order, and then Alaska in order. Golly, Barnett, this is going to be wonderful!"

Paul Barnett was no worm. "My brain and your drive, we'll have to watch it. That's the way dictatorships are made, if you're not careful."

She did find the house. And she did have a share, with Paul, in shaping the Territory's battle against the rapacious enemy. The house was a time-ravaged and abandoned saloon, known in its heyday as The Placer Gold. The business center of the town had grown away from the once-pretentious two-story building. Now its dirt-filmed broken windows stared out like old cataracted eyes, upon a respectable residence street. Gold Street, three blocks distant, had become the main business thoroughfare. Neighborhood housewives and houseowners had, for years, indignantly demanded that the building be condemned and demolished. But it was one of the many pieces of property owned by the town's most fantastic character, Butterfly Megrue. Even the City Council, the Chief of Police, and the Citizens' Committee for a Bigger Busier and Better Baranof shrank from tangling with Butterfly. Butterfly, fifty years ago, had been a Baranof dance-hall girl in the best fictional tradition of those lively ladies. Fragile-seeming, in those days, her eyes had been a heartbreaking violet, her hair a true golden, her skin pink and white and poreless as Chinese porcelain. Strangers, now encountering Butterfly tramping the streets of Baranof in a mismated pair of men's broken shoes, rags of castoff clothing and a travesty of a picture hat topped by a gangrenous flower, thought that this was, indeed, a Butterfly broken on the wheel. Little did they know of the punishment the wheel had taken. Thriftily and cannily she had come by her real estate in the early days of the gold rush. Now she lived off scraps, she hoarded old bottles and newspapers and cardboard boxes and tin cans. She was said to collect fabulous rents, her taxes were second only to Czar Kennedy's, she lived in a one-room rat's nest. Her invective was blue as a king's blood. Baranof regarded her with every courtesy, compassion and kindness. There was something touching and truly spiritual in the town's protection of this raddled relic.

There was considerable risk attendant on venturing a "Good morning, Butterfly!" She might return the greeting with a smile that would have been poignantly lovely had it not been for the broken brown teeth; or she might envelop you with a spume of obscenity. Once, on a particularly gaudy television program celebrating Baranof's old Sourdough Days, Bridie Ballantyne had rashly invited Butterfly to speak as one of the many guests. The Mayor had spoken; the President of the City Council; the town's leading merchant, Wade Zangs, of the Far North Trading Company; Ott Decker, Secretary of the Baranof Chamber of Commerce.

Bridie cast a tardily apprehensive eye at the next speaker, and went into a somewhat nervous introduction.

"You've listened to what the well-known men citizens of Baranof have had to say. The Old-Timers, the Young-Timers and the Good-Timers. So now let's hear something of the thoughts of a lady who has been a citizen of Baranof since its earliest days—though she doesn't look it. Successful in real estate, in commercial ventures . . ."

Butterfly Megrue had been washed brushed dressed. Even the cruel glare of the camera's eye, and the years of neglect and malnutrition were defied by the triumphantly lovely bone structure of the face. Battered, beaten, degraded, the line from the cheekbone to the jaw, from the brow to the mouth, from the mouth to the chin, still had the indestructibility of marble.

"Butterfly," Bridie cooed, "will you tell us what you think of Baranof today, compared to the town you knew so many years ago?"

Butterfly stared out, a direct and malevolent glare. "I sure will. I'll tell you what I think of those sonsabitchin' government tax collectors——"

Instantly she was off the air. Neither the *Lode* nor the *Northern Light* would use it, naturally. But the mukluk grapevine served as well.

It was this formidable nymph against whom Addie Barnett, the newcomer, was to do battle for a home. The bride had been six months in Baranof and three months pregnant before her desperate eye alighted and lingered, with a horrible yet fascinated speculation, on the gruesome shambles of what had been the old Placer Gold saloon. Its elaborate fretwork, its second-story gabled overhang, the proportions of the erstwhile barroom, set her imagination soaring. She picked her precarious way around to the side of the structure and, partially cleansing a small surface of dirt-encrusted window with a handkerchief and spit, made a shield of her hands as she peered. A high-ceilinged room, surely forty feet long and twenty wide, wainscoted with what actually looked to be mahogany. Remnants of what once had been a mirror still clung to one wall, but the long bar had vanished with the bearded faces that had been reflected. Her heart pumping hotly with excitement she slithered and teetered to the rear of the house, ascended the four steps to the back door, tried the knob, the door yielded. The remnants of a kitchen. Mice droppings, cobwebs, the dust of years. With a fearful glance about her she went into the big front room. For some reason she tiptoed. A broken stairway led to the second floor. She paused. Then, with a look behind her, she cautiously ascended the stairs. One small room at the back. A second room. And at the front a third with a fine semicircular curve that once had been a bay window. That was the overhang she had noted outside. Three rooms. Three bedrooms! In this last room there was a broken slop jar and, on the floor in a corner, a large china washbasin ornamented with a pattern of flowers and faded gilt. As she stared at these mementos Addie recalled having seen a washbowl like it filled with flowers in the window of one of Boston's Arlington Street antique shops. Price, fifty dollars.

She stood a moment, breathing deeply, her eyes shut. She clattered swiftly down the perilous stairs, was out of the house (shutting the back door carefully). Paul Barnett, bent over his desk in the *Northern Light* office, sprang up startled at sight of her. She was breathing fast, her eyes were wide. "What's the matter! What's happened!"

"I've found a house."

"What house?" She described it. He said, "You're crazy."

"It could be wonderful. You know what they've done to old wrecks in Boston. I've got two thousand dollars saved. I'm going to buy a lathe. You were going to buy a car. What do we want with a car! Nobody can drive more than twelve miles out of Baranof in any direction, and you know it. Car! We can have a house. Three bedrooms!"

She was crying. Her eyes were wide open, the tears were streaming unheeded down her cheeks.

"Butterfly Megrue won't sell any property. She won't repair anything and she won't sell anything."

"I can try. Will you let me have one thousand dollars?"

"You know you can have anything I've got." Then, at something in her face, "No monkeyshines. No murders."

"Just money and strategy, Barnett dear."

She wrote it, saw it set up, read proof on it, smuggled it in when he was busy elsewhere.

SORE EYES AND EYESORES

> An object of beauty is sometimes called a sight for sore eyes. An eyesore has quite a different meaning. In Baranof, the ramshackle wrecks of what once

> were houses or buildings, now fallen into decay, are eyesores. They not only offend the gaze of the passer-by and give the visitor the impression of an impoverished and neglected town, but they are a potential hazard to lives in case of fire or collapse. There is said to be a movement on foot to petition the City Council with a plan to order the destruction of these buildings. It is rumored that the buildings designated are the one midway in the block on Glacier Drive between Fox and Fifth; another on Otter between Snow and Tillicum, and others at . . .

Butterfly had visited the Federal Building, the Mayor's office and the *Northern Light* before the week's grist of papers was fully off the press. It was said her screeches made the noise of a jet plane just then passing overhead seem, in comparison, like the cooing of a dove. Addie was waiting. "Come on in here," she said, maneuvering the distraught creature into the back room. "Now just sit down, Butterfly, and tell me all about it." For a few minutes she listened quietly to the flood of invective. "Look, Butterfly, I have a plan. You can fool them. If Barnett and I promise to clean up the place, and paint it and sort of mend it, so that it might be lived in for, perhaps, ten years, would you agree to rent it at . . ."

The thing was done. Papers were signed, a payment made. It was not until two weeks later that Thor Storm heard the story, and then it was too late to do more than lecture Addie Barnett on the Alaska code of ethics. Addie had attacked the rehabilitation of the house with a fury of efficiency. Rags, mouse nests, unspeakable mattresses, broken bits of wood, cobwebs, sawdust, paper—all the refuse of a house abandoned for years—had to be not only removed but hauled away. Back-yard bonfires were considered madness in that region of dry air and wooden housing.

Paul and Addie actually were occupying the great front room and the kitchen of the old saloon while the work of reconstruction was going on. They worked evenings, early mornings, Sundays. Thor, newly returned from a two weeks' trip to the north, scanned the two back numbers of the *Northern Light*. He then turned his attention to Addie's tired beaming face and Paul's tired harried face.

"Well, children, I hear you have a house."

"Isn't it *wonderful!*" Addie trilled, with perhaps a shade too many flute tones.

"You happy about it, Paul?"

Paul was silent a moment. Then he looked straight at the man whose loyal disciple he had chosen to be. "I'm happy to have a house. There are other aspects of it I'm not so happy about."

"That's good." He smiled his strangely sweet childlike smile. "I'd like to talk to you a minute, Addie. And Paul."

"Now!" She rattled the sheets of copy paper in her hand. "I'm just trying to get this stuff out, we're going to press at three——"

"No, not now, Addie. Not here. I'll drop in on you at the house tonight about eight."

"Oh, dearie, it's a mess! I don't want you to see it till it's all——"

The smile left his face. A compassionate sternness carved lines upon it.

"I'll be there at eight."

The long days had already begun. Eight in the evening was bright daylight. They had had their supper in the kitchen, they were busy with measurements which, calculated to cut off a twelve-foot section from the long front room, would provide a partitioned dining room.

"Oh, dear, he probably remembers this place from the bad old days." Addie was being pert in an attempt to conceal her nervousness. "Will he reminisce?"

Paul, in shirt sleeves and work pants, balancing on a ladder as he jotted down figures, gazed down upon her with love and tender reproach. "I hope so. But he doesn't do much of that. I think he has something else to say, tonight."

"Sh! There he is. Come in, come in!" She ran to the door. Paul heard her say, perversely, "You've probably come through this door a lot of times, in the old days."

"Not as many as I should have, perhaps." He entered the big

room, he stood looking about it, a giant of a man, ruddy, the shock of yellow hair silvered now. "In those days"—Addie threw a triumphant look at Paul—"the saloon was the warm pleasant place that welcomed you for the price of a drink—or no drink. It was the clubhouse, cheerful and hospitable. And the girls were a comfort and a help to many a lonely man." He stopped abruptly, he measured the room again with his encompassing gaze. "Paul, this is a fine room. It can be a good home for you and your family, until you can build one."

Addie began to talk with great vivacity. "Do you know what I've noticed since we began to clean and scrub up! On dampish days the most delicious saloony smell comes out of the floor and the walls and the woodwork. It's a smell of bad whiskey and tobacco juice and cheap perfumery—I hope it's patchouli, it always is in the novels—and sawdust and beer and cigars. Maybe it's ghosts."

The two men were looking at her quietly, fondly. Her voice trailed off. Silence for a moment. Here it comes, Addie thought.

But Thor Storm only remarked, as though suddenly recalling a message, "Oh, I saw Ross Guildenstern, he was pilot on my trip up to Oogruk. He told me to tell you he wants to give you a polar-bear rug if you're going to put in a fireplace. Or even if you're not. He shot it himself this past winter."

"How wonderful!" Addie trilled. "I saw him only last week. He didn't mention it."

"Eskimos don't like to be thanked."

"How interesting!" Addie murmured.

Paul came down from the ladder. "I'll bring you a chair from the kitchen, Thor."

"No, I won't be staying but a minute."

"Tell her then. Or do you want me to?"

"You're young and in love. I'll say it."

"What in the world are you two talking about!" Her tone was a little shrill for the smile that accompanied it. "Have I murdered somebody!"

"Murder and rape and theft and all the sad crimes committed Outside are to be found right here in Alaska. I have no jurisdiction over those. I just report them in the columns of the *Northern Light*. But the conduct of the newspaper—the physical and ethical conduct—that's my business, and Paul's. We accept paid ads and announcements if they are respectable. But the news and editorial columns of the paper can't be used for personal gain. You're a newcomer to Alaska, Addie——"

"Oh, you're all so snobbish about your Alaska. I know what you're going to say. But what have I done that's so terrible! An old wreck of a house that was falling down——"

"You are on the staff of the paper, and you used its columns for your own personal gain. You ran a news item that was entirely untrue. You knew it was untrue."

"But people *are* complaining. Just last week Ott Decker told me that the Chamber of Commerce and the City Council——"

"That was after your article," Paul interrupted, quietly.

"It's a good thing, then. Now maybe they'll do something about it."

"What you did wasn't a good thing."

"You two are making a fuss about a tiny little nothing."

"That tiny nothing, blown up in the *Daily Lode*, could undo everything I've tried to accomplish for the good of Alaska in the past fifty years."

She turned to her husband, she grasped his arm and shook it as though to rouse him to her defense. "Tell him, Barnett! I had to have a house. I had to have a place to live in! Do you think I'd bring up my child in the back room of a newspaper office! Maybe what I did wasn't exactly according to the newspaper code. But my reason for doing it was right. Tell him, Barnett! Tell him! You two standing there like prophets out of the Bible or something."

"Security," Thor said, quietly. "All women want security. And they're right, in a way. But the whole country may go down to ruin if people want security more than anything else."

"I don't know what you're talking about!" Addie sobbed.

Paul's arm came round her, he grinned fondly down at the distraught face. "Yes you do, Addie. You're just playing dumb. Remember what that writer said—I've forgotten his name—but he said: 'You can't go on the street to earn a trousseau.'"

15

It was June. Three months of Arctic summer, three months of daylight twenty-four hours around the clock before the wintry autumn came. The rapier rays of the constant sun forced every growing thing into fabulous maturity. A month ago there was ice on the rivers and lakes and inlet. Now they were merry with the shouts of swimmers. The cabbages, the roses, the rhubarb, the delphinium seemed to spring overnight (or overday) from seed or bulb to full-grown product. Christine Storm, too, in those blindingly brilliant months, emerged from the chrysalis of girlhood into womanhood.

"In a way, then," Thor had said that first week in June, "these next two years belong to me, so far as Chris's education is concerned. In a way."

The two men were conferring warily in Czar's little private apartment on the top floor of the Lode Building. No one would disturb them there; no cat-footed Gus, as at Czar's house; no Bridie bursting volubly into a meeting planned without her; no Chris sauntering in with a fondly amused, "What are you two evil guardians plotting against your defenseless grandchild?"

"In a way?" Czar repeated Thor's words. His gaze was directed coldly past and beyond Thor, as though surveying with distaste the two years that lay in the future. "I can't see that. In what way?"

Quietly, patiently, Thor reviewed the facts so well known to both. "We know she's going to be at Baranof College for two years. That was what I had hoped. Christine had decided that for herself. I was pleased, naturally. It's understood. So nothing has to be settled about that."

"Nothing?"

"Of course there's her tuition and her other expenses. They'll be paid by me. If she prefers to live out at the college I'll pay her board and room at the dormitory."

"Dormitory!" Now at last Czar turned his gaze full on the other. His eyes were agate.

"When she goes to Seattle two years from now she'll be on her own. Those are your two years. It may be that here at school in Baranof, too, she'd like to be free of two old men."

"Free of two old men!" Czar shouted.

Now Thor broke into a roar of laughter. He threw back his fine head, the blue eyes all but disappeared behind the lines etched at the temples. He wiped his eyes while Czar glared. "Sorry. But perhaps you don't realize that for the past five minutes you've been repeating the tag end of every sentence I've uttered. Like an echo." Now he threatened to burst into laughter again, but controlled himself.

"Very funny." Icy cold, unsmiling. "Am I to understand you are planning to have my granddaughter live at a college dormitory here in Baranof! When all her life her home has been the finest house in town!"

"Part of my granddaughter's life has been spent with me in the very fine log cabin I've lived in for fifty years, off and on."

"It would be a disgrace. It would be the talk of the Territory. Czar Kennedy's granddaughter living in a barracks at Baranof College—if you can call it a college."

"I didn't say she was going to. I said, if she wanted to. She's a woman now, even if you don't admit it. I think she should make her own decision."

"And you have the money for all this? Two years of this?"

"I will have, from month to month."

"Your paper is in a state of permanent bankruptcy, I understand."

"I wouldn't say that. We have a fine circulation, but never enough advertising to balance that. Perhaps you know a little more about the reason for that than I do. Long ago you barely prevented them from stopping my advertisers altogether with threats. My tardy thanks for that, Czar."

"Who told you that!" He stopped himself, abruptly. "That's ridiculous. Why should I bother with such small potatoes? Even if I wanted to."

"That's the catch in being a plotter, Czar. You're plotting with plotters, you never can be sure that one of them isn't plotting against you."

"You haven't any money—that is, what I'd call money."

"You're right, Czar, old boy. Not money as you think of it—you and Husack and Caswell and Kleet and all the yacht-and-Cadillac crowd. But a living. And the *Northern Light* is a living for the Barnetts, too, and the others in the front office and the back shop. It earns its way. I don't take much out, myself. Anything that comes in to me I try to feed back into the paper. Keeping it healthy and functioning. It isn't just a newspaper, you know, Czar."

"I could wipe it off the map tomorrow by lifting my hand."

"You could, once. Maybe you still could. I'm not so sure now. And even if you did, another one would come to take its place. Lately there's been a little tremor—a barely noticeable shakiness—in that hand. Figuratively speaking, of course. All over the world, I mean. If you'll excuse my calling attention to it. Perhaps you may have noticed it, yourself. Almost everybody's got the shakes, in one form or another. Yours might be called the lobby shakes. Virulent in Washington D.C."

"Commie talk," Czar observed, not even taking the trouble to be disdainful. He rose, now, like royalty ending an interview.

"Wrong there, Czar. They've got the shakes worse than any of us."

"Let's be practical. I'll do this for you—or for her, rather. She can live part time at the house, as she always has, and part time at your shanty, though it's a bad arrangement, now that she's a young woman —as you say."

"She'll decide that for herself—as a young woman."

"You can't meet Christine's expenses for two years."

"She'll have everything the other girls have. The salmon fishing brings me in quite a bit, if it's a good season, and your friends' fish traps don't take them all. Writing a piece now and then for one of the magazines, Alaska's getting to be quite fashionable, Bridie told me there was a piece about it in *Harper's Bazaar,* she says Florida and the Riviera are now out. Bridie knows about these things. It's wonderful, all the things Bridie knows."

In restrained fury Czar knew that he was being gently ridiculed by this visionary giant. "Sometimes lately, Thor, it seems to me you're showing a kind of early senility. Try to keep your mind on Christine, will you, for a minute. Now, during the summers——"

"I'm glad you brought that up, Czar. I was just coming to it. Christine will spend her summer vacations with me, and the winter ones, too. We'll travel, vacation times. She's going to see Alaska and hear Alaska. For two years she's going to eat and drink Alaska. She's going to love it and hate it, like all good Alaskans. But when she's finished she'll know Alaska from Point Barrow down to Juneau; from the North Pole to the Banana Belt. Then she'll be ready for your Outside crowd. Ready. Armed. Prepared to make her own choice. And that's what you'll have to agree to let her do. You have agreed."

"I could stop you now, before you ever start."

"No you couldn't, Czar. Look!" He stretched his two great arms straight before him at shoulder level, hands parallel to the floor, fingers outstretched. "See that! No tremor there. No shakes."

Czar tapped his own forehead, eying Thor significantly.

"Nor here," Thor added, and brought his hands up to touch his brow.

Bridie managed to piece together this conversation in which she had had no part. "Do you know what they're like?" she said to Addie Barnett that autumn of Chris's freshman year. "They act just like a husband and wife that's divorced. Pulled apart but kind of sticking together because of the child. And in the end the child ruined. But I'm going to try to see to it that Chris ain't."

A strange pair—the massive old man and the lovely young girl—

as they traveled the next two years up and down this glittering almost mythical world of the Arctic. Sometimes Bridie joined the two, a vivacious and gallant third in her modish clothes that defied cold, discomfort and occasional danger.

"I can rough it looking civilized," she argued, stoutly. "Time I was up to Ottawa and Montreal, three winters ago, I didn't see anybody going around dressed like bears. Sweden either, I bet, or Finland, though I've never been. But I will, someday."

"Alaska isn't like those places, Bridie, really," Thor said, gently.

"It will be. And better. Give it a chance, that's what it needs."

Christine learned.

Thor talked. Thor pointed to this and that and those. He was not too voluble, not too insistent, he was rarely prosy or boring. He spoke with passion and power and knowledge and purpose. He talked as a lover talks of his beloved. This was his life, his dream, his Alaska.

Casually Thor would say, "The Eskimos are dying off, of course. Killed by civilization. Overheated houses, canned food, alcohol, motors, starches, inaction, infection."

"But some of them—there are a lot who—like Ross Guildenstern, for example."

"Yes, the breeds survive pretty well. That mixture of Eskimo and Scandinavian stock, or Russian stock, or German or English or American. That is pretty sturdy stuff."

"Like me."

"Like you, my child. Soon there won't be an actual Eskimo left—that is, an Eskimo with no Caucasian strain. Long ago the Russian and the Scandinavian and the English explorers and hunters and whalers took the Eskimo women. Then the American gold hunters. And now the new rush of construction workers, the technicians, the flyers, the lonely men in the army bases, isolated. The whole modern crew. It ought to make a pretty good specimen of American. It has, through the years. You know—the mixture as before. When the railroads were first strung across the country a lot of the Irish immigrant section hands married Indian girls or Mexican girls, or had them.

Now take young Ross Guildenstern you spoke of. He'll probably marry a girl who isn't a breed at all."

"Oh?"

"Their children will be one fourth Eskimo. Their children's children one eighth. First thing you know, we'll have an Eskimo strain President of the United States."

"Grampa Czar says mongrels. When he's mad at me. Not often."

"Tough stuff, mongrels. Usually nimble in the mind and on the feet. Look at all those dark-skinned black-haired brown-eyed Englishmen of Cornwall. Even after five hundred years, when the Spanish Armada was wrecked off the English coast."

Sometimes he was wrong, sometimes he was right. But she learned.

Chris was stuffed with Alaska lore like a Strasbourg goose with grain. They traveled by plane—single-, twin-, and four-engine planes. They traveled by dog sled. They even used trains once or twice. The rest of the world traveled hundreds, thousands, tens of thousands of miles by automobile, but Alaska had few roads other than those built by the Army. The thousands of automobiles in Alaska were a symbol, a fetish.

"It doesn't matter so much—yet," Thor explained to Chris. "People here don't have time to ride around and around, just to be going nowhere, as they do Outside. It takes all the scrambling we can do to crowd the day's work into the day, men and women. You know that, Christine. Work. Food. Keeping warm. Getting from place to place somehow, if you have to. The dog pack to feed if you're traveling by dog sled. Just living is a kind of triumph from day to day."

Up north where the ice blocks were stacked mountain high in July on the shores of the Arctic Ocean. Down south where the mosquitoes tortured you in jungle heat. A sourdough's log cabin in the wilderness with its gun and fishing rod and radio. Crab-meat salad, charcoal-broiled steaks and an orchestra in the Bubble Room of the Baranof Hotel in Juneau; and dinner prepared by a French cook at the Governor's Mansion.

"Why did they build a white colonial with columns as a Governor's house in Alaska?" Chris asked. "It's so un-native."

"Nobody knows. A stab at elegance, I suppose."

Juneau, the capital, and Anchorage were different. "They're Alaska luxury towns," Thor explained. "Tourists visit them and think they've seen Alaska."

"I like them. I'm having a lovely time. Juneau must look like a little Swiss town—of course I've never seen one, but I've seen the movies. A valley, and little narrow winding streets, and kind of quainty."

For a week in Juneau they attended the sessions of the Alaska Legislature daily, all day. They pendulumed from the sessions of the Alaska Senate on this side of the Federal Building to the sessions of the Representatives on that. Men and women. They talked, they pleaded, they presented, they argued, they quarreled, like all free legislative bodies, but their voices went unheard Outside. The women members particularly fascinated Christine. They wore well-cut suits and smart hats, and when they arose to speak they sounded clear, composed and terribly in earnest.

"It must be kind of fun, being a member of the Legislature, Grampa Thor. Maybe when I'm their age." To Chris they seemed quite ancient—forty, fifty, even sixty. "Somebody said they're trying to get Bridie to run for Representative from our district. She'd be wonderful, wouldn't she! She'd tell 'em."

"Yes," Thor said, rather sadly. "But sometimes, in politics today, especially in Alaska politics, not telling 'em is more effective. Just doing. . . . Look at these names, Christine, on the list. They make a kind of cross section of Alaska history . . . Gunderson . . . Kasilov . . . Petrovich . . . Krause . . . O'Shaughnessy . . . McCutcheon . . . Taylor . . . Ellis . . . Utukok . . . D'Orsay . . . Russia, Scandinavia, Germany, Ireland, France, England, Canada."

"That's not so different, is it? That's like every other place in the United States, isn't it?"

"My darling girl!" She couldn't imagine why he seemed so happy about what she had said.

The planes alone were a liberal education, their paths in the air were the roadways of Alaska, they bore such cargo and such human freight as could scarcely be encompassed by the believing eye. Young Eskimo women in modish slacks and pale blue toppers, their feet in loafers and neat white socks. They always carried a baby in their arms, and the baby was resplendent in pale blue or pale pink satin coverlet, a pink nylon and lace dress, lace-trimmed panties, bootees of soft pink kid. Dark slanting eyes in a startlingly pink-and-white face might regard gravely a gray-haired grandmother whose spare New England figure sat so erect beside the daughter-in-law and the grandchild that she now was seeing and visiting in a daze of unbelief. The wife and child of her son Donald, the lieutenant in the United States Army stationed in Alaska. The wife and child of her son Arthur, born in Akron, Ohio, Engineering Cornell '51. The wife and child of her son John, why didn't he stay home and build houses in Bridgeport, Connecticut, even if the pay wasn't so high, and marry that nice Betty Walworth that was so crazy about him. She settled her hat more firmly on her neat gray head, the severe little American Midwest or New England elderly hat. Her daughter-in-law was hatless, her hair done in a modish coiffure.

At lunch time, "What is your formula?" the plane stewardess would ask.

The young Eskimo mother with the plump baby on her lap would say, "One half canned milk, one half water."

The bewildered grandmother was shocked into protest. "But you fed her just an hour ago. And you've got another bottle right there in the bag."

"One half canned milk, one half water," the mother would repeat, smiling up at the hostess.

"Cold?" doubtfully.

"Cold."

The olive-skinned young mother thought this old lady, her husband's mother, must be a strange one. A bottle of food for the baby, free—and not take it! She had her people's respect for the old, but throughout her childhood in the tiny Eskimo village where she used to live she had learned that nurses and doctors and dentists and formulas and sometimes even housing and food all were provided by a beneficent thing called the Alaska Native Service. And she knew, too, that for centuries and centuries before this day the fathers brothers sons and husbands of her people had wrested a bitter living from the snowy wastes, from the icy seas, often at the cost of their lives. Whale. Seal. Caribou. Fish. Bear. Owl. Loon. Squirrel. Ptarmigan. Walrus. Anything. Anything was food that could be eaten and digested. To refuse offered food was not only bad manners, it was madness. When her own lunch came round on the cardboard tray—good thick cheese-and-meat sandwiches wrapped in wax paper; with deviled eggs and olives, carrot sticks, cake, hot coffee, a feast and free, she ate every crumb, she drank every drop, happily. She was horrified to see that her mother-in-law left more than half her food on the tray. She would have liked to eat that, too, but good manners forbade. Finished, the young woman thumbed the pages of a women's magazine, eying the toothsome pictured recipes as she smoked a post-lunch cigarette.

Every pilot of every plane, whether single-, twin-, or four-engine, seemed to know Thor Storm. This rather surprised Chris. The plane stewardesses knew him, too—those pioneer girls weaving across the continent in the modern covered wagon.

"Hi, Mr. Storm!" they chirped. "You haven't traveled with us since last January. I was beginning to think you'd gone to the dogs." An old Arctic travel joke.

Chris began to feel more stable in the air than on the ground. She had had her first flying lessons, though she never had flown solo. Not old enough, they said. Besides, Czar Kennedy had forbidden it.

"I didn't know you had so many buddies in the air," Chris said. "You never told me. You seem to know every pilot between Seattle and Barrow."

"I like talking to them. They know more about Alaska than the Secretary of the Interior ever will. I don't mean they just know geography and topography and weather. Everybody who sets foot in Alaska sets foot in the air, at one time or another. These boys see them all."

"They certainly see you, Grampa Thor."

"You sitting beside me isn't exactly a handicap," he said, fondly.

After the plane was up and running clear each pilot undoubtedly did seem to follow a routine pattern. He would emerge from the cockpit and stroll casually up the aisle toward the old man and the young girl. Quite formally, abandoning momentarily the Hi! that served for ordinary encounters, the young man in uniform would say with careful courtesy, "It's good to see you, Mr. Storm. Glad to have you aboard." His gaze on the girl.

"Hello, Bob! . . . Captain Tyler, Christine . . . my granddaughter, Christine Storm."

She would smile up at him. Good-looking. But then, all men looked handsome in a pilot's uniform.

He would look ardently down at her, unaware that he was looking ardent; a wife at home and three kids and that was that. Quite a dish, though. Black eyes and they slant a little . . . I wonder . . . no . . . golden hair . . . maybe a paint job . . . no, that's genuine Alaska gold hair.

"Would you like to come up forward and have a look around, Miss Storm?"

Thor Storm had planned carefully, carefully. South Alaska first, the accustomed comfort and even luxury of Juneau, with the Alaska Legislature in session, embattled, serious; the reactionary and the liberal locked in combat.

She had seen Anchorage, sparkling, gay, modern, a city of homes, shops, libraries, museums, hotels, parks that seemed magically to have sprung complete, overnight, from a tent town.

From Juneau they had bounced over to Sitka in a tiny amphibian that rollicked its start through the waters, lifted itself, an audacious speck of metal over the menacing ice-sheathed mountains. They had no sooner been plumped down in the harbor than Chris began to say, "I remember! I remember!" as though she had been there before.

"Remember?" Thor said, mystified.

"Everything you told me. What was I? Eight? Nine? Ten? Anyway, I remember it all. When it was the capital of Alaska for a whole century. And the Russians. And Baranof that our town was named for. That seems strange now, doesn't it? And then Seward's Folly, and the Russian flag coming down and the American flag going up! Like a movie or something. But it seems real to me, just the same. Maybe because I've remembered it so long. All my life."

"All your life," Thor repeated, smiling down at her. He was happy. It was like renewing his youth, just to watch her. She stood wide-eyed before the altars of the old Russian cathedral with the vestments and icons and vessels of a long-gone day. In the little chapel of Our Lady of Kazan was the painting of the Madonna and Child framed in silver *repoussé*. Chris nodded her head as if in affirmation of a familiar object.

They visited the Old Pioneers' Home where old, old men were living out their lives in physical comfort and inner rebellion. They had fought the Alaska wilderness in their youth, they had lived with danger, old age had seemed a distant thing, they had not realized that this was the one inevitable danger they never could conquer. In their faded eyes was a look of puzzlement.

Thor seemed to know them all, they greeted him, croakily, with a kind of admiring affection. They crowded round him and Christine felt a moment of panic as though they might somehow, by their very numbers and their eagerness, take him with them into their now futile lives. Thor brought her into the tiny neat private room of the Oldest Pioneer. His hair was absolutely white and very clean, and his eyes were curiously bright and blue and Christine wished they were not so merry. They made her uneasy. He was courteous to her, but distant, not interested. The crumpled face was pink and white, like a baby's.

"Well, Thor, when you coming with us?"

"Any day now, Swan. Any day."

Smiling, the eyes still glassily merry, "I never thought I'd live to die sitting in a chair by a window in an old pioneers' home."

It was a standing joke, a routine dialogue, Chris learned later.

"How would you like to die, Swan, if you had your choice? Eaten by a bear? Frozen on the trail? Starved in a cabin?"

"I'd like to be shot dead by a jealous husband."

Ha-ha-ha! said Thor. And ha-ha-ha! said Swan.

But when they left, Chris said, "I don't want to live to be old."

"It's not so bad," Thor said. "I just ignore it."

"But you're not old!"

"I'm old, Chris, my dear child. And Czar is old and Bridie is old. You're just used to us, that's all. You've had to skip a young mother and a young father and sisters and brothers, so you don't know the difference. That's why I want you to be ready and prepared, perhaps a little ahead of time, so that when we're not here you can make your way, alone."

"That sounds scary."

"No. Life isn't scary. It's the most exciting experience you'll ever have. But it's better if you're prepared a little."

Then he said a curious thing. "When I'm really old, Christine, and ill and useless, don't let them put me there, will you? It's a good place, but not for me."

She was genuinely shocked. "You! Why, Grampa Thor! What a thing to say."

"I haven't much money, you know. None, really, except from week to week."

"I'll have money. I'll work. And Grampa Czar has lots of money. He wouldn't let you."

"Just remember what I said, dear child."

Ketchikan, Wrangell. Cordova. Valdez. Nome. Even little native Indian villages. Hoonah. Yakutat. Then the bustling city of Fairbanks, exactly mid-center, neon-spangled and thriving; The Golden Heart of Alaska, it called itself, wistfully, Baranof's civic rival it announced, proudly.

"There isn't much time," Thor said. "Next trip we'll head north. That's the real Alaska. Oogruk and Kotzebue and Point Barrow. There's nothing like them in all of North America. But first I want you to see the fishing. Then you'll understand why I'm fighting the Outside crowd. Overnight at the Suewok Cannery, and then out on the tender to the fishing grounds with me. How does that sound?"

Privately she thought it sounded dull. "Mm-hm. That'll be fun."

He glanced at her almost ruefully. "I want you to see it," he said, again. And again, "There isn't much time."

"Grampa Thor, you sound as if you were running a race against something."

"I am—in a way. In many ways, Christine. I want you to see it all."

"Bridie says you and Grampa Czar are so mixed up you can't tell which is me and which is Alaska. Bridie kills me."

"My God!" he said, stunned. "Maybe she's right."

By now it had become almost routine. They were taking off for the Suewok Cannery and the salmon-fishing grounds. There at the airport was the usual twin-engine DC-3, somewhat shabby but still gallant, though vintage. There, too, was the plane stewardess, not at all shabby or vintage. Gerda Lindstrom, a Baranof girl they knew well.

"Someday," Chris said to Thor beside her, "I'm going to have my own little plane."

"Why not!" Thor said, companionably. "Why not!"

They were up, they were leveling off, Gerda Lindstrom was making her announcement in a losing struggle against the noise of the engines ". . . welcome you aboard . . . Miss . . . Lindstrom . . . your pilot . . . Guildenstern . . . hope you . . ."

Christine's heart gave a little lurch. When later, the blue-uniformed figure came through the forward doorway, as always on these trips, he too repeated the formula. "Nice to have you aboard, Mr. Storm. Hi, Miss Storm." Then he, too, was looking ardently down at her, unaware that he was looking ardent. "Would you like to come up forward and have a look around? In about half an hour we'll be due over Anaktuvuk, it's one of the most primitive villages in the region, of course you won't see much from up here."

"They don't build those doorways high enough for me," Thor said. "I always bump my head. You run along, Christine."

The co-pilot relinquished his seat to her, she noticed that he was the older, Ross Guildenstern the younger.

"You're a captain now, aren't you?"

"Yes. I don't fly the freight crates any more."

"I should hope not! After all, a man who flew in the war."

"Oh, that doesn't pull any weight. There are a lot of us buzzing around in hedgehoppers. Do you enjoy flying?"

She was a little disappointed. Politely she said, "I love it."

"Are you comfortable now? I think you don't get the real feel of a plane anywhere but up here."

"Yes," she said, demurely.

"Perhaps you'd like to know a little bit about it. I don't mean I'm going to bore you with a lot of mechanical details. Now this"—his hand indicated the board—"is the instrument panel. In the old days they called it the dashboard, like a car. Of course the big new jobs —I mean, this is a dated job, but I like it."

"It sounds fascinating."

"Of course it would be great to fly one of the big Pan Am planes, but I'd never get a captaincy there. You ever been up to Point Barrow?"

"No."

"You ought to go. It's rugged, but it's really Alaska."

"That's what Grampa says. We're planning to go."

"When?"

"I don't know. Grampa says July is about the best time. Cold, but you can stand it."

"I get that run occasionally. Oogruk and Barrow. I was born in Oogruk. Look, do you know the date?"

"Grampa does."

"Because sometimes, up there, if it's a fair day and nobody's in a hurry, and if there's Brass on board, or a VIP like your Grandpa, I ask them if they want to have a look at the Diomedes. You know about the Diomedes?"

"A little bit. They're two islands off the coast of Siberia, aren't they? And the Big Diomede is Russia and the Little Diomede is United States. And never the twain shall meet."

"Good girl! Scientists say they used to be part of the mainland, thousands of years ago. Now, from the air, they look so close it seems as though a kid could jump across. I always explain that we can fly over the Little Diomede, barely, but just an edge over the Big Diomede and we get shot at. That always rates a screech from the women passengers. And when I say that that black shore line just beyond is the coast of Siberia the passengers say Siberia! Like a bad word. Most tourists never even heard of the Diomedes, or realize that Russian territory is really right up against us Americans in Alaska."

She was disappointed. He was talking too much. Then, even as she thought this, he said, "I'm talking too much."

"Oh, no."

"Do you know why? Because I've hoped you'd get on one of my planes. And today you did. And now I'm shock-happy. Look, do you want to take the controls for a minute? Nothing can happen, I'm right here, you might get a kick out of it."

Momentarily embarrassed, she stared at him, and in the next moment a look of awful realization darkened the brilliance of his vivid face. He covered his eyes with his hand. "Oh, God. I just remembered. I heard. You've logged about a billion miles and they'll give you your license next year when you're out of diapers. And you didn't even stop me."

"I was interested, really."

"You were enjoying it."

"But I *haven't* seen the Diomedes, and I *do* want to see them, and it's fun to talk to you again."

"And you let me sit there blabbing. Oh," he muttered, "this is the instrument panel it used to be called the dashboard do you enjoy flying Miss Storm you get the real feel of a plane up here. Pardon me while I break a window and bail out."

They began to laugh then in a whoop of exuberance. He reached over and for a moment covered her hand with his.

"How long are you going to be in Suewok?"

"Just a day and a night, I think. Two days at the most. Grampa has to load up for the trip to the fishing grounds. I'm supposed to stay at the cannery, Grampa wants me to see it, but he won't stay there, he's feuding with the cannery crowd. I feel sort of funny about staying there."

"Just you relax and do as he says. He's a great old boy. He's the most outstanding man in Alaska."

"I think so, too. Most people think Grampa Kennedy."

"You lead a kind of double life, don't you?"

"Do I? Anyway, I've loved it." She edged her way out of the seat. "Thanks for the scenery."

"Look, when are you taking off for Oogruk? Maybe I can wangle the flight if I know the date."

"It may not be this summer at all. Grampa might put it off until next year."

"Do you mind if I ask him? That is, if you——"

"I don't mind." Primly. "Especially if you'll throw in another travel talk."

"My Oogruk talk," he said, earnestly, "is illustrated with lantern slides."

Seated again beside Thor Storm she said, "I wonder what makes their eyes so clear."

"Whose eyes?"

"Pilots. I mean Ross Guildenstern's and–uh–Gerda's are, too. The whites of their eyes are blue-white, like a baby's, and absolutely clear and clean and shining, like a light."

He glanced at her thoughtfully, then his eyes went to the brilliance of sky and mountain. "Flying so much, I suppose. Altitude, clean air. They're up in the air more than they're on the ground. Winged things always have eyes like that. Birds. And gods. And angels." He smiled at her. "And now, even pilots."

16

"Why do they eat all the time?" Chris asked Thor. The plump little fishing scow was bouncing its way across the waters from the cannery to the distant fishing grounds. "They eat and eat and eat. Six meals a day. It's frightening. They can't be hungry all the time. Why do they eat?"

"Lonely, probably," Thor replied. "Out of their accustomed element. Not secure. We'll talk about it this evening, maybe. When we've got things shipshape on the boat."

She had asked the same question of Bor Maunch, the cannery manager. Maunch had just grinned. "We feed our workers good and they like it."

Bor Maunch wished she'd shut up and not ask so many questions. Why? Why? Why? He was sick of it. She sure took after old Thor Storm, nosey like him. Of course she rated the Special Treatment, being Czar Kennedy's granddaughter and all, and anyway he had had written instructions before she came. Visitors didn't come often but when they did you showed them around, gave them a good meal, a couple cans of the best grade red salmon and that was it. But not this kid.

Why don't you use Alaska workers instead of all these people from Outside? Why do the Filipinos eat apart from the rest? Could I eat one meal with them, I like to taste different kinds of food. . . . Your Grandpa wouldn't like that. . . . But Grampa Thor would love it! . . . I mean your Grandpa Kennedy wouldn't like it. . . . But I'm here with Grampa Thor.

Bor Maunch was sick of it.

On her arrival they had given her an astonishing suite, there in that wilderness of water and mountains, with only the cannery looming out of the water on piles, like a monster on stilts, to mark the hand of man. Amazed, Chris surveyed a sitting room, bedroom and bath. A white bearskin rug on the floor, chintz curtains, a radio, deep-cushioned chairs, a couch, lamps.

"But it's absolutely luxurious!" Chris had exclaimed at sight of this splendor. "I thought it would be like a camp." Somehow, she felt disappointed, resentful. "I might as well be at the Baranof Hotel in Juneau."

"Nothing's too good for Czar Kennedy's granddaughter," Bor Maunch assured her. "This place was fixed up like this for the Big Boys like Dave Husack and Kleet and those. General Cass Baldwin came once. They don't get here once in a hundred years, but they like it this way when they do come."

"I think I'll sleep on the boat where Grampa Thor is."

"No! No, you can't do that, Miss Storm." There was genuine alarm in his voice. "Czar would have me——" His tone changed to a wheedling jocularity. "You're better off here, Miss Storm, that's a fact. Anyway, Thor's busy loading up, he can't be bothered with anybody on board now. They're due out Tuesday morning. You're staying here."

"I am not. I'm going out on the tender with them."

"That's too rough for a young lady like you."

She was rather surprised to hear herself saying, "I like it rough."

He wagged his head in an unconvincing imitation of admiration. He laughed mirthlessly. "Well, say! Chip off the old block! Now, if there's anything you want, why, the place is yours, you as good as own the place, along with Czar and the rest. How's that!"

"I don't want to own the place." Then, ashamed of her own rudeness, "I mean, it's nice of you to be so hospitable. I'd love to see everything."

"That's fine," Bor Maunch agreed. "I'd take you around myself, only I'm busy with a lot of paper work has to go in the mail boat to Suewok. I'll get one the boys——"

"Could I try working in the cannery? Just anything, I mean, for a little while? Packing or something, just to try it."

Horrified, he backed away from her. "Get a finger cut off or something! Czar'd kill me!"

"Czar Czar Czar! I'm here with my Grandfather Thor Storm, he knows more about canneries and fishing and Alaska than anybody in the world! He's the most wonderful man in Alaska!"

"Well, sure. Sure." Placatingly. "He sure does, he sure is. I'll have one the boys show you around——" He had vanished.

When, that evening, she reported this to Thor, having made her way down to the tender being provisioned at the dock, he heard her out, after which he said, mildly, "Yes, Bor Maunch told me, and everybody on the boat here told me, and the cannery workers told me, and the waitresses, and Mrs. Gulick the matron. This is like a village, Christine, only it's more remote than a village, so any news is news, and news travels fast on an empty road. I brought you here to see, not to talk. You can do your talking later, perhaps five years from now."

"I don't know what you mean."

"Pretend you're a seed. Just absorb. Blooming comes later."

She was guided through the desperately concentrated labor of the cannery by a blindingly handsome and suave young man named Juan Pico. He was employed, not in the actual canning area, but as cook's helper; slim, elegant, incredible. Chris first saw him after breakfast on her first day at the cannery. In a corner of the vast bright dining hall he was bent over some work spread on a bared table. He was sewing. Then Chris realized that the long leisurely gesture of the man's arm was that of embroidering. Juan Pico was engaged in the seemingly endless task of creating a *gros point* carpet. An imposing section of it was completed. Chris saw that its pattern was not the conventional roses and wreaths. Violets strewed the fabric, and pale pink and delicate lemon-yellow small blossoms unfamiliar to her, intertwined with trailing green vines and moss like the earth pattern of a fragrant fresh woodland in the spring.

"Juan Pico'll take you around, won't you, Juan," Bor Maunch said by way of introduction. "I guess you know this is Czar Kennedy's granddaughter, you take her around show her the works and I guess you know anybody is Czar Kennedy's granddaughter they're entitled to the run of the place."

"My name is Christine Storm," she said, with more *empressement*, perhaps, than the occasion called for. "I'm here with my Grandfather, Thor Storm."

Juan Pico bowed. "It's a privilege to take you around, Miss Storm," he said. He then stabbed his needle into the heart of a violet, rolled up the canvas, tucked it into a corner, and looked critically at Christine's feet. "Got any overshoes? Not mukluks, but galoshes or something?"

"That's right," Maunch said. "You don't want to slip, it's pretty slimy, places. And look out when you're up on the catwalk."

She must put the first question to him before they had crossed the dock between the dining room and the cannery.

"Mr. Pico—"

"Juan."

"Juan, what was that you were making—sewing, I mean?"

"Oh, that's a carpet, a copy of a seventeenth-century Aubusson in an old French château. Chambord, I think it is."

She could not help herself. "But why are you doing it? I mean, here?"

"To get away from the fish. And the food. And this stuff." He made a gesture that included the cannery, sky, water, mountains.

"Then why are you here at all?"

"Money," he said, and smiled, a flash of white teeth in the creamy face. Chris had thought him very attractive. Now she decided he wasn't really handsome, after all. Something missing. She thought she would take that up later, with herself, when she had more leisure. The fishing boat.

"Do you live in Alaska?"

"God, no! San Francisco. This is my third summer, and money or no money, I can't take it another stretch. Too depressing. Of course, in eight or ten weeks I earn enough to last me the rest of the year. There's no way to spend money here. I get transportation and my meals and my room. Cigarettes, that's about it. We're not paid here at the cannery. They hand it to us in a lump when we get back Outside, see. . . . Up these stairs, Miss Storm. Watch it."

As he talked they had passed through a dim cavernous warehouse. Boxes. Ropes. Nets. Floats. Now the top of the stairs brought them into a world that clanked and whirred and thudded and clattered and rattled. Over and through and under everything was the smell of fish. It was more than a smell; it seemed an actual tangible substance.

Juan Pico, momentarily removed from his violet-strewn world, was factual and detached. For the first time in her life Christine felt disembodied, without dimensions.

"This is the assembly line, see. Those girls are on piece work. . . . Those others there are patchers. . . . Those guys cleaners . . . cutters . . . stuffed in a can with salt . . . the air's extracted that way, see . . . this machine spins the top on . . . the cans go into this high-pressure steam thing . . . this pastes the label on the can, it's a real pretty label, and you buy the can, and that's it. All this stuff used to be done by hand—anyway, that's what they tell me—now it's mostly machinery. Chinese used to do a lot of it, but not now since the War, and anyway the union won't stand for it. Now they call this machine the Iron Chink, that's kind of cute, don't you think?"

"Awfully cute," Chris said.

The women were standing at the long counters in the wet slime and grease, their feet in rubber overshoes, their hands in rubber gloves, their bodies covered with rubber aprons. Their faces and heads, in contrast, were startlingly coquettish and modish. They wore earrings, their faces were carefully made up with rouge, lipstick, powder; their hair was dressed with a painstaking permanent. They did not glance at Christine or at her handsome guide, they did not once lift their eyes from the line that moved so relentlessly past them, they were on piece work, the line moved inexorably like the stream of life, there was no stopping it except by complete annihilation. The patchers deftly snatched the packed can as it twinkled by, their unerring eye had caught the grayish bit that was not toothsome enough for the top layer; with an incredibly swift gesture they substituted a more splendid bit of plump red salmon meat, they set the can back into the life stream as a mother smooths a child's hair or twitches her skirt to rights before sending her off to school.

The men at the long tables caught the whole fish as it flowed through the machinery stream, flowed as endlessly and unhurriedly through the air and metal as though this were a salmon's natural element. Steam hissed, iron clanked, knives chopped, metal thumped, water swished, cans clashed. No one spoke, no head was lifted, the relentless process had a nightmarish pursuing quality.

Now, through the clamor, Juan said, "Follow me. And watch it." He pointed to the catwalk, crossing above complicated belts and pistons. Standing there she could view the entire pattern, the motions of the arms, the heads, the movements of the machinery, so orderly, so repetitious, so inevitable; a ballet of labor. Someone was coming toward her, she wondered nervously how he could pass on that narrow strip of footing. He stood beside her, a big-framed man, tired-looking, with the eyes of a seaman, clear and farseeing.

"Foreman!" Juan mouthed, through the clamor. Now the man leaned toward her and shouted in her ear. Something BERGSTROM! Bergstrom smelled of fish oil and salmon even more distinctly than this temple of salmon itself. It was as though his pores had absorbed the effluvium through the years, soaked it in like the spongy floor boards of the cannery, and now exuded it.

Bergstrom shouted "Thor Storm!" and nodded and smiled and pointed dockward to where the tender lay moored. His expression was unmistakably friendly and admiring. "First time in years!" he bellowed. "Thor don't favor fish-trap country."

Chris nodded and smiled in turn, she pointed toward the hive below the catwalk. As though she had pressed a button that activated a machine, numbers began to rumble forth. ". . . Alaska output . . . four million cases . . . only two million cases . . . six million cases . . ."

Chris shook her head. "People!" she yelled. "Those people. Are they Alaskans! Where are they from?"

But now Bergstrom had difficulty in hearing, he indicated his ears, politely but helplessly as he backed away. But Chris still had a shriek left in her lungs. "You hire them, don't you? You're the foreman."

Bergstrom found his voice. "No, ma'am, they're hired Outside. Seattle. San Francisco."

"My Grandfather says——"

"You speak to him, miss."

Bergstrom had vanished down the catwalk steps.

Juan Pico evidently considered the tour ended. He preceded her down the stairs, guided her across the hazards of the slimy floor into the outer air that came across mountain and water and that here smelled only faintly of fish. She stood on the dock, breathing deeply.

"Anything else you'd like to see?" Juan Pico asked, with the impersonal politeness of a formula.

"No. Thanks a lot. Uh, Juan, this is only one cannery. There are lots of others, aren't there?"

"That's right."

"Hundreds and thousands of Outsiders working and getting the wages and taking the money——"

Juan Pico raised a hand in a gesture of parting. "Well, be seeing you, Miss Storm. I've got to get back to work."

Absurdly she threatened. "I'm going to tell my Grandfather."

"You do that," he said. Then, with an air of the most casual curiosity, "You a Commie?"

In an overwhelming flash of anger she reverted to a childhood phrase. "Would you like to have your face slapped?" she said, inadequately. But Juan Pico, too, vanished. All the Suewok Cannery employees, like jinns in mythology, seemed to have miraculous vanishing powers. One moment they stood before you, smiling, polite, even deferential. You asked a question. They vanished.

Thor would not vanish. You could turn a battery of questions on him, she thought, and he would sit there considering them and answering them, thoughtfully, as though you were a grownup. You are, you fool! she said to herself now, fiercely. You've been playing itsy-bitsy all your life, you're spoiled, that's what, by three people who made you think you were more important than anybody else in the world. Don't make me laugh.

So now, as the little boat chugged its way across the waters, she began to discern the pattern that Thor Storm had etched so tirelessly all these years. You could say why why why endlessly. He never rebuffed you, he never vanished, he was there, solid, indestructible, towering over them all, like Mount McKinley.

In its own cosy way, the boat had turned out to be as unexpectedly comfortable as the Suewok Cannery suite, and much more to her liking. Squat as a plump middle-aged matron it bumped and waddled its way to the fishing grounds. The galley, with its small adjoining nook that passed for a mess room, was warm and snug. Her sleeping quarters were little more than a slit in the wall. A vast pot of hot coffee scented the air all day, all night. To step out on the wind-swept deck of the little tender into the clear brilliant daylight or the clear brilliant night light was, Chris thought, like stepping out of an air-borne plane into space. I must ask Ross about that. I must ask Grampa Thor when we're going to Oogruk. I must ask Grampa Thor. I must ask Grampa Thor.

"Why do they feed them so much at the cannery? They eat all the time. Like Henry the Eighth or something. They can't be hungry. It sort of turned my stomach. Breakfast was huge. Meat and eggs and fish—though they didn't serve much fish. Isn't that strange?"

"No. No, not after you've been all day——"

"Oh. Yes, of course. And hot breads and fruit juice and hot and cold cereals and fried potatoes and pancakes and jam and jelly. Then at ten in the morning they ate again, they had rolling tables there at the cannery piled with cakes and sandwiches and coffee. At noon they had soup and meat and vegetables and salads and pies and cakes and puddings and relishes, but they ate again at four and then at six they had dinner all over again. Even lamb chops! Imagine, all those lamb chops, in Alaska! And at ten—you won't believe it—they brought out platters and platters of cold meats and cheese and pickles and cakes again and pies and everything, as though they hadn't been given a bite to eat all day. It was repulsive. It must cost thousands and thousands. Why do they eat all the time?"

"It keeps them satisfied. Temporarily."

"But I mean, they can't be hungry!"

"Not that kind of hunger. It satisfies another kind of hunger, or they think it does. It's lonely there at Suewok, there's nothing to do but work. And eat. They're cut off from the rest of the world. They're city people, mostly, they get restless and nervous. They don't even have their money until they're flown back Outside. The cannery owners have learned that people who are lonely or frustrated or resentful eat a lot, even if they're not actually hungry. Food is a narcotic, in a way, like alcohol. And the cannery workers can't smuggle liquor in—at least, it's pretty hard to do. They'd have to go into Suewok itself to drink—that is, drink. And the cannery boats just don't take them into Suewok. Did you ever notice the eyes of fat people? Really huge fat people, especially with that chuckling laugh. They laugh, laugh. And they munch all the time, meals, between meals. But their eyes look frantic. They're like babies, having the nipple stuffed into their mouths to stop crying."

She was to remember that cannery trip all her life, though it had the quality of unreality. She read in the stuffy little cabin. The books on the shelf beside her bunk turned out to be Bergson and Bernard Shaw and Tolstoi and Flaubert and Ibsen; a handful of rebellious post-World War II novels; *The Decline of the West; The Oxford Book of English Verse*. She knew that Thor had carefully placed them there; she was not interested. The first day she read a little, she even marked a passage in a page here and there, to prove to Thor that she had been reading. It turned out that this practice he considered an outrage.

"Remember this, Christine. Never mark a book. It's an impertinence to the next reader. Books should be cherished, like children, books are for the next generation, like children, like history."

She was less impressed than once she had been by these pronouncements and philosophies. Throughout her strange childhood she had thought Thor and Czar and Bridie infallible, they were infinitely superior to all other human beings. But lately she had noticed that Alaskans were referring to them as "characters." They did this admiringly and even fondly, wagging their heads and smiling. "Yessir, Thor sure is a character. . . . Czar's a character, all right. . . . Bridie Ballantyne is a real character. She kills me!"

If the crew found her presence a handicap in the confines of the little boat they gave no indication, they behaved toward her like indulgent uncles. The cook even allowed her to turn out a batch of sourdough pancakes and was not too resentful when they actually proved to be superior to his.

"Thin," Chris explained, very graciously. "And delicate. Everybody makes pancakes too thick. Especially men. Like big flannel poultices."

Curiously enough, she remembered that salmon-fishing trip as an exhilarating time. It did not occur to her that her manner of life differed from that of other girls except, perhaps, in the matter of enhancement. Here she was, gay and yet relaxed, she could not account for it, she did not try. She would turn on the radio and now and then something would come through—a squawk of news, a crooner's whine. She was in and out, buffeted by the cold wind, soothed by the cabin's coffee-scented warmth.

"I feel as if I were floating in a vacuum," she said.

"You're afloat, all right," Thor said. "I hope. Maybe you're drinking too much coffee. Scandinavians and Alaskans are coffee drunkards. You inherit from both sides."

"Are we going to Oogruk this summer?"

"Depends."

"Ross Guildenstern said that if he knew the date ahead of time he might wangle things so as to pilot us."

He looked at her, thoughtfully. "Perhaps we'll put it off until next year."

"Oh, no!"

"We could do Oogruk and Barrow both. We might invite Bridie to come along, if it isn't too rough a trip for her."

"But why! Why!"

"Bridie's got common sense. Bridie knows what's good for you better than I do."

"You promised."

"I promised we'd go. And we will. Next summer will be your last summer before Seattle. You'll be older."

"Older? For what? You don't have to be old to go to Oogruk."

"Why are you so crazy about Oogruk all of a sudden?"

"I've always wanted to see it. It sounds fascinating." Then, naïvely, "Ross Guildenstern was born there. He knows everybody in Oogruk."

"That would make it more interesting," he said, rather flatly. "Of course I know Oogruk pretty well." He was silent. She waited. "We'll see. Far North Alaska is a big bite to digest. Next summer might be best."

At the fishing grounds the vastness of the salmon catch stunned her. The silver horde, she thought. She knew now what it meant. The mass lay piled and glistening in the boat. Thor and the crew had worked unceasingly through the days and the white nights; they had worked, not like men, but like machines, they had not slept, they scarcely had eaten. The sight of men working at top speed was familiar to Chris. She had seen this all her life in Alaska where everyone—men and women—worked with tenacity and dogged courage for actual survival. But this labor at the salmon-fishing grounds was an orderly frenzy of activity. Thor and the crew ignored her. Throughout this brief period of intensity, if she spoke to Thor, he looked at her absently and did not reply. There was no time for living, there was only motion in the pursuit of this brilliant swirling mass of quicksilver.

Now, loaded to capacity, the return run must be made swiftly.

As the loaded boat moved off they stood at the deck rail, the old man and the young girl, shoulder to shoulder, looking down at the gleaming cargo.

"Silver," Thor said. "Silver like that is the gold of Alaska today." He flung his arm out in a gesture of exultation. "There it is, dear child! The silver that will pay for your years at Baranof College. But this catch is nothing compared to what they get in the salmon traps."

"Do you ever use one?"

"No. No, Christine. Would you like to know why?"

"I remember you said they were bad. But I kind of forget—"

"Fishing traps are criminal, but they're legal in Alaska, my dear. No state in the whole United States permits them."

"Show me one."

"I don't think I can do that. It wouldn't be wise for this boat of mine to go near one of the fish traps."

Why? Why? Why? Why? Her brilliant face eager, her mind as absorbent of this somewhat dry factual story as that of a child listening to a fairy tale.

"Well, I'll try to explain, not making too much of it, I'm busy. They're wooden things, the fish traps, about a hundred feet long and maybe fifty wide, fastened to piles, or sometimes floating. The bottom of the wooden structure is sealed by netting. And fastened to that is what they call a lead, it's hundreds of feet long, the lead, and sometimes thousands of feet, out at right angles from the shore. A webbing. Can you picture that in your mind?"

"Webbing," she repeated, dutifully. "Like a great big tennis net?"

"Something like that, yes. Do you know what happens then?"

"The net catches the fish."

"But it isn't as simple as that. They put that webbing in the waterways where they know the migrating fish will pass on their way to the spawning streams. Salmon are wonderful creatures, you know. No one understands why these noble fish live and die as they do, in nature."

"Yes. Well?" The child saying go on, go on, though she was no child now.

"The webbing stops them, like a flexible wall, you see. They can't go on. So then they turn outward, they sense they'd encounter the shore if they turned inward. They travel along the lead, thousands and millions of them, and they are led by this into a V-shaped opening, a wide one. But this wide opening leads into a second inner opening, and that's V shaped, too, and as they make their way, the V opening gets smaller and smaller, of course, until finally they're into the tunnel and then into the big wooden trap that has a rope web floor that can be lifted up and out, and all those thousands of salmon dumped into the scow, and then they're on their way to the cannery."

"It sounds quite efficient and smart. Isn't it all right? You're catching salmon, too."

"Not with traps. Traps don't just catch salmon. They exterminate them. Fishing is a fine thing, it could make Alaska rich and prosperous. But pretty soon there won't be any fish to catch or trap. They grab too many of them every year, and every year there are less. The trap is there, it works day and night, no one needs to see to it, all they need to do is to come out and pull up the web floor when the trap is full. Who cares? The cannery people don't care, the owners, I mean, they live in Seattle or San Francisco or Chicago or even New York. Ten years more—fifteen—twenty—then it will be finished. No one stops them."

In her naïveté she demanded, "Why don't *you* stop them! You can write more editorials in the *Northern Light*. You can stop anything you don't like, that you think is wrong."

"Money, my darling child. Money. Millions of salmon make millions of money for the people who catch them."

"But not you."

"No. You know better than that. For the canneries."

"But if it's wrong?"

"Smart men in the capital at Washington are hired to make it seem right. It's a little complicated to explain to you. It's a kind of trading they do. You do this for us, we'll do that for you. Congressmen and Senators, and smart lawyers, and Big Business men. It isn't considered dishonest, it's called lobbying. I don't want you to get a wrong idea of your country, Christine, it's the most wonderful free country in the world. But there are certain things. Alaska, you see, has no standing, it has no vote, it has no power to defend itself, it is a big strong giant tied and bound and gagged."

"Like Gargantua."

He laughed his great rollicking laugh. "You've been reading my Rabelais."

They chugged back to the cannery, the great silver mass of fish gleaming in the scow. Thor and the crew seemed content. "Three or four more like this catch," Thor said, "and your schooling for this coming year will be paid for."

Miserably she said, "It isn't worth it. I'd rather never know how to read or add two and two."

He stared at her in amazement. "Isn't worth what!"

"How can I go to college—how can I have anything, when I know you've worked for it like a—like a horse!"

"You've never seen a horse." This was true. To her consternation, he was laughing. "Now if you said worked like a dog, an Alaskan would know what you mean."

In a fury she said, "You're laughing at me! At least Grampa Czar doesn't laugh at me."

"Christine, my darling child, I wasn't laughing at you."

"You were pulling and hauling like those slaves in the pictures that hauled the stones for the pyramids. I can't stand it! Why don't *you* use a lobby, then? What's a lobby, anyway?"

"Here, we'll look it up in the dictionary. Now then, it says, simply: *A Lobbyist. A person who tries to get legislators to introduce or vote for measures favorable to a special interest that he represents.*"

"Oh, that's like Mr. Sid Kleet. And that Shaw Gavin. And those men in Seattle."

"Perhaps. But there are others—lots of them—that you don't know and never heard of."

"It doesn't sound honest."

"It's so considered. It's as well to have it legal and out in the open as behind closed doors. At any rate, people know it's going on, and how it's done."

"But you can do anything. You can tell the world. About the fish and the forests and the metals and the taxes and the—"

"Child, the world isn't interested in fish, it only sounds comic, and the world isn't interested in Alaska, and the world isn't interested in me. It's as simple as that. Alaska salmon is just something in a can. They don't know it's millions and millions of dollars, almost untaxed, to men who never have even seen Alaska. Alaska itself, to them, is an iceberg peopled by Eskimos and polar bears who eat each other. The forests, the metals, the great fishing industry—it's all the same, it goes Outside, it's owned Outside, the world doesn't hear about it, or care, it isn't very dramatic, anyway, people don't want to hear about fish and forests and minerals, it isn't front-page news. And they wouldn't believe it if they did hear it or read it. It's part of a past era, like the old days of the grabbers and what they called the Robber Barons. It's still going on here, full blast, with Seattle and San Francisco and the lobbyists in Washington as the power plant. But who cares!"

"You do! And—and Paul and Addie and even Bridie, I suppose, and some of those people we saw in Juneau, in the Legislature, I mean. They'd listen to you. And the people Outside would, too."

"Outside doesn't read the *Northern Light*."

"The work you've done just now—is that all right? Is it all right, I mean?" She was very solemn.

The old man's clear steady blue eyes looked into the girl's perplexed dark eyes. "If it weren't, Christine, I'd rather leave you as unschooled as a savage. You know that, don't you?"

"Then I don't see why you don't go to Washington as those men do. Go there and do something about it."

"You can't just go to Washington and stand before the Senate or Congress assembled, and yell."

"I would. I'd go and yell at the top of my voice."

"You'd only be thrown out, you foolish child. It takes money and money and money. Millions, because all the rich things in the Territory are worth millions."

"People would listen if you told them. I'm listening. I'm interested."

"No they wouldn't."

"Why! Why!" The child again, asking questions.

"Because I'm what they call a do-gooder. Do-gooders are considered tiresome. They're not dramatic. The average person—if there is an average person—at least, the everyday human being—has admiration for ruthlessness and boldness. Especially in a virile country like the United States. What makes the front page? Crime and war and ruthlessness. People like to read about them and hear about them and look at them in plays and moving pictures and on this new television. Robin Hood and Jesse James. And then the Railroad Kings, the Land Kings, the Wheat Kings the Oil Kings all the Money Kings of America. The marauders. The Robber Barons of the United States. People marveled and wagged their heads, and they weren't altogether wrong. These bold highhanded men settled the land, in a way, and harnessed the rivers and chopped down the forests and worked the great metal deposits of copper and silver and ore. I don't think any other country in the world could have survived such depredation, but there was so much here. It seemed inexhaustible. But it wasn't. It isn't. Not any more. It's going. Even Alaska, the unknown place, the last frontier, isn't a frontier any more, rich as it is it will soon be done for. The new Robin Hoods and Jesse Jameses have it, clever and bold and ruthless and power-hungry, just like the old days, the bad old days. They will leave this wonderful country barren, like a woman who has had to bear too many children in her youth. The forests are dwindling, and the waterways, and the millions of creatures of the sea and the forest—the salmon and the seal and the bear and the moose and the deer."

He was declaiming now, she knew he was quoting from his book, the book he had been writing ever since she could remember, though she never had seen a line of it. Suddenly she saw him, a prophet without honor in his own country. "Don't, Grampa darling. They'll read it. They'll know. They will."

But he went on, he seemed not to have heard her. "They have marched across a continent and now they have reached far into this great ice palace and plundered it. It's the last treasure-trove, it's the end. No one stops them. Perhaps someday this incredible America will be like India, like the barren over-populated countries of the East, like China, and only the few will know what it means to have a satisfied full stomach once a day or once a week or even once a month. Who says it can't be true if this keeps on!"

He had forgotten the girl, he had forgotten the boat, the time, the reason that had loosed the flood of words. He was shocked into awareness by a sound from her. Christine was weeping. Unchecked, the tears brimmed and ran down her cheeks. Stricken, he stared at her.

"My darling girl, what is it! What's wrong! What have I said!"

His great arm about her as though she were a little child.

"I hate them!" she sobbed, hysterically.

"Who? Who?"

"Those men in the office."

"What men?"

"Those men in the office. Years go. They thought I didn't hear. They were talking about you. Grampa Czar was with them. I hate them. And the ones you just talked about——" She was hardly coherent, she was weeping again.

"Don't, my little one. I didn't realize. I was thinking about my book. I'd forgotten you were here. Forgive me." The merry pink face was stricken.

The tear-drenched eyes looked at him accusingly. "Why don't you finish it, instead of talking about it! You've talked about it and talked about it for years and years and years." She was, suddenly, the older wiser one chiding the younger.

Thor Storm covered his eyes with his hands. "What have I done to you! Maybe Czar was right. You should have young people and fun and luxury. An old man on a stinking fishing scow in the wilderness. I'll send you home. Bridie will know what to do. Forgive me. Oh, Christine, forgive me."

She wiped her eyes, she blew her nose, there was about her the air of finality which marks not only the close of a scene but the end of a period in a life. "You can't send me back now. It's too late."

"How, too late?"

"You should have thought of that fifty years ago, when you first came to Alaska. You're stuck with it, Grampa Thor. You're stuck with Alaska and you're stuck with me."

17

Seattle said that Bayard Husack hadn't adjusted. They did not phrase it that way. As Seattle put it, "That young Husack—Bay, they call him—hasn't taken hold since he came home."

He had returned from the War in late 1945, handsomer than ever, feminine Seattle agreed. And not a scratch on him, male Seattle added. But six years had gone by, he was thirty-one, and whatever it was that he had been supposed to take hold of had eluded him. Millions of young men had endured pain and shock and had inflicted pain and shock and death on other millions of men. They had seen wholesale horror, they had known fear that turned the blood to water and the bones to mush. They came home from the War and changed their clothes as they might after a hard day at the office or the shop. They pretended the past four or five years had never been, they appeared to drop the memories of war with the garments of war, they functioned, it seemed, normally.

. . . I'm going to wash the car before supper. . . . No, look, diaper the baby first, will you, while I dish up, supper's almost ready, the Gabbetts are coming over after, I forgot to get some Coke, she don't drink, jump in the car and go down to the corner for some Cokes, will you?

Bay's mother said to Dave Husack, in defense of their son, "It takes time to get used to everyday life after an experience like that."

"About ten million other boys have."

"How do you know they have? You're not their father. Bay's more sensitive than most. He'll take hold in time."

Louise Husack loved her son blindly, and believed this. Dave Husack loved his son, with reservations, and rejected this.

"Time! He's been playing around for six years now."

"He's at the office every day."

"Two hours for lunch. When I say I want him to go to Alaska for a few weeks, learn something about where all that dough comes from he spends on cars and boats and stuff, he says, No, thank you very much, as if I'd made a joke."

"It's so wild and uncomfortable."

"I said how about running for Congress right here in this state, he could swing a lot of stuff for us down in Washington, Sid Kleet could set it all up for us, all the young fellas seem to be going in for politics lately. It used to be you had to be old, but look at Nixon, sharp as a gimlet, and that Neuberger, and kid governors all over the country like Michigan and New Jersey, and Dewey ran for President. President! Damn near made it, too, if it hadn't been for that damned cockalorum. But no, none of that for our Bay, he's more sensitive than most. Who's going to take over when I'm gone!"

"Gone! Why, Dave Husack, you're only fifty-eight."

"Never mind about that. I was twenty-five when Bay was born. And that ended it." Grimly.

Louise Husack's eyes misted. "You know I wanted another child, Dave. I'd have given anything for a daughter. That's why I was so happy to have Dina here, almost like a daughter to us. I've hoped and hoped that Bay would fall in love with her. I know she likes him."

"She say so?"

"She said she thought he was a dear boy."

"Uh-huh."

Whenever Dave took these matters up with his son, Bay listened in a polite but detached way which infuriated the older man, whose boiling point was, at best, low. Dave, seated at his office desk at the end of the day, glared at his son standing there at the window staring out at a city that lay, a pink opal, encircled by the sparkle of water and mountains. Dave's desk was the uncluttered and imposing barricade behind which the middle-aged successful American businessman defends himself. No papers, no pads, no baskets marked In and Out, not even the ugly base of a telephone. This hung suspended and out of sight below the desk's surface. Here was the battlefield of a man who carried his schemes in his head, and his accomplished plans neatly filed elsewhere behind steel. Like Mort Caswell's desk in the office building next door, like a hundred thousand desks presided over by the successful, this polished expanse bore a photograph in a foot-square handsome standing silver frame. And like the thousands of others, it pictured a black-velvet-and-pearls wife against whose knee a child leaned. Louise Husack with Bay at the age of six. When angry—as he now was—Dave had the habit of picking up this heavy frame in one great fist and slamming it down on the desk. This he now did. Dave would have been shocked if some one had told him why he did this. Again, as in the Mort Caswell office, the photograph was an office fixture like the glowing colors of the oriental rugs, the pictures of ships, the ship models on the carved oak mantel. A handsome old-fashioned room that resounded now to the boom of Dave's voice.

"You just don't seem to give a damn!" Dave roared now. "What do you want, anyway!"

"Not a thing, Dad."

"You ought to be married by now and have two three kids and be in shape to run the business—if necessary. Which," he added hastily, glancing down at himself and flicking an imaginary speck off his coat sleeve, "it isn't. But if this doesn't interest you, as a job, what does? Name it. What would you like to do?"

The handsome head did not turn away from the window toward the older man. He spoke casually, a quiet and detached amusement lurked in his tone. This Dave Husack found maddening.

"I just told you. Not a thing. I know I ought to say I've been wanting to write a book, or go into politics, or take up ranching, or paint like all these disturbed ones, or travel, or manufacture something, or go back to school and become a physicist. Everybody's a physicist. This business is all right, it's legitimate and successful, but there's no gamble in it, no margin for error. It's like a bullfight. No matter how much he paws the ground and bellows he's a dead bull before he sets foot in the ring. There's all that fish and timber and metal and stuff in Alaska, but no matter how much Gruening and the rest of them roar it's all yours. Of course there's an art in it, as there is in every sport. And if the first *torero* doesn't kill the bull there's always a second. I guess I'm just not interested in being a bullfighter. I'm more the audience type."

Dave Husack's face was dangerously empurpled. He whipped out his handkerchief, he stood up behind his desk, he seemed to pound his face as he angrily dabbed at it with the scented fine linen.

"You've got a hell of a gall talking to me like that—you and your bullfights. For a fellow who's so bored with the way his father gets it you spend a hell of a lot of money. If you don't like money——"

"I do. I haven't said I didn't. I think it's great. I'm just not interested in the art of getting it, I suppose. I don't even feel guilty about it, the way a lot of rich men's sons do, always trying to give it away to foundations and stuff. I suppose that's taxes. But they're always apologizing for it. Joining movements and protesting. I'm no second- or third-generation Rockefeller or Lamont or Marshall Field. I think money's fine."

Dave Husack's voice started low because he felt as if he were choking, but it rose triumphantly in volume.

"Why, you skunk, you! I've a good notion to sock you, big as you are, and I would, only now I think you're crazy. I think something happened to your head in the war, and you didn't tell us. Or else you're a fairy."

Bay shook his head, he rejected this equably. "No. I seem to be normal enough. But I feel and behave a good deal like those kids who are running the streets in ducktail haircuts and zoot pants and sideburns, only I wear tailored suits and ten-dollar ties."

It was now that Dave Husack's voice rose to a bellow. "You stinking little rat! Standing there grinning and telling me you're normal. Normal!" This was almost a screech. "You crazy contemptible——"

There was a sharp rap at the door. It opened.

"Come in," Bay called.

"Stay out!" Dave yelled. The door opened wider now, and Dina Drake entered.

"They can hear you down as far as the fourth floor. There's quite a nice little crowd in the hall on this floor standing there letting the elevators go by."

"You keep out of this, will you!" Dave roared.

She ignored this. "Will one of you battlers drive me home? I mean home to your house. My car is busted and I promised Aunt Louise I'd come in at six." She was looking directly at Bay. "I promised to do the place cards and the flowers for the dinner party."

Dave's face was contorted with inner conflict as he endeavored to wrench his frenzied thoughts from finance to flowers. "Dinner party. I'm not going to any dinner party."

"Yes you are, Uncle Dave." She placed a sheaf of papers on his desk. "And sign these." She placed a pen beside the papers. He seated himself, heavily, he began to scrawl his signature as she picked up each sheet. "Drive me home, Bay?"

"Why not?" Bay said.

"Don't gush," she retorted.

Dave Husack did not look up as his hand moved jerkily across paper after paper. "I'll go along with you, call Emilio and tell him not to come for me."

"He's probably started," Dina said quickly.

"I'll be gone."

He was as mercurial as a child, and as emotionally shallow. This girl could almost always distract him from the irritation of his angers, his problems. She knew this. He did not. He stood up now, he fingered his florid tie and patted his pockets. His face was magically cleared of the rage that had twisted it a few moments ago.

Ten minutes later the three were cosily seated side by side in Bay's car. Any casual observer would have seen three extraordinarily handsome people, relaxed, pleasure-bound, solvent, in a sports car whose size and power and chromatic charms even the snob-magazine illustrations did not exaggerate. The girl sat between the two men, her knee pressed Bay's lightly, Dave's knee pressed hers heavily, the three had in common one thing. Seething frustration.

Dina Drake was the Husacks' official protégée, everyone in Seattle knew this. She's like a daughter to them, they had said in the beginning, because this was Louise Husack's repeated phrase. She's like a daughter to us, she couldn't be dearer if she was our own. Of course her mother and I were brought up almost like sisters in Kansas City, up to the very day I married Mr. Husack. She was my maid of honor. She married Ed Dracker and they stayed right there in Kansas City to the day they died in that awful crash. Dina was in Hollywood—of course her real name was Dorothy Dracker but she changed it to Dina Drake when she wanted to get into pictures. They didn't appreciate her in pictures, I don't know why, with her lovely looks and all, but I guess it's all having pull, or worse. We kept in touch after the tragedy, she always called me Aunt Louise when she wrote. Then when she kept writing how tired she was, and lonely, I asked her to come here and pay us a visit and she did. And now I don't know what we'd do without her. She stayed right here in the house, we loved it, but after six months or so she said she felt she was imposing, she'd get a job and she did, modeling for the big stores. I didn't like that, and neither did Dave. I said she might be subjected to temptations but Bay said he thought it was all right. We fixed her up with a little apartment of her own and Dave got her to take a kind of secretarial course, and then after my little illness—it wasn't really a stroke, it was just a kind of fatigue that settled in my right side for a while, I hardly notice it now but I have to be careful—Dina began to kind of help out—pinch-hitting, Dave calls it—for me as hostess here at the house and even for Dave when he has to entertain business friends. She's like a social secretary and a business secretary and a daughter all rolled into one. She's got what Dave calls know-how. She's always there ready to pitch in and help. Dina's closemouthed, too. Sometimes I think maybe too closemouthed. She never told me she'd been married in Hollywood, it only came out when the fellow was killed in a car crash just like her mother and father's, it's as if she was haunted by tragedy. I hope not. She doesn't complain. Dina's no relation, but I always say, she's like a daughter to us.

In the past year Louise Husack had ceased to repeat this oft-told tale. In the past year or two Seattle's eyebrows had gone higher and higher until they threatened the very hairline. Bay Husack was the most eligible bachelor in Seattle, now that young Mort Caswell was married and had on his desk his own black-velvet-and-pearls silver-framed photograph, complete with child. Dina Drake may have been sweetness and light to the Husack household, but she rather antagonized the matrons and daughters and even the sons of the Husacks' social set.

She was, they admitted, lovely-looking. She had enormous natural style. She did not make an effort to be more than barely polite to them. For this she had two reasons. She was concentrating with all her charm, energy, intelligence, and ambition, on Bay Husack. And she was scared to death of the memory of those months in Hollywood when she had known such insecurity and fear and cruelty as to mark her for life. These girls she met at the Husacks' and elsewhere, so secure and serene and protected, were young goddesses poised permanently on the amazing hills of Seattle. They wore their good expensive clothes with quiet assurance, they expertly drove cars in which they sat like toothsome turtles in a shell with only their heads sticking out above the car's protective crust. They sailed boats that were really ships. Their skin was fine and fair under the moist kiss of the Northwest fogs. They never had known fear. They never had run around lugging that round patent-leather hatbox. Maybe their mothers talked as much as Louise Husack, Dina thought, though she doubted it. Maybe their fathers were old goats like Dave Husack. Not likely. Though Dave was more human than Bay, at that. At least you knew where you were with him and could handle him. Sometimes she thought she hated Bay. Lately Mrs. Husack talked a great deal about her nerves. How about *my* nerves, Dina thought, grimly, just consider that a moment while you're up, will you, madam?

So now she spent some hours weekly at the Husack offices, she was on hand to take Visiting Big Business Wives shopping or touring the city. She supervised Louise Husack's eternal dinner and luncheon parties. She accompanied Dave and two or three business associates to dinner or lunch at the Olympic or the country club, ostensibly to take notes when necessary, but there was no denying she added a touch of unbusinesslike excitement.

"Some secretary you've got there, Dave," they would say, tentatively.

"Dina! Oh, she's like a daughter to Mrs. Husack and me. We've practically adopted her since her parents were killed. Very sad, very sad business."

Sometimes Dina even accompanied Dave on his business trips, now that Louise was more or less incapacitated. No one but Dina and Dave knew how pure in deed, at least, these business trips were. Dina was completely determined and relentless. Security was what she wanted and would have, she wanted no frolic in a big, uninquisitive, luxurious chain-hotel suite.

Dave's trips were, for the most part, to Washington, San Francisco, New York. There were occasional little side trips to Portland, Tacoma, Spokane, but this was small stuff in which Dina had no part, you did not need to impress these neighboring towns in which Dave Husack was at once a familiar yet almost mythical figure of success.

If Dina, in her secretarial capacity, accompanied Dave on one of these West-East business trips, Dave always returned with a lavish gift for his semi-invalid wife.

"Brought you a little trinket, Lou," he would say. No one else ever called Louise Husack Lou. "They said in New York it was the thing, Dina helped me pick it out. I'm scared of those salesladies, they could sell me anything, but not Dina. She knows."

The gift might be jewelry, a mink wrap, a cashmere coat soft as cream, lingerie, even occasionally a dress.

"Why, Dave!" Louise would exclaim with a bad simulation of surprise as she lifted the treasure from its velvet or satin or tissue cocoon. "It's lovely, just perfectly exquisite!" A week, two weeks, perhaps a month would go by. There would be a secret session between Louise and her protégée. "Dina dear, I don't want to hurt Mr. Husack's feelings, or yours either, goodness knows, because you helped him pick it out, but I've got no use for these things, I've got more stuff now than I know what to do with. He forgets I'm not the young bride he married, he gets me things that are meant for a young girl. I know. He used to do the same when I went with him. White mink." She held it up, she shook it smartly so that the glistening hairs sprang to still more luxuriant profusion. "How would I look in a white mink cape!"

"Why, Aunt Louise, that fur looks lovely against your skin."

She was not altogether without humor, Louise. "Thanks, dear, but the important thing is, how does my skin look against that fur." She laughed ruefully at her own joke.

In another week or thereabouts Louise would venture, tentatively, to shift the gift to a more vernal background.

"David"—no one else called him David—"David, I just love that mink stole"—or sapphire and diamond clip, or alligator bag or French lingerie or dozens of pairs of filmy stockings—"but honestly, maybe it's my imagination, but I think it isn't right for me, beautiful as it is. White makes me look yellow. . . . David, all those chiffon stockings are just exquisite but my old veiny legs, and you know I have to wear those old rubber stockings under them for my old swelling ankles, so do you mind if I give them to Dina? Anyway, they're a teeny bit big for me. I must say I never was a beauty, heaven knows, but I always did have a nice small foot and a high arch, you remember when we were first married you used to say I must have Chinese blood in me, my feet were so small. Maybe Dina could wear them or exchange them . . . white mink with her black hair . . . all that jewelry in the bank vault I don't wear half of it, it just stays there. Dina wears those slinky black dresses so much, a good clip just sets the whole thing off."

To Dina she once said, perhaps quite innocently, "I always hate to see an old woman loaded down with jewelry." She used a rather revolting word picture to demonstrate her feeling. Possibly she was beginning to grope her way, with reluctant steps, toward the truth.

"Whenever I see a wrinkled scrawny old woman plastered with jewelry I can't help thinking of a mess of garbage. The best of it's been used and the rest cast off. You wouldn't trim a plate of garbage with fresh parsley or capers or mushrooms. It would be sheer waste on waste." She looked at Dina, whose face bore an expression of shock. "I tell David he should hire somebody to wear his presents for me, like a kind of clotheshorse."

"Did you say that to him?"

"Yes. I don't think he liked it, maybe I shouldn't have said it. He scolded me. But then he laughed."

To her own friends Louise would say, "David brings me the craziest extravagant presents, I can't make him stop, he sees me through rose-colored glasses. . . . Dina dear, show Mrs. Ballinger the new fur piece. . . . There. Doesn't she look lovely! I tell David he can imagine I'm wearing it, kind of by proxy."

"And what does he say?" Mrs. Ballinger asked, with awful composure.

"Oh, he laughs."

"I bet," said Mrs. Ballinger, biting off the two words, with a look at Dina.

It was the growing opinion among Mrs. Husack's friends of her own age that somebody ought to wise up Louise. No one cared to assume this delicate mission.

"Hard as nails, that girl," they said. "But Jo says there's absolutely nothing between her and old Dave. Jo as good as put it to him. Not in so many words, I don't mean. But roundabout, and Dave told him confidentially that Bay and the girl were practically engaged, he said nothing could make him and Louise happier, Dina was like a daughter to them and had been ever since she came. Well, figure it out. I can't."

Sometimes the quietly cynical and observant Bayard Husack thought he, too, could not figure it out. Dina pursued him with the relentlessness of a prey-stalking tigress. Her little apartment was the convenient background for their occasional love-making, but Bay never had said to her, I love you. Once, in a particularly moody moment he had said to the girl, almost lightly, "You sleeping with my old man, too?"

She was honestly shocked. "Bay, how can you say a thing like that! You know I'm not. How could I!"

"No I don't. I don't know anything about you, really. How about all that junk he's always loading you up with? That for free?"

"It takes a quiet one like you to be as vulgar as that. You know perfectly well your mother gives it to me. I don't even want it."

"Who selects it for him?"

"I do. He asks me to. I suppose I could choose ugly dowdy things, but I can't, I have to choose things that seem to me to be beautiful, that's the way I am."

"Dad's the virile type. I know it isn't your moral sense or any schoolgirl stuff like that. I know you well enough for that, anyway."

"Would you really like to know why? It's because I want to marry you and I want you to want to marry me, and you wouldn't under the circumstances you—well, under those circumstances."

"Ma'am," he said, "how right you are!"

Now Dave Husack and Bayard his son, and Dina Drake, sat seething in the over-sized sports car, knee to knee to knee. The Husacks had stayed up on the Hill overlooking the bay and Puget Sound, that was the thing when he had built, years ago. Now the trend was toward Lake Washington or even out of the city altogether. Like the rest of the world's communities large and small, traffic and planes and the oily fumes of new industries had marked even the Seattle hills for their own. Family after family moved to outlying districts, away from the throbbing cars zooming up the steep winding roads, around the curves, flashing their huge lights into your plate-glass windows. But Dave's house had been his first substantial proof of stupendous financial success. It was a beloved symbol necessary to his self-sustenance. He had put mahogany into it. Brass. Silver. Even gold. It boasted a wine cellar, though Dave himself drank only bourbon. He liked to mark the growth of the trees that had been planted when the house was built, and that had so flourished that now they periodically had to be trimmed to avoid obstructing the view; the monkey trees, the birches, the madroñas. He liked to fancy that from these heights he could see the Pacific one hundred and twenty miles distant—an absurd notion. The place, inside and outside, was kept in the most exquisite order; of its ugly old-fashioned, comfortable and overstuffed kind, it was perfection. You could not imagine adding anything to it or taking anything away. It was as complete as Buckingham Palace, as the Taj Mahal, as Mount Rainier, as an anthill.

Louise Husack came toward them as the three entered the hallway that cut through the entire house, front to back, and that had the dimensions of an assembly room. Her face was alight and eager like that of a child or a lonely woman. She was full of news and disjointed conversation.

"Well, I didn't know what had happened to you, 'Milio's down there probably waiting for you to come down, David, you'd better try to get word to him, he'll just sit there at the curb all night if you don't. . . . Dina did you order yellow roses I said pink they sent yellow you know I'm superstitious about yellow even if it does go with the gold epergné. . . . I want to show you something, David, you too, Bay, guess who's coming here to school at Washington U. next autumn—Czar Kennedy's granddaughter! Here's his letter, he says she'd like a little apartment near the U., and would we kind of keep an eye on her, she's just a young girl, I'd like to write him I'd just as soon she'd come and stay right here with us, all this room and it certainly would be lovely to have a young girl around the house. I think I remember her. Didn't that Czar Kennedy leave her here with me one afternoon when he had a business conference? A little girl."

"Heh, Mom," Bay said. "Just hold everything. We don't want a kid around the house next year—or any year."

"He sent a picture of her. Look. She isn't a kid. She's grown up."

Dina Drake, on her way to the dining room, turned and joined the three. "In a parka I'll bet."

But she wasn't. "Say!" Bay exclaimed.

"I remember," Dave said. "Nice little kid. I saw her once when Czar brought her along for a meeting or something. In my office, she sat as quiet as a mouse—no, it was Caswell's office—anyway she sat there, didn't budge, she couldn't have been more than eleven or twelve. Bright yellow hair. And the blackest eyes. Now how did I happen to remember that!"

"You're not the boy to forget a blonde," Bay said.

"I know now. When the meeting broke up—she'd been asleep through it—waiting there for Czar to finish—she said good-bye, polite as you please, and then she looked at me as if she didn't like me. Real mean look, I mean."

"Now, David, you're not going to hold that against her, for heaven's sake! A child. I'd be bored, too, and mean-looking if I had to sit and listen to you men yak-yakking about business. Why, I remember when I first came to Seattle a bride——"

"We can put the yellow roses in the library," Dina said, "and have a fruit centerpiece instead. Do you think she'll stay here with you?"

Louise Husack followed Dina into the dining room, she referred again to the letter in her hand. "It says here, no. Czar's letter says a little two-room apartment near the U., she likes to be independent."

18

As she and Thor stood at the Baranof airport exit awaiting their plane's flight announcement, Chris saw him as he swiftly crossed the strip and ran up the loading stairway.

"There's Ross," she exclaimed. "He got the run." She turned now to Bridie who had just bustled up to join them. "Ross is going to pilot us as far as Oogruk. I just saw him go into the plane. He didn't even know last night. Isn't it wonderful!"

Bridie Ballantyne jerked her hat forward and settled her shoulders and jiggled her handbag in a series of twitches. "Maybe, if he keeps on flying. When I'm on a plane I don't want any pilot to be giving a floor show, visiting around spreading the charm and explaining the scenery and so on. Let them fly the plane and I'll find my own scenery."

The twin-engine plane was an ancient but respectable DC-3. Humbled in service but still proud, still functioning gallantly, it gave the outer effect at least of a *grande dame* though inside the cabin the seat springs sagged and indeed one whole side of the passenger space might be filled with incredible species of freight, lashed together with rope.

As Thor and Bridie and Chris entered (the stewardess again was Gerda Lindstrom, who greeted them like a hostess welcoming guests to dinner) they saw, without thinking it at all remarkable, that the seats had been removed along one entire side. This space was packed with the frozen skinned carcasses of moose mingling affably with the chilled passengers across the aisle. A too-hasty passenger might bark a shin against an ice-hard moose leg protruding to trip the unwary.

To offset this slight informality the old plane asserted her social position by equipping herself with the young and pretty stewardess Gerda Lindstrom, garnished with a manicure, a recent coiffure and a figure-following blue uniform; a pilot and a co-pilot; snacks served at practically all hours; somewhat cracked loud-speaker dissertations on the weather, the scenery, the history and the natural phenomena of the Territory of Alaska.

It was too early in the season for the tourist tide. The plane was less than half filled—unless one counted the aloof moose destined later to re-enter the stream of life through the digestive tract of meat-hungry residents of Oogruk and other Arctic Circle villages. There were a handful of construction workers, a half dozen young men in army uniform, and a middle-aged couple with graying hair and apprehensive faces. Palpably tourists, these last. Chris wondered what whim or chance had brought them here, she knew she need never ask because Bridie would have a dossier on every passenger in the plane within an hour after taking off, including the weight and destination of the moose. The woman tourist, fiftyish, wore long dangling earrings, a pale blue coat and a flower-bedecked hat, a sort of Miss Havisham on a honeymoon, Chris thought, having early devoured the set of Dickens in Czar's parlor. The man was plump, eyeglassed, almost comical in a Basque beret, a city topcoat, and good gray gloves.

They'll be miserable, Chris thought. It turned out she was wrong.

In the forward seat facing the wall sat a young Eskimo huddled in a blanket. He appeared curiously aloof and almost fragile. He had no books, he had no magazines, he spoke to no one. He munched a chocolate bar, glanced once out of the window with the distrait eye of one to whom ice-capped peaks and illimitable space are merely the back yard. Gerda Lindstrom was making what Ross termed her pitch. The passengers (including moose) muffled against the plane's icy interior, listened with a concentration due more to necessity than politeness, for the old carrier's engines made declamation difficult

. . . welcome you aboard . . . Arctic . . . DC-3 . . . pilot . . . Guildens . . . co-pilot . . . call attention . . . at left . . . plainly . . . magnificent view . . . lucky to see . . . Mount McKinley . . . coffee will be ser . . .

"That McKinley!" the plump male tourist shouted jovially, setting the tone of the trip. "It jumps around like a jack rabbit. It's like the Empire State Building in New York, you're coming in, going out, there it is sticking up in the sky."

"I'm going to help Gerda with the coffee," Bridie announced and bustled off like a friend at a neighbor's bridge luncheon. "She never gets it hot enough, anyway."

Two of the young army men were already asleep, they had been air-borne for many hours. While the plane soared over the wastes of this incredible landscape their faces in repose under the pitiless scrutiny of the brilliant Arctic light were as unmarked, as defenseless, as the faces of children. In their good clean army clothes they lay sprawled, their excellent watches on their strong brown wrists, their ties knotted correctly, their boots like mirrors; though their dreams may have been violent the expression on their faces was seraphic.

One of the six in uniform was seated alone. He sat alone and talked a great deal to anyone or no one; to his mates, to the passengers in front of him or behind him, to anyone passing up or down the aisle, to the busy Gerda Lindstrom. He spoke with a rather charming Tennessee drawl.

"Nerves," Thor said to Chris. "The boy's nervous and probably the tense type that can't slough off into sleep like those others."

Bridie, on her way, paused to talk to him, he looked up at her though his gaze flitted and flicked from her to Chris at the rear of the plane or to Gerda forward, he even glanced out of the window from time to time as though fearful of missing something. In three minutes Bridie had his name, age, destination, hopes, plans, background.

"Come on over here, Chris," she called out, "talk to this boy. I guess he thinks he's going to a place like Detroit or something, the way he talks."

"Sh! Bridie!" Chris whispered as she joined Bridie quickly.

Bridie was impervious to shushing. "This young lady has lived in Alaska all her life, born here. Chris, this boy used to be a telephone lineman on a repair gang in Nashville, Tennessee, can you imagine! Sending these thin-blooded Southern boys up here!"

"You'll love it," Chris said, too briskly, as Bridie moved away. "You'll get used to it in no time. There's hunting and fishing, it's warmer in July, and——"

"Yes'm," he agreed, politely. "I sure like hunting, I sure would like to get me a bear, one those big white jobs you can th'ow on the floor or nail up on a wall, head and all, they weigh over a thousand pounds—live, that is—the hide would just about cover a good-size room. I sure would like to get me one of those, send it home to my—send it home."

Gerda Lindstrom's voice. "Please fasten your seat belts. We are coming into Tocktoo, please keep your seats we are only stopping to take on passengers."

The giant Tennesseean peered out into the infinite expanse of tundra below. The guileless eyes turned toward Chris. "Ma'am," he said, softly, "can you tell me what size city this is we're coming in to?"

They were descending near a huddle of four or five Quonset huts encircled by stupendous mountain peaks that cut off the universe. No roads, no entrance no exit no anything but a haphazard landing strip toward which the plane was tiptoeing gingerly. The plane touched, stopped, its maw opened and swallowed two waiting construction workers; soared again. The construction men carried their precious tool bags. Wordlessly they relaxed on the spring-sprung shabby seats and were asleep almost instantly. Beat beat beat beat sounded the pulse of the plane again as they leveled off and were again on the way to Oogruk. The young Eskimo had pressed the buzzer and Gerda had brought him a red woolen blanket in addition to the one he already had tucked about his knees. He had not taken coffee, she had brought him a glass of milk.

"Well, say," the young Tennesseean drawled, "I thought you said that guy was an Eskimo. How come he rates an extra blanket and drinking milk? I thought they lived in snow houses and ate blubber and raw fish."

"They do," Chris said, "when they have to—that is, would if they had to. That young man's name is Frankie Ipoluk, he's hurt his leg, he pulled a ligament or something, he's going home this vacation. Frankie is the basketball champion of all the Alaska High School League teams. He's been going to Baranof High but his folks live in Oogruk."

"Champion! No kidding! Say! I'd like to talk to him. Does he talk English?"

"Oh, yes." Politely. "Frankie's planning to be a teacher—a schoolteacher. He won a scholarship and he's going to Baranof College next year." She returned to her seat.

The middle-aged man in the eyeglasses and the Basque beret had been padding up and down the aisle peering through every window except that which belonged to his own seat. He now stopped beside Chris and Thor.

"How do you do, sir," he said, very formally.

Thor cheerfully returned the greeting as one who, for fifty years, has been addressed by strangers.

"You made this trip before?" the man asked.

"Yes. Many times."

"Is that right!" He seemed relieved at this. He raised his voice to address the woman of the flowered hat. "Irma, this gentleman here has made this trip a lot of times." He turned again to Thor. "All right, is it? I mean, this plane," he indicated the moose stacked layer on layer to the cabin's roof, "and those mountains out there, Irma thought it might get to be kind of rugged. But you say it's all right?"

His grayish face, his graying hair, the eyeglasses, the gray gloves, the topcoat, gave him the look of a retired insurance salesman, perhaps, or an accountant who had cannily invested in an annuity.

"You can relax and enjoy every minute of the trip," Thor assured him. "The record of this line is just about perfect. And the land around here is what they call permafrost ground. It's frozen all the year round. You can put a plane down on it anywhere, any time."

"Say! I wouldn't want to do that." Uneasily he looked out at the formidable landscape. "You live around here?"

"I live in Baranof."

"You Alaskans, you're great kidders." The man's laugh was as uneasy as his glance had been. "We played Baranof. Maybe you caught our act?"

"No," Thor said. "You mean——?" His mind rejected it.

The man extended his hand. "Polar is my name. Alwin Polar. My wife Irma back of you there."

"Storm. Thor Storm. This is my granddaughter Christine Storm."

"Happy to make your acquaintance," the man said. "We played Juneau Anchorage and Baranof so that makes us old sourdoughs I tell Irma. The Roller Polars our act is called, we do an act on roller skates, so the title isn't only catchy, it describes the act."

"No!" Thor exclaimed, stunned.

"We've toned it down a little the last few years, I don't whirl Irma by the heels any more like I used to, you could do that those days when you had a real stage you could work on. Nowdays, those nightclub little stages they're like a postage stamp. The old days I remember the audiences some of them, down front, used to try to duck under their seats they thought I would lose my grip and let her fly right over the footlights into their laps."

Bridie minced precariously up the aisle now, a laden paper plate in either hand. Thor stood up. "Bridie, give one of those to Mrs. Polar there, will you? And you keep the other and sit down beside her, she's never taken this trip before. Though," thoughtfully, "after the kind of work she's—well, anyway, you visit there with her, will you? Mr. Polar and I are going to have a chat in one of those vacant seats."

For the first time in her life, perhaps, Christine felt deserted. Well, she thought, we'll be in Oogruk by four and it certainly looks as if

Bridie is getting her wish about not wanting to be entertained by the pilot. She stared out of the window at the blue and crystal universe. Bridie's voice chattering through the beat of the engines was like piccolo notes through drumbeats. Christine closed her eyes. Beat beat beat beat went the engines. . . . From the seat behind her, Bridie's voice . . . You don't say! Well, it sounds like a hard life but you certainly have seen the world. . . . Settle down . . . Chicken farm in Jersey, oh, you'll never like that.

Last night Ross had said, I want to show you Oogruk, I specially want to show you Oogruk. The voices behind her ceased. She must have slept a little. Someone sat in the seat beside her, she opened her eyes instantly. It was only Bridie, who leaned close, her voice vibrant with the eagerness of one who imparts news.

"Those two," she confided. "They've lived the most interesting life. They're theatrical people, that's what she said, would you think to look at them. They used to be in vaudeville, she says vaudeville is dead, she can't understand how it happened, they've been known for years from coast to coast, the Roller Polars they're called, and now they play the night clubs, they're taking this trip because Barrow's the farthest northern town in America and they want to brag to their theater friends they've been farthest north and farthest south and farthest east and west. People are wonderful." Her voice rose. "Just wonderful!"

"What's wonderful?" Thor had finished his chat with the male half of the Roller Polars, he stood now beaming down on Bridie and Christine. "This trip is wonderful, I say, inside and outside. How did you make out with the Army, Christine?"

"He wants to shoot a polar bear," Christine reported. "He and the others are on their way to Imiak. For a year. He thinks it's a town."

Thor glanced toward the lad, thoughtfully. "A Dew Line Installation. A hilltop—a mountain, really. Mountain and tundra, no human foot or man-made thing ever touched there until the Distant Early Warning crew moved in. No place is more nowhere than Imiak. Yet how important it is. When I look down and see tracks down there I think, maybe there's a Hereafter that the righteous are always pining for, but it can't be more exciting and unpredictable than Alaska today."

"Oh, you!" Bridie scoffed. "You've been in love with Alaska for fifty years, it's getting to be a scandal."

The ruddy face looking so thoughtfully down at them creased in a rueful smile. "But the question is, does she love me?"

The forward door opened, Ross Guildenstern came through. He paused to chat a moment with Frankie Ipoluk. He came toward the three now. "Hi, Mr. Storm. Hi, Mrs. Ballantyne." He looked at Christine. "You want to come up front, take over for a while?"

"No, she don't!" Bridie trumpeted. "I'll get off if she does." They laughed agreeably at this timeworn joke. "And I wish you'd go steer this thing and not let it run wild in the sky," Bridie went on. "You want to chat with us, wait till we all get to Oogruk."

"That's what I wanted to know." He was still looking at Chris. "Where you going to be?"

"The Trading Post," Chris said. It was the first time she had spoken. "Is that right, Grampa?"

"Yes," Thor said. "Raffsky's Trading Post."

"It sounds rough," Chris said, happily, "and like old sourdough days."

Thor and Ross broke into shouts of laughter.

"What's so funny?" Chris demanded.

"You'll see," Ross said. "Look. After I drop you people at Oogruk I have to take these boys on up. I'll be back tomorrow morning, or maybe even late tonight. I've wangled it so I can stay a day and another night and fly you up to Barrow on the Wednesday run. I'd love to show you Oogruk and Barrow, too, I've got cousins all over the place, my grandmother lives in Oogruk, of course if you've got other plans—"

I am talking too much, he thought again, I always seem to when I'm talking to her, I wonder why, you know damned well why.

"I just want Christine to see something of this part of Alaska," Thor was saying. "Bridie, too, of course. September will be the end of it for two years, for Christine."

"No it won't," she said, quickly. "Thanksgiving vacation I'm going to come back up here with you, Grampa, and Ross said he'd take us on a polar-bear hunt, I'm like that boy who's going up with the Dew Line, I want to shoot me a thousand-pound polar bear, one of those big white jobs, he said, that you can th'ow on the floor."

"What floor?" Thor asked.

"Our cabin in Baranof. I think it's beginning to look awful."

"Do you?" Thor said, thoughtfully. "I'll have to fix it up. I don't know about Thanksgiving, though. Maybe Czar has other plans."

"There you go!" Bridie exclaimed. "Start pulling again, you'll tear her apart, mark my words."

Mildly Thor said, "I think I'll go talk to that Dew Line lad for a few minutes. They must have briefed him but perhaps it didn't take." He turned to glance at the soldier from Tennessee. "The backs of their necks look so young," he said. "It always upsets me a little." He was off down the hazardous aisle.

Bridie began to fidget, she tucked her blanket tighter, she took her compact from her bag, surveyed herself critically in its mirror, poked at her hair, sniffed very audibly, and, leaning back, shut her eyes.

Ross grinned. "I'm going, Mrs. Ballantyne. But everything's under control, really. The co-pilot's up front."

Bridie's eyes flashed open a second, closed again. "If he was as good as you are he'd be pilot. Nobody ever sold me a substitute. Look at those peaks, we just missed that one, this narrow valley."

"Watch for the sea," he said. "About another hour." He looked at Chris, his face was serious and intense out of all proportion to the lightness of his words. "The Guildenstern tour tomorrow. See Oogruk with a Native. The Strange Customs and Habits. Fishing Through the Ice. Weird Dances."

"Not if you're going to be like that," Chris said.

"I won't." He was off, he shut the cockpit door, disappeared.

The interior of the plane was colder now, you lifted your feet from the floor and wrapped the blanket around them, you turned up your coat collar and tucked the little pillow into your neck if you were seated beside the window. The cold seemed to cut through the closed door, the windows, the floor boards. "Might as well be flying in a sieve," Bridie said.

Gerda Lindstrom was entertaining the night-club entertainers.

. . . and the word Eskimo means Man Who Eats Sea Animals, they say. . . . Oh, yes, they still go whaling in skin boats but things have changed, nowadays sometimes they just step into a little bush plane, set it down on an ice floe, harpoon a whale and fly back the same day. . . . No, we don't fly over the North Pole. . . . Well, say, there's a town a little ways outside of Anchorage, Irma and I went out there in the bus when we were playing Anchorage it's called North Pole, that's the name of the town, I bet we must have sent a hundred post cards we bought there with North Pole on them, to our friends back east. . . .

Christine touched Bridie's arm. "Bridie, I think we're beginning to come down. My ears."

Gerda Lindstrom ceased being the hostess. Her voice took on the tone of stewardess authority.

"Fasten your seat belts, please, we will be in Oogruk in about ten minutes. Fasten your seat belts please."

19

There were a few young Eskimo loungers down at the airstrip waiting to see the plane from Baranof come in, just as, perhaps sixty years earlier, the boy Zebedee Kennedy had hung around the railway station in the little Massachusetts town of his birth, to see Number Eleven go through on its way to or from the great world outside. Oogruk did not boast an airport building. There was only the strip. You stepped off the plane into another century. The little one-street Eskimo village squatted on the shores of Bering Strait. Oogruk never had seen a train. Oogruk boasted one automobile only. Oogruk traveled by dog sled or by airplane. The centuries met and mingled in Oogruk.

"Why am I so excited?" Christine demanded.

"Travel," Thor said. "When you stop being excited by travel you've stopped being interested in the world."

"It's Alaska," Bridie announced, loyally. "More north and nearer the Pole. They say it sends out rays that pull you."

Late June and very cold. Mountains. Tundra. Sea. In the clear air the little wooden houses a mile distant were dark dots on the gray of ice and land. A station wagon awaited the passengers. It resembled a precarious assemblage of weathered driftwood.

Standing apart with two local airplane-company employees, Ross Guildenstern was checking his papers. Luggage was being unloaded. A slim young man stepped languidly out of the decrepit station wagon. There was about him an indefinable but actual elegance, his skin was golden, he was wearing gray slacks and a fawn-color pullover cashmere sweater, he looked vaguely Columbia University sophomore whose highly solvent father (in the wholesale dress-manufacturing business) pampers him.

Ross, glancing up, saw him, he threw an explanatory word to the two men with whom he had been talking, he came swiftly to join the men who now were piling bags on the car top.

"Hi, Norman! Here, let me help with those." Wordless, the young man lifted a palm in greeting. "Mrs. Ballantyne, this is Norman Raffsky—Mrs. Bridie Ballantyne, one of Baranof's most important citizens. . . . Miss Christine Storm." Norman Raffsky inclined his head in the slightest of bows. Thor Storm joined the group now, he put a hand on Norman Raffsky's shoulder.

"Hello, Norman, my boy." He did not pause for a return of this greeting, he did not seem to expect an answer. "There are two more passengers, they're not staying at your place, they're going to the Airline House, it's open early this year, isn't it?"

Norman fluidly transferred himself to the driver's seat, the Roller Polars, breathless, scrambled into the back, Bridie and Christine already were seated, Thor climbed in beside Norman Raffsky. Ross stuck his head in at the window at which Chris sat, he gestured toward the plane. "I'll be back tomorrow, sure, and maybe late today if I push it." He hesitated a second. "Norman's only eighteen," he said to no one in particular, his voice very low. He turned away abruptly, he ran swiftly back to the waiting plane.

The car started with a series of convulsive jerks, then they were off in a roar that subsided into a succession of snorts.

"Why did he say that?" Chris whispered to Bridie.

Bridie sniffed. "You know perfectly well why he said it."

They were nearing the huddle of houses and shacks, they skirted the shore. "Say!" Alwin Polar quavered from the rear seat, "this sure looks like the end of the world—or maybe the beginning, like the history books say, before it begun to thaw out."

"Wait till you see Barrow," Thor shouted back, "you'll think this is Chicago. No offense, Norman. See this while you can, it's the last of the American wilderness. Ten years from now there'll be night clubs and movie houses and Five-and-Tens and traffic lights, and tourist bureaus, and automobiles going nowhere, just like the rest of the world."

But the others were not listening. Their faces were stamped with a look of bewilderment. The station wagon seemed to be standing still. The world was rushing by. "Wait a minute!" Bridie yelled. "What's happening!"

Gently Thor said, "Stop a minute, Norman, will you?" The station wagon shivered to a standstill. The world rushed by even faster than before. They were on the beach path, and Thor pointed toward the ice-packed water.

"Why, Bridie! And you, too, Chris. You ought to know. You've seen the spring breakup often enough. Here it's later and bigger and swifter. That's the ice going out. Now that we're standing still you can see it isn't the globe that's whirling. It's rushing down from the Arctic to the Bering Sea. Did you ever see a current like that? You never will, anywhere. If you were to hop one of those big ice plateaus whirling past us there, you'd get a free ride to Nome in no time—if you stayed on."

Norman Raffsky, sitting moodily at the wheel, now spoke for the first time.

"We have a night club," he said, icily, "and a movie, and the barbershop has a man who does women's hair. Every girl in Oogruk has a permanent. The Dew Line gang is coming in next month, they'll be here years. Engineers. Mechanics. Carpenters. Truckers. Cat-skinners." He started the car again, it leaped into the air like a bronco spurred. "Traffic lights!" His voice rose above the engine's snarl.

"No!" Thor roared. Then, "That's good. That's good. At least, I hope it's good."

The car rounded a slight curve and stopped with a final snort and rattle, before a neat white-painted two-story building. Oogruk's skyscraper. In large black letters the sign painted on the front read:

RAFFSKY'S HOTEL
AND
TRADING POST

"But it isn't a trading post at all!" Chris protested. "It's as big as the Pole Star Hotel back home, and better-looking. I thought it would be a log cabin, with wolves howling outside."

"You sound like a tourist, Christine," Thor said, almost crossly for him.

Bridie stepped gingerly out into the blinding late-June sunshine, the icy late-June air. A woman from Mars, on Fifth Avenue, could not have seemed more incongruous than this modish matron in the midst of Oogruk's bleak wastes. She straightened her hat, wrapped her coat more firmly about her.

"I've known Isador Raffsky for thirty-five years. The only wolves around his place are the skins he's bought from the trappers. He's come to the Pole Star Hotel every spring for all that time, till just lately." She turned to Norman Raffsky, silent, remote in the front seat. "Why'n't you ever come with your father, see a little city life and bright lights?"

Christine, waiting for his reply, found herself fitting adjectives to this young man, and discarding them.

"City life does not interest me," Norman said.

The Roller Polars' anguished faces peered through the car window. "I wish we were staying here at this place," they pleaded. "We'd rather stay here with you folks." Norman threw the car into gear. "No room." Then, over his shoulder to Thor, "Back with your bags in a minute." He drove on.

In the doorway of his vast store stood Isador Raffsky, trapper, fur trader, merchant. He had come from his native Poland at seventeen. He knew every infinitesimal Eskimo village in the Arctic. He had mushed a dog sled hundreds—thousands of miles. He had frozen and hungered, he had battled the blinding blizzards, he had slept in Eskimo huts and gratefully eaten rotted meat. His credit was sound from Point Barrow to New York. As he stood now in the doorway of his huge store, a grizzled, compact, ruddy little man welcoming his guests, he looked like a thousand other compact shrewd and friendly men standing at the doors of their shops in Fargo, North Dakota, and Houston, Texas, and Cleveland, Ohio, and Appleton, Wisconsin.

He made a little bow now, it resembled in a warmer way the courtly inclination that his son Norman had made at the airport.

"Thor, my boy!" He, not Thor the older man, became the patriarch, Thor, the young David. "Mrs. Ballantyne! After all these years you are here."

For the two men this seemed to be an occasion of importance. Thor spoke with serious formality. "Christine, this is my old friend Isador Raffsky. . . . My granddaughter Christine Storm, I've brought her up here at last."

Isador Raffsky clasped his hands behind his back, he stood looking at Christine as one would survey critically a painting in a gallery. Chris was not embarrassed, she was rather drawn to this little man, she had, through the years, been surveyed thus by numberless grizzled Alaska contemporaries of Czar and Thor. She thought, Now he's going to say he knew my father and mother and my grandfathers and grandmothers, and I'll say, oh, did you, Mr. Raffsky, and then he'll go off into a long do about one time when.

Isador began to shake his head now, in agreement with his inner findings. "The Norwegian and the New Englander and the Westerner and the Eskimo. They're all there, mixed together. What a country! What a country!"

Bridie had had enough of this drama. "Now, Isador, this isn't the Fourth of July. I want Chris to meet Mrs. Raffsky." She raised her voice to reach a woman who was standing behind the counter in a corner across the store. "Leah, you being high and mighty with me! I haven't seen you in—what is it now—anyway five years." She was crossing the store to the counter, talking as she went. "I guess you've been by-passing us for Seattle."

Mrs. Isador Raffsky was wrapping a hunk of Cheddar cheese, two cans of mushroom cream soup, a pound of hamburger and a cellophane sack of hard candies. An Eskimo woman in a red calico bag-like garment over her long fur parka picked up the paper sack. An infant was pouched on her back, inside the parka. A boy of two or three walked at her side, another child was palpably on the way. Mrs. Raffsky manipulated the cash register, nodded to the woman with as much manner as she now displayed in greeting Bridie. Strangely silent, like her son Norman. Bridie, always articulate, seemed more voluble than ever, in contrast.

"My, you haven't changed a bit, Leah, not a line in your face, I've got a whole new set of wrinkles. Chris is dying to meet you and the girls, where are they, anyway, I thought they'd be down at the airport . . . Chris, here's Mrs. Raffsky wants to say hello to you. Say hello now to Leah Raffsky."

Christine stared, unaware that she was staring. One simply did not say hello to Mrs. Raffsky. One does not say hello to the sculptured head of Nefertiti in a museum. By some inexplicable alchemy of the centuries Leah Raffsky's darkly luminous slanting eyes, her high cheekbones curving down to the delicately sensuous mouth, the carriage, the manner, all might have been copied complete from ancient Egyptian royalty. Untutored in the lore of royalty, ancient, Egyptian, or otherwhere, Mrs. Raffsky was totally unaware of this resemblance. Amidst the cheeses, the canned goods, the housewares, the hardware displayed in the well-stocked trading post, Mrs. Raffsky was wearing a short boxy lemon-yellow jacket with a small standing collar, it was cut with reticent elegance like a Chinese woman's coat; fine black wool trousers and tiny black flat slippers. Her skin was somewhat warmer than ivory, her black hair was pulled back tightly in a knot at the nape of the neck.

Now she inclined her head and smiled a little in acknowledgment of the jovial introductions. Christine, to her own discomfiture, found herself babbling a bit. "Mrs. Raffsky, what a wonderful store! I didn't dream it would be anything like this, I want to see everything, why, there's absolutely everything here."

This certainly explains Norman, she was thinking.

Mrs. Raffsky smiled faintly, was silent.

"Name it," Isador Raffsky said. "We got it."

"I'm sure," Christine murmured. "Grampa didn't tell me. I thought it would be wolf skins and mukluks and bacon."

"Those we got, too."

Christine had been trained to observe. Her years with Thor, her familiarity with the workings of a newspaper, her friendship with Addie and Paul Barnett, had taught her not only to look, but to see. Now her eye, swiftly traveling the big orderly close-packed trading post, was baffled. Modish dresses, whole hams, jewelry, bath towels, a turret lathe, ripe olives, white fox furs; potatoes, *Time* and *Life* magazines, sirloin steaks, frozen strawberries; shoes, chocolate cookies, lamps, pink plastic tables; frying pans, double boilers, mukluks, gloves, bolts and screws. Impressed but disappointed, her baffled gaze turned toward Thor. Her expression was vaguely reproachful.

"This is the new Alaska," Thor said, as though she had asked him a question. "We knew the old one, didn't we, Isador? It's gone. This is your Alaska, Christine. Take over."

"Whoever's Alaska it is," Bridie retorted, "they can run it but I'd like to go up to my room, if you've got one for us, that is."

"Now, Bridie," Thor chided her. "Now, Bridie."

"You and Isador want to do reminiscening you can go off and do it on your own time, later. I get off a plane, I don't want to have to listen to yarns about the good old dog-sled days."

With a gesture Leah Raffsky indicated that they were to follow her. As they ascended the stairs their bags awaited them in a neat row on the landing. There had been no sound of Norman's return.

Christine had visualized bunks, prickly gray blankets and oil lamps. The walls of this upper hall, wide and bright, were painted pink. On either side the open doors revealed neat bedrooms furnished in modern light wood, you glimpsed bedside lamps and pale blue coverlets and flowered chintz. The windows were tightly shut, but from the bare yard of the unpainted little house across the way, where they sprawled or paced, you heard the high grating snarl and whine of the Malemutes.

Leah Raffsky made a little gesture toward this room and that.

Chris and Bridie and Thor peered in. Bridie took over. "Now, Chris, if you want to take this one—it's the cutest—I'll take that one on the other side. Thor, which one you having?"

Thor was enjoying the look of incredulity on Chris's face. "Any one. They're all too luxurious for me, I'm not used to all this roughing it in the wilds of Alaska. Next year they'll probably have a television in every room." He swung the bags into the bedrooms and clumped down the stairs. When Bridie and Chris turned to speak to Leah Raffsky she had disappeared.

"What goes on here!" Chris demanded rather crossly.

From the far end of the long bright hall came the sound of muted music, there were girlish giggles and laughter and high young voices. Permeating all else, the air was fragrant with the scent of tender things being roasted, of sweet things being baked.

"It's the Raffsky girls!" Bridie said. "I was wondering. Come along, Chris." She rushed down the hall, Chris, following, saw her throw her arms about two girls in the doorway at the far end. "Chris, meet the two Raffsky girls, this one's Elinor and this one's Nancy."

"Hi!" the two said, in unison. Each looked exactly like the other, and both looked exactly like Isador Raffsky. And Norman, Chris thought, looks just like their mother; it should have been the other way around. She now said hi in turn and was conscious of a slightly dazed feeling, inured though she had been since birth to the incongruities of Alaska.

She looked about her. On a vast blue velvet couch, a book in his hand, lay the elegant figure of Norman Raffsky. He did not glance up. A phonograph just beside the couch was playing a Philadelphia Symphony Orchestra recording of Rimsky-Korsakov's Scheherazade. On the floor was a deep-pile fawn-colored carpet that made a pleasant background for the blue chairs and couches, the pale pink walls. Half of one entire wall was a window of thick plate glass through which, separated only by a narrow strip of stony beach, you looked out across the gray shifting surge of Bering Strait and the dizzying ice floe just below.

"What an attractive room!" Chris said, rather lamely. She was bursting with unanswered questions, her lively curiosity had, all her life, been fostered by Thor. She wanted to find him now and ask him questions and questions and questions.

Bridie, meantime, was doing pretty well in that field. "Why'n't you girls meet us at the airport, I looked for you, and downstairs in the store."

The Raffsky girls, in features, manner and deportment, were like two nice plump upper Bronx girls you might see having an ice-cream soda at Schrafft's at five, now transplanted, incongruously, to the frigid wilderness of the Bering Sea.

"Mama doesn't like us to go down in the store much, except to help out, of course, when they're busy." Elinor's tone made plain that this arrangement was family battleground. "Or the airport, either."

Nancy Raffsky took up the theme in a tone equally aggrieved. "She says—and Papa too—that when the Dew Line gang gets here——"

Norman shut off the phonograph, shut his book, rose and left the room. Chris stared. No one else seemed to find this behavior strange.

"Something smells elegant!" Bridie called out. She had sauntered into the dining room and had then vanished into the kitchen.

"Come on," the two Raffskys said, happily, and linked arms with Chris. Friendly, outgoing as they were, Chris decided for a question or two even on such short acquaintance. Anyway, she could stand it no longer.

"Were you born here, I mean, have you always lived here? . . . Can anyone use these rooms, I mean do the roomers or guests use this as a public room, I shouldn't think. . . . Are there parties or . . . Where do you go to school . . . ?" She longed to ask about Leah Raffsky, but refrained here, at least. "Are there other girls—and boys of course"—she almost had said like you, but substituted—"your age, I mean . . . ?"

The Misses Raffsky, their father's daughters, had no secrets from the world, they were as voluble as their mother and brother were uncommunicative.

"We're going to school in Baranof next year, Mama wants us to, Papa doesn't but we are. . . . He wants Norman to go to M.I.T. that's Massachusetts Institute of Technology but Norman says he knows as much as they do now. . . . I love your dress did you get it in Baranof or send to Seattle . . . we've invited some people for dinner tonight to meet you, we love company."

"Tonight!" Chris said, doubtfully.

"Ross can't make it back by dinnertime," Nancy said immediately, with the aplomb of a mind reader.

"How did you know he had planned to get back?" Startled.

"Oh, everybody in Oogruk knows everything about everybody, it's the mukluk grapevine. There's two girls here from Philadelphia, they're coming for dinner, and their husbands are schoolteachers here, they're both Princeton men, the girls don't like it very well here, I think, but here their husbands earn about five times as much as they could in the States, they say they're going to try to stick it out for three years. . . . Lowell Aragrook is coming to dinner, too, he and his wife, he's in charge of all the Alaska reindeer herds up here, but he's been fishing for beluga. I heard he got the first catch of the season maybe he'll try to beach them tonight, I hope not because you might want to see it and there's going to be some Eskimo dancing especially for you, maybe Lowell won't beach them until tomorrow morning. . . ."

"Chris!" Bridie called from the kitchen. "Come and see this."

Reindeer herd. Belugas. I thought I knew Alaska. Grampa Thor brought me up here to learn. "What's a beluga?"

But the Raffsky girls had propelled her into the kitchen under their own power—a kitchen that was modern, metallic and pastel as a *Ladies' Home Journal* double-page ad.

"Just throw your eye over that, would you," Bridie said. Her gesture, as she indicated a mammoth cake—a Mount McKinley of a cake—amounted to a formal introduction. Iced in pink, with chocolate arabesques and pink flutings, it bore a message on its massive bosom. Welcome Thor and Christine. "There wasn't room for another name,"

Nancy explained, apologetically to Bridie. "We'll bake another cake tomorrow, just for you."

"Tomorrow! There's food enough right here this minute to last fifty people a week. A turkey in the oven the size of an ox. You must have every room filled and everybody coming for dinner."

"Roomers! We don't cook for roomers. They eat at Lena's Lunch down the beach, this is a dinner party for our friends to meet you," Elinor said.

"I call that lovely. Isn't that lovely, Christine! Who all's coming, now?"

"The reindeer herder," Chris began, blithely, "and two Princeton men and their wives——"

"And Doctor Kramer from the hospital," Nancy now added. She had opened the oven door and was basting the turkey. "And Mrs. Hoagland the Visiting Nurse, and Father Gilhooley——"

"We know about him, don't we, Bridie?" Chris said.

"—and Ross Guildenstern if he gets back in time but I don't think so, and Bob Shelikov's up from Klawock——"

Now her recital of the guest list was muffled by a sudden whirring and clanking. Elinor had turned a knob.

"What's that?" Bridie yelled.

"Electric dishwasher!" Elinor shouted. "That's why we didn't hear you when you came, it was going. Would you like a cup of tea or coffee now, dinner isn't until six. And a piece of cake." Then, as Bridie cast a look at the towering confection in the corner. "Not that one. That's for dessert with vanilla ice cream and hot fudge sauce. Though maybe if I cut you a little bit of a slice now, from the side . . ."

"I'll wait," Bridie decided.

Nancy seemed the more practical of the two. "Did somebody tell you where your rooms are, and everything? Mama never bothers. Sometimes people take a room and come back and find out somebody else is in it. You know which is your bathroom?"

"Not really!" Chris said. "Not our own——!"

Nancy giggled. "No, Papa wasn't that wild, anyway. But there's one for the men and one for the women, and a separate john besides. Papa said he was going to have the most up-to-date place in the Arctic Circle."

"He sure got it," Bridie said. She peered into a pink-tiled and porcelain bathroom. "When your pa used to come to Baranof every year he used to tell me about you two girls, and Norman, and then he'd go on about how he was going to build everything up-to-date, and all of you were going to college. I knew he'd done like he planned, but I never dreamed it would be like this. Did you, Chris?"

"On the way up I said that this trip might be too rugged for you and you let me say it."

"Maybe it will," Bridie said, "wait and see."

"Where's Grampa?" Chris demanded, wrathfully.

"He's probably downstairs with Papa," Nancy said. "Look, if there's anything you want, just ask Elinor or me, but now I've got to go and set the table."

Contritely Chris said, "Let me help you—that is, I'd like to in just a minute, but first I want to say something to Grampa."

Bridie shook her head. "Now, Chris, don't go asking a lot of your questions, your Grampa's busy. Wait till after dinner or tomorrow——"

"I can't wait," Chris said, as a simple statement of fact. She was off down the hall to the stairway. The Tanagra-like figure of Leah Raffsky was there at the store counter, she was wrapping a large club of bologna sausage for a waiting Eskimo boy. Male voices and the scent of cigars led Chris to the open door of Isador Raffsky's cluttered office. The two men sat, smoking, talking; relaxed to the point of aloofness. It was clear that Chris was not at the moment necessary to their well-being.

"I never saw you smoke a cigar before," Chris exclaimed, inadequately.

Thor removed the cigar from between his lips and surveyed it with a detached admiration. "Isador's private stock. I don't get a chance at one like this very often. Just once a year, when I come up here."

"Grampa Czar smokes cigars all the time."

Isador Raffsky squinted up through the haze. "A cigar is special. Something special. You smoke a pipe alone, you smoke a cigarette alone. You smoke a cigar with a friend."

Thor looked at the girl's puzzled face, he knew the questioning look, he had never, since her early childhood, ignored it.

"Something you want to know, Christine?"

"Well, you're busy—I thought maybe you'd be just walking around——"

"If it's about the Raffskys, just ask it. Isador'll tell you anything you want to know, won't you, Izzy?"

Chris was genuinely embarrassed. "Another time will do. Later."

"Sit down sit down." Isador indicated a chair by throwing its burden of papers to the floor. "So what you want to know? I came a boy here from Poland, I didn't have a zloty. I ran around on a dog sled buying the stinking skins from the Eskimos, when I think what I paid them—well, those days it was different in Alaska. Say, Alaska! No different from other places. Vanderbilt was a fur trader, wasn't he, and Astor, and all those dudes in the Hudson's Bay Company, those pelts they traded had the same stink mine did. I could write a book about it, if I could write a book. Say, Thor, am I in your book, maybe?"

"Yes."

"It ain't all good. And it ain't all bad. But good and bad, it's history, we're history, you and Bridie and me and all the old-timers. But it's over now. Who knows Alaska, only us! My children are going to get an education because it's going to be different. I can smell it. Not like me and Leah had it. It's going to be another world."

Chris made up her mind to stop this foray into the future.

"Mrs. Raffsky?" she ventured.

"What you want to know about Leah?"

"I mean—she's so lovely-looking and—and different. And young—and kind of—well—mysterious." She glanced rather apprehensively then at Thor, but he was smiling and listening, amiably enough.

"Sure she's young, Leah was twenty years younger than me when we were married. I guess she is yet. Leah's mother was half Eskimo, her father was a missionary up here in the old days in the Arctic Circle. And what do you think he was? A rabbi! Did you ever hear before of such a thing! Catholics and Presbyterians and Quakers and Methodists and Baptists you've heard of, missionaries. But Leah's father was a Jewish rabbi and a missionary. From Russia. It's a story."

"I've always wondered why they didn't do more proselytizing," Thor mused. "They're so stiff-necked about their religion. Leah's father is the only Jewish missionary I've heard of since Jesus."

20

Ross Guildenstern had not appeared at dinner, he had not come in during the evening. The evening lengthened to nine, to ten o'clock. Dinner finished, the women sat in the big pink sitting room. The men had remained in the dining room, they formed a close little huddle at one end of the table after the dishes had been cleared away. In the manner of masculine groups their voices were low, their interest concentrated. For the time the world of women had ceased to exist.

Chris drifted over to Bridie on the couch, she stood behind her ostensibly to pat into place a waved lock of fashionably slate-gray hair which did not need patting. Chris pitched her voice low for Bridie's ear, but not so low as to be drowned by the constant music of the phonograph.

"What do you suppose they're talking about in there?"

"Alaska."

"Such old-fashioned behavior. I feel like a harem inmate. I'd like to go in and hear what they're talking about."

"You're in Eskimo country."

The ten o'clock night sun glared boldly through the wall of plate glass. From outside came sounds usually associated with daytime; the high voices of children, laughter, the yapping of dogs, the tattoo of a hammer pounding on wood. The Raffsky girls were handing round coffee for the third time since dinner. The remains of the massive cake, reduced now to a Roman ruin, lay dejectedly on a side table. Chris found herself listening for the sound of an airplane in the clear Arctic air. She wandered over to the window that faced the water. Under that bright sky the beach path was busy as a boulevard. For Chris there was nothing remarkable about this activity during the summer-night hours. Baranof, too, tried to cram a year of sun and fun and work into two summer months. Eskimo women, their ugly bright-colored cotton shifts covering their parkas, paced the path with their curiously waddling gait. Almost invariably a solid round lump protruded at the back, from waist to shoulder blade. A sleeping baby tucked away cosily, with a cushion of moss for a diaper and mattress. Bands of small children screeched and ran and played, they skipped stones into the open water beyond the ice blocks, the older boys jumped onto the swift-moving frozen blocks and were borne perilously downstream, though a single foot-slip might seal them forever beneath the ponderous rushing plateaus. An Eskimo was working on his boat, he had mounted it on trestles, it was his hammer that rang clearly. Two small girls were bumping up and down on a haphazard seesaw with a flimsy box for a fulcrum. But they were not seated. They stood upright. Each time the board hit the pebbled beach they yelled with happy shock. The length of the beach, as far as the eye could see, was etched with poles and racks on which hung the diamond-shaped pieces of seal blubber and seal meat, out of reach of the hungry leaping sled dogs. Oogruk wasted little time on sleep during the precious sun nights. The long months of black winter days and starlit winter nights were the time for sleep and sleep and sleep.

Chris turned away from the window, she thought it would be fun to stroll down the beach; to stop and talk with the men and women and children. That's what you're here for, she said to herself, feeling very frustrated. The wife of one of the Princeton men was describing the clothes depicted in the last number of *Harper's Bazaar*.

"My sister gave me a year's subscription for my birthday. I meant to bring this month's over, but I forgot. The baby was crying and the sitter came late as usual. You'll die when you see what they're wearing. I'm going home in August with the baby for two whole months and I won't even take anything with me except what I stand up in on the trip. I wrote Mom if she didn't present me with a whole new wardrobe I'd bring along my parka and just wear that. This is the first time I've been Outside in two years. I can't wait. Outside! Imagine!" She closed her eyes in ecstasy.

Bridie was wearing one of the modish silk dresses she had bought at the Hollywood Shop in Baranof. She plucked at it now, she sat very straight with a preening effect. "A person would think you were serving time in jail. Outside! Outside! People feel that way about it, they ought to do with less and stay Outside and leave Alaska for those that love it."

"Now, Bridie," Chris chided. She glanced around at the women's faces—resentful, friendly, uncomprehending, cautious, amused. "Mrs. Ballantyne is even more loyal to Alaska than I am. We're both worse than the Texans. People in huge remote areas are usually provincial." She smiled sweetly at the company. "I learned that in my freshman year at Baranof College."

The young Easterner was a well-bred girl, she had been taught not to be pert with her elders. To her, Bridie was a relic of a past century. Christine she considered definitely goofy.

Chris had been accustomed from childhood to an atmosphere of male or mixed conversation. Baranof men and women worked together, they shared the town's social life together, of necessity they often had to devise their own amusements. Conversation in Baranof was likely to be pungent, fresh-minted and thoughtful. How do you pass these long dark winter months in Alaska? Chris recalled now the standard joke in reply to the summer tourist's standard question. Talking and reading and breeding babies.

Lowell Aragrook, the reindeer herder, was speaking as she glanced again toward the quietly conversational dining room. He was wearing a good navy blue suit and a bow tie. On entering before dinner Chris had seen his parka just before he took it off. It was of finest seal, bordered with an intricate design in white ermine, she never had seen one so beautiful, she knew the value of these things, the time and labor that went into their making. This was, she knew, a museum piece. Mrs. Aragrook, in the sitting room, was taking absolutely no part in the women's conversation. Amiable, half smiling, she simply sat like a good-natured bronze idol in a good black crepe dress and a good gold brooch and a pince-nez.

Oh, dear, what are they talking about in there, Chris wondered, with their heads close together? Not *Harper's Bazaar*. All this long flight up to Oogruk and now *Harper's Bazaar* indeed! The wilds of Alaska. I didn't come up here to eat ripe olives and ice cream with chocolate sauce and creamed mushrooms and turkey. Impulsively she walked into the dining room, pulled up a vacant chair, and simply sat there.

The men stopped talking.

"Something you want, Christine?" Thor asked.

"Yes. I want to know what you're talking about."

Only Thor appeared not to be startled by this statement. The other men smiled uncertainly; or their faces hardened in disapproval. They were silent a moment. Bob Shelikov, Territorial Senator up from Klawock, became jocular in the political tradition. "You fixing to run for Territorial Congresswoman, Miss Christine?"

"Not just yet," Chris said, and as determinedly jocular as he. "But maybe by the time I'm old enough and know enough it'll be United States Congresswoman I can try for."

Bob Shelikov was one of the conservatives who contended that Alaska wasn't ready for statehood. "Mmm, pretty girl like you will get married and have a family long before that, Miss Christine."

She sensed that Thor was displeased with her. But now he answered her question briefly and soberly.

"We were talking about something that wouldn't interest most women. You've heard it all a hundred times." He turned to the men. "You know, Christine was raised by two newspaper-publishing grandfathers. So political talk and Territorial arguments were her Mother Goose. Uh, let's see. It may sound pretty dry, just condensed. We were talking about Outside labor—you know—you've heard it all. From way up here, Seattle and San Francisco seem far away and not very important. Up here, if you can get a whale or a seal or two, or enough moose or reindeer meat, you're set for the winter. Or it used to be true. So it didn't matter, up here, if the big union heads in Seattle wouldn't allow Alaska labor to do Alaska work, and brought in seasonal Outside labor instead, boatloads of them and now planeloads of them. Thousands. And paid them in one lump after they got back Outside at the end of the season. But now it has begun to matter, even up here, and it's going to be more and more important. Alaskans like you, Christine, and the Raffskys, and Bob Shelikov here, and Czar for that matter, and those children yelling down there on the beach, we've all been Americans now for almost a hundred years. I've been trying to tell these young college men here"—he indicated the two young schoolteachers—"that maybe the time has come for a Boston Tea Party right here in Alaska."

A hubbub in the sitting room. "Ross!" shouted the Raffsky girls. He stood in the dining-room doorway, he was still in his pilot's uniform.

"Anybody want to see the Eskimo dances?"

Bridie had had enough of the pink sitting room. "Sure do. Where?"

"At the Company Hall down the beach. In about half an hour." The room had come alive, there was movement and purpose. "I brought some passengers down with me from Barrow. They're just here overnight, a bunch of engineers going back Outside. Look, I've got to change, I'll see you there." He was off down the hall.

Half the company decided against joining in this festivity. Their various reasons were legitimate enough. The baby sitters had been engaged until midnight only. Sleep. An early plane out. Tomorrow's work. Bob Shelikov wrapped it up neatly for the negative side when he said, "And anyway, if you've seen one Eskimo dance you've seen 'em all."

Certainly Bridie and Thor had seen these ceremonies countless times at winter festivals in Baranof, in Fairbanks, in Anchorage. They were as familiar as they were to the Eskimos themselves.

"Well, half an hour," he said now. "But I think we could do with a little sleep. Doctor Kramer's showing us through the hospital tomorrow, and you'll want to see the schools, and Father Gilhooley has some magnificent ivory and wood carvings and altar pieces. Then there's the dental clinic, too. Wonderful young couple there, the Native Service dentist and his wife. She's a nurse. In the winter the Eskimo patients come in by dog sled from the villages hundreds of miles away. The whole family. Even now you'll see more bad Eskimo teeth and good Eskimo babies in that office than—"

"Oh, Grampa, let's not be so worthy tomorrow, first thing in the morning, I mean."

"What do you want to do?"

"Just wander around and look at things and talk to the people on the beach. Can't we do your program in the afternoon?"

"You'd think Ross Guildenstern was paying for this trip instead of your grandfather," Bridie said, with considerable bite in her tone.

But Thor only asked, mildly, "Just what have you got in mind, Christine. What do you want to do? This is your holiday, you know, not mine."

"Chris is all mixed up. Tired, I guess," Bridie said.

"I'm not tired! You didn't bring me all the way up here to sit on a blue velours couch and listen to a phonograph. Good heavens!"

"What's the child talking about?" Thor asked.

"She means, I suppose," Bridie explained, "that Ross Guildenstern's got some plan to show her around Oogruk. I can't see that it's any different from other Eskimo villages, only bigger."

"He was born here," Chris said, defensively. "He said his grandmother lives here, and the aunt and uncle who brought him up after his parents died. He said he wants to show us around tomorrow morning. I don't know why he made such a point of it."

"I do," Bridie said, grimly.

"Evidently you two are carrying on some kind of woman warfare that I don't understand. We'll see about half an hour of the dancing —after all, we've seen it all before, though not here. We'll get some sleep. You do exactly what you want to do in the morning. I would like you to see a little of my plan in the afternoon."

She was contrite at once. "It was rude of me to come stalking into the dining room that way."

They were walking down the beach path. They could hear the Eskimo drums now. The door of the Company Hall was open. A group whose ages ranged from six to sixty clustered there. Periodically they were shooed away by someone inside, immediately they returned. The dark faces were merry and unresentful.

"Why don't they let them come in?" Chris wondered.

"Costs a dollar," Thor said, "each. Eskimos don't dance for nothing in the tourist season. They've caught on to civilization, right enough. After the dance has really started they'll let these neighbors slip in free."

Arctic daylight at night streaming through the unshaded windows, combined with the artificial glare of electric bulbs overhead, gave to the room an effect half eerie, half sordid. At the far end of the long room the Eskimo drummers sat cross-legged on the floor, the great flat circle of their walrus-tissue drums spread before them. Their voices rose and fell in a chant timed to the beat of the drums. In the center of the floor a group of men and women—twelve or more—were moving together in a slow mystic dance which each individual dancer seemed, nevertheless, to be performing solo. Though the air of the room was close the dancers wore fur and hooded parkas ornamented with intricate designs, and on their shifting feet were mukluks. The dancers were not, for the most part, young. A few perhaps were thirty or forty. Others looked seventy or more. Now and then a child of eight or ten would step into the rhythmically moving group.

"Hi!" There, to greet them, was Ross Guildenstern. By some miracle, or a native knowledge of short cuts, he had changed from his pilot's uniform to khaki pants and leather jacket and was there at the hall ahead of them. "How about these seats? All right?"

"We're only staying about half an hour," Chris said, somewhat on the stately side. "Bridie's tired, and Grampa has a lot of plans for tomorrow."

"Tomorrow morning at nine you're starting out with me."

"Well, say!" boomed a familiar voice. "This is great! How you making out?" It was Alwin Polar of the Roller Polars, together with his gifted partner, still in the beflowered hat. But reason and the Arctic air had prevailed; she now wore over her pale blue coat a parka borrowed from the hotel guide. She and Bridie greeted each other like long-lost sisters. How you making out? . . . We're real comfortable, I don't say it's any Waldorf, but you wouldn't ask a nicer room . . . what they call shee-fish for dinner Mr. Polar isn't much of a hand for fish but real tasty . . .

Alwin Polar clapped a hand on Ross's shoulder. "Pardon me, ain't you the young fellow on the plane? The pilot on our plane?"

"Yes."

Polar looked intently at him, he stared at the faces of the dancers, the chanting drummers. "Say! I didn't know you were—uh—you look different," he finished, lamely. "It was the uniform, I guess."

Ross smiled his charming smile. "Same fella."

"They told us about this dance back there at the place we're staying. You run these dances?"

"No." Agreeably he went into a polite explanation. "Usually the dances don't start as early in the season as this because the tourists aren't here. They run them every evening in the season." With a gesture he indicated the dancers and the drummers. "They make a little money this way. So I rounded up an audience."

Bridie took over. "It's real interesting, isn't it? Specially if you haven't seen Eskimo dancing before. I've seen it a lot of times. But it's real interesting—for a little while, that is."

Alwin Polar now surveyed the slowly shifting gesticulating group with the coldly appraising eye of the professional.

"Twenty-five years ago they could have made it, maybe, on the small time, snappier costumes, of course, white fur and so on for the women. But the whole act needs pepping up. Variety. Pace."

Now Thor, his tone kindly, his eyes amused, took up the impromptu explanation on a more scholarly note. "Eskimos never used to dance for money. It started as a ceremony, they danced to express themselves. This kind of public entertainment came with the tourist trade. These dances act out a story. Every gesture of the arms, the head, the feet has a meaning. Every gesture follows the story the drummers are chanting."

"You mean they're saying something—those men there with the drums?" Polar turned to Ross. "You understand what they're saying? What's it mean?"

Ross was silent a moment, he turned away from the clumsy friendly man and his well-meaning wife. His attention concentrated on the drummers and on the women's chorus seated on the floor behind them; on the stylized postures of the dancers. Years later Christine was to see the performance of a group of touring Balinese dancers in a New York theater and realize that their movements, form, even characteristics were akin to this dancing Eskimo group now weaving a dream story across the floor of the shabby Arctic hall.

Now Ross turned back to the tourists. Chris was startled by the curiously protective maternal feeling that surged through her as she looked at the merry upturned face, the laughing eyes.

"It sounds kind of foolish when you tell it, a literal translation. Well, this hunter went out to get food for his wife and his children, they had had no food for days because the man had been pierced weeks before by the tusks of a walrus when the man was on the sea in his kayak. And now as he walked toward the sea he saw a wolf, but as he prepared to kill the wolf the wolf turned into a caribou with antlers and it sped toward the water and as it ran the hunter saw that the antlers were turning into tusks like those of a walrus and he knew then——" Ross broke off, his smile a little rueful. "Well, you get the idea. It wouldn't interest you very much. Tribal stories never are very interesting."

"That isn't always true, Ross," Thor argued, as though they were conversing cosily in a lamplighted sitting room. "The Bible is largely made up of tribal tales told first by word of mouth through hundreds of years. Very dramatic, too, many of them."

"Now, Thor!" Bridie remonstrated. "That's blasphemous."

One of the group down from Barrow touched Ross on the shoulder. "Cap, you know how to do those dances? Yourself, I mean."

"Yes, some of them. I used to try to do them when I was a kid.

You just follow the story as the singers tell it. This means wolf, see. And this means caribou. And this——"

He stepped forward then and in a moment he had mingled with the dancers and was indistinguishable from them as they moved and turned and gestured and postured, children and ancients and those of middle years.

The next moment, to Bridie's horror and to her own surprise, Chris too stepped forward and joined the dancers. She kept her eyes on the dancer just in front of her, she raised her arm thus, she turned her head thus, she shifted her foot this way, that way, she too was almost indistinguishable among the shifting dancers except, perhaps, for the shining gold mass of her hair as her parka hood slipped back to her shoulders and the brilliant shafts of the midnight sun pierced the weather-beaten windows of the little Arctic village Eskimo hall.

21

Ross Guildenstern came down the beach path on the run.

Nine-thirty in the morning. He had said nine. As he ran the small fry of Oogruk trailed him like the tail of a meteor.

Bridie and Chris, too, were trailed by a like following, but not disturbingly. A swarm of black-eyed brown-skinned boys and girls had somehow sprung out of the earth as the two women had turned into the beach path. They came out of huts, they emerged from behind beached boats, they were merry as sprites, they were haphazard but not ragged, they pointed at Bridie's pillbox turban, at her high-heeled pumps, her modish coat. They were not jibing or offensive. They had seen and become accustomed to visitors who came to Oogruk on the daily planes, a strange race known as Tourists. But Bridie was something special, they sensed this as they beheld her elegance, her blue-white hair, her spirited face with the guileless dabs of rouge and the vermilion lipstick.

"Hi!" they yelled, as they ran alongside, as they ran ahead, backward, as they trailed, the smallest of them trailing. "Hi!" Like any child from California to Maine. They stared at Christine and Bridie with the embarrassing inescapable gaze of children.

As they ran they pointed and said something that sounded like "Booga." They pointed, not at Bridie or Chris, but at something further down the beach.

"What do you suppose they mean, for heaven's sake," Bridie said.

"Ross could tell us."

"Ross." Bridie rolled the r and hissed the double s. "He said nine, it's nine-thirty or more now, and he hasn't showed up. There's plenty to see, Ross or no Ross, and I don't mean hospital clinics like Thor said, either. I didn't come all this way up here to see hospitals, I had enough of that time I was nursing. Not that they ain't a fine thing, with all this T.B. and worse the Eskimos have."

"Booga! Booga!" chanted the children. One of them even tugged at Christine's parka.

Chris bent over the child. "What do you mean, booga?"

"Hi!" shouted an adult male voice from a distance. He came on the run up the beach with a stream of merry impish black-eyed children trailing him.

"I'm sorry. I got an A.C.S. message. I had to go out to the airport. Are the kids bothering you? I hope you didn't give them anything. They're not supposed to do this."

"But they didn't do anything," Chris said. "They're just children."

Ross put a hand gently on the head of the littlest girl, now they clustered round him, they looked up at him suddenly mute. He said something to them in their own language, softly. Their faces changed, they looked thoughtful, the tallest among them, a boy of about nine, skipped down to the beach, he searched a moment among the stones, he picked up a bit and ran with it to Christine and proffered it. It was one of a million like it.

"Thank you." This plainly was expected. "What did you say to them, Ross?"

"I said you were visitors, that the polite thing is to offer gifts to visitors, never to take gifts from them. They know that. They've been spoiled by the tourists throwing them pennies. As if they were little beggars."

"But they didn't. They were just saying something we didn't understand. Booga, or something like that."

His face cleared. "Beluga. Lowell Aragrook is beaching a couple of big ones. Come on. Come on, kids."

"You're upset about something. There was something in the A.C.S. message."

"Look, Chris, do you think you could go to Barrow late today instead of starting tomorrow?"

Bridie addressed herself to the world in general. "He's gone daft."

"I mean you, too, Bridie, of course. And Thor. I wish you would. Otherwise I can't fly you up. I just got orders, I have to pick up a bunch in Nome. You weren't going to stay more than a night and a day in Barrow, anyway. Then I'd fly you back here—that is, if you want more time here in Oogruk."

The two were alone in the midst of a ludicrous company. Bridie marching ahead in the splendor of velvet and fur and gloves like a parade commander. Eddying all around them the raggle-taggle sprites. Dogs had joined the little procession, or yapped from every compound as they swept by, the pale Malemute eyes staring balefully. Racks of meat and fish were drying on the beach. There was excitement in the air, the midget entourage was swelled now by the adult figures of striding Eskimo men and waddling Eskimo women.

"Of course I'd love to have you show us around Oogruk, Ross."

"Us?"

"Me, then. But if you can't you can't. I don't see why you're so grim about it. I've never seen you like this."

He laughed then, his face clearing like a child's. He is a little like a grown-up child, Chris told herself, suddenly. He always knows what he wants to do and then he just goes and does it. So she said this aloud. "You decide you want to do a thing. And then you do it."

"Isn't that all right? I've made up my mind I'm going to show you Oogruk today. My version of Oogruk. And then Barrow if I can. I'll do it if it costs me my job."

"I honestly don't know what's the matter with you, Ross Guildenstern."

"Yes you do."

In the half-shelter of a single strip of raised canvas on the windy beach a pretty girl was bent over a mysterious task. A young Eskimo girl. Two small boys sat with her on the pebbled strand. They were absorbed in watching her at her task. She glanced up as the little procession came by. "Hi!" she called to them.

"Hi!" Ross called in return. "Bridie! Stop a minute, will you? Come on down here, Chris, I want you to meet somebody."

The girl squatting on her heels on the beach was wearing modish black slacks and a tailored red shirt neatly tucked into her belt. On her small feet were white socks and stitched loafers of red leather. She was expertly cutting up a dead seal with an ulu. The two small boys sat absorbedly watching her.

"Joan," Ross said, "this is Mrs. Ballantyne, up from Baranof. And Christine Storm . . . my cousin, Joan Kungok."

"I'm happy to meet you," Joan said, prettily, and indicated the sharp bloody implement in her hand. "Excuse me, won't you, for not getting up," she said politely to the older woman.

"Well, for land's sakes," Bridie exclaimed, inadequately.

"How—how wonderful!" Chris said, and meant it. "I mean, imagine being able to—do you mind if I watch you a minute?"

"Of course not," the girl said. "I'm not very good at it, I've just learned how, really. You ought to see my mother do it, or my grandmother, they can do in ten minutes what takes me an hour."

The instrument in her hand was shaped like an old-fashioned meat chopper of the kind that cooks once used to mince food in a wooden bowl. Its blade was curved, her hand grasped the handle, with miraculous deftness she held the carcass with her left hand while she sliced the thick layer of blubber from the skin, it rolled down inside the skin as you would separate the meat of a melon from the rind. The seal looked mournfully up at her.

"What are you going to do with that?" Bridie demanded.

"Eat it," Joan Kungok said, blithely. "Next winter. I don't like it any more, but the old people and some of the grownups do."

"I'd starve sooner," Bridie said tactlessly.

Chris covered this with a rush of words. "Hunks of raw meat never look very appetizing. I can't bear to look at those whole lambs hanging up by their heels in the butcher shop, with the neck sticking out. But lamb chops are delicious and this probably is too. . . . How do you cook it?"

Ross stood in silence. Joan Kungok went deftly on with her work.

The dead seal stared up at the group, its whiskers drooping, its teeth bared in a grimace of resentment. "There are lots of ways of cooking seal meat. You can eat it fresh or salted or dried. The old people like to eat the blubber. Maybe that's why they didn't die of tuberculosis years and years ago, the way so many of us young people do now."

"Hold it, Joan." Smiling down at her, Ross raised an arresting palm. "These ladies are Alaskans. They know the score. Mrs. Ballantyne used to be a nurse. Tell her what you're studying for."

The girl's serious young face became suddenly brilliant as she smiled up at Bridie. "I'm in training at the hospital here."

"Look at that, now! Bless you, child."

One of the small boys who had been peering into the open mouth of the seal now touched the jagged brown teeth with one plump forefinger. Then he wagged the finger chidingly at the creature as a Native Service Nurse must once have wagged a disapproving finger at the boy himself. "Too much candy," the child said, sternly. "Eat too much candy."

Christine's laugh rang out, and Ross's, and Bridie's high hoot.

"You darling!" Christine said, and stooped to kiss the top of the child's head. The tense situation of a few minutes ago had vanished.

"Come on, come on, girls." Ross waved them up the beach.

Joan called to them as they left. "I hear Lowell brought in the first belugas."

"Everybody," Bridie observed, "knows everything anybody's doing around here."

"You know everything everybody's doing in Baranof, don't you, Bridie?" Chris said.

"Well, yes, I guess I do. But I wouldn't think just a big fish would make such a ruckus in this town."

"It means summer up here," Ross explained. "The first beluga catch of the season. Anyway, a beluga isn't just a fish. It isn't even just a whale. Did you ever see a beluga?"

"What's it like, then?"

"You'll see."

The town seemed to be streaming toward the beach. Men, women, children, dogs. The electricity of excitement was in the air. Ross began to run, then he remembered and dropped back with the two women. Wordlessly he and Chris each thrust an arm through Bridie's left and right, they whisked her, laughing, protesting, along the rutted stony path toward the crowd gathered around the objects in the water below the sloping beach.

"Grampa Thor's not there," Chris said. She knew he would have towered head and shoulders above any crowd.

"There's the show folks," Bridie panted as she was whisked along. "The Polars. Her hat."

It was a strangely quiet crowd. Even the dogs had ceased their keening. As Ross approached with the two women the crowd parted to make a path for them. The children gazed up at him with shy mute admiration. The muscular stocky men, the women in their bright calico slips over their fur parkas turned their bronze benign faces toward him in friendship.

"Hello there!" the Roller Polars called to them. "Say, this is worth the trip." Irma Polar's earrings swayed and flashed and the flowers in her hat bobbed. Alwin Polar's ludicrously urban face beneath the Basque beret was a trifle pinched with the chill morning air, but the myopic eyes behind the glasses were wide as a child's with excitement. "Say, where's your Grandpa, he sure don't want to miss this."

"He's seen it. He's seen everything in Alaska," Christine called to them, breathlessly, as Ross made their way down to the water's edge.

Lowell Aragrook was standing hip-deep in the water. With him were two men. The three were lashing ropes firmly around the circumference of three white incredible objects that floated in the sluggish surge of the icy waters.

Lowell Aragrook, glancing up from his task, called to him. "Heh, Ross, give us a hand." And flung at him the end of a long thick rope. The men at work with him in the water flung another rope and another and another curling toward other strong deft hands on shore. And now the three weirdly beautiful objects that lay so dreamily on the water were secured at last and would pass through the final act that would forever end their cycle in the Arctic seas.

They lay gleaming white as ermine, the male and the female great white whales. The third was not white like its elders, its coat was pale gray, it was an infant, it still wore its baby fur. Half submerged in the shallow water they were eerie, spectral.

"Take hold here and pull," Ross said. A dozen—twenty—thirty hands were at the ropes now. Bridie's heels dug into the stony sands as she pulled, the Roller Polars were leaning their weight against the white monsters, Chris, in line just behind Ross, tugged with all her strength.

"Greek mythology," she panted in Ross's ear, "at Baranof."

"That was a bull," Ross replied over his shoulder.

"I know now. *Moby Dick*. Melville."

Now the improbable spawn of the sea lay inert on the beach, the water just lapped the edge of the snowy skin. A final tug at the ropes and the three were beached, high and dry, the little aquatic family together in death as in life.

"Hi, Ross!"

"Hi, Lowell! Pretty good."

Lowell Aragrook had waded ashore, he stood looking down at his Herculean catch as a sportsman would look at a satisfactory basket of trout. "I'm sorry about the little one. But it was too small to make out by itself, anyway, just yet, so perhaps it's just as well." He glanced casually down at his dripping mukluks; his little bow to Bridie, to Chris, was both in greeting and farewell, for now he strode briskly up the beach to the path. The crowd, too, dispersed like an audience when the show is finished. Puzzled, Chris realized that now there remained, besides herself and Bridie and Ross, only the swarm of children, the Polars, and one stout middle-aged woman in a bright red calico slip over her parka. She wore steel-rimmed spectacles which kept slipping down and which she automatically pushed back into place with the back of her wrist. As she did this the metal object in her hand glinted in the sun and Chris recognized it as an ulu somewhat larger than the one with which Joan Kungok had so deftly sliced the seal. In spite of the calico wrapper, the spectacles and the brandished ulu, Chris recognized the woman as Mrs. Aragrook, the Raffsky's dinner guest of the night before in neat crepe dress and gold brooch.

"Why did he go away?" Chris asked. "Lowell, I mean."

"His work is done," Ross said. "The rest is woman's work."

Staring, Alwin Polar said nervously, "Heh, wait a minute. What's she going to do?"

Mrs. Aragrook, by her next movement, unconsciously answered his question. With a sweep of her arm the ulu laid open a great gash along the shining white skin. Another gash at right angles, and then another. The ulu flashed, the woman grasped the flesh with her left hand and under the blade in her right the thick roll of blubber curled down like gigantic shavings under Paul Bunyan's knife. Now the purple meat lay exposed. She freed the massive square of fat now and flung it onto an oilcloth that lay on the beach just above the carcass.

"In a half hour she'll have the whole beluga cut and skinned," Ross said. "Come on. Let's go."

But now the children, as though they had been given a signal, rushed upon the massive white creature. In their hands were small knives. With these they skillfully sliced and hacked at the tail. They crammed the bits of rubbery gristle into their mouths, they were blissful as another child might be with a lollipop.

"Try a piece, Chris?"

"Love to."

He sliced a sliver of the tough white tailmeat. "It's called the flute, this tail piece, and the kids would rather eat it than candy."

But when the Polars and Bridie and Chris tried to chew it, it resisted them like hard rubber. Hastily spitting it out, the three older people began to explore their mouths apprehensively. "You trying to work up business for the Native Service dentist?" Bridie demanded.

"I can't make a dent in it," Chris said, "but I'll chew it awhile, like gum, just for exercise." She took it out of her mouth, looked at it to mark her progress, and put it back.

"Christine Storm!" Bridie exclaimed, as though reproving a child.

Chris said, cheerfully, "Not bad, really. Tastes a little like celery. With a dip in the salt."

The Polars glanced up glanced down the bleak little beach path. Oogruk was going about its daily business again. The wind blew chill across the mountains and water to the little cove in which they stood now alone except for the children, the woman intently working over the massive white mounds, and the three who evidently were about to be on their way.

"Where you folks going now?" Alwin Polar inquired, sociably.

Oh, no, Chris thought.

With candor and sweetness Ross said, "I am taking these two friends to my grandmother's house. I am sorry that I can't ask you to come with us."

Simple enough, and direct, and honest, Chris decided. The guileless Polars, too, seemed to find this reasonable enough. "Well, sure, you wouldn't want strangers barging in," Alwin Polar agreed, cheerfully. "We'll just ramble around. I'd appreciate it if you'd just advise us what there is to see, and so on. Like that dancing last night, and these whales this morning, that's something you don't see back in the States."

Gravely, Ross agreed to this. "I'd take you around if I could. But I've made some plans for the day—I've just got this one day. There isn't anything very terrific to see, unless you're interested in the way Eskimos live and work. This is just an Eskimo town, you know. Everybody works like mad in the summer, getting ready for the winter. Nobody sleeps much. If you happen to see something or somebody that interests you, just stop and look at it, and speak to whoever it is. Everybody's friendly here. They're used to tourists. They like them."

"Yes, everybody's real friendly," Mrs. Polar agreed. Worriedly she gazed around her at the bleak little Arctic village, at the woman slashing the sea monster, at the immensely vital swarm of children, at the fish racks extending like an endless arbor along the beach, at the purposeful dark-skinned men and women plodding along the beach path. "I feel real useless here," she confessed, as though thinking aloud. "I feel like I ought to pitch in and help. I never feel like that in New York or Chicago or San Francisco. They're real busy there, goodness knows, but it's different."

She looked terribly displaced and somehow touching in her pale blue coat and her earrings and her flowered hat. Bridie, urban though her garments were, had the authoritative air of the accustomed.

"Down there"—Ross pointed down the beach—"where those tents are, you can see some of the Eskimos carving ivory. You don't have to buy any. They come from very tiny villages, they stay for the summer, selling their ivory to the tourists, and fishing for the winter supply. You can visit the hospital, I think, they'll let you see the public rooms like the dining room and so forth. You can get a really good cup of coffee at Lena's Lunch there down the beach. . . ."

Chris said, very low, "Let the poor lambs come with us, they're lost."

"No," Ross said. "No."

A strangely quiet species of panic possessed Bridie as she stepped along the rough beach path with Ross and Chris. She conducted a somewhat frantic conversation with herself. This isn't just boy-and-girl stuff any more. He's really in love with her, he's ten years older than she is, well, that's all right but she isn't going to take him seriously if I can help it, and I can. He's up to something, so quiet and smiling. Czar was right, I guess. It's time Chris got away and saw something besides Alaska. Czar is wrong most of the time, to my way of thinking, but this time he's right.

"If you'll come back in the autumn," Ross was saying, "that's when it's really good. And I'll take you and Thor out on a polar-bear hunt. In a little Cessna, flying low, you can spot them from the air even against the ice and snow."

"I always think it's sort of mean and unsporting, shooting bear from a plane."

Listen to that, would you, Bridie now fumed, silently. And her own father killed by a big brown. Aloud she said, "Chris won't be coming up in the autumn because she'll be in Seattle learning something besides shooting polar bears from airplanes, I hope."

It was disarming to hear him say, "You don't like me today, Mrs. Ballantyne."

They stopped at a one-room shack connected by a ramshackle passageway with a decent frame house. The door of the little dwelling was open and inside and outside, small children and big dogs were playing and scuffling and yapping and shouting. They became quiet, quiet as Ross stopped at the doorway, the children's faces were upturned with the mute adoration that had been reflected in the faces of the children on the beach.

From his pocket Ross took a little sack of candy, he opened it and counted out a handful of hard bright balls. "One for each of you, that's all, because sugar is good for you but too much is bad for your teeth. The rest of it is for my grandmother."

"No teeth," one of the boys said quickly.

"That's right. Now out, kids, stay outside until we leave, I'm bringing visitors to see my grandmother."

"Tourist?"

"No."

He looked directly at Christine. "Grandmother lives alone because that's what she wants to do, and she works because that makes her feel she isn't a burden. In the old days, if food was too scarce in the winter, they sacrificed the old for the young. That isn't true now, but she remembers it, I suppose. Or maybe it's an atavistic thing. My uncle and his wife live next door here, and they look after her. She's almost blind, but she wants to be as independent as—well, as you want to be I suppose, Chris."

Standing in the doorway, peering into the dim musty room, they saw that Ross Guildenstern's ancient grandmother was seated on a small tin oil drum which served as a chamber pot. She looked up brightly as they entered, her withered yellow face creased into a smile of a hundred wrinkles as she recognized his voice. She spoke his name.

"Wait just a minute, will you?" he said to Chris and Bridie.

"Grandma's on the can. I'll put her back on her bed in a minute and then you can come in."

"Oh, I guess I wasn't a registered nurse all those years for no reason," Bridie said, briskly. "Just let me in. You wait a minute, Chris."

"I wish people would stop treating me like a feeble-minded child," Chris said. The children stared at her, she looked at the children, feeling rather cross, then one of the small girls came to her and offered her the piece of candy Ross had given her. Suddenly Chris, as she shook her head in refusal, felt as though she were going to cry. Ross passed her carrying the tin can, she heard him emptying it in some sort of receptacle at the side of the house.

"Come on in, Chris," he said now, as he returned.

"Why do I like you more for that, and admire you more than if you had just shot a large polar bear?" she asked.

"Sentiment," Ross said.

The old woman had been tidied by Bridie, she sat on a board bed that was like a shelf in the wall. It was supported by wooden blocks at either end and it stood perhaps eighteen inches above the rough littered floor. Her head as she sat on this improvised throne was thrust a little upward and her chin a little forward, and her face wore the uncertain half-smile of the sightless or nearly sightless. The young man spoke to her in the language of her people and then she nodded and smiled in genuine happiness so that you saw the toothless gums. She raised one strangely agile seamed hand in greeting. Then the hands resumed the work on which she had been engaged, she had observed the amenities, she concentrated now with the absorption of a craftsman. Her grandson, whose profession was that of flying an airplane, watched her with affection and pride. She was justifying her existence, she was proving herself still useful in a world of the young and uncaring. He knew this. Instinctively Chris and Bridie, watching her, sensed this for themselves.

"God bless her, look at the cut of her, would you then!" Bridie said. "Working, mind you."

She was making thread for the sewing of skins. The threads would hold together forever the wolf skins, the wolverine skins, the seal skins the otter the fox. Fur parkas for the men and women and children of the Arctic. Mukluks. Hoods. Gloves. Straps and thongs that held together the dog sleds. The thread was made of moose or caribou sinew, and it was the old woman's proud task to roll the strands so expertly together that they made the whole and unbreakable thread.

The three stood watching this aged and ageless example of a strange and gentle and fundamentally civilized people whose remote past was lost in oblivion and whose future was as illimitable only as the human spirit.

The old woman wet the long strands of fine loose sinews with the spit of her mouth, she then drew the strands slowly across her lips, another thin strand, another, moistened in her mouth. She began to roll the threads then together in the cushions of her palms, back and forth, back and forth in the flesh of her hard bony hands, the one against the other, and then she held up the long thin roll of strands that now were united as one and she rolled the thread against her high hard cheekbone, cheekbone to jaw, and back to cheekbone and down again to jawbone, inch by inch, up and down, the friction of the skin of the cheek and the skin of the hand and the oil of the skin united the sinews into a thread that would endure decades after this ancient woman had ceased to be, and her children and her grandchildren.

Her grandson watched her with amused admiration and affection. He had seen the countries of Europe during the last World War, he had seen New York and Hollywood and San Francisco and Honolulu and many strange and exotic places, his world was the globe and the constellations among which he swooped and darted, he would choose never to live anywhere but in this glittering magnetic ice palace in which he had been born. Her world never had been anything other than it now was as she sat rolling the strands of animal sinew as her own grandmother and great-grandmother and great-great-grandmother had rolled them thus before her. She was justifying her existence, she was proving that she was useful still in a world of the swift and the young and the careless. This amiable and industrious little mummy could hold up her head in the presence of the great-grandchildren shouting and laughing in play outside the shanty, no matter how cleverly they read picture books and did finger-painting at school and ate lollipops and ice-cream cones and lettuce and hamburgers instead of muktuk and the leaves of wild green plants, and Eskimo ice cream made of grated reindeer tallow and seal oil beaten and beaten until the mass was white and fluffy, and, mixed with blueberries or low-bush cranberries, so delicious, to her way of thinking.

Ross Guildenstern leaned over the unsavory old woman and touched her cheek with his strong brown hand that bore the Air Force ring, and he murmured something to her in her own mysterious language. The withered mask lighted then with a little flickering flame of brilliance so that for one moment between the young vital man with the vivid merry face and the indomitable old blind woman a curious resemblance sprang into being.

"Oh, Ross!" Chris said, inadequately as they called their good-byes to the children and walked down the road.

"She's all right," Ross said, rather abruptly for him.

"What's that she said when we left?" Bridie asked.

"I was going to tell you that. She said the one who helped her off the can had hands of goodness and that they were work hands, too."

"Now who's being sentimental?" Christine demanded. "It's dark in there, and stuffy, and it can't be healthy. Shouldn't she be in a comfortable place, and not working? And having things done for her? She's so old and feeble."

"Grandma isn't really that old and she's as tough as that thread she's making. She's doing what she wants to do, she's earning her way, she loves it. To her it is a dream life. If you took it away from her she would die."

Caution told Bridie that there now had been enough of Ross Guildenstern's worthy family. "Now what? I'm beginning to be hungry, would you believe it, and not yet twelve! Your Grandpa'll be looking for us, Chris."

"No he won't," Chris said, calmly, "and besides, how lost can you be in Oogruk?"

"I like to know where I'm going," Bridie snapped, "before I go."

Ross pointed to a turn in the rough path. "Right there. That hammering sound you hear is what we're headed for."

"I suppose that's your aunt, building a house," Chris said.

"Not quite. But you're warm."

"Well, anyway, we're certainly seeing the native arts and crafts."

Though Bridie's protective habit where Chris was concerned told her that this Guildenstern family tour had gone on long enough, Bridie was shocked by this display of bad manners. "I wouldn't call that polite, Christine Storm."

"Mrs. Ballantyne, ma'am, you're forgetting that my Grandmother Storm was part Eskimo, even if Grampa Thor never speaks of her, alive or dead. He clams up about her past and his past. In a way that makes me a kind of woman of mystery, doesn't it? I hope."

Ross shook his head. "You're as mysterious as a glass of clear spring water."

She found this infuriating. "You seem quite pleased with yourself today."

"Protective coloration," he said.

Now what are they talking about, Bridie wondered, fuming.

Ross's uncle and aunt were working in the cluttered yard of their weather-beaten house on the road behind the beach path. Six or eight sled dogs yapped and snarled in their compound. The man's hammer strokes sounded an accompaniment to this shrill vocal chorus. As Ross and the two women approached the man at his task of boatbuilding and the woman busy at some mysterious task as she squatted on the ground, the serious intent faces of the two workers flashed into warm brilliant smiles.

Ross threw more charm than was absolutely necessary, Chris thought, into the introduction.

"Hi, Aunt Angeline! . . . This is my aunt, Mrs. Asakluk. . . . Over there working on the boat. . . . Frank Asakluk. Hiyuh, Frank!

. . . Mrs. Ballantyne . . . Christine Storm, they're up from Baranof to see the sights."

Frank Asakluk waved a hammer at them, gaily, he went on building his boat, he did not come forward. Angeline Asakluk did not rise or offer her hand because both her hands and her bare arms to the shoulders were dripping with blood and grease. Her friendly winning smile beamed above the sanguine headless carcass of a seal suspended on a rack in front of her. Now she reached in through the headless opening and pulled out a fistful of entrails; she was busy, she was expert, it was a task to be finished before the end of the day, but she was politely cordial as an Outside housewife caught critically in the midst of beating up cake batter.

"Excuse me," she said now. "I'm making a seal poke. Ross, why don't you take the folks in the house, open up some Cokes. Or maybe you'd like a cup of coffee, I've got a pot on the stove, Frank's a great one for coffee."

"We're on our way to lunch," Bridie said, crisply. "Thanks just the same."

That same protective feeling surged warmly over Chris for the second time. Ross's eyes were on her. Her natural curiosity actually overcame her repugnance to the blood, the fat, the purplish viscera, the decapitated cadaver, and the sight of this pleasant middle-aged woman at her task.

As she put her questions Chris was annoyed to find that her voice emerged somewhat high pitched and that it cracked a little, almost ludicrously, and she laughed a little, and Angeline Asakluk joined her, politely, but Bridie and Ross did not laugh. "I must have caught a little cold on the plane, it was freezing. Tell me, I'm so interested in what you're doing, I know it isn't the same—we were watching Ross's cousin Joan cutting up a seal—and Mrs.—uh—cutting up the whale——" That sounds absolutely crazy, she told herself—"but what's a seal poke? I know what a gold poke is, but a seal——"

"It's the Eskimo deep freeze," Ross said. "Tell Chris how you do it, Angie."

"I'm taking out the insides, you see. Then I'll cut out the meat and the fat."

"You mean you'll open it and slice down the blubber and the meat the way Joan——"

"Oh, no. This is going to be a poke. I just reach through this hole where the head used to be and I cut everything away, very carefully and take it out, you have to be careful not to cut the skin. And then we turn the whole skin inside out by reaching in right through from the head to the tail, and we clean it and we blow it up for drying and we rub it with ashes so that it will dry better. And when it's dry we fill it with meats or berries or green leaf plants in it for storing all through the winter, it makes the best deep freeze you ever saw."

"Now," Bridie observed, "I've seen everything."

"Angeline can do anything," Ross announced, cheerfully. "What a girl! She isn't really my aunt, you know. Frank's my uncle, Angeline's his second wife. Angeline used to teach at the Native Service school, that's how she happens to talk so pretty, eh Angie? Frank's English isn't so hot." Beneath the casual cheerfulness of his tone there was defiance and a kind of exhibitionistic bravado. "Where's Lorena?"

"She's away, she's taking the business and steno course in Fairbanks. The business school. She's going to be a secretary."

"That's great!" He glanced across the yard at the open door of the house, he looked up and down the road. "Where's Rolf? I thought he'd be here."

"He was here a minute ago." Her smile became mischievous. "Rolf! Rolf!" she called, but not loudly.

"Rolf!" Ross shouted.

Angeline laughed aloud, then, and pointed with one encarmined hand to where her husband stood, busy with his boat. Over the rim of the trestled boat's edge a red sombrero rose above a pair of black eyes.

"Hi, Rolf!" Ross shouted again. "Come here."

Over the boat's side there clambered a boy of perhaps six, he dropped agilely to the ground and ran toward Ross. A handsome compact child, the olive of his cheeks was tinted with pink, he was in full movie-cowboy regalia—sombrero, plaid shirt, chaps, high-heeled boots. He carried two toy guns in a holster that was studded with large red, green and yellow stones and as he ran toward the group he pulled out the guns.

"Why, it's Hopalong Asakluk!" Chris said, falling into the spirit of the thing.

"Stick 'em up!" yelled the boy, a gun in either hand. Obligingly feigning terror they raised their hands high over their heads, the boy clicked the weapons ferociously and stuttered an uh-uh-uh-uh-uh far back in his throat in what he hoped was the sound of a rapid-fire gun.

"I don't think he ought to play with guns, Angie," Ross said, though he still held his hands over his head. "I hate to see kids play with guns."

Then he stooped, picked up the boy and held him high, but the small booted feet beat a tattoo in remonstrance against this infantile treatment and Ross set him hastily down.

"Sorry, old boy," Ross said. He laid a hand gently on the child's shoulder. His eyes were on Christine. "Chris, this is my son Rolf. He was named after my father."

22

Bridie and Thor, handsome old landmarks, impressive old lifemarks, were soaring again over the almost mythical Alaskan territory which had so indelibly stamped them in its image. Deep in a discussion of the subject that ran neck-and-neck with Alaska in their thoughts and emotions, they sat together in one of the sagging seats of the old DC-3 churning its way to Barrow on the shores of the Arctic. Christine was not, for the moment, an occupant of the gelid cabin. She was not only occupying the cockpit with Ross Guildenstern; she was competently at the controls.

Bridie's customary sartorial perfection was slightly marred by the temporary victory of the flesh over the spirit. An air-line red wool blanket covered her knees and ankles, another was wrapped snugly around her modish sealskin shoulders, and over her draped blue silk turban she had tied a wool scarf (borrowed from Thor) that covered her ears and was knotted under her chin. From this cocoon her carefully made-up face, with the lively blue eyes, emerged like a modern mummy by Picasso. In spite of obvious difficulties she had managed to work one hand loose and she now was polishing off her second roast-beef sandwich under the quite sound conviction that there would be nothing fit to eat in Barrow.

"You going to let her see this boy like this, all the time?"

"She's nineteen, Bridie."

"I wish you could of seen her face when he said, 'This is my son Rolf.' She just stood there like a statue. But I'll say this for her, good stock will tell. One of those queens you claim you're related to couldn't have come to quicker or more dignified. How wonderful, she says, how can you bear to leave him up here when you get back to Oogruk so seldom. You'd think she was a Visiting Nurse talking, or something. He says Angeline and Frank—that's his aunt and uncle the boy lives with—are crazy about him, the boy needs family affection, his age, and he says when he's ten he's going to bring the boy to Baranof and put him in school there and live with him, so he'll have a real home of his own. Well, just figure that one out, would you kindly? And then give me a ring some time."

"That sounds very intelligent. That's what we tried to do with Chris. We were lucky to have you around to help us."

"Thor Storm, don't you care what happens to Chris?"

"More than anything in the world. More than Alaska, even. And you know I'm considered not quite sane on the subject of Alaska."

"Not quite sane isn't what I think when it comes to your way of treating Chris. I don't mean you're a little goofy like most of us in Alaska. I mean downright peculiar. Chris has got to be guided. She's got the whole world before her."

"What kind of world? Nobody knows."

"My beautiful wonderful Chris! Father of a boy six years old—and never even mentioned him before."

"Bridie, dear girl, you've been helping so many of these Air Force boys and their little brides, you think every girl over sixteen is marrying every boy who buys her a Coke. Chris isn't marrying anyone just yet. She's going to Seattle for two years and she's looking forward to it. You know that. After this Barrow trip I'd say she has seen her own Alaska from tip to tip. Very few girls of her age can say that. Or three times her age."

"That's fine. Maybe she's enjoyed all this dog sledding and airplaning and being shifted around from the time she was a baby, you might say. But what's a young girl want to see Barrow for! A God-forsaken wilderness sitting on the Arctic Ocean, why, men and women who've lived in Alaska sixty seventy years never saw Barrow and never wanted to."

"A strange thing is going on in that Eskimo village. It has jumped in half a dozen years from an Arctic wilderness to a laboratory. It isn't just seal fishing and whale harpooning and moose hunting any more. It's a workshop full of scientists and engineers and Air Force men. Do you know there are Eskimos up there so naturally trained to sound and mechanisms that they can tell whether an unseen plane, miles up in the sky, is an American or a foreign plane? Don't you think that's uncanny?"

"I've been told a dog can hear sounds a human can't."

"Bridie."

"I don't know anything about scientific and mechanical. I only know she isn't old enough to know what's good for her. Do you think that Eskimo boy is good enough for our Chris! Do you?" He looked at her then, quizzically. Horrified at what she had said, she was filled with contrition. "Oh, Thor, I forgot I didn't mean to hurt your feelings. I forgot."

Quietly he said, "If I see Chris making a wrong turn, and she doesn't see the mistake and therefore can't correct it, I speak to her about it. But I suppose there are certain mistakes one has to make in order to learn. It's better to learn by mistakes than never to learn at all."

She could not stop herself, she had wanted, all these years, to know. "Was your marriage a mistake?"

"Yes. In its own way. Not because I married a girl who was part Eskimo. She couldn't adjust to my way of life, I couldn't adjust to hers. We were too far apart in training, in what we call morals, and perspective and habit and customs. Marriage is a terrific adjustment, at best. People say, oh, I wouldn't marry a Negro, I wouldn't marry an Indian, I wouldn't marry a Chinese, I wouldn't marry a Protestant, a Jew, a Catholic, a Mohammedan. It isn't a matter of exterior difference, really, I suppose. Different color, yes. Different religions. But the real difference lies in thousands of years of habit, manners, customs, characteristics, food, standards, morals. All different. Not necessarily better or worse, but different. Perhaps those differences will cease to exist in this world of easy communication. I am selfish enough to hope not—in my lifetime. I love the differences. I'd hate to see a world in which the people were all alike, like the small towns all over the United States now, all the same neon lights, the same movies at the same movie houses, the same gas station, lunchroom, drugstore, supermarket, big glass schoolhouse. All standard and modern and convenient and deadly dull with sameness."

Bridie began to unwind her mummy wrappings as if suddenly emerging into a warmer climate, though as they approached the Arctic the temperature of the plane became colder by the minute. "I'll tell you this, Thor Storm. It's getting so a person asks you a simple question, like do you think it's going to rain, and they get a lecture on Alaska. I start out about Chris and this boy, and I end up listening to scientific laboratories. All right. Where were we at? Oh, yes. Chris has seen more of Alaska than any woman of seventy in the Territory. Then what?"

"Then she's on her own."

"Sometimes I think Czar was right all the time, after all."

"Chris probably will be the only one who'll know that, in the end. I don't know. You don't know, nor Czar. She's different, we all know that. Twenty years from now she may be the most important woman in Alaska. Or she may be just another wife and mother somewhere else. That's life enough, if that's what she wants. How do we know that Barrow won't be the most important spot on the Western Hemisphere next week or next year! Or just an ice-locked Arctic wilderness. Chris has seen the land she was born in. Czar will help her to see the world Outside. But her own life—that's something she'll have to decide for herself."

Shrewdly Bridie carved it all down to the size she could grasp. Cosmic generalities were not for her. "If I had my way she wouldn't be sitting up there in front with Ross this minute, let alone deciding her own life. Anyway, a pilot's got no right to be talking to a girl when he's flying real risky terrain like this. I'm as used to flying as anybody, but I know Chris. I bet she's running this contraption this very minute."

With the too pat timing of a badly constructed play Ross's voice now came over the loud-speaker in the plane's cabin.

"Your attention please. This is an unusually clear day. No fog in the valley. . . . This flight can continue directly to Barrow on schedule but we are a little ahead of time . . . (squawk squawk squawk) . . . or take a brief side trip to see the Diomedes—the Big Diomede and the Little Diomede . . . (squawk squawk) . . . only when we have very important passengers as on this occasion. If you will make your wishes known to your stewardess . . ."

In the cockpit Chris said, "I hope they will. I'm sure Grampa and Bridie would love it. Do you think the other passengers will say yes?"

"Six of them are Dew Line men. They'll go anywhere. Then there're two Eskimos who live in Barrow, they're crazy about flying, they'd go to the moon. And that vaudeville couple that latched on at the last moment. They're game."

"What do you suppose they are? Russian spies or something?"

"No, I think they crave excitement and danger. And now that their act has been cut down they miss the thrills. I've seen a lot of people like that bitten by Alaska. So have you. Next thing you know they'll take claim to a homestead and stay here."

"Grampa Thor says the people who came to America two or three hundred years ago were like that. Adventurous. He says that's why this country is so high-keyed and exciting. Grampa says——"

"Grampa says. You talk like a little girl. I never knew anybody with so many grandfathers."

"You know perfectly well they've been my father and mother and sisters and brothers, too."

"I know, I know. All your life a bunch of people have been cooing over you—not only your family but everybody in Baranof—saying, poor little Chris, got no papa got no mama. You're a big girl now."

"You're nervous. Am I doing something wrong?" She pretended to scan the instrument panel. "Goodness gracious, Mr. Guildenstern, how do you get this thing down?"

"I don't get nervous in planes, Miss Storm. Though I'm going to take over in a minute because buzzing the Diomedes is kind of nervous work. I'd hate to see you try to make a landing in that mush below us this minute, so if you're considering anything we might better crack a nice hard peak and get some drama out of it."

"You don't scare me."

"That's right. After all, there's nothing to flying but taking off and landing. Keep the plane up in the air forever and you'll never get hurt, that's my motto."

"You *are* nervous."

"Who wouldn't be? Isn't it the queen bee—it's some royal insect, anyway—that coaxes the male drone high up in the air for the courting? And after the act of mating is accomplished she gives the poor lunk the *coup de grâce* with a stiletto she wears for that purpose, charming girl that she is, and bingo! He's a dead drone."

"In the first place, I didn't bring you up here, you brought me. I didn't ask you to. You wangled it. In the second place, there's been no act of mating that I'm aware of."

"You'd be aware."

"And in the third place, big girl or little girl, if my grandfathers—Grampa Czar, anyway—were to hear you talking like that he'd call the Territorial Police."

"You're up a few thousand feet, you can't walk out on me and slam the door."

"Yes I can. Right back to Grampa and Bridie."

"Those three old people are going to tear you to pieces."

"I'll be going to Seattle next month. Don't spoil this last trip for me."

She stood up now. He shifted into the pilot's seat. "This time next year you'll probably be raving about Mount Rainier and all those high buildings, and the dances at the Olympic Hotel, and Bayard Husack."

She was standing behind him as he sat in his proper place.

"Why didn't you ever tell me you had a son? It seems so strange you never told me you had a son."

"I was afraid I'd lose you."

"You can't lose what you——" She caught herself. Stopped.

"—what you haven't got," he finished for her.

"Ross, how old was he when your wife died?"

"He was two. Not quite two."

The cockpit door opened. The stewardess, a cup in her hand. "Everybody says they'd love to see the Diomedes. Mrs. Ballantyne said, was it safe, she said she didn't mind being shot, her time of life, but she didn't want to be shot by a Russian. Here's your coffee, Captain Guildenstern."

Idiotically she heard herself saying, "You drink a lot of coffee, don't you? Sort of every hour on the hour."

"They say pilots have no blood. Just coffee in their veins."

"What did my Grandfather say?" Chris asked the stewardess.

"Let's see—what was that he said? Oh, yes, he said nothing is safe from destruction except the spirit of man, I think it was. And he said that even that——"

"Oh dear," Christine said. "You don't think Grampa is getting to be one of those pontifical dramatizers, do you?"

"Call Ackerman, will you, Miss Larson?"

Almost as if he had taken her by the shoulders, pushed her firmly through the cockpit door and had closed the door after her, she felt that he had shut her out of his consciousness for the time, at least. He was looking straight ahead, he was hunched a little over the instrument panel.

"I think you'd better take your seat, Miss Storm," the stewardess said. "And fasten your seat belt. Sometimes it gets a little bumpy around here."

Ackerman, the co-pilot, passed her at the doorway. "Why don't you stay and see the Diomedes from here, Miss Storm?"

"I've been fired."

Bridie surveyed her with a searching ice-blue eye. "You want to sit here with me? Or with your Grandpa?"

"I'll sit back here alone."

"Mhm." Bridie's inflection was a comment.

Miss Larson's cool inadequate voice now came over the loudspeaker at the rear of the cabin, her every important word seeming to be lost in a maddening way by the roar of the engines.

". . . about ten minutes . . . see . . . and Big Diomede . . . Russia . . . Americ . . . villages . . . coast . . . Siberia . . ."

Thor Storm stood upright to his great height. "Sit here," he commanded Chris, his hand on her shoulder so that she met the seat beside Bridie with something of a thud. He strode over to the stewardess mouthing so unavailingly into the instrument. "Ask Ross if I can take over. Don't be offended. I'll explain later . . . I'll ask him." His vast voice ricocheted from side to side of the plane's cabin, it boomed through the aisle, it shamed the engines' roar.

"Ross! Ross out there! . . . Will you let me give this little lecture? It's Christine . . . I want Christine to know about this historic sight while she's seeing it. . . . That's good, my boy. I knew you'd . . ."

"I'll tell you what I think," Christine said furiously, to Bridie. "I think Grampa is getting queerer and queerer."

"He's just getting older and older," Bridie whispered, "and so am I. Pressed for time, he is, maybe. Or feeling so."

"I don't know what you're talking about."

"In a few minutes now," Thor Storm roared, "you'll see a sight few have seen. You'll see thousands of years of history and the world today meeting on two island rocks rising from the sea. They are three miles apart, separated only by a narrow strip of water. Over the Big Diomede flies the flag of the Union of Soviet Socialist Republics. Over the Little Diomede flies the flag of the United States of America. And beyond these you will see a dark cliff of shore line. This is Siberia. These two little islands, so close together, so far apart, are all that is left of what was a stretch of continuous land that once, thousands of years ago, connected and united Asia and America. These islands, jutting from the sea, were first sighted by Vitus Bering, that great and tragic Danish explorer, almost two hundred and fifty years ago, on St. Diomede's Day, and so they came by their name—the Diomedes. These islands are only bleak rocks each rising to mountainous heights, with a sheer drop into the deep sea. Snow, ice, and black water. But people live on these rocks and have for thousands of years. Science has brought the world to those islands. There's a schoolhouse now on the Big Diomede, taught by a Russian schoolteacher, and a schoolhouse on the Little Diomede, taught by an American teacher. They show Russian movies on one, and American movies on the other. It is said that if an American plane flew over the Big Diomede it would be fired on, and if a Russian plane were to appear over the Little Diomede it would risk American fire. Here in this plane we needn't worry. Our pilot knows his craft——"

"I think somebody ought to stop Grampa," Chris whispered.

"Sh! It's real interesting," Bridie said, reprovingly.

". . . but the Natives visit back and forth in their skin boats, they're related, they even intermarry, each tries to tell the other how much better his island is. They have radios, they have phonographs, mechanical luxuries of all kinds. Food. Clothes. Books. They are a miniature example of mankind inhabiting the planet Earth. Once they lived in comparative peace, separated by distance and natural obstacles. Now they are united by the inventions of modern science and torn apart by fear of each other. The Big Diomede Eskimo says to the Little Diomede Eskimo, 'Come, cross the water. Here the Eskimos are allowed to oil the machines, cure the sick, live with Russian women, spit on merchants, go to Moscow, become captains!' The Little Diomede Eskimo says, 'We are free citizens of the great Republic of the United States of America. The fish we catch are ours, and the whales are ours, no one can claim them from us.' But the Big Diomede Eskimos laugh at this and they say, 'We have been told about you, we know you are slaves, all the people of Alaska are slaves, they cannot even say who shall be their President. But rest, be patient, one day we shall come and free you.'

"This is why I wanted to talk to you, passengers with me on this trip. When you look down, like gods, on the Diomede Islands you are not only looking at two little barren bleak islands, you are looking at the whole world today——"

The plane began to bank.

From the Roller Polars then there came a little salvo of applause. They knew entertainment when they saw and heard it, and they gave it its due. But the other passengers pressed against the windows with a complete concentration of attention. Their faces were immobile, even the eyelids did not move. Thor Storm stood a moment at the rear of the plane, a Jovian figure.

"That was really lovely," said Miss Larson.

The Dew Line men and the Eskimo boys had listened respectfully enough. They had encountered queerer than this and would again, they knew, in this wild unpredictable country. When Thor had finished they stared out at the formidable scene below and all about. Only one—the youngest among them—said very low to his seatmate, "The old guy has lost his marbles." But the older man said, "You should be as smart as him when you're his age. Or now, Buster."

Christine, alone at a window, turned and called to Thor, holding out her hand. "Come sit here with me, Grampa Thor. Please."

He sat beside her, he leaned toward her, together they peered out toward the gray sheet that lay ahead.

"It was wonderful of you to do that, just for this little handful of people."

"It's all in my book, dear child. And I'll write a piece about this trip for the paper next week. Maybe, someday, you'll be doing that. And I'll talk a little to these Dew Line boys here before we reach Barrow. I like to know what you young people are thinking."

He smiled down at her and suddenly, high up there in the merciless light of the brilliant polar Arctic day, skylit, sunlit, dustless, refractive, she saw the lines, the vague shadows, the receding of the flesh pads around the eye sockets, the cheekbones, the nose, so that the bone structure stood revealed, the nose seemed larger than she remembered it, the eyes more sunken, it was as though she had not actually seen him for a long time, though she had looked at him daily. He doesn't look very well, she thought, worriedly. And then, suddenly stricken with the thought—Why, he's an old man!

Like a little girl, "I love you, Grampa Thor," she said.

"Thank you, my dear child," he said.

Their heads turned toward the window. Two black rocks jutted out of a gray-black sea. From the plane they were black dots only, with a few tiny black specks upon them. At this height it appeared that only a few inches of water separated the two bits of rocky land.

"Why, say!" Alwin Polar exclaimed, "a kid could spit across from one island to the other."

One of the Dew Line men laughed a trifle uncomfortably. "Heh, I hope our pilot don't get mixed up which is which."

Even as they gazed down, fascinated, the passengers seemed imperceptibly to shrink away from the windows as though, by this distribution of weight, they could veer the plane away from the direction of danger. And then, in the distance, meeting the sky line, they saw across the sluggish icy waste of waters a sinister black cliff-like mass. It was the coast of Siberia.

"Thor Storm!" Bridie trumpeted from her seat, "you tell Ross Guildenstern to turn this plane around and head back where we belong. Sight-seeing is fine, but I don't figure on ending up in any slave-labor camp in Russia. Now go on!"

But already the plane was making its graceful birdlike turn as it circled and banked and straightened out. In that moment of turn the two islands had seemed to rise up and stare through the windows at the shrinking passengers.

"It's all right," said Miss Larson. "We're heading for Barrow, we'll be there in no time. Coffee will be served to any passengers desiring it."

"Well, I'll tell you," Alwin Polar observed, "I'm not a drinking man as a rule, but the way I feel, coffee wouldn't settle me, I could do with a little slug."

"Say, couldn't we all, brother!" said a Dew Line man.

There was a subtle change now in the plane, a sort of settling to the business at hand. The passengers composed themselves in their places. The icy drafts cut through every unseen chink and crevice. Coats and parkas, mufflers and blankets were pulled closer, tucked more tightly. Soon, on either side, rose the formidable walls of the mountains, and below, the tundra that never had known the foot of man. The flat impassive faces of the Eskimos and the young expectant faces of the Dew Line men, and the absurdly urban vaudeville team, and the old man and the old woman and the young girl, prisoners all in this toylike thing of metal and Plexiglas, glanced out now and then at a formidable, a ruthless, a seemingly illimitable wilderness, and thought their own thoughts.

"Coffee?" chirped the stewardess. "Snack? No, those are jelly and cream cheese. These are the meat sandwiches."

They drank the hot beverage, they ate the cold food, they composed themselves again, they seemed, huddled in that bleak little cabin, to be somehow separate each from the other, busy with their own thoughts. Perhaps they felt their own powerlessness to fight Fate if she should feel the whim to turn adversely against this little bubble to which they had entrusted their lives. Boomboomboomboomboom went the engines. Sleepsleepsleepsleepsleep. But they could not in all that clear fine air and that brilliance. But perhaps they did, at least in the more active fibers of the senses. For Miss Larson was saying, "Fasten your seat belts please," and the sign over the cockpit doorway was alight with its message.

Barrow. The Arctic Ocean. "We are coming down in Barrow. We will arrive there in ten minutes. Barrow is the northernmost town in Alaska, and the only sizable settlement between here and the North Pole. You will now notice the Arctic Ocean, the dark line you see is the Arctic ice pack piled up on the shore almost mountain high."

"In July!" exclaimed Irma Polar.

"We have enjoyed having you on this trip," Miss Larson went on, flawlessly, "and we hope you have enjoyed your flight with Arctic Circle Air Line, and that you will fly with us again. Please keep your seats until the plane . . ."

They stepped from the plane into a gray-and-black world whose only flash of color was the United States flag whipping aloft in the wind like a tongue of flame in a bed of ashes.

Bridie on one side, Thor on the other, Chris stood a moment, staring. "It's Mars."

Thor laughed in approval. "That's a good observation, Christine."

Bridie, absurdly inappropriate as to outer appearance, superbly equipped for hardship in spirit and body, hunched her shoulders against the wind. "You wanted to see Alaska."

Christine surveyed the forest of empty oil drums stretching away to infinity, the ice pack stacked high on the Arctic shore, the huts, the weather-pocked frame houses, the Quonsets; the muffled figures clopping across the ankle-deep black fine dust of the road; the vast vehicles equipped with the wheels of airplanes. A town on Mars.

"I thought—I suppose—it would be a little like Oogruk and a little like Kotzebue and Nome and even Baranof. All those engineers and all those scientists and the Army, and the Air Force. What do they *do* here!"

"Protect you," Thor said.

"I'd thank them to protect me this minute," Bridie announced, "with a place where we can get warmed up and away from the wind. What's that place over there? If it's the airport let's get to it. Where we going to stay tonight?"

"You'll be surprised," Thor assured her. "Comfortable and clean. Just wait."

"Chris! Chris!"

She turned. Ross was running toward them across the chiaroscuro landscape.

"I'm going in," Bridie announced, firmly. "Ross wants to talk to you let him come indoors."

Chris waved him forward as they turned toward the wooden structure that served the airport. But, "Wait! Wait!" Ross called.

"Please go on," Chris said. "Take Bridie in, Grampa. I'll be there in a minute." She stood, waiting.

Whether from running or excitement or the whip of the wind there was a flush in his cheeks that heightened his tawny good looks.

"I'm going back," he said. Then, as she stared, uncomprehending, "Now, I mean. I've been demoted for six weeks."

"Why? Demoted to—for——?"

His smile was rueful, but it had a tinge of triumph, too. "You know this wasn't my regular run. I swapped with Ogilvie. I wanted to be with you in Oogruk, to show you——"

Their talk, to a listener, would now have seemed to have the *non sequitur* of a Chekhov play dialogue.

"Your grandmother and your aunt."

"I wanted you to see."

"And the boy."

"I should have told you before, but I hadn't the courage."

"I talk like a little girl, you said. You treat me like one."

"You're going to marry Bay Husack, aren't you?"

"I'm not going to marry anybody. Just now. I can't imagine being married to Bay Husack or anybody."

"Yes you can. Every time you meet an attractive guy you think what it would be like to be married to him. Every girl does."

"It's cold. They're waiting for me."

"That's why Czar is sending you to Washington U."

"I've never seen Bayard Husack in my life. He doesn't know I exist."

"He doesn't have to. It's all arranged. Husack heir, Seattle money; Kennedy heiress, Alaska money. Like royalty."

"How silly! We can't stand here. When are you going to be back in Baranof?"

"I'm in the doghouse. I just heard. They're giving me six weeks on a bush-crate run between Kotzebue and a dozen little dog-sled villages. I'll be carting the Native Service Visiting Nurses and the dentists and doctors and sick Eskimos up and down for the next six weeks."

They stood silent, facing each other.

"You mean you're leaving now!"

"They're fueling up. Look, I'll have to run for it. You'll be in Seattle, probably, by the time I get back to Baranof. Won't you?"

"I suppose so. Oh, Ross!"

"I've got to go. Can you make it to the airport all right?"

"Of course."

"Fascinating ethnological fact. In the Eskimo language there's no word for good-bye."

He ran swiftly toward the waiting plane.

23

"Give in, Bridie. Here's a Company parka, everybody uses them, you can wear it until we leave tomorrow. Look, it's fur-lined, it's got a hood, you'll be miserable here if you don't wear it."

"Christine Storm, I've never worn a parky from the day I first set foot in Alaska, and let me tell you that wasn't yesterday."

"But you've never been in Barrow before, either."

"Never will again, if I've got my senses." She glanced out of the window. The plane that had brought them was revving up now on the runway. "Though I'll say this, I'm beginning to enjoy it, now that I'm here. I'd just as soon take a spin over the North Pole, now I'm this far."

They were in the big over-heated shed that served Barrow as an airport shelter. Aside from its physical crudeness it seemed to be little different from every other Alaska airport or, for that matter, any airport in the world. Men, women, children. White. Brown. The aroma of coffee steaming somewhere. Three people only wore hats and city coats—Bridie and the two Roller Polars. And even now the Polars were shrugging themselves gratefully into the Company parkas that an attendant had offered them. Alwin Polar retained his beret under the parka hood. His spectacled face and Irma Polar's lean visage bedizened with the mammoth dangling earrings peered out from the hoods' shelter like the faces of ancient happy babies.

"I love it!" Irma Polar declared. "I feel like a native. Now one of you've got to take my picture with Mr. Polar in this getup. They'll die back east."

Two jet pilots, pink-cheeked, incredibly boyish, were standing over a box that was being opened under some protest by a round-faced spectacled Eskimo. "I'm not supposed to open it here," the Eskimo was saying.

"Oh, come on," the pilots said. "We're going out. Tell 'em we asked you to, it'll be O.K."

Bridie clutched Thor's arm. "I bet it's some secret explosive or something for that radar stuff," she whispered. "I'm going to speak to them."

"Now, Bridie," Thor remonstrated. "We're leaving, look, the bus is waiting for us."

The two pilots were standing over the box, their faces tense. Bridie, elaborately casual, sauntered toward them. The handsome coat and hat, the paradoxically shrewd yet guileless face, the gray hair, the sparkling blue eyes, made a familiar pattern to these young air gods. The motherly protective type. They had battled it in a hundred USOs.

"You boys ever flown over the North Pole?"

"Yes, ma'am."

"I'd like to go some time."

"I'd be glad to take you, ma'am," one of them said. The other seemed more intent on the contents of the box. "Only we're not allowed passengers."

Bridie beamed on him. "I was saying, there must be something real important in that box, you're standing over it and all. Can I watch?"

"Why, sure, ma'am." They had caught sight of Chris as she and Thor now joined their out-of-hand traveling companion.

"Come on now, Bridie."

"Minute."

The Eskimo had thrust both hands into the opened box, he now held up two slim oblong packages covered with bright paper, one yellow, one scarlet. "You got to pay for them," he said.

"Well sure, what do you think!" one of them replied in an injured tone. "Let me see." He took a box in either hand, he read the labels aloud. "This is Chocolate Fig Crunchies and this one's Marshmallow Maple Rounds. Which do you want, Bowk?"

For a moment indecision aged their unlined faces. "How much are they?"

"Seventy-five cents apiece," the Eskimo said, firmly.

"Any twofers?"

"Nope."

"Well," resignedly, "we'll both take both. Gosh! Four times—and carry the two—it's robbery up here—only a quarter back home—come on, Bowk." They clumped in their heavy gear out of the door and made swiftly for the runway.

"Serves you right, Bridie," Chris said, severely, as though she were the older, Bridie the girl.

Benevolently Thor said, "Let Bridie do things her own way. The answers don't always come out right, but she asks questions. That's one way to learn. Anyway, those boys make their decisions fast enough when they're strapped in those jets that go screaming across our sky."

"Eat too much," Bridie observed crossly as she teetered through the road's black dust toward the waiting bus. "I've watched them, all through the War and now up here. Riding around in jeeps and planes, they never walk a step, and they stuff too much. All that steak and pork chops and roast beef and sweet potatoes and pie and gravy and cake and ice cream and milk and butter. They've got the biggest behinds of any fighting force in the world."

Christine was shocked. "Bridie Ballantyne, how can you talk like that about the most wonderful young men in the world!"

"Sure they're wonderful. I'm crazy about them, as you well know. But pampered. Everybody in the United States is pampered soft. All except Alaskans."

"What's wrong with you two girls!" Thor demanded. "Something's going on that a male can't see."

The bus driver sounded his horn. The three trudged toward the unwieldy vehicle. "Ross can't stay over," Chris said. "He's going to Kotzebue. Now." She glanced up as a silver shape drummed in the sky, banked, circled, was off across the interminable tundra.

"I see," Thor said, quietly. "We'll miss him. He knows this part of our world. Well, you'll have to make do with me, girls."

The bus was an old army truck, canvas-topped, its seating arrangement two backless boards running one on either side the length of the interior. It could negotiate the hub-high fine black Arctic dust only because it was equipped with the massive-tired rubber wheels of old airplane stock.

Like squirrels in a nest the hooded faces peered at them as the three tardy passengers climbed laboriously into the bus.

"Sit here, Christine." Thor indicated a place at the outer end of the bench. "It's windier, but you can see out." He sat opposite. The vehicle started with a lurch, it bumped and swayed and swam through the deep dust like a boat maneuvering its way in a choppy sea.

From time to time Thor pointed out an object as they plowed along. "Skin boats there on the beach, made of walrus hide and hair seal, can you imagine putting out into the Arctic Sea in one of those?"

"But you have. You've told me."

"Yes. Yes, I've done all these things these past years. . . . See the flag whipping away up there, Christine? It stays up for eighty days and eighty nights through these months because there's no sunset up here—well, of course you know all that, I told you when you were a child. I forget, sometimes. . . . Thousands and thousands of empty oil drums, just look at them, it's cheaper to let them rust out here than to try to send them back by air, pretty soon the Arctic will be so filled with empty oil drums there'll be no space left for humans. That would be a good joke on the scientific age, wouldn't it . . . ! We're just passing the Company lunchroom there, it's run by Eskimos, we'll have our meals there."

"Oh, my land, Thor!" Bridie exclaimed.

"You wait, Bridie. It may not be the Ice Palace but it's good and it's clean, and the best homemade bread in Alaska."

"Talk up louder, will you, Mr. Storm!" Irma Polar huddled at the far end of the bus. "We sat here because we thought it would be warmer, but Mr. Polar and I can't hear a word you say." Then a shriek, echoed and redoubled by Bridie as the bus plunged through water.

Reassuringly Thor raised his voice above the clamor and the splashing. "It's all right. We're just crossing the creek, we'll be on the other side in a minute. There'll be a Company guide waiting for you at the Rest House, Mrs. Polar. She'll show you Barrow in style. A nice college girl and smart as they come."

"We'd rather have you."

"These days there isn't quite enough of me to go round. But I thank you, madam."

"Now what did you mean by that, Thor Storm!" Bridie demanded. But they drew up now, with a final swirl, in front of the stark wooden house that was to shelter them. There on the steps was the Company guide, a hearty girl in parka and mukluks and no hat, who took over the Polars in a single gesture. You knew that by noon next day they would know Barrow from the 4-H Club and the Visiting Nurse Clinic to the Will Rogers-Wiley Post Memorial.

There, too, in the entrance, stood a nattily dressed Eskimo in dark-lensed sun goggles.

"Hello, George!" Thor called in greeting. "Bridie, this is George Sootuk. Mrs. Ballantyne. My granddaughter Christine."

"How do you do," the young man said, with enormous manner. "Never see you look so well year sometime, Mr. Storm." He took from his parka pocket a notebook and a bright green pen which he clicked down with professional speed. "Mrs. and Miss, I stand here George Sootuk, am Barrow correspondent for newspaper Baranof *Lode*. What are you do here?"

"Tourists," Bridie snapped, with a tinge of acid.

Christine decided to cover this with charm. As occasional pinch-hitting exchange editor armed with scissors and paste pot in the office of the *Northern Light* she had seen some of George Sootuk's pidgin-English columns, terse, gossipy, outspoken, as they appeared under the heading of Arctic News. "I've always wanted to see Barrow. So fascinating. Grampa brought me up to Barrow—brought us up—because it's an educational tour, too."

It was baffling not to see George Sootuk's eyes behind those black-lensed goggles. The brown face was impassive. "Ross Guildenstern punished for taking you up, penalize six weeks."

Thor was stunned. "Where did you hear that nonsense, George?"

"Mukluk grapevine," Sootuk said, cheerfully. "Barrow mukluk grapevine always true."

"There it is, Thor," Bridie said in a kind of terrible triumph.

An Eskimo woman of perhaps thirty came toward them down the hall.

"You girls run along and freshen up," Thor said, quietly. "It's nearly nine, we'd better have some dinner. Mrs. Awuna will show you your rooms, won't you, Lorena? Mrs. Awuna is the manager." He did not skimp the ceremony of introduction. Mrs. Awuna, in a crisp pink house dress and a permanent wave turned a sparkling gaze of appreciation on Bridie's smart costume. "You look very nice," she said in precise schoolgirl English.

Bridie softened under this. "Why, thanks, honey. I try not to look like a bear."

This sent Mrs. Awuna off into disproportionate cascades of laughter. Still giggling, she showed them two cubicles, side by side. In each a narrow bed, very neat; a table, a chair, a shelf, a curtained row of wall hooks. A window. The night sun was shining upon every object.

"Why, it's just lovely!" Chris said, feeling suddenly gay.

Bridie poked her head out of her doorway, inquiringly. Mrs. Awuna ceased her giggling, an aura of managerial grandeur enveloped her. She pointed down the hall, majestically. "We have two washstands with running water, hot and cold. We have two toilets with water. We have a shower. We are as good as Juneau or Anchorage or Baranof or Fairbanks."

"Better," agreed Bridie as she skipped down the hall.

As they opened their bags they could hear Thor clumping about in his room overhead, almost immediately he could be heard clumping his way downstairs. "Christine! Bridie!"

"Minute!"

In the entrance hall that served as office lolled a big man who was drinking beer from a can. Beside him sat a sallow and careworn woman in an inadequate pink coat and a small-town summer hat. Six unopened cans of beer were neatly ranged on the floor beside the man's chair.

"Come on now, Ernie," the woman was saying. "Here I been waiting for you all day, and now when you come you're like this."

As Bridie and Chris joined Thor now, the man waved his drink in their direction. "Hi, folks! Come on have a couple cans of beer with me. Celebrate. I been here a year, working on this crazy radar. She's come all the way from Nebraska, visit me, whaddyou know! Have a drink. Celebrate!"

"Thanks," Thor said. "We're just going across the way there to have dinner at the lunchroom. We're hungry. We came in on the evening plane."

"That's what I tell him," the woman said quickly. "If he'd just have something hot to eat he'd feel better."

"I couldn't feel better, if I felt better I'd be sick." The man contemplated this witticism a moment, prepared to laugh if the others did, decided against it, took another long draught from the can, placed it carefully on the floor, empty, and picked up an unopened one. "Couldn't eat a bite. Not a mouthful."

Bridie looked at the woman's haggard face. "You come on along with us, have a bite of dinner. Maybe your husband would like to take a little nap, join us later."

Immediately the man turned from good-fellowship to belligerence. "No you don't! You sit right here and like it, hear me! You come all this way up here to see me, you sit right here. No dinner. Who needs dinner!"

Thor opened the door, the three stood a moment on the little porch. The grim row of weather-blackened houses, the black dust of the roadway, had come alive with movement and color. Groups of Eskimo girls stepped daintily through the grinding dirt that had been churned to powder by the giant wheels of four-drive trucks and caterpillars. Their parkas were not made of the skins of Arctic animals or sea beasts, hunted by their fathers, cured by their mothers, and sewn with the enduring threads of moose or caribou sinews. Now, on their way to the Saturday-night dance they wore cotton velveteen parkas of red and blue and yellow and pink, ordered by mail from the Sears Roebuck catalogue, and brought by plane to this icebound wilderness that was a wilderness no longer.

The old man and the two women were silent and thoughtful as they descended the steps and plunged in ankle-deep dust toward the lunchroom. Eskimo boys passed them, in pairs and groups, they wore black leather jackets and tight pants, they were hatless and crew cut, their stiff bristling black hair lending itself to the mode. They did not join the girls, they glanced at them with quick slanting looks. One of the girls rated a second glance, she even garnered a wolf whistle. Her sturdy legs, in the cold Arctic evening, were sleek in sheer nylon stockings like all the others, but about the ankles they were ornamented with brilliant sequins, scarlet and silver and gold, in a pattern of butterflies and flowers that sparkled in the glaring night sun. She was wearing sandals with open toes and a back strap slipped over the heel. Boys and girls on their way to the Saturday-night dance, to the movie, to the lunchroom Coke, there in the polar night, like tens of millions of boys and girls from the Atlantic coast to the Pacific coast to the Arctic coast.

Almost defiantly Christine said, "I think they look darling."

"Who said they didn't?" Bridie retorted. They had come abreast of the sequin-stockinged girl. As though to prove her broad-mindedness Bridie smiled at her as they passed. "My, you look pretty, all dressed up!"

"Thank you." Quite charmingly. Even polar Barrow was inured to tourists by now. "Are you coming to the dance?"

"Me! I'm too old to dance, dear."

The girl stared at the pink cheeks, the snapping blue eyes, she shook her head, smiling. "Oh, no. My grandmother dances. She's much older than you, nobody knows how old, she must be sixty."

As they turned toward the restaurant Bridie pondered this. "It started out kind of backhanded, but it turned out a compliment."

"That poor fellow," Thor mused, aloud. "Stir-crazy, I suppose, more than just drunk on a couple of cans of beer. You see it all the time now, in Alaska. They come here from Outside and they're not used to it. Alone too long."

"Nobody makes him stay, do they?" Christine asked, briskly. "He isn't Army. Why does he stay, then?"

"Money, Christine. Money."

"The way you say money," Bridie said, rather crossly for her, "a person would think it was something dirty."

"Money's just wonderful!" Chris declared. "It paid for this trip, and look at your lovely coat and hat, Bridie, and my education in Seattle when I go. And everything. I like money."

"So do I, Christine. I even think it's more important than you do. I've been fighting all my life to have money earned in Alaska stay in Alaska and pay for all the things Alaska needs. That drunken lonely construction worker or cat-skinner or whatever he is typifies that old saying about Alaska and Outsiders—you know it—*Get in, get it, and get out.*"

"Thor Storm, if you're going to give one of your lectures in the lunchroom I won't set foot, I'll go to bed starving, sooner."

His hand on the door, he smiled down at Bridie. "Wait till you see the prices here, Bridie my girl. You'll probably give a lecture yourself."

Every stool at the U-shaped double counter in the Farthest North Lunchroom was occupied by men and women and children, white and brown, all eating with happy concentration like little boys and girls at a party. Rows of parkas hung from hooks on the wall. The aroma of ham and steaks frying, of coffee and fresh warm bread, enveloped the three like an actual substance as they entered the hot bright room. The Roller Polars together with the Company guide were seated at the farther side of the counter, they were eating steaks, everybody, Eskimo and white, seemed to be eating steaks, the Eskimo faces were blissful. A menu chalked on the wall blackboard read: Sirloin beefsteaks in today $10. There was no vacant seat.

"Hi!" the Polars called, gaily. The three nodded and smiled, everyone in the lunchroom nodded and smiled—all except three small children seated side by side at the curved end of the counter nearest the door. Two small boys and a girl, perhaps eight, nine, and ten. They regarded the newcomers gravely, eating the while, they studied Bridie's hat coat gloves bag blue-white hair make-up with utter concentration and gravity, but a gleam lurked in the older boy's eyes. They were consuming lemon pie and soda pop. The older boy finished, and now in his hand he waved a five-dollar bill idly to and fro.

"Civilization," Thor said.

A plump and pretty Eskimo waitress in a white nylon uniform came down the inside length of the counter, her arms hugging four loaves of freshly baked white bread, the scent was fragrant as flowers. She plumped them down and reached below the counter for a paper sack into which she deftly slid the warm loaves.

"You children finished," she said, "you run along home now. Your mother wants this bread." The two younger ones swigged the remaining soda pop, tiptilting their heads and the bottles. The boy gave her the five-dollar bill, they slid off the stools, their faces flashed into animation as they suddenly smiled at the three waiting adults. They were off, closing the door quietly behind them.

"White bread," Thor groaned in a tone that seemed sepulchral out of all proportion to his subject. "White bread made with processed flour, it doesn't matter how good it smells; and lemon pie, cornstarch-filled, and soda pop. For thousands of years they've survived and been nourished by seal oil and fat fish and whale meat and caribou and tundra greens. A triumph of survival over the most terrible climate in the Arctic. And now the children eat white bread and lemon——"

"Grampa dear," Chris said. She put her hand on his arm. "Grampa dear."

"I'll treat everybody to steaks," Bridie announced.

His tone was gentle, his eyes quizzical. "I'm solvent, Bridie. And maybe these restaurant folks will take an ad in the *Northern Light* to attract the tourist trade. You're a fine independent woman, Bridie, but you mustn't take his manhood rights away from a man. Maybe that's why you and I never married."

"I could have married any man in Baranof or in Alaska, for that matter, fifty years ago, you included, if I'd put my mind to it."

"Perhaps it would have been better if you had, Bridie. For me, at least." But then he looked down at Christine's hand on his arm, he reached over and placed his free hand on hers. "No, I'll have to take that back. Because then there would have been no Christine."

The waitress placed on the counter near them a vast and improbable cake covered with bright green icing, a fearsome sight. Calm, kind, childlike, she smiled at the three. "I saved this one for you, Mr. Storm, the minute I heard you were in town. Nobody's going to get a crumb of it till I've cut you the first slice. Now. What do you and the ladies want? I've got caribou stew and liver and onions and steak——"

"Steak," said Thor.

All about the counter the Eskimo Dew Line workers and their wives and children were eating up the Saturday night's pay. Pork chops and steak, hamburgers and lemon pie, cake and liver and bacon—quietly and neatly they ate away until the pay envelope had vanished. In their faces shone a gustatory delight, like that reflected by the gourmets and gourmands stuffing themselves ecstatically at the Pavillon in New York, Maxim's in Paris, Claridge's in London. Here was a world they never had known or dreamed of. Philosophically, they took it as it came, a gift from the spirits of good. If, tomorrow, all this should vanish—the strange sensitive scientific machines, the airplanes, the powerful vehicles, the monsters that spanned the frozen tundra in the winter, the antennae that so mysteriously received warnings the white man's ear did not detect—all these were real today. They accepted them without question, like children. Their friendly amiable faces reflected their satisfaction in the Distant Early Warning, in radar and four-engine planes, and four-layer cakes, and electricity and beefsteaks. If, tomorrow, all these enchanting things should go as mysteriously as they had come, there, still, was the Arctic Ocean with its riches of whale and seal and polar bear and fish; the tundra with its caribou for meat, its furred creatures for clothing, the dogs for travel. They had been there for thousands of years, they would be there for thousands more.

Thor explained this to the two women, quietly, as they sat perched on the counter stools eating the nourishing meal, the great nickel coffee urn in the corner and the baking loaves in the oven sending forth their aroma; the ice pack on the Arctic shore just outside the door grinding and groaning and crashing in a titanic obbligato.

He was, in a way, talking aloud to himself as he now so often did; a musing audible soliloquy. "It may kill them off, in time. Maybe that's what we want, unconsciously. Perhaps if they can eat enough butter and meat and milk and vegetables it will take the place of the seal oil and the muktuk. But that takes money, a great deal of money, and all this bustle and scramble of building will be finished one day. Of course the tuberculosis rate is higher than ever. The girls go with the workers, Scandinavian, Irish, American, Italian, German-background men. Lonely men, like that poor lad at the Rest House."

"There you go, Thor, making that speech you said you wouldn't. I'm going to have a piece of that cake," Bridie announced, "if it kills me."

"I'd like to go to the dance," Chris said. "To see it, anyway."

"Why not? I'll dance with you both, if nobody else does. I used to be a great dancer at the balls in—I used to be quite a dancer when I was a young fellow."

Bridie threw him a penetrating glance. "I bet. Too bad Chris here was too late for those balls, and so on. I'd like to know what you think Barrow's going to do for her education. It's interesting, I ain't saying it's not, but what can a girl brought up like Chris was get out of it, only sight-seeing. Steak's no treat for Chris. Or Eskimos, either. Now, the Legislature meeting in Juneau, and society and club movements in Anchorage and all that, that's different, you learn something."

Mildly, "You may be right, Bridie. But these were my two years with Christine. I wanted her to see it all, new Alaska and old Alaska. I think that this Barrow we're seeing today, so near the North Pole, is a newer Alaska than anything Christine saw down in the Banana Belt."

The meal finished, they stood a moment just outside the door, blinking in the blatant sunshine. The dance music came to them in the clear cold air. The street was strangely busy with figures passing to and fro, they did not loiter, it was as though they were intent on errands of importance. You heard the high clear voices of children at play.

"I ought to be sleepy," Bridie said, "my age. But I ain't."

Chris pulled a deep breath into her lungs, exhaled it. "I feel just wonderful. Steak, I suppose, and coffee, and all that frightening cake."

Thor beamed down on them, approvingly. "It's only midnight. Just right for the dance."

The dance hall was a long rough shed, the big room was dimmer than any Broadway danceland, red shades covered the electric globes. Boys in duck-tail haircuts and narrow cuffed pants and flamboyant shirts. Girls in bouffant skirts and flat little ballet slippers. They danced exactly as the boys and girls danced at midnight in San Francisco, and Chicago and New York. Between this Eskimo village and those famed cities there were four hours difference in time, five hours, six hours. Thousands of miles. They clung close, they flung their bodies about in the parabolas of acrobats, they stamped and postured. They disappeared into corners, they fled outside into the unkindly glare of the polar sun, they drank from bottles like California or Ohio or Connecticut young rebels in protest against a frightening world.

Chris had pushed back her parka hood. Her hair was like a light in that dim room. No one asked her to dance. The music was a phonograph blasting at full strength. "I'm a wallflower at nineteen."

Thor made a courtly bow before her. "If I knew what they call whatever it is they're dancing," he said.

"I'm too old for it, Grampa. You and Bridie. She's dying to dance, aren't you, Bridie? Look at the way she's tapping that foot!"

Stricken, he looked at Bridie. Too late. Bridie's left hand touched his shoulder, her right hand grasped his left. "Let's give it a waltz, Thor. For old time's sake. I've waltzed in my day to a jig tune. Once around and we'll quit or I'll be dead on my feet." In a sort of stately court minuet they moved off into the maelstrom.

As they moved precariously away, "I'll see you at the house!" Chris called. For the first time in her orphaned life she felt terribly alone. She ran down the road in the brilliant sunlit night. There were people all about, as they passed her the gentle friendly faces, the laughing eyes flashed in greeting. Hi! they said. Men women children. Hi! Savoring this brief cold bright handful of days and nights that was their summer.

But the Rest House, when she reached it, resounded with the imprecations of Ernie. A verbal torrent of obscenity, profanity, of wild raging against the world, against his wife, his life, his job. The woman's placating weary murmur was the twanging of a loose wire in a thunderstorm.

"Oh, no!" Christine said to herself, aloud. She walked the length of the hall as noisily as possible, coming down hard on her heels. Was no one interested in sleep in all this honeycomb of tiny bedrooms? Her own room was bright as day, but a lifetime of Baranof summers had accustomed her to this. The window was fastened and nailed tight against the cold. She was used to that, too. A yellow window shade, futile against the sun. Oh, well. Hastily she scrawled a note and pinned it on Bridie's door. Good night Bridie dear simply bushed see you morning Chris. She dashed to the lavatory and back to her room, she shut her door just as Bridie and Thor returned, she stood very quiet, visualizing their startled faces as they entered the bare little front office to a blast of profanity and howled complaint. As the ravings ceased for a moment Chris could plainly hear

Bridie's high crisp tones and Thor's less distinct and soothing murmur.

"Well, somebody's got to stop him, the way he's yelling like a banshee."

"He'll fall asleep, he must be exhausted by now."

"I don't know whether he is, but I sure am. Isn't somebody in charge here?"

"No. Not till morning."

The shouts of anger and protest rose again, died away, the wife's tearful murmur trickled through the torrent.

"Ain't you going to do a thing about stopping him?"

"No."

"Then I will. This keeps on I'm going to knock at the door, I've got some sleeping pills with me, if she can get a couple of those down his big mouth while it's open yelling, and slosh some more of that beer into him, he'll be cooked."

"Not a bad idea, Bridie. Two for him and one for you, and you'll be set until morning. Good night, my dear. And thanks for the waltz."

Bridie stopped at the closed door. Chris held her breath. Now she's reading the note, Chris decided a moment later. Now she's taking out the pills. Oh, wouldn't it be wonderful! I can't stand a night of this.

The shouting rose and fell. Mutterings and groans from the occupants of the other cubbyholes. Then Bridie's high heels tapping along the corridor's bare floor and her three determined raps at Ernie's door. Bridie's incisive instructions, the woman's murmured doubts, her tone, then, of reluctant acceptance.

Bridie's, "I'll do it, then."

"No, no! I will. I promise. I'm sorry, I'm sorry."

Chris lay in her narrow bed, now the sun rose full blast, its glittering swords thrust themselves through the space at the sides of the ineffectual window shade. She turned her face to the wall, she thought of her bedroom her bed her yielding luxurious mattress at Grampa Czar's, her pink sateen pillow with the good linen slips still miraculously surviving from the absurd trousseau of Czar's bride, the grandmother she never had known; the glint of the water and the thundering majesty of mountains against the blue sky from her Baranof bedroom window. Gus's breakfast coffee and little Swedish hot rolls. Seattle . . . Husack heir, Seattle money, Kennedy heiress, Alaska money. Like royalty.

How ridiculous. But anyway, this is the last of this. Barrow. What was it that man said? Who needs—uh—it was something—well, anyway, who needs Barrow! Oh, listen to him, oh he's worse than ever! I can't stand it I just can't stand it all night I'm going to ask Bridie for one of those sleeping p . . .

It was Sunday morning, it was ten o'clock, there actually was hot water, the toilet worked, the house was too hot but all Alaska houses were too hot. Slacks, mukluks, sweater, parka. Bridie's voice somewhere down the hall. Breakfast. The lunchroom. I'll have some of that lovely light home-baked bread, toasted, and they'll have canned orange juice and maybe bacon——

In the little hot front office Bridie was chatting with the scrawny wife. The woman was wearing the crumpled pastel pink coat and the straw hat as on the night before.

"You don't say!" Bridie was exclaiming as one enthralled, while the woman poured out her fears and resentments as people did under the beneficent radiance of Bridie's encouragement.

"Four children," the woman was saying.

"Well, now, that's lovely."

"Lovely! But in the street is where they have to play, that's why he had the idea to come here in the first place."

"How's that again?"

"Five hunderd a week, they said. Ernie read where they'd pay that, they were putting up a thing up here, you can tell what's coming at you a thousand miles away. Planes and rockets and like that. I don't understand those things, anyway, he does, he told me and I said what's the world coming to, it won't be fit for the children to live in, pretty soon. Five hunderd a week, he said. He wouldn't make that in a month in Detroit, even overtime. We figured it out about the pay up here, he said six months, five hunderd a week, he figured twelve thousand, can you imagine! We could buy us a house and pay for it, and a yard for the kids to play. I said right away, we'll make out, the kids and me, go on up, you say your fare's paid and all, what's six months, suppose it was a war! First he didn't seem to mind, he said it was cockeyed, the cold and all, and then the daylight all the time, and everything secret, he never did know what he was doing he just did it. Then he kept writing it was lonely, you just laid in your bunk and looked at the ceiling. So I kept writing stick it out for the kids' sakes, it's only six months then it's a home for all of us forever, no rent. But then he sounded real desperate, so I got my mother to come in, I took a plane the first time in my life, I thought we'd never get here and here I am and now look at the way he acted last night."

Chris, dressed and standing at the door, apologetically at first until she saw that the woman was past caring who heard her, thought it must be awful it must be unbearable to be married to a man like that. She recalled the filth the obscenities that had seemed like an actual stench in the hot little Rest House. Marriage could be horrible, she thought. How could you know what it would be, beforehand?

"Tell you what," Bridie was saying, her usually penetrating tones now low and confidential. "Tell you what, Miz—what'd you say your name was?"

"Cowgill. Mrs. Ernie Cowgill, his mother was a Wouter, there isn't a better family in Michigan, he never behaved like this, well, he'd have a drink now and then, but he never was a drinking man, not like this. I don't know what's got into him, if it wasn't for the kids I'd leave him."

"Tell you what. If I was you I'd figure like he'd been sick and when he wakes up he's well. I'm a nurse by profession. I've seen it a thousand times. Look. Five hundred a week, five thousand a week, it don't mean a thing to a man who's lonesome. He can't talk to it he can't sleep with it. I bet your Ernie was so keyed up thinking about your coming he couldn't take it in, it knocked him flat, he took a couple of beers before your plane got in, maybe a whiskey on top of that, next thing all the poison he's been storing up these months has got to let loose. That's all. Pay it no mind. Come on over have a cup of good hot coffee with me, get yourself fixed up, and when he wakes up maybe he'll get some coffee down. If I was you I wouldn't throw last night in his face, just talk about the house you and the kids are going to have——" Then, as the woman's face hardened, "A man who'll give up his home and his friends and his whole way of living to come up here and work in this Godforsaken place, why, that's a man who loves his wife and kids."

To her own amazement Chris heard herself saying, "This isn't a Godforsaken place."

She opened the door, closed it, stood a moment on the little gritty porch. Along the pathway plodded the muffled figures. Far down the road, as they reached the creek, she saw that they took off their Sunday shoes and donned the waterproof mukluks they carried in their hands, and waded across the icy shallow water that divided the little settlement. On the opposite shore they left the boots on the creek bank and put on the shoes. They walked on. A row of boots, dozens of them, strewed the ground. How could they tell them apart when they returned for them? Older men and women. The pink and blue and green velveteen parkas were sleeping after last night's dance.

The church bells rang across the wind-buffeted July ice pack. Catholic bells. Methodist bells. Baptist bells. Presbyterian bells. The neat white-painted mission houses of worship. They all sounded alike across the crystal clear air, across the dust-fine Arctic sand, across the grinding ice floes.

24

Letter from Czar Kennedy to Dave Husack

August 12
1953

Dear Dave—

I am writing this long hand and mailing it to the house instead of the office because I figure there are some things that even Etta Gurkin does not have to know. You know an old watch dog like Etta sometimes they get so use to guarding the boss and screening everything and everybody that comes in, why they get mixed up and are likely to bite a friend by mistake. Usually I dictate letters as you know, I am not much of a hand for writing even if I do own the biggest circulation newspaper in Alaska. I don't pretend to be a writer like old Storm the publisher of that handbill called the Northern Light. *My education quite when I was twelve years old back in Massachusetts, so I let the reporters and the editors do the writing and I just stick to the unimportant things like the papers policy and the money end. I am pretty good at that as you might have noticed and I am not too proud to use a dictionary when I come across a word I am not sure of. Well there I go again I find latly I catch myself rambling a little that is an old man's trick and I am not what you could call an old man yet so I better watch myself. You probly do the same thing and don't tell me you don't because I have caught you at it and too polite to call your attention. Anyway I am better at talking or clamming up than writing.*

Here is the thing. This letter is for you and Louisa both. That is another reason why I am sending it to the house. It was mighty kind of you both to offer to take my Christine in to live at your beautiful house during her first year at the University at least, and I want to thank you for this again and tell you I won't forget it. I would have liked that fine and it would have been a wonderful thing for Christine but you know how young people are nowdays. Independent they have got to be independent they say but I notice that when it comes to taking the money handouts they kind of overlook the independents for a minute.

So Christine says she wants to live in a college dorm—they won't permit private apartments. She says whatever I can afford or say she can do I will say this for Christine she never tries to put the squeeze. Bridie Ballantyne says a young girl should not live in an apartment alone going to college but Christine is all for it and then Bridie says well young people nowdays if they want to act modern why an automobile is just as handy parked as an apartment in my day she says back in Ireland it used to be a haystack and if you are going to misbehave an apartment or a haystack or an auto it is all one but Christine is not that kind of a girl she says. By the way, Bridie is getting to be a kind of a niusance running things and all I hear she is going to run for Territorial Congress and she keeps yapping her head off about statehood and all that slop a lot of good it will do her eh Dave old boy?

The thing is to come to the point I have got that old puffpot Thor to let Christine come to Seattle a little early before school really starts so she can get settled and look at a place to live and get some clothes she needs and kind of get settled in and comfortable and I would like to bring her down myself about August 25. I can only stay about two days and I will be at the Olympic as usual but if Christine stays on like we plan then I would be mighty thankful to you if she could visit at your place just till we get things set up for her and all, her apartment and her clothes and college connections and so on. Old Bridie says the clothes here in Baranof are as good looking as the clothes you would buy in Paris or anywhere, the bossy old girl is getting kind of like the fellow says the harder the arteries the softer the brain. Old Thor Storm is getting to be the same, I must tell you some of the latest about the old Viking when I see you, his trip north I mean he dragged Christine from the Banana Belt to the North Pole with him that was his way of educating my wonderful girl.

I won't beat around the bush, another reason why I want to come down I want to get a look at the Buccaneer. *I know she made that trial trip in good shape and I understand she will be tied up at the Seattle docks waiting to go into dry dock for stripping for next season. I sure have to laugh when I think of those big fine brocade saloons and cabins and decks and all covered with fish and slime and stink, I bet old B. T. Gates is whirling in his grave like a top. I have only seen pictures of her she sure must have been a humdinger of a beautiful yacht in her day, yacht hell she was like an ocean liner, well her champagne and caviar and Rivera days are over, they strip her down in drydock get those satin drapes off and all that heavy expensive woodwork and snakework and so on, get the excess weight off her, why I bet she can carry more fish out of Alaska and into the hoppers than any twenty tenders and thats a fact. Christine would like to see her too, I bet, so we will make a kind of party of it, my treat, come and bring the children like they say in the ads. Let me know if this visit I mention is inconvent and I will make plans otherwise.*

Faithfully yours,
Zebedee (Czar) Kennedy

25

"They're good," Louise Husack announced at the end of what Dina termed the Style Show, "but they're dowdy."

Dowdy. Christine had never actually heard this old-fashioned term used before, and certainly never as applied to her own clothes. As she stood now in her good black nylon slip edged with sturdy black lace her face reflected a shocked unbelief. This adjective was used to describe her Baranof-bought college outfit. Instinctively, protectively, her bare arms hugged herself, a palm cupping either elbow. The narrow black line of the slip's shoulder strap accented the firm fine beauty of her arms and her breast. Her hair, as the result of having had dresses and blouses and pullovers dragged over its lavish golden mass, now tumbled in a confusion that might have seemed Medusa-like in an older woman but that only enhanced the lusciousness of this girl's dishabille. As she had pulled garments off and on before the critical gaze of Mrs. Dave Husack and Dina Drake she had become warmer and more uncomfortably warm (like a true Alaskan, she found Outside temperatures tropical) and increasingly disturbed and even resentful, this last a rare emotion in a girl usually so good-tempered. Her face had taken on a flush unusual in that clear peach-colored skin. The high cheekbones wore a brilliant patch of deep pink as though an inexperienced hand had applied an injudicious dab of rouge.

Dina Drake, staring pitilessly at this girl standing before her in Louise Husack's overstuffed rose-colored bedroom, realized that here was a human structure as nearly flawless in youth, health, intelligence, beauty and artlessness as such an example can be. She felt a sudden sharp stricture as though an unseen needle had darted a stitch through her heart.

Chris remembered now what Czar had said before she had left Baranof for Seattle. "Listen, Bridie. I want Christine to have the best. Dresses and coats and so on. None of this parka and mukluk stuff. That's fine for Alaska, but Seattle is different."

Now standing before her two Seattle inquisitors, Chris flung her arms out in a gesture of explanation and protest, mingled. "But Bridie and I bought them just before I came here, we get the new autumn styles early in Baranof because it gets cold the end of August or early Septem—why, the Hollywood Fashion Shop and the Miss and Mrs. Baranof Shop—they advertise Miss and Mrs. Never Misses —get the newest California sports things and even New York styles ordered absolutely direct."

The brocade rose-colored bed, the satin chairs, the handsome inlaid fruitwood tables were atumble with dresses, sweaters, blouses. No hats.

Dina looked at the girl's hair. Her eyes narrowed, she smiled amusedly, though her tone was kind. "Poor kid, you'll have to chop that stuff off, to begin with."

"Chop what?"

"That floor mop. Honestly, child, I haven't seen anything like that since they stopped reading me 'Goldilocks' or whatever her name was, and the 'Three Bears.'"

Louise Husack, who had been examining a pink silk party dress (Chris's absolute best) that lay in her lap, turning it inside out to inspect the seams and shaking her head over the crude finish, now looked up at Christine as though actually seeing her for the first time and then, slowly, her gaze turned toward Dina and that gaze, too, had in it a quality of new vision.

"Why, Christine's hair is lovely. Just lovely." She spoke deliberately. "Don't you let anybody cut it, Christine. It's the kind of hair you don't see now, it's the kind of lovely long hair a man would like to choke himself with winding it around his neck—if he had the chance."

Dina stood up. She pulled herself up very high from the waist, out of what she sometimes referred to as the rib cage. She adjusted her waistline and stretched her neck from side to side as though bored and finished with it all.

"Let me know if I can help. Most of the good shops and the department heads and so on know me. I get a professional discount, you know. From when I was in pictures and"—humbly—"one of those little models with the patent-leather hatbox." She turned away with a small properly stifled yawn, then turned back to face the girl. "But if you're going to buy some things that aren't tacky you'll have to take off some of that fat, first."

"Fat! I wear size twelve!"

"I'm an eight."

There came a discreet knock at the closed door. "It's the coffee," Louise Husack's tone had the greedy anticipation of the caffeine addict. "Come in! I sure need it."

Christine Storm covered her face with her two hands in what was to her an unprecedented feeling of inferiority.

"What's going on here! The trial of Joan of Arc?" Bayard Husack leaned against the doorway. Dina walked toward him, she just placed her fingers against his cheek, gently, as a wife might greet a husband home from a day at the office. "What timing, Bay!"

Louise Husack was scandalized. "Bayard Husack, get right out of here!"

"Why?"

"Because Chris is trying on clothes, that's why."

Christine did not cringe or wrap herself in her arms, or otherwise display maidenly confusion at being viewed by male eyes while wearing a black nylon lace-trimmed slip that came well down below her knees and well up above her breasts. She was cross and upset. "Hi, Bay," she said, spiritlessly.

Bay remained negligently leaning against the doorway. Dina now put a hand on his shoulder and, just as negligently, leaned against him.

A dull unbecoming flush so rare in the elderly now suffused Louise Husack's ocherous cheeks. She gave a poor performance of shocked propriety. "Barging into my bedroom and staring at a young girl!"

"Ladies," Bayard Husack said, "pardon my mom. She's got a dirty mind. The truth is, Christine—or should I say Miss Storm—I'll take that up later—anyway, the truth is that girls in slips and girls in those strapless evening jobs and even girls in bikinis and a couple of clam shells—in fact, *especially* girls in those sordid gadgets—simply don't attract me. It's a deviation in me, or perhaps a perversion. But just let me see a girl who's wrapped up from head to foot like a laundry bundle! That brings out the beast in me."

From the pile of garments on the bed Christine now dug out a bulky navy blue chain-knit sweater with a turtle-neck collar. This she pulled over her head thrust her arms into the thick sleeves, and jerked its folds well down over her hips.

"I brought three parkas with me from Alaska," she announced. "Looks to me as if one would do it."

Dina gave a definitely bad performance of an indulgent laugh. "Don't pay any attention to him, Chris. He's just a sheep in wolf's clothing."

"And don't think," Bay added, genially, "that when Lucrezia died the whole Borgia line passed out."

Dina turned her head, already so near his own, their faces were now an inch or two apart. "You're getting to be as catty as a woman."

He reached up and gently took her hand from his shoulder. "What's going on here!" demanded a bewildered Louise.

"Here's your coffee, Mom," Bay said. The maid bumped her inexpert way into the room, a laden tray in her hazardous hands. "Here. I'll take that."

He looked about him at the burdened tables, Chris cleared a low stand and dragged it with some effort to the side of Louise's chair. "My!" Chris said, red-faced and surprised.

Bay set the tray down. "Teakwood. Good girl! Weighs a ton."

"Who wants coffee?" But even as she asked, Louise Husack poured herself a cup and drank half the steaming beverage without the ceremony of cream or sugar or hostess. She put down the cup and exhaled a deep breath.

Chris had learned something of the ways of the elderly in her almost twenty years of life. "Would you like me to pour it? Would you like a cup, Dina?"

"No, but I'd like a drink. I'll stop on my way downstairs. I'm late. Coming down, Bay?"

"Nope."

Dina had turned to leave. Now she stood a moment, arrested in the doorway. Louise Husack picked up a sandwich, she opened one of its thin flaps and peered in, cautiously. Then, with a smile of purest anticipatory pleasure she took a large semicircular oozing bite. "Coffee, Chris dear? Try one of these." Thickly.

"No thanks. But I'd love a Coke. I'm thirsty after all those clothes."

"It's an act," Dina Drake said, cryptically. She was off down the stairway.

"A Coke." Bay Husack repeated the word paternally, almost fondly. "She wants a Coke. Come on, kid. I'll get it for you."

Louise called after them, "Remember you've got to be dressed and ready by six, your Grandpa and Mr. Husack are meeting us at the dock, and then dinner at the Olympic. You coming down with us just this once, Bayard?"

"Why not!"

Christine picked up an armload of the rejected dresses. "I'd better not bother about the Coke, thank you."

"Here, give me those. You pick up another load. What is all this stuff, anyway?"

"They're my clothes—they *were* my clothes—for the winter. And now they're tacky."

He looked at her over the pile of garments. "As far as I'm concerned you're wearing a parka this minute."

Laden, they staggered down the hall to her bedroom.

"Where do you want these?"

"Just throw them on the bed."

"She's all right, great friend of the family and kind of social secretary for both Mom and Dad. But you're not taking her seriously, are you?"

"I was, just for a minute there. Not now. She's a real old-fashioned girl, the kind I used to read about in the novels in Grampa Czar's bookcase. She ought to have a rose in her teeth and a knife in her garter."

He dumped the dresses on the bed. "Say!"

"She's going to marry you, isn't she?"

"Look, infant, you're supposed to answer the questions, not ask them."

"I've asked questions all my life. I was brought up that way."

"Get into one of the tacky dresses and drive down to the dock with me, how about it?"

"I'm going down with Aunt Louise—she told me to call her Aunt Louise—and the others, whoever you are."

"More fun with me."

"Look, I'm here in Seattle to go to school, I'm just here as your guest for two weeks—and mighty nice of you as Grampa Czar says —but please don't get me mixed up, would you please?"

"Do you always talk like this?"

"Like what?"

"Like a kind of verbal prize fighter. Do the Alaska boys like it?"

"They love it. Ask anybody."

Now he was leaning against her doorway as he had in his mother's room. Chris was hanging the despised garments neatly in her closet, jabbing the clothes hangers into the sleeves with more force than was necessary.

"Why don't you stay on here at the house. Heaps of room. Mom and Dad would love it."

"I'm dying to try living alone."

"Sounds ideal as preparation for married life."

"I've always lived with Grampa Thor or Grampa Czar. They've

been wonderful to me. But living alone must be dreamy. Uh, thanks for lugging the dresses in here."

He stood a moment longer in the doorway, he took a handful of keys from a pocket and jingled them in his palm and thrust them back. "We'll be leaving about quarter of six. The boat's going to be slimy and the Olympic dining room dressy, so that poses a nice question for you. Maybe one of your medium tacky numbers. Do you want that Coke?"

"I'd love it. I'll go down."

"I'll send Kea up with it." He turned away. "See you." He closed the door behind him.

On the drive down to the docks she found herself seated beside him. This rather surprised her. She had meant to be with Mrs. Husack in the back seat. Now Dina was there. Dina had demurred, certainly, though *sotto voce* and Bay had said with what Chris considered very bad manners, "Stop wrestling and do as I say or we'll be late. I hate being late." How precise and fussy he sounds, for a young man, Chris thought.

There was silence in the car as they sped down the twisting hill road. She felt vaguely uncomfortable, but her desire for information always had been stronger than her caution.

"The *Buccaneer*—tell me a little about her, will you? I know she was a beautiful yacht—one of the biggest in the world. Grampa Czar says they're going to gut her and use her for a fish carrier."

"That's it. She was the finest privately owned ship in the world, in her day. Nobody wants a ship like that these days. It cost millions to build. She's been lying around useless for years. She. A buccaneer isn't a she. But a ship always is. You ever hear of a lady buccaneer, Dina?" He turned his head a little to one side.

"The ocean's full of them."

"Do you think we can go for a little ride on her tonight, before dinner?" Chris asked. "I'd love it."

"No you wouldn't. Wait till you see her. They took her out on a trial trip for capacity, before they started to strip her. She's a real mess now."

"I don't see how they could do it."

"Oh, it's simple. Knock down partitions, all that fancy woodwork, the saloon and bedrooms were lined with satin brocade——"

"I don't mean that. I mean I don't see how anyone who cares about ships—I mean a ship that was the most beautiful yacht in the world——"

"Fish companies aren't quite that sentimental. Right, she was a queen—foolish, but a queen. It's quite a shock to see her now. Like Marie Antoinette after they chopped her head off."

The ship lay at the dock—the once bustling colorful docks over which the glinting airplanes now flew so tauntingly, so derisively, with their roar or screech or piercing whistle. Those docks had known ships from India, from China, from Japan, from exotic islands and tropical seas. Seattle no longer was host to these strange craft, or Skid Row to their yellow-skinned crew wearing queues, or to the lascars whose gold hoop earrings shone against their dusky cheeks.

The *Buccaneer* lay at the dockside. Neglected and idle for years, scabrous now and dirt-dimmed, deposed and degraded, the bone structure and the lines were still there, the breeding and distinction persisted. She looked vast, even now, among the little fishing boats and the squat tubs in from Victoria or the islands.

The four occupants of the Husack car—Louise Husack, Bayard, Dina, Christine—had a glimpse of the ship from the hilltop. As they drove down to the docks and into the Company pier itself two rubber-booted figures came toward them down the gangway. Czar Kennedy and Dave Husack, grinning, jubilant, waved a greeting and called out to them before the others had descended from the car.

"You'll have to wear boots," Dave yelled. His color, always roseate, had the purplish tinge of excitement. In one hand he carried what seemed to be a gold picture frame, and jumbled in his arms were miscellaneous articles of footgear. "Here. We scrounged a bunch of old mukluks and boots and stuff, it's pretty mucky, places. You girls better pin up your dresses a little." He pitched the boots into the floor of the car. "You fit 'em onto the girls, Bay, best you can."

Dina looked with disdain at the clumsy dirty boots. "I wear fours. And I'd rather ruin my pumps than get into those horrors."

Chris stuck out her foot. "Six and a half. I'd never even make the ball."

Cradled in one arm Czar Kennedy carried a dark-green gold-topped bottle. He held it up now. "Champagne. Domestic, but champagne all right. We'll have the real stuff at dinner, to celebrate, but you're going to break this over the bow, Christine, for luck."

Something in Chris was outraged at this. Like pinning an orchid on a raddled old woman, she thought. "You only do that when the boat is young and—and beautiful!"

"She's better than young," Czar said. "She's old and rich, she rates a bottle of champagne, she's worth her weight in gold—or silver salmon, anyway."

Dave turned the gold frame so that the picture it enclosed faced the newcomers. He thrust it in front of them, laughing. "Look at that, will you! It was hanging in one of the stateroom closets on a hook turned to the wall, can you beat that! The whole crowd of muckamucks, you'll die!"

It was a group photograph showing a party of men and women on deck. They seemed strangely naïve in their costumes of another day. The women wore long skirts and little jackets with broad revers and floppy hats with floating veils. The mustached men wore yachting caps and tight suits. The party was toasting someone or something and the whole effect was unnautical. There was nothing domestic about the vintage look of the plump dark bottles on the table or protruding from a silver ice bucket. "Look at the date!" Dave yelled. "That's the day the *Buccaneer* was launched. Look, there's old B.T. himself, and that's Rosalie Garrett, the actress——" And that one and that one and that one. "They're all dead now. Good and dead. But we ain't. Come on, folks. We'll take a look around and then over to the Olympic, I'm so hungry already, by God, I could eat a small boy with the measles. But first you're going to bust this bottle over the bow, Christine."

Clumping along in the clumsy misfitting boots Christine protested mildly. "I don't know how. I wish somebody else—"

"Don't look at me. Thanks." Dina linked an arm through Bay's.

He extricated his arm, apparently to remove a handkerchief from his pocket. "Here, we'll have to wrap a couple of handkerchiefs or something around the bottle and tie them. Somebody give me another. Dad?" Dave snatched a fine linen square from his pocket. For a moment the fishy dock smell was lost in a wave of spicy eau de cologne. "I don't want any broken glass making hamburgers of Christine."

The little party stood now looking up at the scrofulous bow of the old ship. Gingerly Chris took the bottle in one gloved hand. She seemed suddenly very small in the shadow of the structure looming above her; a trifle absurd, too, what with the clumsy boots and the blue silk dress that she had chosen as being the least tacky, and the matching blue coat that Bridie in Baranof had pronounced just the thing for Seattle August evenings; and the handkerchief-swathed bottle in her hand.

The others were grouped around her, their smiles a little stiff now. As she swung toward them they instinctively drew back a little. She swung her arm forward then, the loosely knotted handkerchiefs fluttered to the ground, the big bottle slipped in her gloved hand and fell with a smart smack into the waters of the bay below.

"Christ! That's bad luck!" Dave Husack shouted.

Czar's voice. "Easy now, Dave. Easy."

Chris closed her eyes a moment, opened them wide and wet. "I'm so sorry." She set her jaw a little, she looked at Dina. "I'm sure you could have done it beautifully."

"Forget it, Christine," Czar said, shortly. "Good thing it was only domestic, at that."

Louise Husack seemed relieved to the point of happiness. "I'm glad it's over, it was a silly notion anyway. I'm getting cold in this damp place, if we're going over the boat let's go and get through with it and have dinner."

Christine stood a moment staring down into the water as though expecting to see the big green bottle bobbing and taunting her there. An arm, friendly and protective, brushed across her shoulders. She looked around at Bay.

"You did that purposely."

"I did not!"

"I don't mean you did it purposely on purpose. I mean you wanted to do it and you couldn't help it. It was done when Czar first gave you the bottle."

"Oh." Did he think she was a little idiot who knew nothing about Freud and Jung and everything after two years at Baranof College! "Oh, that. Psychologically . . . Yes, I suppose so." She dusted one gloved hand with the other to rid her hand of the memory, as she had seen people do it in a play.

"You get cuter by the minute."

"Oh, do shut up." Suddenly she felt older and wiser than he—than anyone in the group now plodding up the gangway.

"Is that the way you talk to the Baranof boys?"

"I'm not in Baranof."

"But you wish you were."

She glanced quickly around, they were at the foot of the gangway, the others were ahead of them, Dina turned to wait for them, studiedly.

"No, I don't. I thought I would. I did, for a little while. But now I don't."

Czar turned at the ship's rail, he made a gesture of urging to the two loiterers. His voice sounded a little hollow for so big a man; or perhaps the ghostly empty ship sent back a cavernous note. "Come on, come on, Chris! Don't keep us waiting, too." Too.

"Can we go for a ride?" Christine asked as she stepped on deck.

They laughed tolerantly at this. Dave Husack thrust one great paw forward and pinched her cheek between two vise-like fingers (already she had learned to dodge that sadistic demonstration of affection, but this time she had not foreseen it). "Listen to the kid! The *Buccaneer's* going out at eight o'clock, headed for dry dock, but we're not going out on her. We'll be eating a good thick steak at the

Olympic, I hope." He stuck his head in at the door of the great saloon. "Heh, boys, I brought you company. Ladies."

The wreckers were working overtime. They hacked with hammers and crowbars and drills and acetylene torches and they had almost finished stripping this once magnificent room down to its aged bones. It had been gutted. The saloon and smoking room and cabin partitions had been torn away to make room for the millions of fish that would bring millions of dollars to the Husacks and the Caswells and the Kennedys and the Kleets and the men at the directors' tables in Washington and New York and San Francisco. Already the white enamel, the teakwood, the mahogany, the satin and brocade hangings, the deep-pile carpets were unimaginable. The rooms that had known the luxurious beds, the perfumed bodies; the passageways and dining rooms that had held the aroma of exquisite foods and vintage wines, the scent of rich black cigars, the prick of frosted cocktails, now reeked of the fish that had piled up on that first wildly successful trial trip when tons of them, like living silver, had choked the caverns of mahogany and silk. The caverns were cribs now, and men in hip boots slid and slipped on the slime of the floor.

"Take your ma's arm, Bay, you dope!" Dave said.

"Watch out there now, Christine." Czar's cautioning voice.

Now and then the ship seemed to quiver as with a chill. "It's the blowtorches," Bay explained as his mother looked around, nervously. "I don't think they ought to use them until they're in dry dock."

Dave Husack corrected this with a hoot of derision and triumph mingled. "No it isn't, dopey boy. This machinery in this little skiff was built like a watch, like one of those fine Swiss watches. That's why it cost the old boy about a million a minute to run her. Well, our fish ain't so delicate. We yanked out the delicate works first thing and we put in some good serviceable secondhand junk that will make the old tub go and that's all we need. But she's temperamental yet, she gives us a shiver now and then the way you would"—he laid a heavy hand on Dina Drake's shoulder—"if somebody was to take that pretty little mink doodad off of you and wrap you in burlap instead, see?" He did not pinch her cheek, though. His hand rested just a moment still on her shoulder. Then he turned away. His heavy hand descended now on Czar's hunched shoulder, he did not notice the little flame of dislike that flicked out at him from Czar's deep-set eyes.

"Give in? You ready to concede, Czar, old crab?" He was at his most jovial. "I been telling you all along, and the other boys have too, there's no damn sense in carrying a spoonful at a time in little tubs when an old pro like this can load ten times as much. She'll pay for herself in two three trips, like I said. Any old grease-monkey can run her engine now. She's good for another ten—fifteen—maybe twenty years. Man!"

Dina's skirts were lifted high above the slime of the decks, she had picked her way so fastidiously from place to place that her pretty black pumps were spotless, her lovely silken legs unflecked. She had come upon an empty wooden box and this she had mounted, still holding her skirts clutched high in one hand. "Uncle Dave, you're just a wizard." She placed one hand on his shoulder as though to balance herself, she stood a little above him on her perch, smiling down on the big beefy face.

Czar's cold voice, "You familiar with the cannery business, Miss—uh——?"

Dave's laugh boomed out somewhat hollow in tone. "Say, she ought to be by now, she's handled enough correspondence and heard enough gab about it."

Louise Husack sometimes surprised you. "Wizard or witch, we've seen this ship now, smells and looks like any other old stinking fish boat, only bigger." She placed one hand flat over the region vaguely supposed to shelter her heart. "Enough's enough. I'll take my salmon at the Olympic with a nice martini cocktail on the side."

Ill and old and raddled as she was, a kind of tonic decency emanated from her. Bay grinned, he tucked her hand under his arm. "That's telling 'em, kid." He steered her toward the gangway, he threw a glance over his shoulder at the others. "Come on, you young fry."

"Right!" Dave bellowed. "Anyway, they're pushing off for Spruce in another hour, we'll find ourselves in the middle of Elliott Bay if we don't watch it."

The head waiter at the entrance to the handsome main-floor dining room was a name dropper. Good evening, Mr. Husack. We have your table, Mr. Husack. This way, Mr. Husack. There were red roses in a bowl on Mr. Husack's table, two dark-green bottles, wire-capped, stuck their necks just above the wine bucket's bed of ice. A round table laid for six. Pink-shaded lights. Though its circular shape did not provide for a head or foot, Dave Husack gave the effect of being at the head of the table. Louise at his right, Christine at his left, Bay, Dina, Czar, in a neat ring.

"Three men three women." Louise, the perennial hostess. "If there's one thing I like, it's a balanced table."

"If there's one thing I like," Dave boomed, "it's a great big steak *that* thick. How about it, Emil? Say, take away those roses, will you, boy? They always give me hay fever or rose fever or whatever it is, in August. And get those pink lights off too, while you're about it. I can't see only the top of Dina's head."

Two deep lines extending from nostrils to chin seemed carved in the gray-white of Czar Kennedy's face. His eyes were flat, gray, expressionless as oysters. He lifted one forefinger, he stared at Emil the head waiter and the man found himself staring back as though hypnotized. Though Czar did not raise his voice he was plainly heard.

"You. Come here." The man skirted the table, he stood at Czar's side. "Kennedy," he said, "is my name. I am giving this dinner. I ordered it this morning."

"Yes, Mr. Kennedy. Certainly, Mr. Kennedy, I wasn't here at the time, but—when I saw Mr. Husack—he's one of our regulars of course, sometimes lunch *and* dinner——"

"Listen to me. Mrs. Husack, I have taken the liberty of ordering the dinner, I find scattered ordering unsatisfactory, but if there is anything you do not approve, it can and will be changed. . . . Don't take those lights away, man. And stand still. . . . I have ordered imported caviar, black—and I don't mean salmon roe . . . martinis or vodka, though I'm taking bourbon and so can anyone else. . . . Three-inch steaks, so there'll be plenty even for you, Dave, rare, medium, or well done. Those baked potatoes the way they do 'em here, mixed up with chives and little bits of bacon and brown on top. Mushrooms and peas. A big salad with Roquefort dressing. And for dessert of course"—he looked around the table, he suddenly turned on them his winning smile like a light flashed on a dark room—"a baked Alaska."

"Yes sir, Mr. Kennedy," Emil agreed, smoothly.

Well, Chris thought, that's telling 'em, Grampa Czar. She looked at him, a sparkling glance of impulsive admiration.

Czar looked at the girl, he spoke casually. "When our drinks arrive we'll have a toast——"

"—to the *Buccaneer!*" Dave finished for him.

Smoothly Czar continued as though Dave had not spoken "—to our most gracious friend, Louise Husack. And after that I'll be glad if perhaps you, Bay, will propose a toast to our little student here, in good wishes for her first year at the great Washington University in Seattle."

A moment of somewhat eerie silence fell upon the table.

"I love a man who can order a delicious dinner," Dina said. Czar, seated at her left, did not turn his head. He seemed to be carefully considering—and rejecting—certain replies to this, none of which were flattering.

"Say, Czar, you must have been living high off the hog up there in Alaska," Dave said.

"No. No, not exactly, Dave. We eat well, but plainly, you'd call it. There's enough of most things, and more than enough, usually, but food comes high up there and we eat it with respect. I remember when the girls used to save the lettuce and use it for the next party, nobody'd be so mean as to eat it at a friend's house."

Emil put a tentative hand on the rose bowl, with an inquiring glance at Czar. Czar nodded, wordlessly. "Too bad," Louise Husack said, with a somewhat poisonous glance at her husband. "I bet you don't see roses like that up in Alaska."

Christine's low charming voice seemed to clear the air of embarrassment. "Not like those, Aunt Louise. Such dear little things. That's the trouble with all our Alaska flowers, I suppose, except the tiny ones that grow on the tundra. The cabbages are as big as bushel baskets, the strawberries are three inches around and the delphinium grows nine feet high."

Bay said, "I hope the Husack family knows when it's licked."

The cocktails, the caviar, the steak, the champagne—an hour—two hours had gone by. The company was relaxed now, and without rancor. The orchestra that had been playing what is known as dinner music now broke its tempo into fragments suited to dancing. Bay, who had regarded the musicians with an eye remote to the point of obliteration, now asked Chris to dance. This rather surprised her, she rose with alacrity, whisked to the tiny dance floor, his arm came round her. She said, "I've been simply dying to dance, I haven't had a——"

Bay said, "Sh-sh-sh-sh." They danced the remainder of the number in silence and returned to the table.

Dave sat back, replete, and belched delicately with a napkin to his face. He glanced around expansively, he caught the eye of an acquaintance across the room and greeted him with an open jerk of the hand. He looked across the table at Dina, so silent, so contained. He frowned as though suddenly crossed in the midst of satisfaction. His eyes rested on Christine's flushed happy face.

"Well, Miss Chrissy, you haven't told me what you think of the ship."

"I think it's horrible."

His start was almost a jerk, like that of a bad actor in a play. "Say, wait a minute!"

Czar looked at her keenly. He often had seen that expression in her eyes when she began what he called one of her Thor speeches. "Now Christine," he said, gently, warningly.

"I guess you don't like fish, Chrissy girl," Dave said. "That it?"

"It was like seeing a race horse hitched to a garbage wagon."

Very leisurely, Czar seemed to hum rather than actually speak.

"I don't recollect that you've ever actually seen a horse, Christine."

Dave leaned forward, his enormous hands gripped together on the table. He had shoved his plate away abruptly so that the knife fell off and spattered the white cloth. "Listen here. An old race horse hitched to a garbage wagon is doing something useful. He's hauling garbage that has to be hauled—or anyway used to have to be, before trucks and incinerators. What did he do before! He just ran. I like a good race as well as the next fella, but what's a race horse good for, when you come right down to it? What did he do? He just ran."

Chris felt helpless and rather foolish, but, somehow, in the right. "He was beautiful. I've never seen a race horse, but I know they're beautiful, especially when they're running. And they do too prove something. Anything or anyone that can do something better or more beautifully than another is valuable. Just by existing and making people feel the way they do when they do it, they're valuable." She was growing somewhat incoherent, but she persisted, earnestly. "Like a painting. A piece of music. A poem. A race horse. It has nothing to do with everyday usefulness. It—it's beauty."

Czar was deeply annoyed with her. But he laughed now, a short laugh, but tolerant-seeming, as he glanced around at the others. "Don't let her get your goat, Dave. That's what I call her Thor talk. He's a great one, Thor is, for this beauty stuff and so on. Not that I don't like beautiful things myself, but if you don't mind I'd like to take this minute to clear this with Christine, here, seeing that I'm leaving tomorrow, and all. Now then, this ship was beautiful, the finest of its kind in the world, I guess, in her day. And one of the richest men in the world went all over the world in it, with beautiful women and, from what I've heard, handsome successful men. Actresses and so on. Place called the Rivera, up and down the Mediterranean Sea. What good was that! Millions of dollars for the pleasuring of a handful of foolish men and women."

Dave interrupted. "That's right, Czar. You've put it just on the button. Of course, a nice little boat to run around in, that's something else again. My boat, for example, of course compared to the old *Buccaneer* she's a minnow next to a whale. But this old hulk, she's earning her living now."

Louise Husack, somewhat soporific, what with rich food, alcohol, and a heart that had been strictly forbidden these, now became sufficiently aware of the argument's trend to wish to take part in it.

"Christine dearie, you never saw the *Buccaneer* when she was in her prime, any more than you did a race horse. So what are you driving at, not knowing!"

"She was the most beautiful and perfect ship of her kind in the world. That was excuse enough for her living."

Sotto voce Bay said, very close beside her, "Give it up, Chris. You can't win."

Now the vast dessert arrived, a ceremony, almost a ritual, with three waiters and Emil as acolytes and priest. Baked Alaska, golden, mountainous, at once hot and cold in some miraculous way. Plates were being handed round.

"This is Alaska, all right," Czar said as his fork went into the rich confection. "Layer of cold and layer of hot. Cold and sweet, hot and sweet. Ice cream and cake. People Outside think it's all cold. Well, let 'em. We know better, don't we, Dave!"

But before Dave could agree to this with more than a preliminary chuckle, a boy in hotel uniform crossed the great room and stopped beside Dave's chair.

"Telephone for you, Mr. Husack."

"How's that? Oh. Take the number."

"They said very important, it says." He glanced down at the slip of paper in his hand.

"Oh, now, David!" Louise Husack turned protective. "You finish your dinner and tell them to call the house later. They're after him, day and night," pridefully, "Washington and San Francisco and New York and I don't know where all."

"Go away, boy."

Czar Kennedy viewed this power performance with detachment. Smoothly, he picked up the table talk as though the bellboy had not interrupted. He even managed a fond tolerant laugh. "My little Christine isn't used to champagne."

Surprisingly, Dave was receptive to this. "Me neither. Filthy stuff. It never did agree with me. Stick to whiskey. Champagne is for chorus girls."

"Chorus girls of your day, Dad. They don't go for stuff like that now. They're like you, they stick to scotch."

"My son's quite a stage-door Johnny."

"What's a stage-door Johnny?" Chris asked.

A laugh went round the table in which Chris found herself joining ruefully. "Did I say something?" But even after it was explained she seemed puzzled. "Just goes to show how far away Alaska really is," Dave said. "Far away and out of step."

The bellboy was at Dave's elbow again and this time he was fortified by Emil. "There are two or three gentlemen—that is, men from the newspapers—out there to see you, Mr. Husack. And the telephone. I could have it plugged in here, of course, though in this dining room we generally prefer not——"

"Do you want me to go for you, Dad?"

"Nah."

Dina pushed her chair back. "Let me, Uncle Dave. It's probably Washington. They said tomorrow, but they've probably had a meeting, it's about midnight there."

"I'll go, I'll go. They can't make up their minds because they haven't got any brains, you can't make up minds with——" He sounded far from fit to cope with Washington long-distance affairs. His face was flushed, he crushed his napkin into a ball and threw it into the dessert plate of melting baked Alaska. Standing, he grasped the chair back a moment, then weaved his way among the tables with superb accuracy and speed, he even saluted a group here and there as he went.

"A liqueur, anybody?" Czar inquired, grandly. He said likweer, but not a muscle moved in the three young faces. "How about a nice cream de mint, Louise?"

She laughed, plumply. "Now, Czar, I guess you think you're out with one of those chorus girls."

Dina was glancing toward the great doorway. She turned back now to the table. "I've eaten such an enormous dinner, I think I'll just have a brandy, Mr. Kennedy."

"Brandy, eh? Anybody else want to keep Miss—uh—company?"

"I'll try one, Grampa Czar."

"No you won't, my girl. You've never tasted brandy."

"Grampa Thor would say this is a good time to try it, then."

The little white flame leaped from his eyes. "Thor has had his day. This is mine. Understand?"

"I'm sorry, Grampa. I didn't think you'd be cross about it. You asked."

But now Dave Husack came swiftly toward the table and behind him like a comet's tail, Emil. Dave's hand on the chair back was shaking, his face was dangerously purple, his eyes stood out like balls from their sockets. "You keep those goddamn reporters out of this room or I'll sue the hotel, hear me . . . !" He sank into the chair, the scented handkerchief seemed unavailing as he dabbed at the greasily wet face.

"David! David! What's happened!"

He glared at them, his lower jaw combative, outjutting, like a troglodyte's. "She's gone. The goddamned ship is gone."

"Gone where, David? She was supposed to go at eight, you said, se——"

"The *Buccaneer*. She sank. Just like that. Sank."

Czar leaned across the table, his face was halfway across it, he pushed aside the pink-shaded lamp with a gesture that rocked it. "Collision?"

"Here," Dina said. She thrust toward Dave the brandy that the waiter had just placed discreetly at her place.

Dave pushed the glass bubble aside, it overturned and rolled a bit, the amber liquid spread on the cloth. "She just went down, I'm telling you. No reason. Daylight. August. Nothing in sight. They say she gave a heave, like, and shivered once, and went down. They saved two men, maybe three. She's gone, absolutely gone. Listen to this."

He unfolded a crumpled wad of newspaper in his hand. "They been trying to get me. The papers. Listen to this swill, will you!"

"David Husack!"

"Aw, what! Listen to this. '. . . She moved out into Elliott Bay, the last rays of the setting sun revealed cruelly every line and bruise and wrinkle and flabby peeling skin of this degraded old hag, once so beautiful, so magnificent, so queenly. Then, quietly, smoothly, calmly, like the great lady she was, she staggered once, righted herself, fell forward like a Victorian *grande dame* in a faint, and slipped into the watery depths with a softly hissing sigh of relief. Or was it scorn?' "

He looked up now. The table was silent.

"Millions," Czar said, quietly. "She was going to bring in millions. . . . Let's be sensible. It was the machinery. Built like a Swiss watch. That's what you said. And you put in cheap junk engines. You try putting a hunk of iron in a Swiss watch. . . . Those men'll sue. And the dead ones' wives."

"Let's go home, David. Let's go home."

Husack's bloodshot protuberant eyes found Christine's shocked face and rested there. "Bad luck. I told you it would be. When that bottle slipped out of your goddamned silly hand. Bad luck."

26

Meeting Thor Storm on Gold Street, or dropping in at the *Northern Light* office with a bit of news, or to insert an ad, his Baranof townsmen would say, "What's the news of Chris? She given us old sourdoughs the go-by for good? I hear she's going to marry Dave Husack's son."

"Christine hasn't written me about that. Nor Bridie. She writes each of us a long letter twice a month. You know Christine. She makes up her own mind about what she wants to do, and she usually does it."

"Yeh, well, pretty girl like that, all the money in the world—or will have when Czar kicks off—she'd be a fool to stay here in this icehouse the rest of her life. Ice Palace, hell! And the Glittering North, like the ads say. I'd get out myself if I could."

"Why can't you?"

"Well, I don't know, I been thinking about it, my old lady keeps beefing about it."

"You've been here in Alaska a long time now, haven't you, Mel? How many years is it?"

"Let's see now—it's—ten—twelve—gosh, going on fifteen years! Say, I'm an old sourdough right. Maybe, like they say, the spell of the magic North has got me, but don't mention it to the old lady, she sure would like to swap it for a spell in California."

From its days of almost utter isolation, Baranof—and all Alaska—had retained its love of gossip. It was not so much gossip, perhaps, as interest in all local and territorial manifestations. Science, World

War II, the Dew Line, the vast peacetime Army Bases, Alaska Communications Service, and airplanes airplanes airplanes daily—hourly in cities such as Juneau, Anchorage, Baranof, Fairbanks—had brought Japan and all Scandinavia and the North Pole and California and Hawaii and Seattle within a few hours' reach of almost any Alaskan settlement, from the remotest Eskimo village squatted on the tundra to the capital of the Territory. But all Alaska still retained its love of local news, its pioneer curiosity in the small private details of its neighbors' lives.

"Drove past your place the other day, Thor. See you're making some improvements in your cabin. You fixing to get married, now Chris is off your hands?"

"Oh, sure, sure. I figure it's about time for a young fellow like me to settle down."

The town was curious about it. Chris had been away well over a year and in all that time she had not once returned to Baranof. At the end of her first year at Washington University she had gone to Europe for three months with a guided student group. Baranof was all but smothered by a chromatic snowstorm of post cards depicting kaleidoscopic cathedrals, châteaux, canals, castles, parks, forests, uniforms, restaurants, ruins.

"That old shack of yours must be about the oldest house in Baranof, they tell me. How old is it, anyway?"

"Only about fifty years. That isn't old, really. Of course Baranof itself isn't much older than that. But in this country—uh—I mean to say, fifty years isn't old for a good sound building."

"Ha! Good sound—I don't want to hurt your feelings, Thor—no offense I hope—but I wouldn't think that old log cabin would rate putting any more money into it. Not a dollar, I'd say. You're even adding on a piece there at the back I see. Lots of old rat-ridden log cabins around town, I hear the City Council figures they're unsightly and a hazard, they're going to tear them down to make way for new modern buildings."

"Too bad. Tourists might find them interesting."

"Tourists! How many tourists do we have! Not enough to count, and never will have."

"You'll be surprised. All over the United States, things to be seen and studied—battlefields and Indian mounds and Spanish missions, and Paul Revere's house, and that old opera house up high in the Rocky Mountains, and the iron lacework of New Orleans——"

"Yeh, yeh, sure, that's right."

They said that old Thor was a great old boy but getting kind of—— A circular motion here, with the forefinger, in the region of the forehead.

He was deft and clever with his hands and he went to work on his log cabin, situated there so near the water with a pleasant bit of land around it. He had little spare time, what with the *Northern Light* and the salmon-fishing season and the book on which he had been engaged (to Baranof's fond amusement) for years and years. Must be bigger than the whole encyclopedia by now, Baranof said. He left the exterior weather-blackened logs much as they had been in actual appearance, though he treated them with a preservative. He added a bedroom, a bathroom and a kitchen. He installed a furnace. The little bathroom was tiled and it shone with stainless metal. The kitchen was fitted with modern appliances. One small space that had been his sleeping room and living quarters—little more than a shed, really, at the rear, he kept as it was, untouched. His iron bed, his chair, the washstand; a little splayfooted iron stove; his guns, his fishing tackle, his cherished specimens, his books books books on rough shelves, in boxes, on chairs, tables, the floor. Except for his battered and dated typewriter the room might have been—was, in fact—exactly as he had occupied it, the young blond earnest giant of half a century ago. A saucepan on the stove, a chamber pot under the camp bed; a calendar on the wall, a half-bald fur parka on the hook.

But the main room—that was a different matter altogether. For this he had removed a partition and turned two rooms into one. He scraped and sandpapered and rubbed and waxed the old blackened interior logs until they shone with a mellow golden glow, walls and rafters. "Taffy," Addie Barnett said, viewing the rich patina of the wood. "Or cream caramels. It looks as if you could eat it with a spoon. What in the world did you put into that waxing formula, Thor? Molasses and melted gold and a few strands of Chris's hair? It's like—like—it's almost apricot, like——"

"Like Chris," Ross Guildenstern said. He sometimes came in and helped Thor with certain mechanical jobs, he was very good at this, he could take apart or put together any kind of mechanism. Paul Barnett was not much good at these manual or mechanical tasks but he puttered about amiably, he sometimes brought the children with him, he said that Addie could drive a nail straighter than he could, but he was better at keeping the kids from falling into the water.

Ott Decker, too, got into the way of dropping by, ostensibly to see what progress Thor was making, and to admire his handiwork. Usually he took off his coat and fell to work. Thor was, in fact, rather embarrassed by the number of Baranof young men who seemed suddenly to take an interest in his handiwork.

"Chris coming back?" they asked, casually, as they drove home a nail, painted a bedroom wainscoting. "You're fixing this up for her, aren't you?" It was as though, in working for her comfort or delight, they somehow moved closer to her life.

"No sign of her coming back," Thor replied. "I'm planning to live here myself until somebody else moves in. Live here as I always have, in that one room there at the back. I'll move out altogether if —when—someone else takes over."

"You will! That'll seem funny. Where?"

"There's a one-room cabin down by the water, I bought it a couple of years ago."

Paul Barnett said, one evening when the late-summer daylight still lingered in the midnight sky, "Furniture. Addie and I wondered where the furniture was coming from to go with all this Devonshire cream."

"Blue, don't you think?" Addie suggested. "The couch and cushions blue, or maybe a pair of chairs. Blue against all this golden wood. Heavenly! And Chris being so blond."

Surprisingly, Paul Barnett disputed this. Usually he was too wise to battle the ironclad Addie. "She isn't a blonde at all. She's tawny, like a leopard, like a lioness."

"Like an apricot," Ross Guildenstern said again. He was down on the floor tinkering with an electrical outlet. "Blue is too washy for Chris."

"Just a minute, you two boys." Addie laughed. "I'm kind of a tawny type myself, if you can spare me a look, but I don't see anybody battling about whether I'm a lion or a tiger or an apricot."

Thor was installing bookshelves on either side of the fireplace. He spoke, now, over his shoulder, quietly. "Christine is in Seattle, and likely to stay there. So don't fight about whether she's flora or fauna. I'm the one who's living in this log house."

Addie crossed the room to throw her arms around the great shoulders, gaunt now rather than massive. "Any color is just right for you, you big beautiful Swensky you!"

Czar, learning of these changes, came by to see for himself, driving at his accustomed twenty-five miles an hour. He passed, staring; turned at the end of two or three digesting blocks, and came by again. The seaman's keen blue eyes had seen him. Thor came to the door.

"Come in, old pardner, come in!"

"I hear you're fixing to be married," Czar called from the car window.

Chattily, Thor leaned against the doorjamb. "That's interesting. Anyone we know?"

"Might be." With apparent reluctance he left the car and walked leisurely up the path, surveying the house with the remote and casual glance of a stranger. "Could be. Bridie, say. She always was stuck on you."

"I thought it was you, according to the old story."

"Or maybe one of the girls along the Strip. Or maybe you're bringing home an Eskimo bride—again."

"Come in, come in. Have a look around at your old diggings."

"Must be fixing it up for some woman. Look at it! Who're you fooling? Not me. I'm smarter than you are, always was. Who's the—girl?"

"Thanks for the compliment, Czar. I'm a little on the vintage side for marriage—you and I, both."

"I don't know about you," Czar retorted, a little coarsely for him. "You being such a dreamer and all, all your life. But if I was so minded I could increase the population of the Territory pretty considerably. If I was so minded."

"Perhaps," Thor mused, rubbing rubbing with a slow rhythmical motion the curved surface of a wall log. "Perhaps it might have been better for the Territory—and for you—if you had done so. You've compensated, they call it in the new language—you've taken out your natural human urges in a passion for power. Power passion. Many men do that. It doesn't always work out too well. Hitler——"

"Why, you dirty old drooler, you comparing me to Hitler! You're crazier than I thought, and everybody knows how crazy you are. Crazy as a coot!"

"Czar, Czar, I'm sorry. I was just thinking aloud, I sometimes do. We've known each other for fifty years. Cooped up together in this locked-in land. There aren't, after all, many secrets we have from each other, are there?"

"It isn't any secret that most of the time you don't know what you're talking about. Or doing, for that matter. This shack, for example." His face, in its cold seething anger, was like the ice breaking up in the late spring, a crashing destructive jumble of fury. "You're fixing this place up for somebody besides yourself."

Thor went on with his polishing, methodically, lightly, the wood shone like pulled taffy. "To tell you the truth, Czar, I may do some traveling, later, Outside. Outside the Territory. I've been here a long, long time, it's time I went away. In all these years I've scarcely been Outside. I could rent this place at a good profit now, in case I stayed away for quite some time."

"Uh-huh. You going to pay a visit to those royal relatives you spun that tale about! Up there in Norway, in the Swensky country? Valhalla, you used to call it. Valhalla. Old Thor, the god from Valhalla."

"I might at that. Valhalla. That's just about the idea, Czar. You've just about hit it."

Now the ice mass broke with a crash. The fine gray eyes were almost white, the color drained from the cheeks, leaving them clay. "Listen to me, old crackpot! You're fixing up this place for Christine. You think she'll come back here to live. Well, stop kidding yourself. She isn't coming back. Not yet, anyway. She's marrying Bay Husack and she may come back to Alaska at that, for a spell, but she'll be the wife of the Governor of Alaska. And then the Senator from the state of Washington. And then the First Lady of the Land. The wife of the President of the United States maybe twenty years from now, maybe even less. So you can stop rubbing that old kindling wood and making out like you're fixing up this shack for rental."

Thor went on rubbing the wood lightly, he even breathed on it a little and then resumed his rubbing and cocked his head, gazing critically at the glow of the spot on which he was working as though to compare it in rich color and sheen to the section next it.

He straightened his big frame, he glanced meditatively out of the window to the water beyond. "Little Christine in the White House. First Lady. She'd be refreshing, but she wouldn't fall in with the ideas of your crowd. There hasn't been a President's wife since—or before—Eleanor Roosevelt that had the courage to be herself. Franklin's wife showed them there was more to being the President's wife than giving dinners to stuffed shirts and stuffed bodices. Bodices. I'm caught with an old-fashioned word, they don't use it any more, I'm told. They don't use the gold service much any more there either, I'm told."

Czar turned to leave. "Gabble on, gabble on. Half the time I don't know what you're talking about and I don't think you do, either."

"Could be. Could be, Czar. But it's cheap at the price. Outside I'd have to pay a psychoanalyst fifty dollars an hour to sit and listen to me gabble. I don't pay you a cent. Thanks, pardner. And when I gabble to myself it comes even cheaper. In fact, I gain by it, if the truth were known."

27

Christine Storm was The Fashion. No matter what she said now, they laughed uproariously, admiringly. "Did you hear Chris Storm's crack?"

Certainly Christine had not meant this to be. In the beginning she had merely been honest. She had had no intention of startling them with her replies to questions. A strange new world. Only a few hours' plane distance from Baranof, this city of Seattle, this city of New York, this city of San Francisco, Paris, London, Rome. But a world lay between. And especially, in the beginning, Seattle.

At a dinner party, or a dance, or in a college group:

"Baranof? Where's that? Russia?"

At first Chris would wait a moment before replying because she found herself possessed by an emotion rare in her. Anger. Behind her teeth the little silent voice cautioned her to remember what Thor had said. "Just be honest and polite, the way you are here at home. If they ask questions, answer them. Remember, they don't really know you there as everybody knows you here from the day you were born—and before."

So she waited a moment before answering, her lips slightly parted in the small mirthless smile of social intercourse.

What language do they speak in Alaska?

Do they live in igloos?

They eat raw fish and guts and whale blubber—that right?

They get sewed up in bearskins for nine months in the winter, don't they? How do they—well, I guess we'd better not go into that.

Mostly Eskimos up there, aren't they? Except the Army Bases, I mean.

How did you happen to live up there, Chris? Your father Army?

Born there! Look, Chris was *born* up there, she says.

It was at that time, the beginning of her Seattle experience, that she had got into the habit of giving them what Bay Husack called the old caribou routine. I was born in a caribou in a blizzard up in the Wood River country. Her hearers' faces would register incredulity.

"Quit kidding. I'd like to go to Alaska some time, all those Eskimos and stuff. I really would."

"I'm Eskimo."

"Yeh, and I'm an Arab chieftain."

"My grandmother on my father's side was one quarter Eskimo. So my father was one eighth Eskimo. That makes me one sixteenth, if I'm any good at arithmetic—which I'm not. And of course I only eat raw fish and seal oil and muktuk. I'm sewed in for the winter, too, as you see."

She might be wearing, at the time, a strapless while faille dance dress in which she looked so appetizing that her male interrogator had to caution himself not to take a bite.

"Look, Chris, let's start again from the beginning. Baranof, you said. If it isn't Russia where is it?"

"It's a town in the Territory of Alaska, and Alaska is part of the United States, though it isn't a state. Not yet. By the way, what language do you speak here in Seattle?"

"What do you mean—what language! English, of course."

"Oh. Well, we speak it better in Alaska, if my ear is correct."

But she had a splendid time, for the most part. Certain things shocked her unpleasantly; most things stimulated her pleasantly. In Alaska she had been aware of the high percentage of senseless crimes and misdemeanors in a rough country, but Outside seemed no better, and with less excuse. Baranof's solid middle class fostered an almost Puritan standard of conduct, perhaps because a society so close-knit must, in self-protection, be decorous. But here the standards of many of the young men and women of her own age startled her. She was genuinely horrified at the mild amusement and even disrespect with which her generation Outside regarded old people. They sneered openly or they were tolerant with an obvious patience which was more galling than uncontrolled impatience.

Bay Husack, for example, who was almost ten years her senior. His attitude toward Louise Husack was that of an adult toward a not very bright little girl. Toward his father and his father's associates he displayed a quizzical contempt. Chris, sensing this, criticized it in the form of a generalization.

"I don't see how we can call ourselves civilized. Civilized countries respect and revere old people. Look at the Chinese and the East Indians."

"Yes, look at them!" Bay jibed. "They're in fine shape. They're so civilized that only a few million die of starvation every year. And I've always heard that the Eskimos take their old people out on the ice and let them sit there until they freeze to death."

Her resentment of this was, Bay thought, out of all proportion.

"Perhaps, years ago, when they needed what food there was to keep the young people alive. The hunters and the workers. Your ancestors, hundreds of years ago, probably hit the old people over the head with a club. Ross Guildenstern's grandmother is treated with the most tender respect."

"Ross what!"

"It doesn't matter. In Alaska the old pioneers are respected. They're considered valuable citizens. The three most important and beautiful people in Alaska are over seventy."

"You're like Queen Victoria, brought up by a bunch of graybeards. So far as I can figure it these two grandfathers of yours you're always quoting and this Juliet's Nurse—Birdie or Bridget or whatever it is—anyway, you're all in love with one another, and each of you is in love with Alaska. I never saw such a bunch of Oedipus wrecks. You're out of stir now, you're living alone, doesn't that put ideas into your head?"

"There are about fifty other girls living in my building. Why don't you try ringing doorbells?"

"They don't go around telling everybody about the toothsome sourdough pancakes they make for breakfast. From an old family wad of dough. It sounds pretty repulsive, but I'll come—if you'll let me come early enough before breakfast. About midnight, say, the night before."

"Do come. And bring your fiancée, Miss Drake."

"She isn't my fiancée."

"She told me she was."

"That's odd. I thought you were."

"You talk like Louis the Sixteenth."

"You're going to be an old maid if you're not careful—you and your frozen north ways. Don't say Uncle Bay didn't warn you."

"Bitter boy, you hate the world."

"Maybe I do."

"But why? It's wonderful!"

"You tell me all about it some time."

"I can tell you now."

"All right. Let's sit down here, real cosy, and I'll put an arm around you, and you talk and I'll listen."

"You're afraid to listen. You're afraid to talk."

"I know it. But I'll listen to you. There now. Isn't that comfortable? Now talk. Or don't talk. It's soothing just sitting here like this. Maybe soothing isn't the word, exactly."

She had been asked to dinner at the Husacks'. She often came to dinner at the Husacks'. Just the family, Louise Husack said. You're like one of the family, Christine dear. I wish you'd come to dinner every night. We all love having you—Bay and all of us.

Not Miss Dina Drake, Chris thought. Any dinner now I expect to find arsenic in my soup. I must write Bridie about her.

Bridie had written in reply. ". . . That girl had clear sailing with him till you came along. Like they say, if you can't fight her join her. She won't know what you're up to. . . ."

Oh, won't she though! Chris thought. You don't know Dina, Bridie dear. Besides, I'm not up to anything. I just don't like to be patronized.

Suddenly now, as she sat with Bay in the dim handsome Husack library, so rich in shelves and shelves of lovely leather whose contents no one read, she suddenly felt relaxed and at ease with this rather frightening young man. His arm was about her, her hand was in his. It was surprising.

"For the first time in all these months I feel comfortable and cosy with you, Bay."

"Women always have to talk about their emotions. All right. You feel that way because you think you're going to say something that will help me. Women love that. Gives them a warm glow."

"You're an upset person. You came home from the War, upset. And angry at a stupid horror and you decided to stay that way. That was ten or eleven years ago. I know lots of men in Baranof who are like that."

"You been around a lot, Miss–uh——?"

"And you don't like your father, lots of people don't like their fathers. And you're bored with his business. If you cared more about people–I mean if you knew what's going on. Here in Seattle you're all so old-fashioned!"

"That's a refreshing one. I'll have to tell that to Pop."

"Please do. He's the most old-fashioned of all of them. It's the middle of the twentieth century–past the middle–and they're still behaving as if it were the nineteenth. Robber Barons! It couldn't be more old-fashioned."

"Like your Grandpappy Czar Kennedy–who's paying your bills here at Washington, I understand."

"Yes. Like him, too. And don't think I don't feel guilty. I don't know what to do. But at least Grampa Czar lives in Alaska and loves it and does things for it."

"Such as what?"

"Newspapers. And banks. And shops. And coal. And the Ice Palace."

"What's that?"

"A building. An apartment hotel. Fourteen stories."

"You babe! You kill me!"

"At least he isn't an absentee millionaire. The first Alaska absentee millionaire was Peter the Great—and then Catherine the First. There've been lots of absentee millionaire landlords since then, and your father is one of them."

"Yet you come here to dinner!" His tone was mock horror.

"I know. Aunt Louise has been so good and kind."

"Are you sure it isn't me? I'm not good and kind, but I'm interesting."

The honest merry eyes regarded him searchingly. "I've thought of that. You're a kind of challenge. Like converting a drunkard."

"Better be careful. You might get seriously involved in the process. You know—like the woman who tries to cure him by taking a drink every time he does. Next thing she's right down there in the gutter with him."

"I'm stronger than you are."

"Sugar, you'll never get a husband if you talk like that."

"I'm not worried."

"Are you bespoke, ma'am?"

"Not at present, sir."

"You might be any minute now if you'll forget that high-school chatter."

Very stiffly, "Oh, I neglected to tell you. That challenge I mentioned doesn't really interest me."

He began to laugh, then, and he pulled her closer to him. "Dear sweet kid, I don't care about those things. I don't give a damn. Don't try to make a noble character out of me, I'm really a son-of-a-bitch. I think the world stinks and I want no part of it. I'm a rich man's son and I enjoy it in my own way. But no responsibility, thank you very much. Like a clerk in the shipping department—I only work here."

The library door opened; Louise Husack came in. The two sat facing her, Bay's arm about Christine, Christine's golden head so close to his. They did not move, they did not appear embarrassed because they weren't.

"Hi, Aunt Louise! I'm leading your son astray."

All the wattles and lines in Mrs. Husack's face seemed to melt into one radiant smile. "That's nice." She cast about the room a cursory glance that would not have discovered a packing case. "I thought I'd left my glasses—but no." She stepped hastily back into the outer hall, she closed the double doors gently behind her, there was a sort of happy haste about her movements.

"Mom's up to something," Bay observed. "When that little mind of hers begins to work it's as obvious as watching a six-year-old trying to run away."

Dreamily, as though thinking aloud, she said, "I suppose it's too easy here. Everything that's difficult in Baranof is easy here, and taken for granted. Keeping warm. Dressing in winter without being buried in layers of fur and wool. Food. A place to live. Getting from place to place. You can't imagine how wonderful it seems to me to be able to get into a car and just drive. Drive anywhere! Anywhere you please."

"What's so wonderful about that?"

"There are no roads in Alaska—at least, none to speak of, considering how big it is. From town to town, I mean."

"What's that highway you hear about?"

"Oh, the Alaska Highway. Yes. That was the War. The Army. But I mean from town to town. Of course we have the planes. That's wonderful. It's like freedom after being in prison."

"If you want roads why don't you build them?"

"With what?"

"Why don't you yell for them?"

"Because your crowd chokes us if we try to yell."

"Now listen, honey, you're really a little queer about all this, aren't you? A nice attractive girl, but a little tetched in the head."

"I know it sounds foolish to you. But we can't get a word of publicity, we really can't. There's so much money—so much Outside money spent to keep everything very, very quiet. My Grampa Thor described it to me and I'll never forget it. I remember it almost word for word, he can always describe a thing as though it were a picture, and you can see it just like that. He said the thing the Big Boys want is No Publicity. Every other person and every other organization and every other business setup in the whole country seems to be yelling for publicity, but Grampa said that's exactly what these men don't want. So every Alaska bill and every Alaska measure and every Alaska voice is killed killed killed. Quietly killed. Alaska, just let it lie there, everything quiet and frozen. Then he said, you've never seen a bear fishing. They sit hours and hours, so quiet they don't seem to be breathing, watching the water, watching the water. Then, so quick your eye can hardly see it, one big paw goes in up to here—snatch—and up the paw comes with a big fine salmon. Quiet. Quiet. That's the Boys Outside. Grampa Thor said."

"He must be quite a boy himself."

"I wish you could see Alaska. Though you'd probably hate it. Lots of people do—even people who live there. Even people who've lived there for a long time."

"But not you, h'm?"

"You're laughing at me, but I don't care. It's heavenly and luxurious here, and it's rough and pretty uncomfortable there, sometimes. But everything is still to be done there, and maybe that's why I like it better. The old pioneer spirit, inherited. Isn't it tiresome! But that's what makes it exciting for me. Here you just take everything for granted—water and electricity and concerts and high buildings and oil burners and stuff. Here the cities are all finished. You just keep on adding trimmings. You take up the old water pipes and put in bigger ones—or the electricity coils or whatever they are. You tear down the enormous buildings that are perfectly good and just put up buildings more enormous. Bigger. More. More. Maybe I'm kind of homesick. Isn't that unadult!"

"The masochistic type, aren't you? You want to be uncomfortable. Tell you what I'll do for you. I heard Mom say at breakfast that we're having Cornish hen for dinner. I'll take you down to Greasy Jo's in Skid Row instead."

"We can get Cornish hen at Nick's Caribou Café."

"Where's that?"

"The Ice Palace."

"Where's—oh, you told me. No more travel talks, please. And all that wise old philosophy you've been brought up on."

"Go on—sneer! But I wish you could meet them."

"Meet who? Oh, your—the one you call Grampa Thor, and that old nurse of yours?"

"Yes. Yes. They're different from the people Outside. I don't mean better—I mean they want something terribly but not just for themselves, it's a cause, it's a crusade, it's like the Spirit of '76—that sounds stuffy——"

"I'm afraid it does."

"Not if you knew the Alaskans I mean. Paul and Addie Barnett and George Sundborg—he's an editor in Juneau—and the Atwoods in Anchorage and Herb Hilscher and Eva McGowan in Fairbanks, and the Nordales, and Bob Bartlett our Delegate, he's just the most wonderful—and Ernest Gruening—he was our Governor, you know—no, you don't know, I suppose—they live in Washington anyway, those two—I mean Washington D.C., not your Washington—I wish you could—I love them——" She stopped jerkily as she looked, wide-eyed, at the dry cynical eyes regarding her. He was staring at her with the gaze of a man who loathes the first sign of hysteria. And then she was weeping. "I'm sorry. How idiotic. Homesick—at my age! And I was going to keep a stiff upper lip."

"No, don't. A stiff upper lip never gets kissed." His other arm came round her. He kissed her as one would kiss a weeping child, tenderly, to comfort her.

With an unerring sense of the dramatic Dina Drake came into the dim quiet room. She did not apologize.

"Bay, you bad boy, what are you doing to that poor kid!"

"Kissing her," Bay said. "Very nice, too."

"I should think it might be. But hardly fair—an old gent like you."

"Clever girl."

"No wonder Aunt Louise sent me in here on some fool errand about her glasses. I was typing one of her dinner lists, I suppose she thought it was time somebody interrupted this little snuggle."

She pretended to be searching for the mythical glasses, ignoring Christine as though she were a child.

Chris lifted her head, extracted a handkerchief from Bay's pocket, wiped her eyes with it, blew her nose, and stared at Dina Drake with a look surprisingly baleful for a girl ordinarily so sunny of aspect.

"Oh, go away, Dina," she said. "I'm not trying to steal your gent. But I could if I put my mind to it."

"Isn't that darling, Bay! If she put her mind to it. I love the way you Alaskans talk."

"Yes-s-s!" And now she was being very Oxford English, unconsciously, as Thor Storm was when he was very angry. "So quaint. So different from you Kansas City girls."

"Not worthy of you, dear," thus putting Chris directly in the wrong, "and I'm sorry," Dina said. "I guess Aunt Louise was just worried, that's all. She knows that Bay sometimes—I don't mind because I'm used to it, I let him smooch around with other girls if he wants to, I don't have to be jealous, but I think he ought to pick people his own size, who can protect themselves."

Bay stood up, he shook himself a little, a kind of shrug into his coat collar. "This is getting kind of sordid." He shook his head as Chris mutely offered him his somewhat used handkerchief. "Laundry . . . Listen, Chris. Mom tricked her into coming down here—good old dumb Mom—so she'd see that I've fallen for somebody—a little stumble of a fall, anyway—if I ever could fall for anyone. Which I doubt. Well, you gals clobber it out between you. But watch out, Chris, she won't fight fair, no holds barred for *that* rassler." He was gone.

The two women stood facing each other only for a moment. Dina Drake's tone was friendly, almost casual, like that of one imparting self-evident information. "I think you ought to know that Bay Husack and I are going to be married. It was arranged long before you came."

"I think you ought to tell him, then. He denies it."

The resourceful Dina tried another tack. "It's easy enough for you. You've had those rich people all your life in Alaska, and now here, cuddling you up and handing you around. I haven't got anybody. Leave him alone, won't you!"

"That's what Bay meant when he said no holds barred. You don't fight fair. Listen. I'm going to finish my time here and get my degree and then I'm going back. And I think it's sickening to see two grown women snarling over a man like two huskies over a chunk of muktuk."

"Huskies—mu——"

"Never mind." She turned at the door. "Don't forget Aunt Louise's glasses. She had them up on the top of her head when she came in."

She had seen various Alaskans occasionally as they flew to or through Seattle. Czar had flown in twice, Bridie once, Thor never. She had seen Ross twice when he had managed to wangle the flights. She had Louise Husack and Bridie to lunch. She was delighted to see that the two women got on marvelously together, dissimilar though they were. They discussed Chris, approvingly, in her presence, while they were served rock crab followed by cheese soufflé followed by baked peaches and sour cream, which the two elderly women consumed with protests of enjoyment.

"Do you notice any change in our Christine?" Mrs. Husack's question was accompanied by a possessive, yet coy, glance.

"She looks a little thinner to me, I guess they do a lot of gym work and swimming and so on at the U. Or maybe she isn't getting her sleep, studying the way she does. Chris, you getting enough sleep?"

"Loads."

"Or maybe," Mrs. Husack simpered, "she's in love."

"I am," Chris said. Bridie jumped noticeably. "I'm in love with Seattle and Alaska and life and the world." Bridie relaxed.

"I want to invite you to my home, Mrs. Ballantyne," Louise Husack said, spaciously. "We've loved it all these years—anyway, Mr. Husack has, he's a man loves his home—and I'd like you to see it while I'm still there."

"Aunt Louise!"

"My goodness, where you going!" Bridie demanded.

"Oh, I don't mean what you mean. The truth is, I'd like to travel if I can only get Mr. Husack to see it the way I do. I love Seattle, goodness knows I've got a million friends here and all, but here I've been stuck all my married life, you might say. Mr. Husack just wouldn't stir. San Francisco Chicago New York Washington D.C., on business, of course, but that isn't what I want. Mr. Husack says there's everything a man could want right here in Seattle—water mountains planes fishing hunting and so on. Maybe that is everything a man could want but I want to see Paris and Italy and all those places. Greece, even, and Egypt. We've been right on the edge of starting a dozen times, but then something always comes up—business or a war or something. But now I told him, we're *going*. Let Bayard and Christine take over the house."

"Aunt Louise, what in the world are you talking about!"

"You know perfectly well Bay's crazy about you."

"He isn't crazy about anybody."

"That's just his way. You don't know him the way I do. A sweeter more loving child doesn't live than——"

"He isn't a child."

Bridie had heard enough. "Now just a minute. If you please. Is this some kind of royal marriage or something that's being fixed up between you Husacks and Czar?"

Chris laughed, but not very mirthfully. "No, Bridie darling. You're just sick of housekeeping, aren't you, Aunt Louise?"

"I am. I'm good and sick of whether we should have leg of lamb or chicken or a four-rib roast. I didn't mind when I was younger. But now I'm older, I've been keeping house for almost forty years and I'm good and sick and tired of it, and that's the truth. I'll be glad and willing to move out of that big place into one of the new little eight-room apartments. You can't get decent help any more. Dave says if we move out we'd lose face. Face! My features are all worn out from keeping face. Let Bay do it. The girl that marries Bay won't need a thing. Not a thing. There's linen and silver and china and glass enough to set for a hundred. We *have* set for a hundred, many's the time. You and Chris come to dinner tomorrow and I'll show it all to you, it's a treat to see if I do say so. Any woman would be wild over it."

Bridie jerked her hat, which she had worn throughout lunch, she straightened herself in her chair, she sniffed. "I live in one room in the Ice Palace. From choice. I'd think two rooms a burden. I've got six dinner plates, six cups and saucers, six glasses, six salads, six soups, six knives and forks—and so on, and two luncheon sets I got that time I was in Hawaii, they're as good as the day I——"

Crisply Christine cut in. "Can't come to dinner tomorrow night, thanks, Aunt Louise. I'm going to the sorority dance, it's the big dance of the year."

"With Bay?"

"I did ask him. Just to hear what he'd say. He said he didn't go to children's parties because chicken-and-sweetbread patties and chocolate ice cream didn't agree with him."

"What did he mean?"

"Nothing. He invited me to drive out to Spruce with him and eat dinner at Fishermen's Wharf."

"You going?"

"Ross Guildenstern's going to be here." Now Bridie looked up, sharply. "I've invited him, I wired him, I haven't seen him in months and months and months."

"I'd think," Bridie suggested, "there'd be plenty of nice boys right here in Seattle, wouldn't have to be imported."

Ross Guildenstern telephoned from the airport five minutes after his plane had landed.

"Chris!"

"Ross! I don't know why I even speak to you. I haven't heard from you for months. That's why I started running after you."

"See, the guy was right, absence does make them come whimpering."

"Eight o'clock, and some of the kids are meeting here for a drink first, so come early."

"I had my tux pressed——"

"Don't call it tux."

"Dinner clothes, Seattle. Dinner clothes. Anyway, it makes no difference because I tried it on, I haven't worn it in four years, and I'd be arrested. Inches too small."

"Rent one. You have to wear dinner clothes, it's the one very important party——"

"I won't disgrace you. I hope. I'll rent one with stripes down the side of the pants and everything."

The rented suit looked frightful on him, though Chris did not say so. He was too muscular, too stockily built, too square-shouldered to look his best in evening clothes; rented evening clothes. But he turned out to be a hit. The young men and women, clustered around him, seemed to find in this olive-skinned smiling young man a certain frankness and freshness that had attracted them to Christine.

"Where do you live, Mr.–uh–Guild–no! Not really Guildenstern! Like in–I love it!"

"I live in Baranof–that is, when I'm on the ground. . . . No, I was born in an Eskimo village called Oogruk, it's on the Bering Strait. . . . Now it's quite a town. . . . No, we don't live in igloos. . . . In Baranof I live at the Ice Palace, most of the pilots . . . it's an apartment hotel . . . no, Alaska isn't what you think, you ought to come to Alaska some time. . . ."

At the end of the evening, "You going to stay here, Chris?"

"I'm going to finish, of course."

"I mean stay."

"I don't know what I'm going to do."

"In Baranof they say you're going to marry him."

"Ross, I don't know what I'm going to do. I feel so mixed up."

"Fly back with me tomorrow. You don't need a college degree."

"*You* have one."

"I wasn't mixed up."

"I'm going to Washington next week. Washington D.C., I mean."

"Alone?"

"Oh, no! With Uncle Dave and Aunt Louise, and Bay, and Dina Drake's going too—she's his secretary—Uncle Dave's, I mean—the Alaska bill is supposed to come up, it's so exciting—a lot of Alaska people will be there. Maybe this time Alaska will make it. Oh, Ross, wouldn't it be wonderful!"

They flew across a continent. Christine was accustomed to flying, certainly, yet now as she passed over a mighty land she was as elated as though she never had flown before. Mountains rivers plains prairies forests. It was a miraculously clear day, over the whole land there hung a dream-like opalescent light.

Their hotel was jammed, Dave Husack seemed to know everyone from the doorman to the hearty bellowing men who thronged the lobby. Christine was introduced to many men at the hotel, in the Senate lunchroom, in the halls of Congress. The men Dave knew seemed to be divided into three kinds only. There were the big bellowing kind like Dave Husack himself, usually they were middle-aged or older, they were jovial and they laughed a lot even when nothing very amusing was going on. They greeted one another with affectionate abuse and name-calling. Why, you old son of a gun! they said, fondly. You old hoss thief, you old crook! They flung an arm about the shoulder of the man they greeted, they were always touching anyone to whom they happened to be speaking—an arm, a hand, a shoulder as though, by actual physical contact, they could hold the attention of the other. If you were not wary, Chris found, they could back you into a corner and paw you like an Alaska brown bear.

Then there were the quiet crafty secret ones. Like Sid Kleet, she thought. He was there, too. These talked in a low voice, their eyes were turned to the corner with a listening look. Sometimes they talked behind their hands, their faces were like those Christine had seen in the portraits on the walls of Italian galleries, depicting thirteenth-century Florentine political plotters, the look, the gestures, the planes of the crafty faces were the same.

The third sort was made up of younger men, they looked a good deal like Bay Husack; disillusioned, Christine decided, and striking but not as handsome as Bay. They smiled down at you in an appreciative sort of way, they were a lot like the boys at the university, really. They were well dressed, not sloppy at all, but not sharp, either. Serious, pleasant, agreeable. They looked like young businessmen or lawyers or advertising writers, and sometimes she was rather startled when she heard their names or recognized them from newspaper photographs. They were so young to be so well known and nationally successful. Yet as they talked with her, if she happened to look up at them suddenly, instinctively sensing a loss of attention, she found that while their heads were still bent admiringly toward her, and they still were laughing easily and saying, "Yup. Yup. Oh, now you're kidding me, Miss Storm," their eyes had an anxious strained look and they were listening, not to her, but to two men who were conversing a few feet away.

At lunch the first day of their visit one of the hearty men of the shoulder-thumping type came by, his clothes seemed markedly western; well made.

"Well, Dave, you ol' son-of-a-gun, you here again, I hear Alaska's coming up, what you trying to get your big paws on now, ain't you got enough!"

"Look who's talking! Sit down, sit down. You know Mrs. Husack and Dina here, and my son Bay. And this is Czar Kennedy's girl—Congressman Doorpost, Chris. Watch out for him."

The Senator's eyes bunged. His mouth fell open. He stared at Chris. "Well, the old reprobate! Say!"

Then something in the face of the older man, and the fresh sparkling look of the young girl, her pretty manner as she acknowledged the introduction, caused him to stop, fumbling for words.

Bayard Husack laughed suddenly, a short bark of laughter, and mirthless. His manner became a blend of urbanity and stiffness.

"Miss Storm is Czar Kennedy's granddaughter. Perhaps you know him."

"Why sure, sure. Happy to meet you. Please remember me kindly to your Grandpaw, I've known him for years. Well, say—uh—nice to see you all." He fumbled away from the table.

"You certainly pulled a honey that time, Dad. If that gets around, Chris will not only be the toast of Seattle but of Washington, New York, Chicago, and all points west."

In the three days of their stay in Washington Chris tried not to complain about the heat and the breathlessness. "I find myself trying not to breathe," she said to Bay. "I feel exactly as if I were walking under water."

"That's practically what you're doing, considering the humidity in this town. And you're in over your head in a lot of other ways too —I hope."

She had showered Baranof with post cards of the White House, the Capitol, Washington Monument, the Lincoln Memorial, the Senate, the Mint. But to Thor and to Czar and Bridie and the Barnetts she sent telegrams.

ALASKA BILL COMING UP SEVENTEENTH AM HERE EVERYTHING WONDERFUL HARDLY WAIT WILL TELEGRAPH YOU RESULT LOVE CHRISTINE

They sat in the first row of the visitors' gallery—she and Bay and Dina and Louise and Dave. To the others the imposing room, the men seated like outsize schoolboys at desks, was not a novel sight, but to Christine it was breath-taking, it was dramatic, it was history. She sat leaning well forward, her eyes were shining, enormous. She seemed almost as though poised in flight. Bay thought, suddenly, that if the Winged Victory at the top of the Louvre stairway had been seated instead of standing she would have looked like that—the swell of the young breasts, the line of the throat, the head set so well upon it, the slimness of her long waist, the way her thick blond hair curved away from the forehead.

"When are they going to bring it up, Uncle Dave?"

"Any minute now."

Bay said, "Don't expect too much. You're here to see Washington, not for Alaska politics. Take it easy."

He turned to his father and said something, low-voiced, as though in remonstrance. ". . . a dirty trick." At least, it sounded like that. Dave Husack leaned well toward her then, he spoke with earnestness. "It was your Grandpa Czar Kennedy suggested this visit to Washington, you know, Chris. For you, I mean. I was coming anyway, we thought it might make a nice jaunt. But Czar suggested you come. I guess he thought you might learn from seeing things in the—in the making, politically speaking."

Chris's face was sparkling, radiant. "I'm so glad he did. Thanks, Uncle Dave——"

But now there was a sound of scuffling and startled voices from the dignified chamber of government below. The men at the desks and the man on the raised platform stared, startled, their faces reflected unbelieving shock. Chris, leaning far forward, saw suddenly, terribly, the giant figure of Thor Storm striding down the aisle while other smaller men clung to him, impeding his desperate progress. One great arm was upraised like that of a prophet of the Bible, he spoke in a voice of thunder, but then the clinging men succeeded in confining and twisting his arms, and they turned him around like a bundle and rushed him up the aisle. They disappeared with him. In the midst of the melee a man rose in the House and said something above the uproar as though he had been waiting for this moment. You just caught the word Alaska. There was a mumble. The man sat down. That was all.

Chris scrambled wildly out of her seat. "Grampa Thor! Grampa Thor!"

"Sh-sh-sh! Sit down!"

"That was my Grampa Thor! What did he—what are they doing. I'm going down to him. I'm—what are they doing to him!"

Dave Husack yanked her into the seat. "He's all right. Sit still. I've tended to that. They'll let him go. That's all. That settles Alaska for two more years, anyway. That's all."

"You knew about this! You—Grampa Czar—that's why——"

"Come back here, and keep out of it. He's all right, I tell you. The delegation's with him. Serves 'em right. After lunch you can—say, how about lunch, anyway! What d'you all say, lunch?"

Chris pressed both hands flat to her stomach as though she were about to be sick. "All!" she cried, her voice so high and clear that the gallery turned to stare at her even as they began to move out and up through the exits. "All! No! No!" She fought her way forward, she leaned far over the balcony, she flung out both arms in a gesture that seemed command or supplication or both.

"Listen to him! Listen to him! That's my grandfather, Thor Storm! You men! Listen! Alaska must be free! Alaska! Alaska!" Like the old-day suffragettes, like Charlotte Corday, like Betsy Ross, like Joan.

She was, of course, hysterical.

Dave Husack gathered her up with one great paw and pulled her down into the seat, she felt his moist soft palm clapped across her mouth, stifling her. She could not dislodge the hand, she heard Bay say quit that Dad or I'll sock you, she managed to work her lips back somewhat from beneath the pressure and she bit the hand hard so that she was gratified to feel the bone as her teeth crunched into it and she heard his howl of pain and rage as he jerked his hand away. Then he slapped her.

28

There were eighteen for dinner, Christine had planned for ten only. At the last minute she had had to serve buffet-fashion a dinner which had not been designed for this informality. Even the after-dinner conversation around the fire, usually so stimulating at Territory dinner parties, turned out to be rambling, aimless, what with the entire company's efforts to work over Bayard Husack, who, according to mukluk grapevine rumor, was incredibly slated to be the next Governor of Alaska.

"There'll be ten for dinner," Chris had said, "not counting Grampa Thor, he's just coming in for a minute after dinner."

"He'll come in for a minute and speechify all night. What's got into him! The way he behaved this noon with the General there and all those Seattle Big Bugs. They've always said we're nothing but wild Indians here in Alaska. They'll use it against us. The way they did that Washington fracas."

"Bridie, I'm worried about him. He does all those spectacular things, I spoke to him about it after the luncheon and he said there isn't time any more to be just patient and polite. And he looks so thin, so almost wasted. Today when I took hold of his arm—it's always been like a column of iron—there just wasn't anything there."

"It's his living alone in that little shack. Men don't eat right when they live alone."

"He's lived like that most of his life."

"He's just getting older. Aren't we all! I've just begun to realize it myself. Here in the Territory they keep yelling about how young they are and how young everybody is, and how young everyone has to be to keep what they call the pace, like it was some special gift. I suppose it is a gift, being young, but it isn't special. We've all got it, early in life. The thing is, it slips away from you when you're not looking. What're you having for dinner? Here it is, middle of the afternoon, how are you going to scrabble food together for a crowd?"

"Addie's coming in to help. And the Toklat girl is going to help serve and wash dishes."

"I'll pitch in. I'll dress early and get over here. What time did you say?"

"Eight."

"Eight!"

"Bay and Dina are used to late dinners. Anyway, I can't help it."

"What you having?"

"An all-Alaska menu."

"They'll hate it."

"Not this. Alaska smoked salmon first, with the drinks. Then a caribou broil, parsley and butter sauce——"

"Tough."

"The steaks are marinating now in oil and vinegar."

"I want to see that Dina Drake's face when she hears it's caribou. If all belonging to you were dead you'd still have to laugh, I bet."

"Home-grown Alaska potatoes, Harvard beets, rhubarb-and-cranberry relish, salad, ice cream with frozen strawberries. Every bite of it grown right here in Alaska. Coffee around the fire."

"Home-grown too, I suppose."

"Now, Bridie, don't be cranky."

"All that to do between now and eight! Why you want to run yourself ragged cooking for those two I can't see."

"Bay's my friend—or was. And his mother was so good to me—she still writes me to come and visit—as though nothing had happened, poor dear."

"I suppose that Drake's a poor dear, too."

"If he's going to marry her at last, why, good for bad old Dina."

"From what I hear, she's earned it. My opinion, she never cared a hoot about him. Old Dave, now, he's more her cup of tea, old as he is. It's a wonder she didn't slip something into Louise Husack's food long ago. Maybe she did, maybe that's why Louise's been so ailing."

"You've been seeing too many TV shows, Bridie."

"She's going to make an ideal Governor's wife. One of those big Juneau receptions, free for all, when a thousand slop in in their mukluks after a good wet snow. And handshaking for all of them. Where're the men eating—Dave Husack and that Distelhorst and Kleet and those?"

"At Grampa Czar's."

"Mm-hm. Not eating out at Nick's Café or any place where they can be heard talking. Oh, no!"

"Grampa Czar's having them at home, I'm having my guests at home, it's pleasanter. There are things I'd like to talk about here, too. It's a chance to tell Bay the facts of life—Alaska life, I mean."

"If they're flying up to Nome and Oogruk tomorrow, like they've planned, and maybe going to Kotzebue and Barrow, this time of year, they'll learn the facts of Alaska life, all right. Sixty below, and that wind off the Arctic, she's sure going to be surprised how thin that mink coat can be. Who's mustered as Public Relations escort?"

"I was. I'm not going."

"Well, I should hope not! They try to say you had to go?"

"I'm not going."

"Christine Storm, I bet you could marry Bay Husack today, if you wanted to. And what a Governor's wife you'd be! Maybe he's changed, maybe he's just going to show old Dave he can't——"

"I was sort of planning to be Governor of Alaska myself, twenty years from now. They don't call them Governess, do they . . . ? I think I'll have the potatoes baked, though it's a lot of work. I mean baked and stuffed, mashed up with butter and milk and stuffed back to brown in the oven, they look so dressy and delicious."

"Who you punishing?"

Christine always found it amusing to see the expression in the faces of guests entering her house for the first time. The cabin's weathered exterior had prepared them for the worst. Over the entrance doorway, where dwellings Outside bore Greek pediments or Romanesque arches or modern beams, there branched the graceful curves of a great moose antler. Visitors, passing under this wildlife harbinger, were prepared for splintered wood floors, smoke-blackened beams, knobby chairs, and, for decoration, yellowed photographs of early gold-rush citizenry in derby hats and whiskers.

The gleaming golden walls and beams looked down upon a soft golden carpet. A great curved cushioned couch could seat ten before the fire. The chairs embraced without engulfing you. Lamps shone upon the soft green of Alaska jade and mellow ivory carvings. A polar bearskin rug. Paintings of Alaskan scenes by Lawrence, etchings by the Eskimo Ahgupuk, lithographs by the Alaskan Machetanz. Books books books. There were no Indian masks or woven baskets.

"Why, Chris!" they always exclaimed. "But this is lovely!" As though they had expected a pine table and iron stove.

Dina, entering the room (wool dinner dress, deep crimson), said the expected, "Chris! But this is lovely!"

Bay stood a moment in the doorway, quite quiet. He looked about the soft golden room. "Whoever did this loves you."

"He still does, I hope. Grampa Thor Storm. He did it while I was at school in Seattle. Isn't it strange! As though he knew——"

"He knew you better than any of us."

"Here it was when I came back. Waiting for me. Grampa Czar wouldn't speak to me. . . . You've met Mrs. Ballantyne . . . Mr. and Mrs. Paul Barnett, they publish the *Northern Light*—with Grampa Thor, of course . . . Ross Guildenstern you've met, too . . . oh, of course, you met them all at the airport . . . Mrs. Gannon and Judge Gannon . . . he looks more like a juvenile delinquent than a judge, doesn't he? . . . Isabel and Matt Berg, they have the most wonderful bookstore in Alaska, everything from Kinsey to Toynbee . . . Ott Decker of course . . . Professor Derwent of our Baranof College . . . Mrs. Cale Korf and Cale Korf, Arctic Circle Air Lines Chief, you're going up in one of his planes tomorrow . . . Mead Haskell, he's a flying missionary . . . Mr. and Mrs. Nate Berman, Nate's our new City Planner we're going to be a mass of palm-lined boulevards and statues someday, you'll see. . . ."

Bridie, determined to get things off to a good start, said, "That's a handsome red you got there, Miss Drake, it's seldom you see a real true crimson, it's the French dye does it."

Dina glanced about her. "I hope the things I've brought aren't too formal. I thought with Bay so much in the public eye—"

Bridie threw her good intentions to the winds. "Oh, they expect Dave Husack's secretary to be a snappy dresser. Anyway, you can't be too dressy for Alaskans. We dress for dinner on the planes."

Dinner was not a success. Caribou steaks and baked potatoes are not fare to be eaten buffet style. Bridie's prediction about the caribou had turned out to be true. The beets were somewhat woody, the strawberries gigantic but watery, Ott Decker spilled red wine on the golden carpet and for a moment the tears came to his eyes, or seemed to as Chris tried to reassure him. He said, "It had to be me. It couldn't be Husack or even Ross. It had to be me. Mother's helper."

"Salt," Chris ordered, cheerfully. "We'll pour a lot of salt on it, it makes red-wine spots vanish. Don't ask me why. Think no more of it, Ott dear." He wished she wouldn't call him Ott dear. She didn't call Ross or that Husack Ross dear Bay dear. In public, anyway.

An evening of talk, Chris thought wildly, was what I'd planned, so genteel. Talk about what! Bay had sat next her, a plate teetered precariously on a small side table.

"When are you planning to be married, Bay?" She had not meant to ask this. There it was.

"Whenever you say."

"Same old Bay, never a dull moment."

"Don't play dumb. You know about this charade."

"No. No, I don't."

"I don't know what I see in you, you're just a Girl Scout. Wouldn't it be a joke on me—and some others—if I really did end up just another White House captive, all because it might soften you up!"

"You can't want to be Governor. Anyway, it's too ridiculous, even for the Seattle crowd."

"I haven't anything else to do, it might be fun."

"These people won't stand for it. Not when they know. You are absolutely ignorant of Alaska, you think this is just one of your cynical perverted jokes."

Dinner was finished, they were concentrating on him.

"Mr. Husack . . ."

"Mr. Husack . . ."

"Mr. Husack . . ."

"Call me Bay."

Chris knew that he was grinning inside at his own imitation of the homey politician he despised.

They were talking at him and to him.

Dina Drake did not talk. She sat, glowing in her crimson dress, and glowering, though becomingly. Once she brightened expectantly at the sound of new footsteps at the door, but the figure that entered, wistfully, was that of the redundant Wilbur K. Distelhorst.

"Say, this is more like it!" he shouted. "I snuk out and walked over here, I just remembered you could steer your way by the Ice Palace, they call it."

"You all know Mr. Wilbur Distelhorst. Mrs. . . . Mr. . . . Mrs. . . . Mr. . . ."

"Pretty stuffy over there at old Kennedy's—excuse me, Miss Storm—say! Anyway, they're talking Washington—D.C., I mean—and Seattle and so on, well, I didn't come to Alaska to talk Washington politics. Now you folks, I bet you're talking about stuff that will interest me. Go on. Go right along. Talk as if I weren't here. Or I'm just a tourist."

Bridie: "Tourists tourists, we don't get enough of them because we're not ready for the tourist trade. Folks, traveling, will look at anything if you just lead them to it. Churches. Caves. Tombs. Mounds. The Empire State Building. Chicago stockyards. Cheshire Cheese. Why'n't we fix up some of these log cabins the way they used to be in the old days, instead of tearing everything down! Out to the creeks, get a couple of pans and an old screen and pickaxes and leave them there. That house of yours, Addie, if that had been done up again like the old dance-hall saloon the way it was once—"

Addie: "Don't listen to her, Mr. Husack. It's bad enough as it is. My five-year-old came home from school crying, he wanted to know if it was true he had been born in a bar, he didn't even know they used to be called saloons. Oh, you've never seen my house, of course. It used to be an old gold-rush saloon."

Professor Derwent: ". . . That letter to Major McNally, Storm used it in a *Northern Light* editorial last November. I cut it out, it's memorable. Listen to this: 'We are a very naïve nation, aren't we? That was, perhaps, a rather engaging trait one hundred and fifty years ago. But now we are too old for naïveté. It doesn't become us. And life is too perilous for such a quality in a people. Russia. Hungary. Egypt. Hitler . . .'"

Judge Gannon: "It's the newcomers mostly who can't take it, Mr. Husack. There is endless work to be done. Some of the Johnny-come-latelys come here on the old principle they've heard about Alaska—*Get in, get it, and get out.* But each person is important in a community where there is a constant battle against stupendous natural antagonists—cold, ice, snow, vast distances, few humans. The proportion of insanity is high here. Claustrophobia, I suppose."

Nate Berman: "I've got quite a nice little collection of native curios and artifacts and so on. I have quite a lot of fun with one of them, maybe if you have time you can drop round and see them. Never forget the time I was showing the collection to the General's wife. I've got a short cane about the size of a swagger stick, but much thicker. It looks and feels like old ivory. It's really the penis of a big male walrus. Well, the General's wife let out a squawk. . . ."

Isabel Berg: "Three or four years in Alaska and you're caught. Even if you leave you're marked for life. It's the way you feel about the man you loved but didn't marry. You can marry somebody else and even be happy, but you never forget the other, you're his, in a way, for life. I've known people to go from here to live in California. . . ."

Cale Korf: "The airplane is our First Citizen and Czar Kennedy our Second. No offense I hope, Chris. Without the planes we'd be set back a hundred years. And without Czar Kennedy—well, when he goes the whole Territory will be in mourning—not that he isn't hale and hearty and good for another fifty years this minute. I hope."

Ott Decker: "Gold used to be the medium of exchange, then it was copper, then salmon, pretty soon I shouldn't wonder, oil! Wait till they really hit it here. Zowie!"

Mead Haskell: "The black and the brown people are in the majority now all over the world, and they're learning fast, if you'll just read the writing on the wall. . . ."

Dina: "Look, we're leaving tomorrow, of course I know we'll be stopping by on our way back, but wouldn't it be fun if we could just take a whirl out to what you call the Strip? I mean, I'd love Bay to see it. I hear there's the most marvelous Negro dancer at a place called Dahlia's——"

"Dahlia's place was closed just today, one of the girls there rolled a soldier, the poor kid had three hundred dollars on him." Judge Gannon.

The sound of heavy footsteps in the entrance, a door closed gently. Chris thought, without being aware of her own thinking, He walks more heavily than he used to, though he weighs less. Thor came in. A little greeting gesture of the hand and the head, quiet, almost self-effacing. No matter what he wore, he always, somehow, appeared neater and cleaner than most men, perhaps merely because of the fine pink skin. You could see the path of the careful comb through the once golden hair, silver now. He was wearing a prim blue and white polka-dot bow tie. The boyishness of this sent a sudden pang through Christine's heart.

"Grampa Thor, you know everyone here."

"Everybody sure knows you," Distelhorst brayed.

Thor seated himself near the group, but not quite of it. He dwarfed any chair he might sit in, no matter how ample. There never was sufficient room for the long legs.

"I had some of that caribou steak myself for my supper," he said.

"I wish to apologize to the guests, in the name of Alaska. Tough as a blacksmith's apron."

They laughed a little then at his frankness and at the almost archaic figure of speech, the laugh united the company for the first time. His head cocked a little to one side he sat listening to the talk now, his calm appraising gaze went from this face to that, he listened without speaking. Hydrogen . . . old stuff now . . . Russia . . . shabby genteel old England . . . that so! The most courageous people in the world . . . Hungary . . . Poland . . . Czechoslovakia . . . Israel . . . Egypt . . . Dew Line . . . obsolete a week after they're born all of them . . . Russians are settling their Far North region with forced slave labor forcibly transplanted . . . well, say, maybe that's what we ought to do . . . we are already, aren't we! But not enough of us. . . . You going to be a stooge Governor, Mr. Husack . . . ?"

There was a little shocked silence. In that silence Thor Storm began to speak in that low vibrant voice which Christine had so fortunately inherited from him. It seemed to cut under and through the more plangent vocal sounds. It was almost as though he were ruminating aloud.

"It will soon be finished unless a miracle happens. I believe in miracles. Perhaps it will come from the women. If women ever realize their power and true strength they will govern the world, there will be another matriarchy. We have reached a depth of degradation such as the world has never known. Millions and billions of people are working like dumb slaves to pay for weapons which will destroy them. Every nation is armed against every other nation. Every country's economic stability is based on the destructive apparatus of war. War is a business greater than the steel business greater than the foolish automobile business greater than commerce food clothes education health life itself. War is Death and we bend our necks to it and our backs to it, slaves. Men in the courts of law and decent women in the schoolrooms try to combat with words or with punishment the gangs of children all over the world, boys and girls, armed with knives and clubs and bottles and small guns and bits of metal, fighting against each other. But the example is a world—the entire planet Earth—one huge gangland in a race to be armed with weapons deadlier than the mind of man has ever before dreamed of in its most hideous nightmares. Men in uniform and in neat tailored suits and men in turbans and robes and even in feathers and clubs, meet and discuss this, solemnly, but not reasonably. They say they do not want this, you want it, we do not want this, you want it, each to the other, pointing, like that famous old cartoon of that brilliant cartoonist, Nast. Nast. I learned of him when I was a very young man in Norway, it was he who introduced the cartoon donkey for the Democratic party so many years ago, and the elephant for the Republican, and the tiger symbol for Tammany Hall. Perhaps another Nast could change the world now, with rapier ridicule, perhaps it could be as simple as that. Another Nast. Another Jesus, with a resurrection of the spirit. Clear-eyed simple men of good will. Now the greatest minds in the world, the magnificent brains of the scientists and the minds of inventors and of men of business and of teachers and politicians and writers and rulers and manual workers are concentrated on creating more and more deadly instruments of war. They insist that these are not instruments of war—they are instruments to prevent and forestall war. As well place a box of matches and a stick of dynamite in the hands of a child to keep him quiet. This is childish, this is madness, this isn't proper behavior for Man, the highest form of animal life, the one creature endowed with the thing called the spirit." He rose with effort. "I must be maundering a little, I find I do occasionally, now." He walked through the room as though no one were there. "What a lovely world. The loveliest. We've had it, a gift, for a million million years, and now we're throwing it away. A pity." He went to the doorway, almost blindly. "Alaska, the arsenal. It should be free."

As Christine rose swiftly to go to him there was a heavy knocking at the door, then the outer door slammed, heavy footsteps in the entrance. Thor had disappeared through the doorway, now he reappeared, he was strangely alert again, and incisive, as though fully awakened from a dream. And at that moment the telephone rang with that strange note of urgence with which the insensate instrument seems to presage a message of importance.

"There are a couple of Territorial Police outside, they want to take you back to the Ice Palace right away, Bayard Husack," Thor said.

Uncertain laughter, rather bewildered raillery. Say, Bay, you're a fast worker! Got here this morning and the cops already——

Ross Guildenstern had answered the telephone, he turned to the room now. "It's your father, Bay. It sounds very——"

"What——!" He picked up the telephone, he heard, he hung up. "My mother."

"Bay!" Chris cried.

He nodded. One of the Territorial Police stood in the doorway. "Excuse me, sir. We're taking you to the Ice Palace, Mr. Husack. They're trying to connect with a plane and a pilot, but this time of night——"

"I'll get you the plane," Cale Korf said. "Come on, let's get going."

Ross Guildenstern came forward. "I'll take it–if you need a pilot."

"Let's get going," Korf said.

Half an hour later Bridie, the guests gone, cushions plumped, ash trays emptied, glasses rinsed, was limping her way in too-high heels out to the car in which the faithful Ott Decker had returned to take her home. Her arm rested on Chris's.

"He said," Ott reported, not happily, "that they'll be back this spring, probably April or May. That's what he said. So I guess they mean business."

"That girl's look!" Bridie said, settling herself in the seat beside Ott. "I was looking straight at her when the news came. It was like a candle had been lighted behind her face. Radiant. That's the only word for it. Radiant. Governor's wife, me eye!"

Through the open door the sound of the telephone again. Chris ran up the icy path and into the golden room and snatched the receiver.

"Chris!"

"Yes, Bay."

"Wait for me."

29

All through the spring Thor spent odd moments working on his new boat. It wasn't a powerboat, it was nothing at all modern. It was an old-fashioned square-ended skiff such as fishermen in the old Scandinavian countries and fishermen in the new world New England sat in hopefully, peacefully in the middle of a flat body of water, the line and the flat-bottomed boat both moving almost imperceptibly. It was a boat for a man who, for days or weeks or months at a time, could live happily with, or without, people.

Both Chris and Bridie, as the long hard Baranof winter drew to a close, and the ecstasy of the long golden days and rosy summer nights began to tingle through the sluggish fibers and nerves and tissues and blood and skin of the winter-weary Alaskans—both these women who loved him developed and followed a plan of campaign.

Chris interrupted his boatbuilding.

"But what are you going to do with it? You've got boats as good as that. You're just wasting your energies."

"I thought I wouldn't fish this year—with the tender, I mean, and crew. You're earning money, I don't need much myself—just the few dollars for food and tackle and my little jaunts around the Territory."

"That's what I mean. You could come with me to California. Or perhaps Honolulu. We'd fly, it only takes a minute."

"Everything only takes a minute. Now. What's the hurry? Where's everybody going in such a rush?"

He talks like an old man, Chris thought. A tired old man. "We wouldn't have to rush. We could stay away for a month. Until the middle of May. Until the ice goes out. Just sit in the sun on a beach."

"You're not a girl for sitting in the sun on a beach."

"I can try it, can't I? So can you. I'd like, just once, to stand treat. Darling Grampa Thor, you've paid my way all my life, until these last two years. You and Grampa Czar."

"You run along, dear child. Or take him."

"You're already sorry you said that, aren't you? What are you going to do while I'm gone?"

"I could take this new little skiff, and some grub, and just skirt along the shore, very easy, pretend I'm Steller just discovering Alaska, and looking for new greens and birds and creatures."

She could not say, But you look too thin and almost feeble, you're too old for that sort of thing now. Alone.

Bridie, in her new spring tweed topcoat for which the Baranof temperature was still far too low ("Nothing shows up a fur coat like that spring sun after a tough winter's wear. Ratty.") came occasionally to argue with Thor as he went about his boatbuilding task there by the waterside so near his one-room cabin. She had peered into the cabin before she came down to join him as he hammered, sawed, sandpapered, calked, painted. Everything inside the cabin was neat, orderly, shining. His saucepan, kettle and frying pan scoured, his floor scrubbed, his bedspread straight, his books ranged on the shelves but stacked too, now, in floor corners, his few clothes hanging behind a faded gingham curtain.

"You're a regular old maid," she announced as a charming opening gambit. "I don't know how you ever got along with the Eskimos, slapdash the way they are. . . . Oh, there I go again, I always forget. Excuse it, Thor, please."

"Sometimes I think it's a great waste of time, being neat in your habits. So many things more worth doing than keeping your shoes in a row, toes all pointed one way. But I was brought up to do that in those days that seem so far away in another world."

"You're in this world now, Thor Storm, and I'm here to ask you why you don't plan a holiday for yourself. With Chris, or with Chris and me, or alone or whatever. You could go to the Old Country where your folks are, man like you a prince or a duke or whatever it was you were then. Imagine their faces when they see you, like the prodigal son in the Bible."

"They're probably all dead by now, Bridie."

"You ain't, anyway."

"It's an idea. As you say, they might be glad to see me."

"Oh, no use talking to you. You and Czar both. Stiff in the mind as you are in the joints, both of you. Why'n't you stay elastic like me!" She was off, with a jerk at her new spring hat. Now she turned for a parting question. "What's in that big tin box in your cabin? You got your money or bonds or whatever laying around on the floor like an old miser, when there's banks in plenty in Baranof? I tried to open it, but it's locked."

He laughed then, throwing back his fine old head in a roar of amusement such as she had not heard from him in years. "Bridie, Bridie, we should have married those years and years ago, I'd have been as successful as Czar and Dave Husack combined, and you'd have been Queen of Alaska."

"Maybe I am now, there are folks that think . . . What's in that box, Thor Storm?"

"It's my book."

"Finished! You mean the book you've been writing on all these years! Finished!"

"No book is ever really finished, I suppose. If you care enough about what you're writing—or too much—you keep picking at it and picking at it, trying to write better than you can. But now I think I won't try any more to make it perfect. I've said what I had to say as best I could."

"You don't sound any too gay about it. My land! About fifty years writing it, first and last."

"Yes. There's a little note of explanation in the front of it. I want Chris to read it someday soon. I want Chris to be the first to read it."

Regretfully, Christine bade him good-bye and went off for the first Outside trip she had had since her return to Baranof following the abruptly terminated Seattle experience.

"I'll be away four weeks, but if I don't like it I'll just come home."

"Don't do that. Finish what you start."

"Grampa Thor, I wish you'd live in my house while I'm away. You'd be so comfortable. Won't you? If only to keep the mice away."

"An old fellow like me wants to stay in his own lair, like the woods' creatures. . . . Christine?"

"Yes, Grampa."

"One thing I wish you'd do, I've meant to talk to you about it before now. You never finished your college education. You never got your degree, after that bad time Outside, when you left and came back home. I wish you'd go back to Baranof College for one year and get your degree. Cap and gown, and you standing there with the rolled sheepskin as they call it, in your hand. You began it. Finish it."

"What a strange idea! I've got a job. But I'll think about it."

"It's going to be kind of restful, both you and Bridie gone. Nobody to nag me about food and temper and my howling editorials and my bad behavior."

"We love you."

The square-ended skiff was finished. It was a strange-looking craft, in some small details. It had, for instance, a plug in the bottom which could be pulled out by a linked metal chain, almost like a bathtub plug. On a brisk flawless May day he hauled the skiff down to the water's edge and stood surveying it with the eye of a craftsman and a boatman and a fisherman born. For a full half century and more, from the day he had left his native Norway he had loved the sea, he and his father and his grandfather and generations before them. During the month he and Ross had mixed cement and skillfully laid a new floor for Christine's garage. He now weighted the boat with some of the residue of this mixture, but not too much. The boat was new and shining. Nobody has ever sat in it before, he thought with satisfaction. He himself, eager and alert, was neat and fresh and clean as the boat into which he now stepped as it lay on the water. Leisurely, with a look of utter anticipation and enjoyment, he rowed out to where he could see the mountains white-topped, the almost heartbreaking blue of the Alaska sky, the pines, the glistening water. It was lovely, it was complete. Now he rested his oars and he lashed himself firmly to the boat, pulling the ropes he had brought with him around his ankles, his knees, his waist. It was his favorite time of day, sunset came late now, later and later, soon the daylight days and the daylight nights would meet and blend. The sun was not streaming in bold brassy shafts, it shone golden and warm like Christine's hair.

Now was the time. The handy old hand reached out, it pulled the plug with one firm jerk. The concrete-weighted boat sank so that for one brief instant he was standing upright in the water, he saw the mountains the sky the trees the water—the elements and objects he so loved. The water slid over him—ankles—hips—shoulders—head—like a soft silken shroud.

Though she rebelled at first in an agony of tears and self-recrimination, Chris understood after she had read his letter.

Until now, Christine my dear child, I always have had a mild contempt for people who leave Last Notes. They are like those who stand and stand at the door, saying good-bye, long after they should have left and done with it. I always had put it down to vanity—to a final fling of exhibitionism. But now I think I understand them a bit. There is no doubt that we have been exhibitionistic old parties—Czar and Bridie and myself. Characters, I suppose we'd be called, and have been. We're a little passé. Power people nowadays function more quietly. They're deadlier than we were, though they make much less fuss. Like the barbaric ritual known as war. The drums and the cannon and the guns and even the planes are old stuff now. Now it's just one neat quiet package like a big cigar, a puff of thick smoke, and that's it.

I am maundering a little. I meant only to tell you that I have gone on that journey we spoke of. My increasing thinness (or should that be decreasing?) was, as you suspected, illness. It would have been a long business still, and the pain was becoming too much for me. I thought of you and good Bridie nursing me nursing me through the months. Your money would be spent, and hers, and your precious energies and time. How foolish, how wasteful. This is better and cleaner and more civilized.

My work is done. The book is finished. But my work in my beloved Alaska is not finished. You must carry on with that. Not must. I wish to recall that word. I never have said must to you.

You are the most dear and lovely thing I have had in my life—you and freedom. I leave you all I have to leave. My Book. My love of Freedom. My belief in the Dignity and the Spirit of Man, as long as the Human Race shall persist, and in spite of the power and purpose of the Men of Destruction.

30

Czar Kennedy felt enormously light and exhilarated. He had felt that way for weeks, for months. He couldn't account for it. It wasn't the Alaska dry cool electric air. He was, God knows, accustomed to that by now. It wasn't success. He had known the buoyant effects of that, too, for half a century and more. It wasn't his fundamental health and vitality. He had always been well and forceful. It wasn't even that he and Chris had come together again, grandfather and grandchild, and he had forgiven her—or as good as forgiven her—for her crazy outburst in the visitors' gallery that time in Washington. Of course she hadn't married Bayard Husack yet, or even said she might. But once he was set up in the Governor's Mansion in Juneau, safe and soft, she'd fall into line without even knowing it, smart as she was—or thought she was. He, Czar Kennedy, was smarter. He was smarter than anyone in Baranof. Smarter than anyone in Alaska. Smarter than those big windbags in Seattle, yes, and in San Francisco and New York and Washington, too. Let them have the cashmere coats and yachts and the cars and the private planes and the girls and the three-hundred-dollar suits. The laugh would be on them when he died and they opened his will and saw that he had millions and—— But he wasn't going to die. He felt strangely light and potent. He felt that he could do anything. He felt free and young and powerful.

Now when he awoke in the early morning his first almost unconscious sensation was like that he had had when he was a small boy and school was over for the summer. School was out there in the little

Massachusetts town so many years ago, and he and one of the boys were going fishing. He had not been quite aware of what the lovely thing was that was going to happen, he wasn't yet awake. What is it what is it? Something lovely is going to happen, something lovely has happened. And then he would remember though he never once admitted this to himself, once he was awake and fully conscious. He got up, smiling a little without knowing he was smiling, and rubbing his stomach and scratching in a kind of warm cosy reassuring comfort and satisfaction. He did not give it a name. But he knew.

He had won. He had survived. He, Czar Kennedy, was alive. And Thor Storm was dead.

After Thor's death he had solemnly told her of her grandfather's Norwegian background. He had told Dave Husack, too, and that whole Seattle crowd, the fat cats. How much blue did they have in their blood? Plenty of yellow, that's sure, but no blue. The lawyers had opened the box in the Seattle bank, and there it all was, sure enough, in the documents.

Czar had told Christine the details, she had been shown the documents, she had stared in unbelief and then in compassion and reverence for the man and his great purpose and self-denial. But then, when she heard Czar say, "You're probably a kind of countess or something, your children would be sprung from nobility——" she broke into laughter—vexed merriment, really. "How quaint and old-timy." Then, in a sudden panic, "You haven't told anyone! Please! I hope you haven't told anyone."

"Person would think you were hiding a crime or something."

"They'd kid the life out of me. I'd never know another peaceful moment. Poor wonderful Grampa Thor, how right he was!"

"You ought to be proud of your background."

"I am. I was born in a caribou in a blizzard up in the Wood——"

"Stop that!" he yelled.

"I'm sorry, Grampa Czar. I shouldn't tease you about a thing like that. You're right. Bay Husack tells me that's become my routine pitch, and he's right, too." Ruefully.

He brightened a little at that, mollified. "Does, does he? He's smarter than I thought. Not that I don't think," hastily, "that Dave Husack's son isn't going to make a fine—"

"He'll be terrible."

But the two got on together more equably than they had before Thor's death. They even took little trips together to Alaska's more luxurious points—Fairbanks, Anchorage, Juneau. Occasionally he even consented to take Bridie along. She served as ballast and buffer between the two high-powered creatures.

"I'm going Here," Czar would say; or There. "Want to come along with the old man, Christine?"

Once or twice, if the distance were short (as if that would lessen the risk) he had even consented to having Chris fly him in the little two-passenger bug which she had purchased out of her own savings. He had a kind of pride in his granddaughter's ability to handle a plane, in her reputation for skill and reliability and safety.

Stoutly Czar would say, "I'm as modern as the next one. You got to keep step with the times while you're alive, or you might as well lay down. And I'm sure alive, all right. Nothing to piloting any more than there is to driving a car. Easier, if anything, I'd say."

"That's right," Christine agreed, looking gingerly down at the mountain range past which they were soaring.

On the trip to the Kennedy coal lands Czar himself had suggested that Christine fly him up in her little Moth. It was summer, night and day were one. "I could take the train," he said, "or go on the regular Tuesday plane. I guess I've got so I haven't the patience for anything but air nowadays though I ought to use the railroad, they bring the stuff down. Either way, of course, I'd have to stay overnight. The plane doesn't pick up back till Thursday."

"I'll fly you. I'd love to. It's nothing. An hour or less."

Buzzing along contentedly in the little plane, she asked, above the drone of the engine, "Is there anything wrong at the mine?"

"Not what you'd call critical."

"It can't be too bad if you can fix it in one day."

"It's management. Management. If you don't watch it all the time the costs go up and the profits dwindle, you've got to be on the job yourself. Every little item. That new fella from Outside, he's supposed to know coal mining—machinery—engineering—loading—the works. He couldn't run a kiddy-car. He's overloading, parts wear out quicker than we can replace them. Next thing they'll be bringing coal in from Outside cheaper than I can sell it right here in the Territory."

"Don't let things like that upset you too much, Grampa Czar. They're not worth it."

"What d'you mean, not worth it! What's more important than you get your work done right and run your business in first-class shape!"

"Well——" and she pointed to the vast world below. "That, for example."

"What about it?" Certainly this particular region was not the spectacular Alaska of mountain peaks and great gray waters. It was flatlands that they were approaching. Coal lands.

"It's so exciting."

"What's exciting about it?"

"Being alive, for one thing. And knowing that all this used to be forest once upon a time."

"Who says so?"

"The historians, the geologists. Books."

"Oh—books." He rejected this feeble source. "Thor talk."

"Don't!" she said, sharply. Then, reminding herself that this was an old man, this vital inwardly seething Czar Kennedy was an old man, "They say all this was tropical once upon a time. Millions of years ago. Enormous forests of trees. Because of course coal is just hardened trees and stuff. Carbonized trees."

"I remember that," he admitted, grudgingly. "I never thought about it again, that way. It's interesting, though, real interesting to think about, like you said."

"I can't bear to think about all the things that are going to change in the next few million years—like trees into coal—maybe the coal will change back into trees. Who knows? And I won't be here to see it. I wouldn't so much mind dying if when I came back I'd——"

"Came back!" he interrupted, sharply.

"You know—reincarnation."

"You're crazy."

"How do you know? How do we know? If only we could remember at least some past lives. Perhaps we do, dimly, now and then. If only I could say, I remember that life five hundred years ago—a thousand—a million years ago. I won the Miss Troglodyte Beauty Contest. . . . I was a Viking's bride. . . . I was a slave girl on the Nile. . . . I was an actress—a waitress—a champion ice skater—an Indian squaw."

"Look, Christine, my girl, just get us down before you go clear off your head and start screeching. Lots of people go loony in Alaska, I never thought my own granddaughter would."

Indulgently she laughed, they glided expertly down to the runway and the somewhat apprehensive mine manager from Outside who was awaiting Czar.

"You want to come down in the mine, Christine? I'm going on down before lunch. That's what I'm here for, I want to get a start back tonight if I can straighten out the dumb goings-on here."

"Sure, sure," the manager said, nervously. "Come on down, Miss Storm, everything's going swell, Mr. Kennedy."

"I won't go down now," Christine said. "Maybe after lunch. I don't like coal mines much."

"You like the money from them all right, don't you?" Czar asked. She ignored this. "I'm going over to have a little chat with Mrs. Boone at the store. And I'll fool around with the plane a little bit, we'll be going back so soon. And you mustn't skip lunch, Grampa. Bad for you. I'll meet you at twelve-thirty at Boones'."

Czar turned abruptly with a gesture to the man, he trotted off with an exaggeration of his short quick stride. He did not talk. He would look, he had decided, he would just say nothing but he would look into everything, he would be calm and quiet and ask this and that, pleasant as you please, and then when he had the whole story he would blast. Who did they think they were fooling! An old man! Not by a damn sight. He wasn't old. You were as old as you felt and he felt like a man of thirty. Twenty, by God!

An hour in the company office. Figures. Statistics. "Maybe it's a little too late to go down now before lunch, Mr. Kennedy. Maybe you'd better wait with that till after your lunch."

"Lunch, hell! I'm here to work, not eat. I don't need food to keep me going. I've got a perpetual-motion machine rigged up inside of me, young fella."

"Yes*sir!* You sure have."

"You go on, eat your lunch. I'm going down."

"Oh, no, Mr. Kennedy."

"I knew coal mining before you were out of diapers. I want to ramble around alone. Scat!"

He was enjoying himself, really. This was wrong, that was wrong, the lunks! By two o'clock he'd have it all in line, he'd give them the big or-else and buzz back with Chris in time for dinner in Baranof. What a world. Like Christine said, the kid was right. Exciting. I bet I was one of those Roman emperors.

He watched the chunky heavy-laden coal cars coming down the grade like fat old ladies cautiously descending a hill in San Francisco. He laughed to himself, rather fancying this mental figure of speech. Then he thought, they're not being cautious enough. Look at that! Too fast. So that's how they been wearing them out, and the machinery too. Why don't they brake them like I always used to. I'll jump one of the cars, go down and give them the works right from the coal pile. He waited tense at the side of the narrow track, poised ready to jump as the laden car passed him, to jump aboard as he had a hundred times in his younger days. The car reached him, he jumped, but the muscles had lost their elasticity, they pulled him up but he was short of the goal, he fell under the car with its iron wheels and its tons of coal, the merry little wheels jolted over him and he rolled again and again and again. The coal car scurried on smugly as one who has done a thorough job.

There were no telephones from town to town. Alaska's natural barriers and vast distances had thus far defied this bridging.

Alaska communications service, then. A.C.S. Baranof Baranof. Paul Barnett. The *Lode* office. Bridie Ballantyne. Ott Decker. Territorial Police. Judge Gannon . . . Ross Guildenstern . . . "He's a pilot. If he can get hold of a plane. If he's in. In Baranof, I mean. My little plane won't do, it won't carry—no, I won't fly back without Grampa Czar . . . if Ross can get a plane . . ."

His reply came so quickly that they scarcely had had time for more than two or three messages.

> LEAVING CAN DO ABOUT HALF HOUR PAUL AND GANNON WITH ME DON'T TRY BE BRAVE WATCH SKY WAIT FOR ME ROSS